GRIM PORTENTS

A

NOVEL

BY

CHRISTIAN AKINS

For my wife, Montana,
who has given me the life that
Bill is always fighting for.

And for my best friend, Mike,
who will not read this.

WHERE TO BEGIN…

WE KILLED ANOTHER guy at the Whataburger this morning, which makes three since we started on the road yesterday. I knew to expect the occasional incident before we left, but the frequency was beginning to concern me. I should also clarify that when I say we killed three "guys" I actually mean spiritually possessed host bodies.

The first two attacked together in the Buc-ee's bathroom late last night. I had hoped that the high foot traffic of such a location would buy us a modicum of safety. I don't know if you've ever been to a Buc-ee's, but every visit I've previously made has rivaled the annual attendance of Disney World. That said, arriving at two in the morning thins out the crowd a fair amount.

We were in dire need of both gas and a restroom after our last stop four hours earlier—and if I'm being completely honest, the sound of freshly roasted, cinnamon-coated pecans beckoned to me like a sweet siren song lures sailors to their deaths. Rather than simply grab my snack and be on my way, I decided to take advantage of the thin crowd to use the restroom in relative peace. My two pursuers took the same advantage.

The altercation was over in seconds. I'd like to say that I overpowered them with my superior fighting ability, but the truth of the matter is that I was fully sitting on the toilet when they confronted me and I only gained the upper hand because they recoiled upon opening the stall door. I suppose it was fortunate that the bathroom was situated in such a way that a row of sinks blocked the view of the stalls, because that's what passes for fortune at this point in my life. The other patrons could continue to utilize most of the urinals without seeing anything on the opposing side of the sinks—for instance: a man struggling to stage two bodies on separate toilets with their pants around their ankles. With so many stalls available, and a general odor strong enough to combat the eventual stench, it could be an entire day before anyone discovered the corpses.

The third "guy" was by complete happenstance. Though my companion and I had become targets for all manner of paranormal creatures, a number of them have wisely learned to avoid us. As you can expect from the Buc-ee's bathroom incident, I have a pretty effective means of dispatching them. That said, the third host didn't expect us to walk into the Whataburger the following morning any more than we expected to see them holding the drive-thru attendant upside down over the scalding hot fry oil.

I generally try to deal with these situations without witnesses. I'm a poor liar and supernatural encounters always arouse the type of questions that can't be answered in a succinct or logical way. But short of allowing a teenager to be deep-fried before taking action, there was no way to avoid it this time. As a result, we were subjected to a number of questions from the would-be victim, and even more from the police afterwards, hoping all the while that we had put enough distance between us and the Buc-ee's restroom that the local deputies wouldn't think to make a connection. The entire interaction caused us to lose a day's worth of travel, which meant a second night in a roadside hotel, where I'm writing this now.

So, before we get back on the road tomorrow, I figure I should go ahead and get some of this down while it's still fresh in my mind. Though, I guess if I'm actually going to do this, I should start at the beginning.

1

THE FIRST DAY OF THE
END OF MY LIFE

MY ONLY CONCERN in the hours leading up to my wedding was whether I would be able to adequately affix a bow tie. It's an infuriating garment that likely would have been phased out of fashion decades ago had it not pitifully clung to the wedding industry as a last bastion of relevance. Admittedly, no one was forcing me to adopt such an outmoded accessory, but it wasn't as if I knew how to do a regular tie any better so I figured I might as well opt for the "fancier" option. Had I known that my choice of tie would ultimately determine the fate of all sentient beings in the universe, I would have bought a clip on.

In movies, the groom always appears to be a nervous wreck, asking his buddies if he's making the right decision. I had no worries or feelings of uncertainty that morning, and even if I did, I certainly had no buddies to consult with. I lost touch with all my school friends years ago and I worked from home, so I wasn't forced to interact with my coworkers outside of the occasional call. It was bad enough when someone suggested we turn our cameras on. Even my parents had both passed away, not that I could ever imagine going to them for advice. They were in their fifties when I was born, and according to my father, neither wanted children. That isn't the most comforting thing to tell your ten-year-old son immediately after his mother's death, but it was a pretty good preview of our relationship in the years to come.

By the time of my wedding, the only person of true significance in my life was Grace. A splash of color in my grey-toned existence, she had become the sole focus of my universe since the moment we crossed paths. I was working for a marketing agency at the time, preparing ads for a brokerage firm out in Austin. I don't remember what the ads were for, or much else about the meeting, other than the cute, copper-haired woman I kept exchanging glances with. After the meeting, she approached me to ask if I remembered her. I was a bit let down that she had only been eyeing me out of recognition instead of attraction, and embarrassed to admit that I didn't recall her at all. We had apparently shared a class in high school, but otherwise never interacted—which made sense. As a teenager, I wouldn't have had the courage to speak to a girl as mesmerizing as her. I barely had enough as a full grown man. She asked if I was staying in town, and if I'd like to go get a drink to catch up on imagined times. To be honest, I had never been asked out before and I must have said yes at least four times in one sentence.

"Yeah, that sounds—absolutely, uh—perfect, sure."

I didn't realize that by "drinks" she had meant a tour of every bar on 6th street. Turns out, she had just exited a long-term relationship and mostly wanted some company to help take her mind off it. It was the best night I don't fully remember, and at the end of it, we went our separate ways. It wasn't until the following afternoon I realized she had put her number in my contacts. They say you're not supposed to call a girl right away, so I texted her instead.

The next few years were the happiest of my life. We traveled, we went to concerts and festivals, we once took a summer to try every pizza restaurant in Austin in order to definitively rank who had the best slice. We never did finish that project though. About halfway through July, Grace realized that the intense indigestion she felt all the time was a result of a gluten allergy that she had been heretofore unaware of. From then on, we took on the much more difficult project of finding restaurants that weren't poisoned by cross-contamination, which extended far beyond the summer into the prospective future.

All this to say that we spent every waking hour with one another and were all the happier for it. Finally marrying her was, in my mind, all I could ever desire. And there we were, minutes away from saying our vows and living out my dream life. And there I was, wrestling with my tie, not realizing that at that very moment—I was sealing my fate.

My video tutorial was failing me. For whatever reason, my brain could not process how to move my hands in a mirrored motion of the bowtie on screen. Rather than waste precious minutes locating a better guide, I opted to poke my head out of the dressing room to scan the guests for anyone wearing a similar garment. To my relief, I quickly spotted what I needed. Hovering around the wedding cake with a plate full of appetizers in his hand, stood a tall gaunt man that I did not recognize from the guest list. He was, however, sporting a black bowtie that I prayed he had fashioned himself.

"Excuse me," I gave a meek wave to greet the man as I approached. "This is going to sound like a weird question, but do you know how to tie a bowtie?"

The man swallowed a bite of whatever he had been chewing on and smiled. "Perfectly understandable question considering the circumstances. You are the groom, are you not?"

"That's me," I confirmed.

The man maintained his smile, setting down his plate to present his palm to me. I handed him the loose fabric.

"Turn around," he said, reaching his arms over my shoulders to fasten the tie under my collar. I watched his fingers work with practiced precision, but something about his spindly appendages unnerved me. They looked like spider legs, ensnaring me in their grasp.

"I don't believe we're acquainted," I said, partially to break the tension of this oddly intimate exercise. "Are you with Grace's family?"

"No, I'm with the caterer. Just getting everything ready before the reception."

"Ah, that makes sense," I said, when I actually wondered why a caterer was sampling all of the food in full view of the guests.

"There we are," he said at last. "Perfection." He turned me around to admire his handiwork and his smile suddenly dropped. "Oh dear."

"What?" My eyes bulged. "What's wrong?

"It seems I may have touched your lapel with a spot of sauce. But don't fear!" He swiftly ducked behind a nearby cocktail station and retrieved a small bottle of club soda. "This should do the trick. Just pop into the bathroom and dab it with a paper towel. Dab, do not rub."

"Right." I accepted the bottle, looking down at my tiny stain. "Thanks for your help.

"My pleasure, and additionally, my apologies."

I departed from the strange man, heeding his advice and slipping into the nearest restroom. Upon closer examination, the spot was barely noticeable, but I took great care to dab properly until it disappeared entirely. I inspected myself in the mirror, admiring what had to be the most handsome version of myself I could hope to achieve. It was all perfect. Everything was going to be perfect.

Just before exiting the room, I caught something in the corner of my eye. I glanced at the reflection in the mirror where I thought I'd seen the culprit, but there was nothing. *That's odd*, I thought, turning back to the door. I reached out to grab the handle, feeling that it was ice cold. The hairs on the back of my neck stood up and I could feel an overwhelming fear encompass me, like a thick fog. It was a familiar feeling, a fear that I had experienced only one other time in my life: the night my mother died.

I was ten years old. Most nights, my parents would spend their time on opposite ends of the house, speaking like strangers when they passed one another in shared spaces. When the aneurism occurred, no one was close enough to hear her drop to the floor. I was the one who eventually found her, having finally left my room to ask about dinner.

While my father sat silently staring off into the corner of the hospital waiting room, I wandered off. He was too preoccupied to notice, and I didn't know what else to do to channel my anxious energy. I'm not sure how long I explored the halls, but eventually, I found myself in the maternity ward, facing a window which looked into the newborn nursery.

Now, a child's mind is inherently open to the existence of the supernatural, but that alone isn't enough to see beyond the veil. One must be in the correct mental state at the exact moment that a supernatural event occurs. Unfortunately, as I stood on my toes to peer into the nursery, my thoughts dwelled on death. That's the only explanation for what I saw.

Imagine a silhouette of a man, not fully defined, and as devoid of light as the deepest reaches of space. It appeared to emit the dark, as if that were a physical property.

I stared at this thing, more terrified than I had ever been, and watched as it hunched over the infants. Then, it turned to face me. I couldn't see its eyes, but I could feel them bore into me. A moment later, the figure faded away and I didn't feel paralyzed anymore. I took that opportunity to scream at the top of my lungs and run away as fast as I could, until the staff noticed and returned me to my father.

I told him about what I'd seen later that night, but he convinced me that it was all in my imagination, that I was delirious after losing my mother. Eventually, I convinced myself he was right. The wave of fear that kept me frozen in place was nothing more than a physical response to emotional trauma. But of course, if that was the case, why was I experiencing the same feeling on my wedding day?

What I should have done was fling the door open and run as fast as I could, screaming all the while—just as I'd done as a boy. Instead, I decided to take one last look behind me. It was a public bathroom after all. One of the stalls must have been occupied before I entered. That would explain the presence I felt. But as I turned to look, a brief moment occurred in which I allowed my mind to wonder, *what if?* It was such a provocative thought, so infused with memory and emotion, it broke down all the barriers I built up in my maturity. It placed me back in that moment as a young child, staring in horror at something my mind could not comprehend.

It is only in these moments, in which all doubts and assumptions about the supernatural are set aside, that our brains can process the complete bat-shit lunacy that exists in the world. We may catch a glimpse when we have our guard down, but to see one in its entirety is rare. The reason our minds do not process these images is for our own protection. If everyone could see into alternate planes of existence, they would gouge their own eyes out to stop their brains from exploding in their skulls. Perhaps not literally, but you understand my meaning. Regardless, my mental barriers were down just long enough for me to perceive something more horrible than I could ever imagine.

Standing before me was a beast of pure malice. It had deep purple skin and a thin spattering of coarse red fur. Its jaw jutted out, revealing a row of yellowed teeth coated in some kind of decaying meat. Black, beady eyes sunk into a head with no neck. Its arms were hulking and loomed forward with its fists planted firmly on the ground, like a gorilla. The monster, even on all fours, towered over me—and it was only inches from my face.

I stood breathless, unable to scream. *It's an illusion*, I told myself. *I'm just nervous about the wedding. Really, really nervous.* But I didn't believe that. This was far too visceral to be a concoction of my mind. I could hear it breathing, smell the stench of rotten eggs and roadkill. If I were so bold, I knew I could reach out and touch its scarred hide. This was real.

The true horror came when the beast realized that I could see it just as well as it could see me. It actually looked surprised, then elated. It was an expression that said *Finally*, as if the creature had waited an eternity for this moment. A horrific grin stretched across its monstrous face, revealing the rest of its teeth. I thought the beast would bite me in two, but instead, it lifted one of its tree trunk arms and snatched me from the ground. There was no doubting its existence now. I could feel its grip tightening around my chest. It held me close for inspection and furled its brow, as if to say, *I suppose this will do.*

As I hung in the monster's grasp, I felt as though I could vibrate out of my suit and melt into a pool of Jell-O on the ground. I squeaked a call for help, but could only emulate the sound of a punctured dog toy. One thought suddenly took over my mind. Grace. If this thing wasn't some bizarre hallucination, then it posed a threat to her and everyone else in the building. I feared for my own life, but I refused to leave hers in jeopardy.

As a final defense mechanism, I mustered every bit of strength I possessed and swung my dangling leg full-force into the beast's jaw. To my astonishment, it actually released me from its grasp. When the beast reached out to grab me once more, I managed to dive to the side of the room. Unfortunately, in my moment of adrenaline, I had unintentionally maneuvered away from the exit. If I could get around the thing, I might be able to escape before it grabbed me again.

The insanity of the situation was not lost on me, but if I allowed myself to dwell on it, I'd only freeze up again. If not for my desperation to warn Grace, I'd have probably died already.

The monster struck out its arm with lightning speed and propelled me through two of the stalls before the third one stopped me. All the air left my lungs and I struggled to fill them back up. At least one of my ribs had broken, but I couldn't afford to focus on that. I had to push past the pain and rise to my feet. The monster took another step to the side, leaving a small opening for me to reach the door—if I was fast enough.

The sound of the church organ suddenly penetrated the walls. The monster's focused stare faltered momentarily in the direction of the sound. This was my chance, and I took it.

The next few seconds felt as if they occurred in slow motion. I remember the wheezing noise I emitted as my body lunged forward, the beads of sweat streaking across my brow, the blinding flash of pain as my ribs shifted in my chest. And of course, I remember the feeling of absolute dread at the sight of a thick muscled arm reaching between me and my destination.

Before I could reach the door knob, the monster pierced my chest with three enormous talons. My body went limp, impaled on this creature's hand. It was all that kept me from collapsing to the floor. The pain was gone. I had no need for it anymore. The last thing I saw before all perception faded away was a small tunnel materializing in front of me and a hand emerging from the other side, reaching for me.

2

CLERICAL ERROR

DYING WAS THE most exciting thing I ever did in my life. I'd like to describe the sensation as comforting, my problems and concerns melting away as I embraced a bright light of shimmering peace. Instead, I experienced the excruciating sensation of my soul being ripped from every atom that made up my body. It felt as if all my cells each had their own full head of hair, and every one of those hairs was simultaneously yanked out. My soul was pulled through a narrow tunnel of light and then there was nothing. It was as black as the shadow creature that haunted my dreams as a child. Here I was, in the afterlife, coming to the realization that there was no afterlife. All that existed was a cold, bleak, nothingness.

But that was only for a second.

Somehow, despite being only a consciousness in a dark void, I blinked. My eyes opened to a harsh fluorescent light blaring down on me. I had a physical form, or at least felt as if I did. I was afraid to blink a second time, fearing that I would return to the void, but after about a minute or so of not blinking, it dawned on me that I didn't need to. My eyes felt perfectly moisturized—or however they're supposed to feel, despite the direct assault from the fluorescents above. Deciding never to blink again, I began to examine my new surroundings.

It appeared to be some kind of hospital room. I sat up and found myself on top of a clean twin-sized mattress. There was a suspended TV in the corner, a side table with a flowered vase, and a clipboard hanging off the foot of the bed. There was no window though, which I found unusual. I then realized that I was completely naked. There was no blanket or sheet of any kind, just nudity. Hanging on a hook next to the door, was a light gray suit.

Given the circumstances, I should have been in a state of utter panic. Instead, I calmly rose out of bed and got dressed. I later learned that my reaction was not at all uncommon. The room was actually designed to place people in a serene state as they came to terms with their recent demise.

The suit felt tailored to my body, and extremely light on my skin. It was almost as if I was still naked. Lastly, I grabbed the tie and found no trouble recalling how to put it on, despite needing instructions every previous time in my life, which were admittedly few. I looked over at the clipboard hanging off my bed. On it was an ordinary doctor's chart, but under the diagnosis it read: "YOU ARE DEAD." I'd already guessed that, but when I tried to remember how I died, the whole thing was a blur. In any case, it seemed unimportant at the moment.

I wondered if I had permission to leave the room. It was the same feeling I had in every doctor's office, like if I opened the door I would somehow get in trouble, even though I was a 32 year old man and the worst thing that could happen was a stern talking to. Even still, I couldn't imagine anything I wanted less than to be scolded by whoever ran this place, so I decided to check the clipboard again. Maybe there was a second page I hadn't noticed before?

There was. Behind the blunt "YOU ARE DEAD" page was

another page that read: "YOU ARE ALLOWED TO LEAVE THE ROOM." Convenient.

I set down the clipboard and prepared to exit, but hesitated at the door. I had no idea what to expect on the other side. As far as I was concerned, it could be Heaven, it could be Hell, or it could be a cruel windowless hospital. I took a deep breath and prepared myself for the worst.

It was a hallway.

I knew it wasn't a hospital because the hallway was completely empty and it was lined with that short-fibered carpet that you find in office buildings. As I entered the space, I noticed that it extended in both directions, seemingly forever. Along the walls, were an equally infinite number of doors leading to, I assumed, rooms like mine.

I thought about returning to my room to lie on the bed for the foreseeable future, when a door opened about a dozen down the hall from mine. Out stepped an elderly gentleman sporting a darker version of the suit I was wearing. He looked over at me and nodded. I waved. He then walked forward to enter the room directly across from him, but before he could, I shouted.

"Wait!"

He paused mid step and cocked an eyebrow at me in confusion. I jogged over while he tapped his foot, as if he had some place to be.

"Excuse me," I said. Normally a run of any distance would have me gasping for breath, but I didn't feel the least bit winded. "I'm new here. Uh, could you tell me what I'm supposed to do?"

"Didn't you read your clipboard?" The irritation was evident in his voice. "Enter the door opposite yours."

"Oh. Thank you."

I walked away as he muttered something about young people's attention spans. Upon reaching the correct door, I thought I had better check my clipboard again, for anything else I may have missed. I went back into my room and flipped over to a new page. It read, "DO WHAT THE OLD MAN SAID." I was beginning to understand how the clipboard worked. I flipped one more page to make sure there wasn't any more. "THERE ISN'T ANY MORE. DO WHAT THE OLD MAN SAID."

Slightly embarrassed, I obliged the clipboard and returned to the hallway. Upon opening the specified door, I froze, awestruck. It wasn't so much a room as it was a grand hall. Enormous marble pillars reached up to a ceiling which displayed murals that would make Michelangelo weep. Actually, considering the circumstances, it's possible that Michelangelo painted them. Even the floor consisted of beautiful and intricate tile patterns. Beyond all this, just past the pillars, was a library. The bookshelves were at least three-stories tall and filled to the brim with innumerable volumes. Like the hallway, this all stretched on in both directions, without end.

Thousands of people formed lines, all leading to a row of desks in front of the library. At each desk, a person sat and rifled through various books. I chose the line in front of me and waited for my turn to speak with whoever sat at the end of it. Most of the people in line were elderly, but I suppose that was to be expected. Everyone, men and women alike, wore suits of a similar style, but for some reason, differing shades and colors. Several lines down, I spotted the old man I had met earlier in the hallway. When his gaze turned to me, I waved at him again. He did not return the gesture.

After about an hour or so, even the majesty of the ceiling paintings couldn't keep me occupied. The line was moving with the same enthusiasm as a deboarding plane. I understand that these people were analyzing their entire lives, but one would assume that the afterlife would have a more streamlined process for deciding who was condemned to spend an eternity burning in hellfire, or not. At last, the little old lady in front of me was granted entrance into the beyond, or whatever, and it was my turn to step up to the plate.

"Name?" The woman at the desk demanded.

I don't know why I would possibly think otherwise, but for some reason I asked, "Who? Me?"

"Yes you. You're next in line. What is your name?"

"My name is—" It just occurred to me; I haven't actually revealed my name yet. It's exactly what you would expect if you met me. It is utterly mundane and yet unique in its simplicity. I've considered legally expanding it on more than one occasion, but it always seemed like such a hassle for something so superficial. Besides, what would be the point of changing a name that suited me as well as it did? My name is—

"Bill Baker."

"I need your full name, Mr. Baker."

"That is my full name."

The woman looked up from whatever she had been writing. "Bill isn't a nickname? Short for William, maybe?"

"No, it's just Bill."

"Just Bill? No middle name or—?" She let the question hang, certain there was some kind of addition to my name that I hadn't thought to mention.

"No. Just Bill Baker."

"Bill Baker. Huh. Alright. One moment, Mr. Baker."

She scanned the library cart of books next to her and plucked the thinnest one, which bore my name. I thought to myself, *perhaps it's small because I'm younger*, but in all likelihood, I probably did very little in my life that merited recording. The woman at the desk opened the volume to a random middle page. Just as the correct book had been within her reach in an infinite library, the page she chose presented her with all the information she needed.

She read to herself, mumbling inaudibly every now and then, while I craned my neck to try and read along. After a couple minutes, she looked up.

"Everything seems fine."

"Really?" I grinned.

"Yep. I mean, you're not some saint. You don't volunteer, or give much to charity—"

"Well, you know, we just bought a house and the real estate market—"

The woman gave me a sharp look.

"—doesn't matter. Sorry."

She raised an eyebrow. "As I was saying, you're not perfect, but you aren't bad either. You've never stolen, you almost never lie, you've never cut out early from work? I mean, I do that *here*. It says you don't even like to *think* bad things about people? I had to double-check that to make sure I hadn't misread it."

"It makes me feel guilty."

"So I see. You've done literally nothing that would bar you from transition, so as soon as I finish your paperwork, you're free to move on. But might I suggest, when you get there, try to live a little."

I was taken aback by that comment, but happy about going to Heaven or whatever good version of the afterlife existed nonetheless. She pulled a new form out of her desk and began mumbling aloud as she wrote.

"Baker. Bill. Middle name, not applicable. Cause of death—"

She turned a page of my book and pointed to a random spot. Looking down to read from it, she frowned.

"Well, that's peculiar."

"What?" I asked, concerned.

"The cause of death."

"Why? How did I die?"

"I don't know. It doesn't say."

An image flashed in my mind: *A hulking figure, snarling, raising me high above itself.* And just as quickly, the image faded.

"Did someone forget to write it?" I asked, ignoring the intrusive image.

The woman looked concerned for a moment, which is not something you want to see in the afterlife.

"You'll have to excuse me one moment." She stood up from her desk and disappeared into the library. I heard a chorus of groans behind me and turned to see the entire line glaring in my direction. I turned back, and as fast as she had left, the woman returned, now accompanied by a tall, blond-haired man.

"Hello, Mr. Baker," the man said. "My name is Haniel. Would you mind coming with me, please?"

Everything about this situation screamed that something had gone terribly wrong, but for some reason, the sound of this man's voice put me at ease. He led me past the desks and into the labyrinth of bookcases, taking several turns until no one else was in sight.

"Here we are." He turned to the nearest shelf and pulled a false book. A door swung out, revealing a small, wood paneled office that contained only a desk, two chairs, a computer, and a ficus tree. For such a fantastical location, it was a sad looking room, though the ficus helped liven it up a bit. We sat down on opposite sides of the desk and Haniel smiled at me until I awkwardly returned the gesture.

"So, how are you feeling today, Mr. Baker?"

"Um, well—"

"What am I saying? You're dead! You must be feeling awful. Has it hit you yet?"

"Has what?"

"You know, being dead. Has it sunk in?"

"I don't really know."

"Ah, well then–no, it hasn't."

"How do you know that? Maybe I'm just handling it well."

He nodded encouragingly, "Maybe."

Haniel continued to grin at me like a customer service representative, but somehow, more genuine. In fact, everything about him was really quite pleasant. He had the face of a movie star, and even when discussing my death, I felt cheerful when he spoke.

"Are you from England?" I asked in response to his accent. He seemed delighted by my question.

"Do I sound English? Brilliant. I love the English. Wonderful vocabulary."

"So, you aren't then?"

"Oh no, I'm from here. I'm an angel."

"An angel? Do all angels sound English?"

"No. Technically speaking, I don't either. As a human relations representative here in The Library of Eternity, I've found that it's best to project a calming aura around myself. I both sound and appear however you'd like me to." He smiled even larger.

"So, how come the woman up front didn't sound—" I stopped, worried that Haniel might take my comment the wrong way. "I'm not trying to make a complaint, or anything, but she just didn't sound as—uh, welcoming."

"Oh, she's not an angel. It's very rare for an angel to work the front desks. The woman you spoke to was a high-level afterlife service worker."

"You still have to work in Heaven?"

"You're not actually in Heaven, not what you would consider Heaven to be anyway. You've been categorized into a transition point that most resembles your belief system. Technically this is an in-between world, like a cross-over flight. Have you ever been to Atlanta?"

"Yeah."

"It's like that."

"So, this is purgatory?"

"Eh, no. At least, not in the Catholic sense of the idea. Basically, what happens here ultimately determines where you proceed."

"You mean, what I did on Earth doesn't matter?"

"Of course that matters! In fact, if you're a particularly heinous person, they don't even let you up here."

"I'm very confused."

"Don't worry. You'll pick it up. Do you have any other questions?"

"Well, I have one, but I'm worried it might be offensive."

"Offensive to…?"

"Angels."

"I don't know if any human has ever considered that, least of all to myself." Haniel's smile widened. "Go ahead and I'll let you know."

"Do angels not have wings?"

"Ah, yes we do. We just like to keep them imperceptible."

"Oh. Do they just like… fold into your jacket?"

"More like they fold into another layer of reality. You see, they're quite large and I'm sure you've noticed the size of the room we're sitting in. It wouldn't do well to have two nine-foot, razor sharp protrusions tearing up the walls."

"Do they ever come out?"

"I suppose some angels use them more often than myself. They're mainly for traveling to and from Earth, or in the old days, for combat—which you can imagine, isn't very pertinent anymore. I don't believe I've unfolded my wings in over a millennia."

"Wow. Don't they get sore? I can't even sit at my desk for more than a few minutes without adjusting my legs."

Haniel's smile changed ever so slightly from polite to amused. "I'm sure you've noticed by now that your physical form isn't quite so fragile on this plane of existence. I don't imagine there's much I could do to experience soreness, even if I were human."

I noticed at that moment that I was actively bouncing my leg. I guess some compulsions have more to do with the spirit than the body.

"Is there anything else?" Haniel asked.

"Uh, nope. I think that covers it for now."

"In that case, we should address your problem."

He revealed my thin little life book and flipped it open on his desk. As he read, he began typing information into his bulky gray computer. It appeared to have been built back in the 90's, but like everything else in this afterlife, I assumed it contained qualities that surpassed anything that existed on Earth.

I waited, picking at my nails to pass the time. A few minutes of keyboard clicks went by when a thought occurred to me. *There's something I'm supposed to do today.*

"Excuse me, um—Mr. Haniel?"

He stopped typing and looked over at me, still smiling. "You don't have to call me 'Mister'. Haniel is fine. Can I help you?"

"I was just wondering about today's date."

"What about it?"

"Um, what is it?"

"Oh! Of course! Let's see," Haniel pulled a small flip calendar from his desk drawer and stabbed his finger at a random date. "On Earth, it is June, twenty-sixth. We don't have days here in The Library of Eternity, so it's a bit difficult to keep track in your head."

June, twenty-sixth. There was something important about that day, but I couldn't quite put my finger on it. I'd have to ask Grace the next time I saw her. Grace. *Oh my God.*

The past week flashed before my eyes. The planning, the preparations, the guests arriving, putting on my tuxedo, asking that strange man to fix my bowtie, going to the bathroom to clean a stain. I was getting married today, except—

The image returned. A monster impaling me on its claws, holding my body in the air as my essential functions flickered out. I had been killed and worse yet, that monster was still there, free to incite chaos. I'd been moping around in the afterlife for hours while my fiancée and entire wedding party was in peril. My eyes snapped open and I fell back in my chair, slamming hard on the thin carpet. I began screaming, both in pain and in horror of my realization.

Haniel didn't even react to the outburst. He just acknowledged, "So, it finally hit you."

"I'm fucking dead!"

The angel winced. "Yes, you are. And I'd ask that you watch your language here, please."

"But Grace! I have to go back!"

"Now, now, let's not be hasty. You can't just go back. We still need to figure out how you died."

"I was killed! By a monster!"

Haniel's smile twitched slightly. "Yes. I'm sure you were. I would feel better if we checked the files however, just to be certain." His words no longer had their initial calming effect.

"There's no time! Grace is in danger!"

"I'm nearly done, Mr. Baker. Once I've finished inputting all your information, I'll be able to access a video record of the events surrounding your death. Then, and only then, will we know for sure how you died."

I had no choice but to pick my chair back up and wait as Haniel took his sweet time, happily typing data into a 90's relic. I was mad, really mad, and I don't get mad easily. Unsure of how to direct my aggression, I glared at the ficus tree in the corner of the office. *Why did it get to live when I didn't?* Though, perhaps it was dead and placed in this office as its plant-afterlife, but that would suggest that plants have souls. I should look into that if I ever get the chance, but I'm getting off topic. I was mad at a tree.

I heard one final click from the keyboard and then silence. Haniel's eyes widened, his smile gone. He looked genuinely shocked, which must be rare for beings that have existed for thousands of years. He attempted to regain his composure and turned his attention back to me.

"Mr. Baker, there seems to be a problem with your death."

"I know." I said, doing my best to keep my temper. "That's why I'm here."

"Right. I apologize, but I didn't anticipate—uh, this."

"You mean a monster? I wasn't lying," I said, through gritted teeth. Every second we wasted on polite conversation was another in which the beast was free to run rampant through my wedding.

"Don't be silly, Mr. Baker, it wasn't a monster. You were killed by a demon."

I don't know if that was supposed to make me feel better.

"A demon, like, an evil-angel demon?"

"Ah, no. That's a common misconception. The fallen angels are prisoners of Hell, the same as a human soul would be. Demons are Hell*spawn*. They're native to the Hell dimension, and revel in the torture of both humans and fallen alike."

"So they aren't supposed to leave Hell?"

"It wouldn't be a very good prison if they could."

"But this demon did."

Haniel paused, concerned. "Yes, well, this is a very unusual occurrence. Demons are spiritual creatures. They can project their essence from Hell to possess open minds on Earth, but to my knowledge, no demon has ever breached the physical plane. They technically shouldn't be able to, hence the problem."

"Yeah, hence. So, send me back."

"I beg your pardon?"

"If these things aren't supposed to get out, then I'm assuming I wasn't supposed to die in the first place, correct?"

"It's not that simple. People die before their intended time every day, Mr. Baker. Murder is not part of the grand plan, but these people do not simply get to return to Earth."

"So, there's nothing you can do?" I stood out of my chair. "That thing is still down there! It could be on a killing rampage, and you're going to let it go?"

Haniel clasped his hands together and narrowed his eyes at me. I could see his gears turning in whatever constituted an angelic brain. "I didn't say that. Murderers face judgment for their sins. Demons do not. Technically, there's no protocol for something like this, so it would seem that we have a bit of leeway to work with."

"Is that a good thing?" I asked.

"Perhaps." Haniel stood from his desk and paced around the tiny room, concocting some kind of plan. At last, he turned his attention back to me. "Suppose I *could* grant you your life back, Mr. Baker, would you be willing to do something in return?"

My eyes lit up, "Anything."

Haniel's smile returned to his face. "Wonderful. If this demon remains on Earth for long, it is likely to continue killing and disrupting the natural order of events that have been laid out by my superiors. They would not like that. And unfortunately, even if I report the problem, there is little we can do to stop it ourselves. Angels are forbidden from direct interference in the affairs of mankind."

"Even when demons are directly interfering?" I asked.

"Just because they break the rules doesn't give us the right to. Someone has to set an example."

I wanted to argue against what had to be the stupidest justification I'd ever heard, but I held my tongue so as not to prolong this any further. "What can I do, then?" I asked.

"Humans have been the instruments of the angels for thousands of years. Granted, we usually pick living ones, but as this is a special case, I think you'll do just nicely. You are going to return to earth and put a stop to this demon's rampage before things spiral out of control. While I can't go with you, I will do some research in the Library to aid you in your task. And of course, I will assign a partner to assist you."

"A partner? Who?" I asked.

"His name is Sonny, and he's the man who took your soul."

3

A DEAL WITH DEATH

HANIEL PLACED A call on a seemingly ordinary office phone, but as with every "ordinary" device in the afterlife, this corded hunk of plastic contained supernatural qualities. The phone was able to contact anyone in both the physical and spiritual worlds as a voice in the mind. It provided a literal angel on the figurative shoulder of whoever received the call. Sonny has since described the process as a forcible penetration of his brain and claims that nothing has ever made him feel more violated. It just sounds like listening to Bluetooth headphones to me.

After a few minutes of waiting, a hole opened up in the fabric of reality. As if that wasn't alarming enough, out of the portal stepped the most horrifying man I'd ever beheld. What was left of his skin looked to be in the process of decomposition. It was slimy and peeled in multiple places. He still had hair, but only long, select strands scattered sporadically about his head. Parts of his skull were visible, most noticeably on his cheek bones and the bottom of his chin. He dressed nice enough, in khakis and a cardigan, but that failed to distract from the portions of him that remained uncovered. The floating rip in space-time sealed up behind him and the apparition glared at Haniel.

"Well," Sonny said, frustrated at having his mind penetrated. "You rang?"

"Yes, Sonny. Thank you for coming."

"Always a pleasure." His words dripped with irritation.

"I called you here in regard to one of your reapings. Do you recall Mr. Baker here?"

Without even bothering to glance at me, Sonny replied, "No."

"Well, you collected his soul at nine—"

Sonny held up his hand. "I should be more clear. I have not today, nor have I ever, recalled one of my reapings. I'm in-and-out, no time to take in the sights."

"Well then," Haniel continued. "I suppose that means you don't remember the nature of Mr. Baker's death, either?"

"That's a good guess."

"Despite the fact that he was killed in a manner not seen since the First Apocalypse?"

Sonny scrunched his face. "Am I supposed to know what that means?"

"He was stabbed through the chest by a demon, and while my records show that you arrived during the encounter, you didn't see fit to report the sighting."

Sonny's annoyed expression faded. "A demon? C'mon Haniel, that's impossible. Even under possession, people can't be forced to commit murder."

"It wasn't a possession, it was a full-fledged, physical demon roaming around on Earth."

Sonny tilted his head. "That's even more impossible."

"Now you understand why I called you here. And it raises the question, how did it go unnoticed? I understand that you can be less than vigilant on the job, but a demon is a difficult creature to miss,

Sonny."

"I probably wasn't even in the room, Haniel. Half the time, I'll just reach my arm through the portal."

Haniel raised an eyebrow and began writing something down on a sheet of paper.

"What are you writing? Stop!" Sonny demanded, but Haniel continued, undeterred. "Look, I'm sorry for not reporting this, but if you're thinking of raising my quota—"

"Relax, Sonny," Haniel set down his pen. "We aren't without mercy, but perhaps this will be a lesson to pay closer attention in the future."

"Absolutely," Sonny clasped his hands together, feigning sincerity. "Believe me when I say, this will not happen again. So, may I return to my shift? I'd like to rack up a few more souls before I clock out."

"No, Sonny. And you can stop being so anxious to return. You're being placed on leave as of now."

"Leave?" Sonny's expression turned from apologetic to furious. "That is complete bullshit! You can't do this Haniel! Not when I am so close to finishing this God forsaken job—"

"Please avoid blasphemy while in my office."

"I just want to get back to work so I can finish my quota, the quota you're forcing me to meet! Is that too much to ask? It's bad enough out there with you guys fucking up my hours! I mean you got these Goddamn—"

Haniel's manner changed dramatically. The lighting in the room dimmed and his aura of peace mutated. I felt pressed to the wall, bombarded by waves of radiance and unable to look directly at the angel. When he spoke, his voice enveloped the room, reverberating in my chest. He no longer had a British accent.

"I am an angel, first of creation. I have witnessed the birth and death of a billion worlds before the spark of life ignited on Earth. I will not be swayed by concerns of mere days in the scope of infinity. I will do as I see fit to do and you can accept it, or you can face your eternal damnation." The lights flickered back on and Haniel's presence returned to normal. A few sheets of loose paper gently cascaded back down to the angel's desk.

Sonny had taken several steps back and was visibly shaken by Haniel's transformation. When he noticed me looking at him, he straightened himself and adjusted his cardigan.

"I apologize, Sonny. That was uncalled for." Haniel spoke with his usual jolly inflection. "You know how I feel about cursing."

"Yeah, I'll uh—I'll keep that in mind."

Throughout this encounter, I had been a mostly unnoticed spectator. However, Haniel's full angelic glory had frightened me more than his intended target. I began to feel a lump grow in my throat that would almost certainly prevent my breathing if I did nothing about it. In my panic, I forgot that I was dead and did not, in fact, need to breathe. I made the softest grunt I could manage, prompting both Haniel and Sonny to turn their gaze to me. I took this as an opportunity to enter the conversation.

"So, how exactly is Mr. uh…" I waited for someone to inform me of Sonny's last name, but they only continued to stare in my direction. "Mr. Sonny going to help me with my problem?"

Sonny looked back and forth between Haniel and myself. "What is he talking about? What problem?"

"The demon, Sonny." Haniel said. "I've promised Mr. Baker here a chance to return to Earth in exchange for his service."

"Why? You already know where the thing is. Go get it yourself."

"You know my limitations better than most, Sonny. I cannot directly interfere. You, however, are still technically human and are bound by no such rules. You will take Mr. Baker back to Earth and you will assist in the capture or elimination of the demon."

Sonny blinked. "Capture a demon?"

"Or eliminate." I added, trying to be helpful.

Sonny rolled his eyes at me. "Okay, fine. But if this guy gets his life back, I deserve something too."

Haniel took a moment to consider this. He then retrieved a fresh sheet of paper and pen from his desk and briefly became a blur above the parchment. I'd have sworn he sprung eight hands in that half second he spent writing, before suddenly snapping back to normal. He held up the completed legal document with his own signature at the bottom. "In payment for your service, I will reduce the remainder of your quota by half."

Sonny's expression transformed from discontent to elation. Whatever Haniel had offered him was, apparently, a big deal.

"Does that mean you'll help me?" I asked Sonny.

He tore his gaze away from the contract and looked at me, his thoughts still transfixed by the promise of his reward. "Maybe. Though I'd be much more tempted to help if Haniel offered to fulfill *all* of my quota."

"You get half, Sonny," Haniel told him.

"Seventy-five percent," Sonny shot back.

"I can always find someone else."

"Half sounds great!" Sonny gave a thumbs up to Haniel and slapped me on the back. "Mr. Badger and I will have that demon back in Hell before anyone even notices it's gone."

"It's Baker, actually. Bill Baker," I corrected.

"Whatever."

"Does this mean we can leave now?" I asked Haniel. "I want to stop this thing before it has a chance to hurt anyone else at my wedding."

The room turned silent. Haniel and Sonny gave each other a knowing look. "What?" I asked. "What aren't you telling me?"

"Mr. Baker," Haniel sat down at his desk to meet me at eye level. "It's been nearly four hours since your death. I can assure you; the demon is no longer at your wedding venue."

"So then, it just killed me and left? Nothing else happened?"

"Well—" Haniel's eyes shifted to the screen of his computer and then quickly back to me.

"What's on the screen?" I asked.

Haniel dropped his smile, again. "Now, before I show this to you—"

I leapt out of my seat and grabbed the monitor, turning it to face me. I feared I would see the monster throwing my guests around and causing absolute mayhem. This was worse. Instead of the demon, I saw myself. My own body was terrorizing my wedding, jumping from chair to chair, shouting inaudibly and laughing. Haniel reluctantly turned on the audio, revealing that the shouting was mostly just profanity. The guests fled as this imposter assaulted them. Some people tried to tackle it, but were rebuffed by the creature's enormous strength.

I could see members of Grace's family, falling over themselves to get out of the church. Everyone swarmed to the exit like mice fleeing a sinking ship. In the midst of the chaos, I could see the tall, gaunt caterer who fixed my bowtie standing in the corner, seemingly oblivious to the dire situation. He just smiled and casually cut himself a slice of cake. Better than letting it go to waste, I guess.

Then my heart stopped. Stepping down the aisle and watching this madness unfold, was Grace—my fiancée, speechless at what she beheld. I hoped more than anything that the imposter wouldn't notice her, that it would chase someone else out of the church and leave her be. For a moment, it seemed as if my wish might come true. One of Grace's cousins had thrown a wine glass at my body's face, cutting it up pretty bad. But just as the imposter began to pursue its assailant, Grace opened her mouth and spoke two words.

"Bill, why?"

The demon stopped. It turned towards Grace with a grin so fiendish, I was astonished that my face could produce it. Grace stepped back, looking rightfully terrified. I wanted to intervene, to force Sonny to open a portal and take me there to stop this, but it had already happened. There was nothing I could do.

The imposter leapt across the aisle before Grace could turn to run.

It grabbed her by the wrist and pulled her chin inches from its wicked smile.

"What's wrong sweetheart? It's our wedding day! Try and have a little fun!"

His voice was heinous, and yet still mine. Anybody would tell you we sounded just alike, yet somehow, completely different. Grace tried to pull away, but it was useless.

"Don't tell me you're having second thoughts?"

"Why are you doing this?" Grace pleaded, tears streaming down her cheeks.

"Why? Why!" it screamed at her. "Look at me! I've been living the life of a pitiful nobody for too long. I think it's time I make a change. Now, what do you say we consummate this thing right here and now? It's not every day I get to desecrate a church."

I was about to turn away from the screen when a miracle happened; our officiant tried to kill me. The priest had broken a wooden leg off a chair and stabbed the imposter from behind. I was just as surprised by the act as the demon was. The beast released Grace, who ran surprisingly swiftly for a woman in a wedding dress and heels. The splintered wood poked through the imposter's chest, eliciting genuine fear from my puppetted expression. Then, its smile returned. The imposter pushed the broken wood all the way through my body, to the other side. It examined the bloodied tip of the makeshift weapon while the priest looked on in horror.

"Thanks for that, father. I'd wanted to test how much punishment one of these meat suits could take." Lightning fast, it shoved the bloody wood straight into the priest's heart. "Looks like yours isn't so sturdy." The priest trembled, staring at my grinning face as he went slack. For a split second, there was the flash of a portal behind him. The priest's soul was yanked through, and the portal vanished.

Haniel paused the video and turned to Sonny, who was now watching over our shoulders.

"So, it seems you missed the demon, again."

"Hey, in my defense, he just looked like a guy that time."

"Fair enough. I'll likely be receiving another call about that gentleman in a moment, but for now, let's settle your matter, Mr. Baker."

My eyes were still glued to the screen, staring at my own hellish grin. What must Grace think of me right now? What would she think of me for the rest of her life?

"Mr. Baker," Haniel placed a hand on my shoulder. "Are you ready?"

I pulled myself away from the computer and began pacing the room. "Is she okay?" I asked. "Did Grace manage to get away safely?"

Haniel typed something into his keyboard. "She's fine. Shaken up, but on her way out of town."

I let out a sigh of relief. "Okay. Okay, good. And you promise that if we do this for you, I can go back to her?

"I am an angel of my word."

"Okay. I think I'm ready, then."

"Excellent." Haniel stood up from his desk and came around to face me. A little red light began flashing on his magic phone. "That'll be the priest." Haniel said. "Looks like I'm going to have a busy day. I'll keep my eyes open for sightings of the demon and inform you when it pops up. Then it should be as simple as popping over and luring it into one of Sonny's portals. When I'm through processing the rest of this demon's victims, I'll do a scan of the library database for additional information in case you need to weaken it somehow first."

I cocked my head in confusion. "You don't know how to hurt it? But you're an angel. Haven't you fought these things before?"

"Of course not. I told you, demons are hellspawn. None have ever left that dominion and I've certainly never paid it a visit myself. Given that it's a dimension of unending fire and torture, I would imagine the native creatures are relatively resilient."

Sonny scowled. "Relatively?"

"What about holy water?" I suggested. "Would that work?"

Sonny rolled his eyes and Haniel offered a condescending smile.

"While I'm sure that works in films," the angel said. "It's very unlikely that something so rudimentary would have any effect on a *real* demon. I'll let you know what I discover. If worse comes to worst, there are weapons capable of vanquishing any spiritual entity, but I hesitate to place one in the hands of humans—no offense."

"Offense very much taken," Sonny said.

"In any case, we have a plan B. Just don't forget, Sonny; your quota doesn't budge until the job is done."

"Aye aye, cap." Sonny gave Haniel a floppy salute. "Let's go, Biff."

Before I could try to correct him, he departed the office, shutting the door in my face. I turned to Haniel and gave him a short wave before following Sonny. "Thank you for your help, I think."

"I'll be thanking you if you manage to pull this off. Good luck, Mr. Baker."

4

THE LIBRARY OF ETERNITY

I CLOSED THE door to Haniel's office and turned to see Sonny disappear behind a bookshelf. I had to jog so as not to lose him as he weaved through the aisles like a rat in a maze. By the time we reached a point where I felt thoroughly lost, he stopped.

"This should be far enough," he said.

"Far enough for what?"

"To avoid any snooping angels or other library workers. I prefer to browse in peace."

"Shouldn't we be getting back to Earth?"

"If you'd like to get massacred twice in one day, sure. Personally, I'd like to develop a plan of action before ambushing a creature literally designed to inflict pain and torture."

Sonny began pulling books from the nearest shelf, flipping through the pages, and tossing them to the floor. It confused me, as I had assumed that every book in The Library of Eternity magically opened to the information you needed. I was also appalled to see someone treating books in such an aggressive manner. I bent over to place them back on the shelf.

"You don't have to do that," Sonny told me.

"We can't just leave them down here."

"This ain't your local library, kid. As soon as we leave, they'll be back on the shelf, in pristine condition."

"Does someone come and do that? Or is it like… magic?"

"I don't know. I don't work here."

I set the books back on the floor, still careful not to scuff them, while Sonny continued his search. After his tenth discarded book, I investigated further. "What exactly are you looking for? I might be able to help."

Sonny paused and bit his lip, contemplating an answer. "I'm not sure, yet."

That only left me more confused. "Then why are you looking at all?"

He slammed another book shut and sighed. "If I knew what I was looking for, I would find it. I'm just brainstorming here. Give me a minute"

"Well, we're looking for information on the demon right? Is there some kind of monster directory or hell encyclopedia we can use?"

After tossing yet another book over his shoulder, Sonny rolled his eyes toward me. "Look Ben, I don't like you, and you don't like me—"

"It's Bill, and to be fair, I don't really know you."

"Yeah. And it would be insane to like someone you don't know."

"I guess. Though sometimes preconceived notions—"

"For God's sake, don't fucking split hairs with me. You don't like me, and I REALLY don't like you now. Regardless, we have been forced together for what I hope to be a mercifully short period of time. Now, if we're going to survive the duration of that time, you're going to have to learn a thing or two. The first thing being: everything Haniel says is bullshit. In fact, that goes for all angels."

"Everything? Like even their names?"

"Well, no, not everything. Obviously some things—God-fuck-ing-dammit you're doing it again. Just listen. Angels are company men, alright? They are naive, trusting do-gooders who believe the system they serve is beyond reproach. They have no conception of anything not directly related to their specific duties because no one ever gave them permission to. Every second they're not pulling invisible strings to make my job a pain in the neck, they are just sitting in quiet rooms, staring blankly at the wall with a dumb smile on their face."

"I thought they were supposed to be all-knowing?"

"No, you're thinking of the monotheistic God, if such a thing even exists."

"What do you mean if? Don't you know the answer here in the afterlife?"

"Why would I know? I've never been to the higher realms. I have no idea what's going on up there. With my luck, it's probably just a board room of more useless fucking angels running everything. Which brings me to my point. The angels claim that all knowledge in the universe is contained in this library, but I know that isn't true. Some knowledge is either restricted, or missing."

"Missing? Like checked out of The Library?"

"Missing like nonexistent. Go ahead, give it a shot. Think of a topic."

"A topic? What, like—anything?"

"Yes, anything. Go."

I looked down at the floor, my mind frozen from overwhelming choice.

"Christ," Sonny blurted. "Just watch me. I'd like a book about capybaras." He reached over to the nearest shelf and, without looking, held up the first book his fingers touched.

I leaned closer to read the title. "*World's Largest Rodent: A Study of the Capybara.*"

"Oh look, it can read. Think of a topic yet?"

I ignored the slight and focused on the first idea that popped into my head. I shut my eyes and snatched a random book off the shelf.

"What is it?" Sonny asked.

I opened my eyes and examined the cover. *"Bram Stoker's Dracula."*

"Dracula? What the hell were you thinking about?"

"Dracula."

Sonny raised an eyebrow, but held in any would-be retort. "Right. So we established that it works. Now by all means, retrieve the information you'd like about demons."

It was clear where this was headed, but I decided to humor him regardless. I pulled a book from the shelf, thinking, *I want to know about demons.* The book I pulled was *The Exorcist* with a small sticker on the cover stating "Now a major motion picture!". Perhaps if I asked a more specific question. *How do I kill a demon?* The next book was called *Conquering Your Inner Demons: How to be Your Best You.*

"See what I mean? Missing." Sonny turned away to continue his random search.

"But why? How do entire subjects like this go missing in an infinite library?"

"There are theories, but no one really knows for certain. The angels won't even acknowledge it. And it's not as if the information about *where* the books went can be pulled from the—" Sonny stopped. He had just opened a new book and was staring at the page.

"Sonny?" I asked. "You were saying something about the missing books?"

"Shut up for a second," he said, his eyes bouncing from line to line.

I did as instructed, pacing down the aisle and running my hands over the spines of books. It occurred to me that any question I ever had about the universe was literally at my fingertips. I tried to think of one, but my mind was too distracted. I didn't have existential concerns, I merely wanted to know more about what I was getting myself into. Most especially, I wondered about my new partner. *Who is he, and how did he end up like this?*

As my fingers grazed the book spines, they stopped on one that poked out a little more than the rest. I read the title on the side: *The Book of Benito.* Next to the title was a series of symbols that I didn't recognize. Perhaps it was The Library's way of coding and organizing each book. I was curious and began to pull it off the shelf when I heard Sonny call from down the aisle.

"I think I may have a lead. This book is new, like brand new. No offense, Brad, but you may have died at the most convenient time in a millenia."

"Not my name—and I feel like I disagree, but can I ask why?"

"Because otherwise I may not have discovered what might be the most important book in this entire library."

"What is it?"

Sonny held up a worn composition notebook with the words *Kelsie's 5th Semester Notes* written in Sharpie.

I stared at it in complete confusion.

"Don't worry about it." Sonny stuffed the notebook in the inside of his cardigan. "Suffice it to say, I know where we should go first."

"Okay, great! Where?"

"I'll show you." He walked over and placed his hand on my back, smiling at me. "I should probably ask: you don't get motion sickness, do you?"

Before I could process the question, he yanked me back through the fabric of space-time. And to answer his question: *yes, I get terrible motion sickness.*

5

BORN AGAIN

I ASSUMED THAT spirits couldn't get hurt. After all, pain is just a psychological sensation—a result of nerve signals trying to prevent harm to the body. If souls were immune to these sensations however, the entire concept of Hell would be pointless. I can assure you, it doesn't matter if you have no physical form, having your essence spaghettified from one end of the universe to another feels unpleasant.

I shot out of the portal like a canon, skidding across the ground and moaning in pain. We were back on Earth. A clear blue sky shone overhead and even for my spectral body, the June heat was blistering. Sonny however, could not have appeared more aloof when he emerged, lightly brushing some lint off his lapel.

He offered his hand to help me up and I immediately wished that he hadn't. His flesh was grotesque, yet, a lifetime of social protocol informed me that refusing his help would be rude. So, against my better instincts, I took the hand. It felt like I was grabbing a colony of worms, squirming around a cluster of bones. I gritted my teeth and resisted the urge to ghost-vomit, *excrete ectoplasm maybe.* Now at eye level, he smirked at me.

"What?" I asked.

"Oh nothing. I just determined that I know exactly the kind of person you are."

"In the past twenty minutes?

"Why did you take my hand?" the reaper asked.

I tilted my head in confusion. "Well, you were trying to help—"

"I know what I was doing. You think I'm ignorant of my condition? Why do you think I carry these?" He retrieved a pair of gloves from his cardigan pocket and slipped them over his hands.

"I didn't want to offend— Hang on, why not just put the gloves on in the first place?" I asked.

"I wanted to see what you'd do."

My confusion morphed into indignation. The more I got to know my new partner, the less I cared for him. I only hoped our time together would be over as soon as possible.

He walked past me with a smug smile on his face, and as I turned to follow, I noticed that we were in the courtyard of a hospital. I jogged to catch up.

"Hey! Why are we here?"

"Isn't it obvious? You need a new body. This is basically a body supermarket."

"Oh, right." I said, unnerved by his analogy. "Won't somebody notice you though? I mean, you don't exactly blend in."

"Thanks. What happened to not wanting to offend, asshole?"

"Oh! I didn't mean—"

"Calm down." Sonny chuckled. "I'm just fucking with you, man. This job is going to be a real drag if you don't loosen up."

"Sorry."

"You don't have to apologize. And I swear, if you apologize for apologizing, I'll stuff your soul in the body of a rat."

"Can you actually do that?"

"I don't know, I've never tried."

"You still haven't answered my question."

"What? Oh, will I be noticed? No, and neither will you. Being a grim reaper is hard enough without the people you're trying to reap fleeing at the sight of you. Human brains can't process our existence."

"What about ghost sightings and stuff? Surely someone has seen something."

"Most of those are, in all likelihood, bullshit. True ghosts don't exist, except for you, I suppose. Souls can only be separated from a body by a reaper or an angel, after which they are immediately deposited to the next stage of the afterlife. We can't let them just run wild on Earth, it wouldn't count towards our quota. I suppose it's possible that someone could have glimpsed a reaper—and, of course, there are other things that go bump in the night, but I won't get into all that."

That was the second time my new companion had mentioned some kind of quota, but far more interesting was the last tidbit. I already knew that walking corpses and demons were roaming around in secret. What else could be out there?

We entered the hospital and I attempted to weave past anyone who walked through the halls—a difficult task being invisible as I was. Sonny phased through them without hesitation.

"So, if people can only glimpse spiritual stuff," I continued. "Why was I able to see the demon that killed me? I had like, a full-on duel with the thing."

Sonny shrugged. "The brain has hiccups. It must have stood still too long for your mind to ignore. Or maybe you're just a special little boy who doesn't have to play by the rules. You are here after all, the first human soul free to walk the Earth since the second apocalypse."

"The what?"

"You know, that whole thing with Noah and the big boat."

Every question Sonny answered only raised new ones. If I was the first human soul to return to Earth, then what was he? And if the flood was the second apocalypse, what was the first? Were there any afterwards, or were we due for another one?

I followed the reaper into the stairwell and continued up to the third floor. I wondered why we didn't use the elevator, but figured spirits were unable to press buttons. Still, how we could pass through people and walls without falling through the floor was a mystery to me.

Sonny led us into a dark room. The closed blinds cast a dim light on a network of machines hooked up to a relatively overweight balding man, somewhere in his fifties. He appeared to be in deep sleep, or more likely, a coma—given the state of his surroundings. I looked around the rest of the room and found no one else.

Sonny walked around the bed and reached into his cardigan pocket. He pulled out another magical item: the reaper's list. It was a small yellowish piece of paper, rolled at the top and bottom with only a few words scrawled on it. Assumedly, like the books in The Library, the information he needed was all that appeared. Sonny glanced at his list for less than a second and stuffed it back in his pocket. He moved closer to the man in the bed and hovered his hands over him.

"You might want to stand back," he said.

It was almost too quick to see. Sonny reached into the man's body, grabbed hold of the soul, and ripped it out. I winced, remembering the pain of my own detachment. With his other hand, Sonny swiped through the air causing one of his portal things to materialize in its wake. He then heaved the naked spirit through it and sealed the hole back up with another motion.

The machines went haywire. Within seconds, hospital staff rushed into the room, through my ethereal form, and attempted to save the empty vessel. Amongst the panic, Sonny casually strolled away from the scene. He took me by the arm and led me out of the room, stopping right outside the door.

"We'll wait for them to clean the body. They should do it pretty quickly, otherwise it starts to stiff up."

Having a second to think, it occurred to me that without any consideration for my opinion, Sonny had chosen the body I would temporarily be living in.

"Wait a minute," I said. "Is that it? That's my body?"

"Yeah, wasn't that clear?"

"That was the first room we walked into, what if there was something better?"

"Better? Is this because he's bald?"

I rolled my eyes. "Obviously not."

"I think this is pretty good under the circumstances. I know he's not as ethnically ambiguous as you, but you're both middle-aged chubby dudes. What's the difference?"

"First off, I am not middle-aged. I'm thirty-two."

"In my day, that was practically elderly."

"Second, ignoring the chubby remark, that guy is in way worse shape than me. Aren't we going into battle?"

"Like you're in peak fighting condition as is?"

I scowled at him. "And one more thing, what do you mean 'as ethnically ambiguous as me'?"

"I mean, I'm not gonna throw around assumptions. I don't know your lineage."

"My name is Bill Baker. My parents were the whitest people I've ever met."

"Interesting. You ever done one of those online DNA things?"

"No."

"You might want to look into it when you get your own body back."

I opened my mouth to retort, but found myself lacking a response. My parents' relationship wasn't exactly an endorsement for the institution of marriage. Was it possible that they weren't entirely truthful about my upbringing?

"Look," Sonny finally snapped me out of my stupor, "This is the best body you're gonna get under the circumstances. I had to place you close to our contact."

"Contact?" I asked, pushing my newfound parentage concerns to the back burner.

"Yeah, that's why we came here. That book I found in The Library mentioned a college professor that lives nearby. I think he might have valuable information pertaining to our mission."

"Why do we have to be close to the contact? Can't we just warp through your magic portals?"

"They're not magic, and I can't take you through a portal once you have a body. Only spiritual stuff can travel through them and you'll need a physical body to talk to the contact. Trust me, unless you'd rather wait around for a star athlete to have a freak accident, this is the best option."

The door next to us opened and the room began clearing out. Sonny and I took our opportunity to slip inside. The reaper walked over to the corpse and waited for me to approach. I gazed into the dead man's face, wondering how it would feel to become someone else.

"So, how exactly—" Before I could finish, Sonny reached into my chest and grabbed me by my ghostly spinal cord. He lifted me over his head and plunged my soul down into the body of Herman Powell.

As his brain became my own, I was blasted with a flood of memories and sensations that didn't belong to me. *Herman Powell was a college professor who taught psychology at the nearby university. He was estranged from most of his family, but had recently begun to repair the relationship between himself and his daughter. Yesterday however, the two got into an argument that ended with her declaring that she was done giving him chances; that he would never meet his grandchildren. After the conversation ended, he had a heart attack.*

My new body convulsed as my soul attached itself to all its components. Suddenly becoming 20 years older and ninety pounds heavier is not a sensation you can prepare for. A person's body can change dramatically over time, but transforming in an instant felt like morphing into a werewolf. I wanted to scream in pain, but bit my lip so as not to cause a commotion in the hospital. I couldn't help wondering though, *why does everything in the afterlife hurt?*

The convulsions stopped and I opened my new, matured eyes. My vision was blurry. I thought it was a temporary side effect of returning from the dead, but my new memories revealed that Herman wore glasses. Next to me, Sonny was waving his hands, attempting to grab my attention. As my hearing faded in, I realized he was yelling.

"Hey, buddy! Can you still see me? Can you hear me?"

I groaned a deep and heavy groan, deeper than any noise my original body could conjure. Talking was still difficult, so I nodded my head at him.

"Okay good, I was worried you might lose some functions. Can you walk? We need to get you out of here before the hospital staff shows back up."

I lifted my arm, not to get up, but to make sure I could move. After that, I tried to lean forward, but to no avail. I wasn't strong enough to get off my back yet, so I tried rolling like an overturned turtle. Once on my side, I could see a pair of glasses on the bedside table. *Convenient.* After a few moments of rocking back and forth, I was able to push my body off the bed and balance on my new feet.

"Alright, good job. Now, let's go!"

Herman needed to update the prescription on his glasses, but at least I could see where I was going. I stumbled away from the bed, like a giant baby walking for the first time. Sonny's frustration was evident as he pantomimed pushing me to go faster. My steps became less wobbly with each successive movement and by the time I reached the door, I could pass as a man with a limp.

Thankfully, I wasn't the only person in a hospital gown, but it would only take one member of the staff to recognize the guy-who-just-died to blow everything. Sonny led me to the elevator, tapping his foot as his eyes darted in every direction.

After pushing the down button, I grumbled in the back of my throat until I was able to form words. "Why are you so nervous?" I asked. "I'm the one who's in trouble if we get caught." My new voice was deeper than I expected and hearing it emerge from my mouth was disorienting.

"I'm not nervous. I'm agitated. If you wouldn't topple on the first step, we could be taking the stairs."

"Are you scared of elevators, or something?"

"I just prefer stairs. This is why you're so overweight. You clearly never take the stairs."

I wasn't sure if I should be offended on behalf of a body that wasn't technically mine. Before I could decide, the elevator doors opened and the doctor inside looked me right in the eye. That is to say, he looked at Herman Powell—a man he saw die a few minutes earlier. The doctor was frozen in place, staring at a ghost. Beside me, Sonny was screaming.

"Do something! Anything!"

I panicked. I don't work well under pressure and I had a multitude of better solutions than the one I landed on. I could have told the doctor I'd experienced a miraculous recovery and wanted to stretch my legs. I could have joined him in the elevator and quickly explained the situation, only to run away when we arrived at the bottom floor. I probably could have smiled and walked past him, allowing the doctor to believe I actually was a ghost. What I absolutely should not have done was punch him in the face.

He fell back into the elevator, howling in pain and drawing all eyes to me. I turned to Sonny, hoping that my ancient and world-weary guide would offer a clever solution to this predicament.

"RUN!"

I should have known he would be as useless under pressure as I was, considering his last shriek of advice was "do something". Still, I heeded his suggestion.

My balance hadn't fully returned, so my first two strides involved me toppling into a nurse and knocking over a, thankfully, empty wheelchair. After that, I started to get the hang of it, placing my hand on the wall for support. Sonny was in front, leading me to the stair-well. I looked behind me to see if my pursuers were gaining ground, but all I saw was a few people helping the doctor to his feet. That did not slow my pace however, because as soon as I reached the stairs, I proceeded to tumble forward halfway down. There was no time to wallow in pain. I brought myself to my feet and *carefully* made my way down the rest of the steps. Sonny, who had apparently forgotten that I was following him, rushed back up to meet me.

"What are you doing? We gotta go!"

"Can you not see that I'm trying?" I asked, gritting my teeth.

He looked up the stairwell to check for pursuers, but so far, we were in the clear.

"Okay, I have an idea," he said. "Follow me." I reached the second floor and Sonny led me out of the stairwell.

"Wait, why are we going—"

"Just trust me!"

As I exited, I could hear the door above us open up, followed by footsteps. Sonny made me stand to the side while he peered through the little window on the door. As he predicted, the hospital staff ran right past us and continued down to the ground floor. He breathed a sigh of relief.

"It's a good thing this is a hospital," the reaper said. "Most places would've taken you down before helping the injured guy."

"Do you think he's okay?" I asked, guilt ridden.

"He's fine, everyone could do with a good punch to the face now and then. Keeps you on your toes."

"Now what do we do?"

"Well," he gulped. "They certainly won't be expecting you to try the elevator again."

6

CURSED WITH KNOWLEDGE

THE REASON SONNY wanted to avoid the elevator was an issue with awareness. According to him, spirits can walk on solid surfaces because their mind knows it's there. In fact, they can interact with any solid object so long as they devote their attention to it. The problem comes when a solid object begins to move without their knowledge. For this reason, Sonny was forced to grip the handrails of the elevator for dear life so as not to fall through the floor as we made our descent. He glared at me all the while, as if daring me to poke fun at his behavior—which I genuinely would never have done. Despite our rocky start, we were able to escape the hospital without further incident.

Once on the ground level, he instructed me to wait in the parking lot while he procured our transportation. I'd only been waiting about a minute with my hospital gown billowing in the wind before the reaper returned, jingling a set of car keys.

"Did you steal those?" I asked, knowing the answer.

"What, are they gonna arrest me?" He began clicking the key

FOB until the distinctive sound of a car horn honked in the distance. With a smile, he tossed the keys to me. "Go get in the car," he said. "Your ass is showing."

It was hard to debate such an ironclad argument. We made our way quickly to the white sedan that matched our newly acquired keys—however, as I buckled into the driver's seat, a thought occurred to me.

"Wait, what happens when I start driving? Will you phase through the car?"

"As long as you don't drive like a maniac, no." Sonny said.

"But I thought it was harder for ghosts to stay in a moving object?"

"For starters, I'm not a ghost. Second, it's just a matter of concentration, I can see the car moving in space, so it's really not that hard to orient myself. Now, throw me in the trunk? Then we'll have problems."

With my concerns abated, I pulled out of the hospital parking lot while Sonny directed me towards our "contact" using his magic list. Driving around the college town, I found that I recognized the shops, and could recall personal feelings associated with them. As we passed a local restaurant, I suddenly craved a basket of their specialty: a basket of nacho cheese flavored Doritos with white queso poured over. It took me a moment to realize that I had never actually been in that restaurant and was simply experiencing the memories of my host body. It was uncomfortably intimate to know so much about this stranger. Being inside his mind felt invasive, almost as invasive as Haniel suddenly joining me in it.

It began as a high-pitched ringing in my ears. I looked over to Sonny to see if he could hear it too, only to find him scrunching his face and banging his head against his seat. After a few seconds, the tone was replaced by a friendly greeting. "Hello Mr. Baker, Sonny. It's me, Haniel."

"Dammit Haniel!" screamed Sonny. He pressed his hands against his ears, as if that would silence a noncorporeal voice in his thoughts.

"I apologize. This is the most convenient way for me to communicate."

"Well, it sure as hell isn't *convenient* for me!" Sonny retorted.

The angel ignored him and addressed me instead. "Mr. Baker, I see you've located a body, that's good. I have an update on the whereabouts of our demon. It was recently arrested—still in your body—by the Austin police department. I'm not sure how you're going to get access to it, but for the moment, it isn't going anywhere."

"That's a relief," I said. It really was. If I possessed the memories of Herman Powell, then the demon certainly possessed my own memories. I was terrified that the beast might go in search of the person that occupied most of my thoughts: Grace. With the creature behind bars, hopefully we would have the time we needed to reach her first.

"That's where the good news ends, I'm afraid," Haniel said. "I regret to say, I have been unable to locate any useful information on demons in The Library. It's somewhat baffling." There was an irritation evident in his voice that I'd not yet heard from the angel.

"Well, it has only been a couple of hours," I assured him.

"Precisely!" he complained. "And in that time, I've pulled 547 self-help books, which only spoke of demons as a metaphor. I had to read each one cover to cover, just to be sure."

Sonny and I looked at each other, wide-eyed.

"The only explanation," Haniel continued, "would be that all books on the topic require restricted access. As a Library Administrator, I hadn't imagined that there were any topics restricted to me. Unfortunately, I may need to put in a special request to my supervisor."

"Will it take a long time to get approval, or something?" I asked.

"Not necessarily, I just—" Haniel paused for a moment. "I'd have preferred not to involve my supervisor until we had more to show for our efforts. They can be somewhat... let's say, difficult."

I wondered if this supervisor was actually as intimidating as Haniel made them out to be, or if angels just hated their bosses as much as humans did. "Well," I said. "If you want to hold off, Sonny and I are—"

Sonny shrieked loudly in my ear, causing me to swerve briefly into the wrong lane. "Did you see that?" Sonny asked. "There, uh—there was a deer, uh—in the road. Anyway, Haniel, as Bob here was saying, you got this. Just read another five hundred books and let us know what you find!"

"You're right," replied Haniel, who was too distracted by his own problems to be thrown off by Sonny's outburst. "I just need to visualize my goals and things will work out for me. I think I read somewhere recently. I'll put in the request and keep up my search in the meantime. I'll update you as soon as I have more news."

The echo in my head disappeared. I pulled the car over and Sonny and I looked at each other, sharing the same indignant expression on our faces.

"Why'd you do that?" I blurted at him.

"*You* were about to tell Haniel about my contact!" Sonny fired back.

"So what?"

"So, if the angels find out my contact has secret knowledge, it won't stay secret to them for long."

"What are you talking about? Who is this guy?"

Sonny sighed. He did that a lot when talking to me. "The guy isn't what's important. It's what he may have found. Do you remember what I said about lost books in The Library of Eternity?"

"Vaguely."

Sonny rolled his eyes. "Aside from the fact that I love knowing about things the angels don't, there's a real reason we can't tell them about this. Why do you think there are entire subjects missing from a library of infinite knowledge?"

"Maybe they are restricted, like Haniel told us."

"I'm sure that's what the higher angels want us to believe," Sonny said. "but that's all part of the coverup!"

"Oh boy." I was instinctively suspicious of anything that followed the word coverup. Inevitably, it was always some kind of insane conspiracy theory.

"As we all know, Hell was created as a prison for fallen angels—"

"Wait, Hell isn't for human souls?"

Sonny groaned. "The upper levels do hold damned souls, but the realm's *original* purpose was to keep Lucifer locked up. That's the devil, by the way."

"I know who Lucifer is, Sonny."

"At this point, I don't assume you know anything!"

I wanted to protest, but it was a fair judgement.

"Now, this is all before reapers were created," Sonny continued. "But according to my sources, there was supposedly an attempted jail break. Some angel sympathizers stole the blueprints for Hell from The Library and located passageways where the plane overlapped with Earth. I heard a version that they even changed the blueprints to give them a direct path, and Hell itself changed to reflect it."

"What, like—changing its code? Like a computer program?"

"Why not?" Sonny said. "You think reality was built atom by atom? No, it was written into existence. And those rules can be changed."

I shook my head. "Remind me how you know all this. If there were no reapers around yet, how can you be sure?""

"Oh, you'd be shocked at the kind of classified information that trickles down to service workers. The angels barely notice we're in the room half the time."

I thought about all the random tidbits from our lives that Grace and I had absently revealed to various waiters or checkout clerks without meaning to. "Yeah, that tracks."

"As I was saying," Sonny continued. "When Lucifer's followers crossed over into Hell, they were sealed in forever. The higher ups had been monitoring them the whole time. Afterward, all books that contained knowledge about Hell, or anything to do with it, were removed from The Library—never to be seen again."

When Sonny finished, he looked at me very matter-of-factly. I stared back at him, my eyes squinting in profound confusion.

"...So what does that have to do with our contact?"

"Is every human these days as dense as you? *Obviously*, this guy has found the Lost Books of Eternity!"

"You think these magic books, which contain all the restricted knowledge of the universe... are in Alabama?"

"I know. It sounds crazy. Personally, I never put too much stock in the lost book theories, but when we were in The Library, we were talking about them. The books were at the forefront of our minds."

I nodded, humoring him.

"That's when I pulled this notebook from the shelf." He revealed the composition book tucked inside his cardigan.

"A college notebook," I said.

"Kelsie's college notebook containing transcripts from a class that took a very interesting turn mid-semester. Evidently, her professor started going on insane religious rants in the middle of his lectures"

"Maybe it was part of the lesson."

"Not in an engineering class. From what I can tell, this happened enough times that he was eventually replaced by a new professor."

"It sounds like this guy is just crazy."

"Maybe. But Kelsie took good notes. It turns out, everything the professor ranted about was right on the money. What's more, he wasn't just making this stuff up. During one class, he read aloud from what he called *The Compendium of Ethereal Entities*. From it, he meticulously described what a reaper was, from our rotting flesh to the intricacies of our contracts."

"But why would that be in a lost book?" I asked. "It doesn't make any sense. That has nothing to do with Hell."

"That doesn't, but I'll bet you anything that this Compendium has a section on demons. In fact, I'll bet it can tell us everything we need to know about them."

"I don't know," I said. "I mean, how has no one found this guy before? If the angels wanted these books so badly, wouldn't they have checked The Library for information about them sooner?"

"Sure, maybe a thousand years ago, but these notes are only a few months old. We could be the first ones to find them!"

"What if you're wrong about him? What if the reason no one's found these books is because they really are restricted? Doesn't that seem more likely?"

"If I'm wrong, then Haniel is right. He'll request access and it'll be no harm done. But do you really want to have gone through all the trouble of getting to this professor without at least checking? You punched a doctor, Bob. You stole a car!"

"You know my name is Bill, right?"

"Whatever, fine. Bill."

I was unconvinced, but Sonny had a point. It's not like I had anything to lose by indulging him—and even if we learned nothing about the demons, there were still those special weapons Haniel mentioned as a last resort. Though, if an angel was that afraid of a weapon, I wasn't sure how comfortable I would be using one.

"Alright." I said. "How much further?"

I followed Sonny's instructions to a small neighborhood just northeast of the college. All along the street were perfectly kept, cookie-cutter houses, with nary a lawn ornament to disturb the uniformity. In the center of this Stepford utopia was a decrepit two-story house that appeared to be condemned. The grass had grown to a savage length, usurping the driveway in a war for lawn supremacy. The mailbox nearly buckled under the weight of ignored envelopes. One of the windows was broken and boarded up from the inside. In fact, upon closer inspection, all the windows were boarded on the inside. I kept driving.

"What are you doing?" asked Sonny as I drifted away. "That's the house! Don't you see it?"

"Oh, I see it. It doesn't exactly blend in. We're driving a stolen car and I'd rather not park somewhere that draws more attention to us."

Sonny looked at the house, then at the rest of the neighborhood. "Yeah. Good call."

I parked the car across the street, a few houses down. With any luck, we'd leave before anyone noticed it didn't belong there. I walked up to the run-down home and banged on the door. There was no reply for a while, and I started to doubt that anyone even could live here. Then, I heard a shrill voice call out.

"Herman?"

Sonny and I looked at each other in confusion. "Uh, yes?" I shrugged.

We heard the sound of multiple locks unclicking before the front door creaked open, stopping short on a chain. Through the crack in the doorway I could see a short, pale man peering out. He had the deep sunken eyes of someone who hadn't slept for days and wild Einstein-esque hair.

"What are you doing here, Herman? Is this about that strangely dressed reaper that's following you?"

I took a step back and looked at Sonny. His eyes went wide and his mouth gaped.

"You can see me?" he asked hopefully.

"Of course I can see you! You're standing right in front of me! Herman, I'd be careful. This one looks like he's just itching to nab your soul."

Something in his voice seemed familiar and when I tried to place it, I was hit with another barrage of foreign memories. *I passed by an older man nearly every day while walking to teach my class. He was much better groomed than the figure currently at the door, but there was no mistaking him. Remembering further back, he once asked to join me at my table for lunch. He introduced himself as—*

"Professor Widdick!" I shouted louder than I intended, causing him to wince.

"Yes, that is my name. You're acting very peculiar, Herman. And I don't just say that because of the hospital gown."

I looked down, having briefly forgotten my attire. "I—uh—"

"Nevermind that." Sonny brushed me away and brought his face close to the door. "How is it that you can see me?"

"Because you're nearly touching my nose." The professor broke into laughter, before promptly closing the door on Sonny's face. The reaper stood, flabbergasted and ready to charge through, but a moment later, the door swung fully open.

"Well, don't be shy," Widdick smiled. "Make yourselves at home."

That was easier said than done. The house was anything but homely. There was barely a place to stand amongst the trash littering the floor. Loose and crumpled paper covered every inch of furniture, and this was all only visible because light shone in through the front door. When the professor closed it, the room became almost pitch black. Only tiny streams of light poked through gaps in the boarded-up windows to assist the candle-lit lantern in the corner.

"Sorry about the light," Widdick's voice emerged from the darkness. "I keep forgetting to pay that power bill, among other things."

The light was the least of my concerns. The entire south was in the midst of a historic heatwave and I had no idea how Widdick was able to survive with no air conditioning. I felt as if I would pass out if we stayed for too long.

The sound of shuffling trash helped me determine where Widdick was in the dark. There was a sliding and clunking of drawers on the opposite wall and a second later, light stung my retinas.

"I don't normally use these old flashlights, but seeing as I have company." He waded through the trash and handed me a yellow, heavy duty flashlight. He then continued lighting candles around the room which, given the amount of loose paper, seemed like a recipe for disaster.

"So," I said timidly. "About why we're here—"

"You want me to expel the reaper? Sorry, I can't help you there. I've had enough trouble trying to keep spirits away."

"No, it's not that, and you should probably know, he already got my soul—er, Herman I mean. He got mine too, but I'm not actually Herman."

Widdick paused, blew out his lighter, and turned to examine me. "What do you mean, *you're not Herman?*"

Sonny stepped in-between us. "Yeah, sorry to be the one to break it to you, but Herman is dead. Heart attack, very sad, not important. This is Bill, he needed a short-term body so we could talk to you. He's also dead, but isn't supposed to be. Are you following so far?"

Widdick scrunched his face. "I think so. Bill, dead, reborn; Herman, dead, vessel."

"Exactly!" Sonny gave a wide smile.

"What I don't follow, is why?" Widdick waved his flashlight back and forth between the two of us. "Of course, I know that it is *possible* for a spirit to inhabit an empty vessel, but to my knowledge, it is a highly restricted affair."

"You're right about that." Sonny said. "In fact, Bill here is the first approved possession in—well, ever, as far as I know."

Once again, Professor Widdick brought his face within an inch of mine and searched my eyes. I held my breath, wondering when the last time he brushed his teeth could have been based on the ferocity of the smell. "What makes you so special?" he asked.

Sonny began to speak, but Widdick snapped at him, "I was talking to Bill!"

Sonny frowned and Widdick focused back on me, his right eyebrow rising high above the other.

"Well, er..." I stammered. It was hard to form a rational thought when I felt as if I could drop from heat stroke at any moment. Widdick shone his flashlight directly in my eyes.

"Well?" he breathed his foul air on me.

"I, uh—I was killed—"

"People are killed every day! What's so special about that?"

"—by a demon," I finished.

Widdick backed away. His flashlight fell from my face and hung limply at his side.

"That's not possible," he said, almost whispering. "Demons are bound to Hell. They could never affect the physical plane. Was it a possession?"

"Nope," Sonny said. "Demons can't force someone to commit murder—"

"Unless that person already intended to kill their victim," Widdick finished. "But how? How could a demon possibly escape from Hell?"

I shrugged. "We were kind of hoping you could tell us."

"And more importantly," Sonny added, "we were hoping you might know how to send it back."

Widdick paced the room. His hands were on his temples and his face twisted, as if he were experiencing a massive brain freeze. Sonny and I looked at each other, concerned. Before Widdick could have an aneurysm, Sonny decided to cut to the chase.

"Maybe the answer is in the books!"

The red drained from Widdick's face. "The books? How do you know about those? Were you snooping around here the other day?"

Sonny turned absolutely giddy. For a brief second, his cheery expression made me forget his physical affliction and he appeared somewhat childlike. "I knew it! I knew you had the books! It was the only way!"

"Oh yes, I have them, though they aren't quite finished yet."

"New information is still being added?" asked Sonny, fascinated.

"Everyday. Why don't you have a seat there and I'll go fetch a few of them." He pointed to a slightly less messy part of the couch with his flashlight. While he went off to another dark corner of the house, I flopped down, wiping the sweat from my forehead.

"He's taking all this rather well, isn't he?" I asked.

"Better than I expected," he said. "But that's a good thing."

"What do you think he meant about you snooping around? He

didn't seem that surprised to see you. Could other spirits be after these books too?"

Sonny looked around the pitch black room. "I doubt it. A creaky house in perpetual darkness is not the best environment for a lonely man in the midst of a psychotic break. He may just be a tad paranoid."

"By the way!" Widdick shouted from the other room. "I never did catch your name, the reaper."

"It's Sonny!"

"Sonny? Odd."

Widdick was silent again, so I continued. "Yeah, I guess, but he didn't even flinch at you. I mean, no offense, but you scared the ever-living shit out of me when you first showed up."

"I do have that effect."

"And why can he see spirits anyway? Don't you have to be dead for that?"

"Not necessarily," Sonny said. "Once you open your mind to what's really out there in the world, you can see just about anything."

"I guess. I mean, I did see the demon that attacked me."

"Right. As for old Widdick here, the knowledge of the lost books must have made him wise, seeing—"

"And crazy."

"Yeah, and a little crazy."

Widdick came back into the room, struggling with his flashlight and several large books. He laid them out on what I assumed was the coffee table, though the trash was piled so high, it was difficult to tell. Sonny eyed the books greedily as Widdick held his flashlight to their covers.

"Now, let's see," said Widdick. "One of these should have what you're looking for."

There were four books on the table, each one the size of a college textbook. Sonny scanned the titles and pointed to the one he recognized.

"This one, *The Compendium of Ethereal Entities*. It might tell us something about the demon's weaknesses."

"It's an unusual name," said Widdick.

"Why?" I asked, dumbly. "Is the compendium not actually about spirits and stuff?"

"No, not that," Widdick waved. "Sonny. That's an odd name for a reaper of your age. You must be nearly two centuries old, judging by the decay."

"Good guess," Sonny replied. "And it's just a nickname, one I got in the afterlife."

This was news to me. "Why did people start calling you Sonny?" I asked.

"Can't you tell? I have such a sunny disposition." He was far more interested in the book than giving a real answer to the question. He pulled the compendium closer to himself and opened it to the center. Upon looking at the page, he frowned. "What is this?"

"It's *The Compendium of Ethereal Entities*," Widdick said, innocently.

"No. I wanted one of the lost books from The Library of Eternity. This is not from The Library."

"How can you tell?" I asked.

"Look at it!" He lifted the book and shoved it in my face. I leaned back and shined my flashlight on the open page.

"Classification: Nephilim. What's a Nephilim?"

"I'll tell you what it's not! A demon! If this book were from The Library of Eternity, it would open on the information we needed! This is handwritten, on printer paper!"

"Of course it's handwritten," Widdick defended. "The power's been out for ages! I had to write them all by hand."

"You? You wrote them?" Sonny asked, aghast. "But that's impossible! You have to have the lost books! How else could you—" He paused. His eyes grew wide with revelation and he pointed a rotten finger at the professor. "You're the book."

"What?" I was at a complete loss. At a certain point, I stopped trying to understand things on my own and just relied on Sonny to explain them.

"There aren't any lost books," Sonny surmised. "Not physically anyway. Somehow, all the knowledge that was in them is stored in his mind."

"That's right!" Widdick confirmed. "And it's a damn pain in my neck! I have to get it all down on paper. If I don't write it all out, it spews out of my mouth at random. It's a nightmare!"

"Do you know how this happened?" I asked.

"No. As luck would have it, that's one bit of information I didn't acquire. I can tell you fifty different spectral creature classifications and their hobbies, but I can't figure out why I know it, or how to stop it all from coming! At first, I didn't even realize it was happening. I would be reviewing a lesson one minute, and the next my whole class would be staring at me. That may not sound unusual in a classroom, but on an ordinary day, at least half of them should be completely checked out. Eventually, my outbursts cost me my job, but on the bright side, it freed me up to record my thoughts."

I looked at the other books, each as large as the one Sonny held in his hands. As my eyes began to adjust to the darkness, I realized the house was filled with stacks of texts. On a desk in the corner of the room, the candlelight revealed a large pile of papers that were in the process of being bound. In fact, what I had taken for loose trash was actually just hundreds, maybe thousands, of crumpled sheets of paper.

"Sonny," I said. "How much knowledge was taken from The Library?"

"I don't know. I never expected this much. The angels would have a field day with all this."

Widdick shined the light on Sonny's face. "It wouldn't be wise to show the angels any of these books. A good amount of them portray the angels in a questionable light. This information could be danger-ous in the wrong hands."

"Hey, believe me. You and I are on the same page," Sonny said.

"I've got no love for those pencil pushers. Besides, in my line of work, information is currency. I'm not letting a word of this gold mine get out to anyone."

"If this is so dangerous," I said. "Why are you showing it to us?"

"Bill!" Sonny yelled. "Let's not change the man's mind."

"It's quite alright," Widdick said. "I won't snatch the book back. The fact of the matter is, even a single rogue demon can be a grim portent of things to come. You'll need all the help you can get."

I didn't like the implications of what he said. As someone trying to begin the next chapter of my life, I'd rather the portents of my future remain positive enough for me to enjoy it.

"Is there, like, a table of contents, or something?" Sonny asked, flipping through the pages of the handwritten text. "This book is enormous, and we really do need to find the section on demons if we're going to figure out how to stop one."

"Well," said Widdick. "It is organized alphabetically."

"Ah, excellent." Sonny smiled.

"But of course, that's referring to the old angelic alphabet."

Sonny stared blankly at the pages as his expression descended into a frown. His eyes shot up to look at the professor.

"But it's written in English."

"Well, I don't know angelic! The text came to me in thoughts I could understand, I didn't choose the order it was sent."

I rolled my eyes. "Oh, just give it to me." I yanked the book from Sonny and started flipping through the pages myself. "Honestly, I'll just skim through it till I see the word 'demon'."

Sonny sighed and grimaced at Professor Widdick. "Fine. I'm gonna go check on the car." He got up and disappeared through the front door.

"He's a bit abrasive, isn't he?" Widdick remarked.

"I'd like to say he grows on you, but I've only known him for a few hours, so it remains to be seen."

A moment later, Sonny reemerged, far less calm than he had been when he left.

"So, Bill," he said too loudly. "How's that skimming coming?"

"It's been two seconds," I said. "Can you give me a minute?"

"We may not have a minute."

"Why?"

"Because the cops are down the street, looking at our car."

"What? Shit!" I exclaimed.

Widdick and I ran over to the window and peered between the boards where I immediately spotted a police cruiser behind our stolen sedan down the street.

"What's going on here?" Widdick asked. "Are you two fugitives?"

"Well, Bill might be," Sonny said. "I think I'm a little outside of their jurisdiction."

"It's not like that," I protested. "We got caught escaping the hospital when I was supposed to be dead. I didn't think they'd send the cops after me."

"You did punch a doctor in the face," Sonny added.

"Not helping, Sonny," I said.

"And you stole a car."

"Still not helping."

"You carjacked a doctor?" Widdick asked

"No, a different guy," Sonny said.

"Guys!" I yelled. "What are we going to do?"

"Just hurry up and find the information we need," Sonny said. "I'll rip your soul out of Herman's body and we'll portal over to Texas and find you a new one."

"And leave the dead body on the floor for the cops to find? What do you think they'll do to Professor Widdick after we frame him for murder?"

"Unless anyone has a better idea, that's the best plan we got," Sonny said.

"You know they'll confiscate the books, right?" I pointed out. "All these crazy writings will be used as evidence of his unstable mind."

"Shit," Sonny said. "What else can we do?"

"Would you two be quiet for a moment! I'm thinking!" Professor Widdick placed his hands on his temples again and both Sonny and I watched him in silence.

"Okay," Widdick said. "They aren't going to start storming houses over a stolen car, but once they realize I'm an acquaintance of Herman's they may get a warrant. You'll just have to take the compendium and go now."

"Go where?" Sonny asked. "We don't have a car. And even if we get away, I can't zap him out of here if we have to carry a solid book."

"You'll take my car. It's in the garage. If you leave soon, the police shouldn't notice you pulling out. I'll go fetch Bill some real clothes. They'll be a little tight, but under the circumstances—" He shrugged.

"Are you sure you're okay with all this? A couple of strangers taking your book, and your car?" I asked.

"And we'll probably need some money for gas, if you have any," Sonny said.

"It's alright." Widdick smiled. "I don't exactly get out much anymore, and as long as those books are out of my head, I don't care what you do with them. You have no idea just what a relief it is to hear that I'm not as crazy as everyone says I am. Anything I can do to help, I'm more than happy to. Just promise me one thing."

"Anything, of course," I said.

"Bring the car back when you're done catching your demon. We still have a lot to discuss."

7

GO WEST, DEAD MAN

I HAD HOPED that the professor's car would be somewhat inconspicuous, and was dismayed to discover a red Corvette awaiting us in the garage. Sonny, on the other hand, lit up as he inspected the vehicle from all angles. It was clear that the reaper was itching to drive it himself, but we'd undoubtedly draw even more attention if we went around town with no visible driver. I pulled down the baseball cap that Widdick had included in his pile of clothes, praying that the cops down the street would pay no mind to the bright red mid-life crisis beacon I was driving away in. Once we turned out of the neighborhood, I allowed myself to breathe a sigh of relief.

Widdick hadn't been kidding about the clothes. The polo he provided was fine, but the shorts rode up far too much if I kept them buttoned, and the shoes were even worse. I was nowhere near his size and had to shove my feet into two constricting flip flops that I immediately kicked off once we merged onto the highway.

We still had no way of tracking the demon, and unless the Compendium provided some way of doing so, we had to rely on the assumption that it was still in Austin, either in the custody of the local police department, or otherwise causing some kind of mayhem that would appear on the news. Either way, until we developed a better plan, my priority was to find Grace and get her to safety. I knew that my fianceé would react poorly to any attempt at explaining my recent actions, but I couldn't shake the feeling that she was still in danger. If there was even the smallest chance the demon would be drawn to her through my memories, I had to do something about it.

So I drove, anxiously digging my fingernails into the steering wheel while Sonny sat next to me—oblivious to any impending danger and pressing every button in the car with childlike jubilation. *The Compendium of Ethereal Entities* lay untouched on the dashboard.

I heard the passenger window roll down and looked over to see my companion sticking his head out, his stringy hair blowing in the wind. When he came back in, he asked me excitedly, "Can you pull over and take the top down?"

"No. If we do that, then you won't be able to read the book, which is what you should be doing."

"Ugh. *Thanks Dad.* We've got like fifteen hours. I'll have time to look through the book."

"Tell you what, I'll take the top down when we stop for gas."

"Fine." He sighed deeply.

Sonny rolled up his window and I turned up the air conditioner to try and combat the blistering summer heat. It was one of those heats where you could see the road shimmer in front of you like a mirage in the desert. Even the trees seemed to shrivel away, leaving only dried out husks of wood that lined the interstate. I knew Texas was in a bad drought, but I hadn't realized it had spread this far east.

"Do you guys have any control on the weather up there?" I asked. "I feel like it hasn't rained in months."

"I'm sure the angels could if they wanted to," Sonny said. "But you heard how finicky they are about direct interference. They'd just as soon let us boil alive before they turned on the faucet themselves."

"Can you actually feel the heat outside? I mean, since you're a—uh—" I stammered.

"Of course I can feel it. I'm a reaper, not a zombie."

"Sorry, I just—" I struggled to think of the proper way to word my question without offending my companion. "You mentioned that I was the first human soul to return to Earth, so I'm not sure what exactly a reaper is. I mean, you look like a person, but—"

"But all fucked up, right?"

"Uh, yeah."

Sonny chuckled, seemingly amused that I agreed with his descriptor. "Alright then, since it seems we have a long drive ahead of us, I guess I can clear some of the air. I am a human, or at least, I was."

"Was?"

"Yes. All reapers were humans who lived questionable lives, or did something particularly heinous to ruin our good track record. I consider myself part of the latter. They used to send people like us straight to Hell, but a couple thousand years ago, there were some big policy changes upstairs. They became a little more sympathetic to the human plight, so they came up with the afterlife service program."

"The lady at the front desk." I recalled. "Haniel mentioned that she was a service worker."

"Bingo. And she's one of the lucky ones. Front desk work is one of the easiest gigs you can get, if you can stomach having to talk to people all day."

"How come they don't look as, uh—" I waited for Sonny to fill in the blank again, but he just stared at me. "—fucked up? Your words."

Sonny smiled in satisfaction. "Shorter service times. The longer human souls spend in-between worlds, the more we start to decay. I think the average contract for a front desk worker is about twenty-five years."

"So you've been at this for a while."

"Longer than I care to think about," he said.

"What other kind of service is there?"

"Lots of stuff. Reapers obviously escort souls to the afterlife. There's also personal assistants to the angels, clerks in the in-between world, selling clothes or food—"

"Food?" I asked. "Do spirits need to eat?"

"We don't need to, but you can't imagine how gratifying it is to have a sandwich after years of no taste at all. It's all imported from upstairs, and it's the only thing us spirits can actually eat. Of course, it's not free. Every purchase could add weeks or months to our service"

My eyes went wide. "Weeks or months? Who would do something like that? I mean it's not like spirits *need* new clothes."

"Bill, look at me. I died in 1847. Do you think I was wearing this?" He gestured to his cardigan and tight-fitting khakis. He wore slip-on shoes and had colorful patterns on his socks.

"But why?" I asked him.

Sonny removed one of his gloves to display his rotting hand. "After looking the way I have for so long, it's nice to feel like a human being every once in a while." His gaze lingered on his fingers for a few more seconds before he pulled the glove back on.

I could sense a melancholic shift in the atmosphere. Sonny always spoke with such bravado, and I hadn't realized how much his condition actually bothered him. I tried to change the subject.

"So there's reapers and other afterlife service workers. Obviously there's angels and demons. What other spirits are out there?" I asked.

"I mean, we got a book full of them," Sonny said. "Do you want me to read the whole thing out loud?"

"Not everything. But there's got to be some interesting ones. What was that one I saw in there earlier, started with an 'N'?"

"The Nephilim."

"Right. What's the deal with those guys?"

"I don't need this book to tell you that *those guys* are bad news. And you should hope we don't run into them."

My interest was piqued. "What makes them so bad?"

"There are lots of malevolent spiritual beings, but the Nephilim are the only ones I'd call true abominations. They were never supposed to exist in the human realm, and they're extremely resentful of that fact. If you ever see one, you'd be better off to just turn and run."

"What do they look like?"

"Supposedly, their bodies are all twisted and wrong, but their true form is concealed by a dense, black fog. If you glanced at them, you'd think they were just a shadow, but up close, it's like looking into nothing. Really messes with you the first time you see it."

I was ten years old again. I stared, horrified, into the absence of light that surrounded the shape of a man, hovering over a crying infant.

My heart felt like it would burst from my chest and no matter how quickly I took in breath, I couldn't fill my lungs. Up until Sonny had explained this creature to me, I had always told myself it was a figment of my imagination, the mind playing tricks. It was just a shadow. But now the monster had been given a name, an identity. It was real. As much as everything in the afterlife had already disturbed me, realizing that my biggest childhood fear actually existed was the worst of it.

I was on the verge of a full fledged panic attack, but before I could begin hyperventilating, I was distracted by something actually worth panicking about.

Out of a portal in the sky, a morbid figure leaped onto the hood of our car, baring his teeth in rage. I yelled at the top of my lungs and jerked the wheel to the right, which at seventy-five miles per hour, caused us to lose traction. The car spun out of control. I looked over at Sonny only to find an empty passenger seat. I could barely hear the horns of swerving traffic over my own screams. Somehow, through all this, the mysterious man held on to the windshield. When the car finally stopped spinning, it was blocking a lane of traffic. Other cars honked as they drove around me, oblivious to the undead teleporter standing on my hood.

This mysterious man jumped off and pointed to the side of the road, glaring at me all the while. I had no business arguing with him, so I immediately pulled to the side, as he directed. Sonny was lumbering towards us after dragging himself from the ditch he had flown into. The sudden spinning of the car had been too much for him to maintain his concentration, and he had been violently ejected a fair distance away.

I exited the vehicle to confront what I assumed to be another reaper. The sound of my greeting was drowned out by the roar of wind and speeding traffic. He stared menacingly at me, while I awkwardly smiled and swayed back and forth, waiting for Sonny to catch up.

For a reaper, the stranger didn't look nearly as grotesque as my companion. There was enough of his skin remaining to discern that he was a black man, likely in his forties or fifties. He dressed like the Terminator, in a leather jacket and black pants—which seemed like a terrible choice for the heat, but it certainly added to his intimidating aura.

"What the hell was that?" Sonny yelled as he finally reached the car. "You trying to kill us, Josiah?"

"How was I supposed to know the human could see me? I merely wanted your attention." Josiah spoke in an unnervingly monotone voice.

"Well," Sonny replied, arching his back till he heard a loud crack. "You have it. What could be so important that you had to show up and scare the bejesus out of my associate?"

"Your associate is precisely why I am here."

"Me?" I asked weakly, once again drowned out by the sound of traffic.

"What do you want with Bill? He hasn't done anything to you."

"It is not Bill that concerns me. It's Herman Powell."

"Oh, shit," Sonny said.

"Herman was scheduled to die exactly nine minutes ago. You can imagine my... distress at finding his hospital room empty."

"You gotta listen, man," Sonny pleaded. "I can explain—"

"I searched The Library database for any reaper who tore open a portal in my region in the past several hours." Josiah took a few large steps towards Sonny and grabbed him by the collar of his cardigan. "You took a soul during my shift; a soul that rightfully belongs to me. I can have you relieved of your service for this. And when I'm done, I will personally escort you to the gates of Hell."

I gulped. This reaper hadn't even spoken to me and I was nearly shitting my pants.

"That really won't be necessary," Sonny told him. "As I said, I have an explanation! I was instructed to retrieve a body for my friend here so that we could complete a special mission. I have clearance from upstairs and everything!"

"How do I know you're not lying to me?" Josiah lifted Sonny off the ground and intensified his scowl.

"You can talk to Haniel! It all checks out!" Josiah did not appear convinced and tightened his grimace, but then Sonny's face lit up as an idea struck him. "In fact, since my mission might take a while. I'll need someone to cover my next two shifts! What do you say? Two weeks of souls in exchange for this one?"

Josiah's scowl vanished. He put Sonny back on the ground and took a step back.

"Are you serious about that? Because if you're not—"

"You're a big scary man, I can fill in the blanks of what you'd do if I lied to you. Like I said, I need someone to work my shift regardless. Can't have people cheating death in my region. There'd be pandemonium!"

Josiah reversed his sour face into a smile. "I apologize for the theatrics. Had I known you weren't trying—"

"Don't worry about it. Believe me, I would've done the same to you!"

Josiah gave out a hearty laugh, causing me to flinch. I hadn't calmed down as quickly as the others.

"Yes, I'd like to see that," Josiah said.

"What, you don't think I could do it?" Sonny asked. "I could pull off a sneak attack, or something. I mean, you're falling apart, man. You look terrible."

"And you look worse."

"Yeah well, I got 90 years on you. You should respect your elders."

The two laughed again as I leaned against the car, silently smiling—like any good third wheel. It was a role I had grown adept at in my life.

"So," said Josiah, still chuckling. "About your associate—"

I perked up. I was being included.

"You're wondering why he can see you?" Sonny guessed.

"Among other things."

"All part of the mission. Classified."

Josiah looked over and examined me.

"This vessel contains a soul named Bill, you say? That means he was restored to life. Are you saying he's a sanctioned possession?"

He looked directly at me as I spoke, but I wasn't sure if I was at liberty to reveal anything. Instead, I waited for Sonny to answer.

"I said classified."

Josiah smiled a thin smile and sauntered toward Sonny.

"So that's what everyone's been whispering about at the cantina."

"I wouldn't know anything about that," Sonny said. "I haven't been there in years."

"Not even for the gossip? I thought you had an affinity for privileged information. You mean to tell me that you've heard nothing about a horde of rogue demons rampaging amongst mankind?"

"It's one demon. Let's not get carried away here."

"Really? I heard otherwise. Perhaps you do know more than most."

"Okay, fine. *Maybe* this has something to do with all that."

"And you two are heading west, to what? Take on the demon yourselves? I assume that means the soul in this vessel was killed by the beast."

Sonny sighed, having somehow given away most of his secrets. "Yeah," he said. "Yeah, that about sums it up."

"How do you intend on engaging it? I highly doubt it's going to just walk itself through a portal back to Hell."

"We're still working on that. We've got a long drive, so I figure if we put our heads together, we'll think of something. Besides, we still need to drop in on my associate's fiancée to get her outta dodge. Better safe than sorry. That'll buy us more time to come up with a plan."

My heart fluttered upon hearing this. Of course I wanted to check in on Grace, but I had assumed that Sonny would prioritize the mission first. Then again, maybe his concern indicated that she was in even more trouble than I'd guessed.

"Well, it sounds like you've got a lot on your plate," Josiah said. "I won't keep you any longer. Good luck with your mission. And thank you, again, for your generosity."

"Just don't go around telling everyone what we're doing. This is a secret operation."

"There seems to be a lot of that going around lately. Goodbye, Sonny."

With that final word, he stepped backward into a portal and was gone. I breathed a sigh of relief. My heart was still pounding from the whole encounter.

"What the hell does that mean?" Sonny asked.

"Huh?"

"Lots of secret operations going around? Does he know something we don't? Cryptic son of a bitch. I'll give you some free advice about the afterlife. Don't trust a soul, or any spirit for that matter. Damn bastards are always trying to get an edge on you."

We got back in the car and I took a few deep breaths to regain my composure. Sonny looked over at me, concerned.

"Are you doing okay over there? Your body's not having another heart attack is it?"

"I'm fine. That was just… unexpected."

"Yeah, sorry about that. Most reapers just whine to Haniel if they have a grievance, but if I'd known that Josiah was working today, I would've given him a heads up."

"Are all of you so protective of your shifts? I mean what's one soul to you guys? Thousands of people die every day."

"All over the world, sure. In one region during a six-hour window? Not-so-much. We do have a quota to fill."

"Yeah you've mentioned that before. I thought you said the average was like twenty-five years for service workers?"

Sonny laughed. "Sure, if you work the desks. Reapers require special abilities to complete our tasks. The angels were apparently worried that we would take advantage of our necessary portaling abilities to slack off, so they decided that we need an extra incentive to stay on task. We have the quota: One-hundred thousand souls before we're allowed to move on."

"One-hundred thousand?" I asked in disbelief.

"We're at the bottom of the pecking order. They make us work harder than anyone to ascend and they pat themselves on the back because they didn't banish us to Hell. Not that I'd rather be there mind you, but it still sucks."

"How close are you to finishing that quota?"

"It's tough to say. Back when I started out, I had about five hundred square miles to myself—six hours, every day. But the more people die, the more reapers there are sharing the same space. Nowadays, I only get one hundred miles, once a week. Back in the 1800s, I was on track to finish my quota by 1960. Now, here I am in the 21st century, with only 70,000 souls to my name, give or take."

"So Haniel's deal—"

"Yeah, it's big. Could take decades off my time, assuming that inflation continues as it has."

"What do they expect you to do the six days you're not working?"

"I suppose they expect us to use that time to contemplate the actions that led us to this existence. I watch a lot of television."

I was beginning to feel that I'd misjudged my decaying companion. If I was in the same situation, maybe I'd be just as antagonistic after 200 years. Afterall, he was willing to put our hunt on pause to track down my fiancée. As I finally started up the car and pulled back onto the highway, I turned to him and smiled.

"You know," I said. "You mentioned before that Sonny is just a nickname. What's your actual name?"

The reaper didn't say anything. I looked over to see that he had pulled the Compendium off the dashboard and opened it so that I couldn't see his face.

"Hello?"

"I heard you," he said.

"So…?"

He sighed deeply. "Why don't we take a break from the conversation so I can read a little? We want to be prepared."

HOURS PASSED. We stopped for gas once before the sun went down, and again some time after. Every now and then Sonny would read out an interesting fact from the book, but without a frame of reference, I had no idea what most of it meant. His eyes never lifted from the pages, but mine were beginning to grow heavy.

At around midnight, I considered stopping at a hotel. I passed by several, slowing down every time, but I shook off sleep and pressed on. A couple hours later, a sign for a rest stop came into view—and that view was growing blurrier by the second. I wanted to keep driving, but my mind was fading. As a matter of fact, I had forgotten why I was even awake. I closed my eyes for just one second—

"You should probably stop there."

My eyes shot open. I suddenly remembered that driving a car was a very good reason to stay awake. I looked over at Sonny, my eyes bloodshot.

"Huh?" I asked.

"There's a rest stop coming up. You should probably stop there. Just for a bit."

"But I gotta keep going—"

"I'd rather not get flung from the car a second time because you fell asleep at the wheel. Just pull over for half an hour. I'll wake you up and we'll be back on the road in no time."

I wanted to argue with him, but I didn't have the energy. I pulled in and found a parking spot away from any other cars. The orange light of a streetlamp shone directly into my windshield, but it didn't matter, I was asleep within seconds.

8

SAVING GRACE

MY EYES OPENED. The sun illuminated our hotel suite, shining on my face. I rolled over in the bed to find Grace asleep next to me, on top of the covers, still wearing her wedding dress from the night before. We must have passed out as soon as we got to our room. I had a vague recollection of a dream where I died, but I was back now. Everything was fine. I got up to shut the window. It was letting in a cool, ocean breeze that I feared might wake Grace. The view of the beach was breathtaking, and I couldn't wait to begin our honeymoon. I turned to rejoin her in bed, but found it empty, the covers neat and tidy.

"Sweetheart?" I called out, but received no answer. I ran throughout the suite and found nothing. There was no trace that she'd ever been in the room. As I began to panic, the room became darker. The sun no longer shone through the windows and the sound of ocean waves grew louder, more violent. Hoping I might find her outside, I rushed to the door.

It opened into our home, the one we'd just moved into together. I tried the light switches, but nothing worked. It was dark and devoid of any sign of life. Once again, I raced through the halls in search of her, but found no trace. Her belongings were gone, and she vanished from all the photos on the walls. I leaned against the hallway, and slowly sunk to the floor. The world darkened further, and a wave of loneliness overtook me.

But then, a glimmer of hope. At the end of the hall, I could see a thin strip of light coming from under our bedroom door. *Surely*, I thought, *she must be here*. I raced down the hall to throw the door open, but as I turned the warm handle, I realized my hopes were in vain. The room was engulfed in flames that spread quickly through the rest of the house. The life I had built was burning, and the heat engulfed me.

"I'VE GOT IT!" Sonny yelled, causing me to jolt awake and bang my elbow on the car door. I winced, at first in pain, and then at the sunlight that was blaring through the windshield. It was sweltering hot and I felt like a turkey in the oven. When I realized where I was, I scrambled to turn the car back on, both in order to check the time and to get some blessed AC.

"Did you hear me?" The reaper asked. "I said I've got it!"

"Sonny! It's 8:42! Why didn't you wake me up?"

"I just did, right now."

"You said you'd wake me up in half an hour! You let me sleep for over six hours!"

"Relax. I just let time get away from me a little. Besides, you needed the sleep."

"You let time get away? The sun is up! Was that not a big enough clue?"

"What's the big deal, man? So you rested a bit."

"The whole point of checking on my fiancée is to make sure the demon doesn't get to her first. In six hours, it could have gotten loose, tracked her down, and killed her before morning!"

Sonny narrowed his eyes, reaching into his pocket to pull out his magic list. "Let me ask you something. Where's the first place you'd think to look for her?"

"Huh?"

"Go on. Where would you look if you didn't have my help?"

"Well, we have a house just outside of Aust—"

"Not there. Next?"

"Her parents live in Salado—"

"Not there either. Do you want to know where she is?"

I was beginning to understand what he was getting at, but I did want to know. "Yes, where?"

"She's in San Antonio, several hours from either of those locations. Do you think the demon is going to find her in the middle of a distant city, after one day of looking?"

I breathed a sigh of relief. Despite his condescending tone, Sonny made me feel enormously better about the situation. Without a reaper to magically locate her position, the demon was as close to finding Grace as I would be on my own.

"Okay," I said. "I'm sorry. I'm just a little groggy. I guess I did need sleep if I'm going to fight this thing."

Sonny tried to maintain his piercing gaze of superiority, but his mouth curved into a slight smile at my apology.

"You always this cranky in the morning?" he asked.

"No, but I normally wake up in a bed, next to the woman I love."

"Well, sorry about the car, but at least you still got to wake up to a pretty face." He winked at me.

I shook my head, chuckling against my better judgement. After stretching my arms and arching my back, I recalled that Sonny had woken me for a reason. "What were you saying earlier?" I asked. "You've got something?"

His face beamed. "Not just something; I've got *it*."

"It? You mean—"

"I've figured out how to weaken the demon!"

He held up the book and shoved its open pages so close to my face, I could barely make out the words. I pushed it away. "Why don't you just explain it to me?"

"Right!" He pulled the book back and scanned the page for the correct passage. "This is it! It says: *where those creations of the Earthly realm may be cleansed and purified by the waters which provide life, so too will the manifestations of Hell be afflicted.* Don't you see?"

"Um, uh," I stuttered. "Say that one more time."

"Cleansed and purified by water? Holy water!"

"Holy water? You're sure?"

"Absolutely. Listen: *Their flesh craves the warmth of flame which gave them birth. They have never known the touch of the rain or the sea, lest they become vulnerable to mortal perils.* The whole thing reads like this, but that's as clear as we're gonna get."

"I thought you guys said holy water wouldn't work? I suggested it before."

"Please, Bill. You don't have to try and take credit for *my* discovery. Though I will admit, I'm a little disappointed I didn't think of it sooner."

"Again, I already did."

"It just seems so silly. I mean, the answer has been in hacky movies and TV shows for decades. Maybe it's just one of those innate things humans know deep in their subconscious."

"Does it say that the water will kill them?" I asked.

Sonny scanned the page once more. "I don't think so. But if I'm reading this correctly, it should make them corporeal."

"Will it at least hurt them?"

"It doesn't matter. In its spiritual form, we're powerless against this thing. It's big, and we're us. But if we can pull it onto the physical plane—"

It finally clicked for me. "Then strength doesn't matter! We have weapons and stuff!"

"Exactly!"

I was newly invigorated. Within seconds, we were back on the highway, tearing down the road towards our destination. For the first time, I didn't feel like we were stumbling our way through the mission. We had a plan now, and it seemed like nothing could stop us.

"Alright," I said, more excited than I'd been since we started this adventure. "Should we head to a church before we find Grace, or after?"

"Why would we need to go to a church?"

"For the holy water. I mean, unless you have the power to bless it yourself—"

"I always forget how ignorant the living are. You can't make holy water. Do you think a priest has the ability to turn water holy? He's just as much a man as you."

"Where are we going to find it then?"

"All water is holy water. It's the life giver and no one can make it more or less holy."

"So, you're telling me I can spray this thing with a soda bottle and the water inside will still work on it?"

"I—well... theoretically—I don't fucking know man. You give it a try and come back to me."

OUR SECOND DAY on the road was exceptionally better than the first. We'd knocked out a solid eight hours already, so the remaining five felt far less daunting. It was a beautiful morning. There wasn't a cloud in the sky—though considering the drought, clouds would have been welcome. I recalled my dream from the night before, and I realized that this pristine summer day was to be the start of my honeymoon. The wedding had seemed like a lifetime ago, when in reality, I had been dead for less than twenty-four hours.

Sonny insisted that we take the top down from the car this time. I would have liked to hear more from the book, but he had already found what we needed to know. The next fifty miles of the trip was like driving with an overly excited puppy. He hung over the side of the car because apparently the wind wasn't strong enough for him already. Even though I couldn't see, I imagined he had his tongue stuck out, flapping freely in the wind. When he finally settled in his seat, he stared at the passing scenery with a grin on his face.

The landscape transformed as we drove from tall trees to flat desert. We had long since entered Texas and were only a couple of hours from San Antonio when I stopped for gas one last time. I went into the Buc-ee's to buy some snacks while the car filled up. I don't think Herman's body had eaten any food in two days and I was about to face off with a rage-fueled Hell-monster. I needed energy. As I walked back to the car, I looked down at the two bottles of Dr. Pepper in my hands and realized the futility of the second. *Maybe I could save it for later.*

I unhooked the gas nozzle and got back into the car, chewing on some beef jerky while stuffing the other bag I bought into the console. Sonny didn't notice that I placed two bottles in the cup holders, nor did he make any reaction when I got back in the car. He just stared at that little list he had pulled from his pocket.

I stopped chewing and asked, mouth full of jerky, "What's wrong?"

His eyes lifted from the paper to meet mine. He started blinking rapidly and stuttered.

"Where um, wha—what did you say was the second place you'd look for your fiancée?"

I swallowed the beef jerky. "Salado. At her parents' house."

"Yeah… That's what I thought," he said, his voice sullen.

I stepped on the gas. We were already on a direct path to San Antonio. If I had known sooner where Grace was going, I could have gotten there at least an hour earlier.

"Dammit, Sonny!" I yelled, shaking the steering wheel and hitting my own head back against my headrest.

"Look! I'm sorry! She *was* in San Antonio this morning!"

"You didn't think to keep checking?"

"Why would she go back? It's only been a day! Does she have

some kind of death wish?"

"Don't go blaming her! If you had checked in sooner—"

"Hey! Don't forget, I'm doing you a favor! There's nothing in my job description about saving your little girlfriend!"

I slammed on the brakes, which of course, made Sonny fly out the windshield and into the street. *I know, I know,* that was an unthinkably mean thing to do, and given my more pressing timetable, very stupid. But it did give me a brief moment of satisfaction. Sonny got back in the car with an unblinking glare and I continued down the highway.

"That was real fucking mature, Bill."

"What? There was an armadillo in the road."

"Yeah, sure asshole."

"Fine, I'm sorry. I shouldn't have done that," I admitted. "Are you hurt?"

"Yes," he said. "Emotionally."

I sighed. "I know it's not your fault. I'm just worried about Grace."

"Oh, well in that case, it's perfectly understandable to throw people out of moving vehicles."

"I know, I am actually sorry. I shouldn't have lashed out. You don't deserve it."

"If I forgive you, will you stop groveling? It's gross."

"Yes," I said.

"Good. And I guess I'm sorry about not checking the list sooner, or whatever."

"Thank you."

A few seconds of silence passed between us, before Sonny finally stopped pouting.

"I'm assuming your girlfriend's parents have a gun or something in the house?" he asked. "I mean, it is Texas."

"Knowing them," I said. "I can guarantee it."

BECAUSE OF MY own upbringing, it was almost jarring to see a family as tight knit as Grace's, and even more so when they extended their affection to me. They instantly made me feel like I belonged, and it was a feeling I had never realized I so desperately craved. That's partially why I was willing to overlook her father's upsetting passion for hunting. Their house was lined with deer heads and animal skins, which I suppose Grace had grown accustomed to. The first time I visited, her father mistook my wide-eyed horror for appreciation. I've had to decline multiple invitations to join him on a hunt, but thankfully, my squeamishness never tarnished our rapport. In the wake of my imposter's recent behavior however, I feared that our familial bonds were now irreparably broken.

We arrived at Salado in record time. I could feel knots developing in my stomach just thinking about the conversation I was now confronted with. I had no idea how to explain any of this to Grace, let alone how I could convince her that I was who I claimed to be. From her perspective, I would just be some insane older man she doesn't recognize, claiming to be her dead fiancé—who she believes is still alive. As I turned onto her parents' street, I slowed the car to a halt.

"What's going on?" Sonny asked.

"What am I supposed to say to her?" I lamented. "*Hey Grace, just swung by to let you know that I was killed by a demon and I came back to life as an old, out of shape guy with a mustache.*"

"You can tell her you're in deep disguise, so the cops don't recognize you."

"Sonny."

"No, wait! Kick open the door and say: *Come with me if you want to live!*"

"Sonny!"

"Alright, alright. How about this: you're with the police. Tell her that her fiancé has busted loose and that you're here to take her to safety."

"That—That's actually a really good plan."

"Of course it is. All my plans are really good. Are you ready now?"

I stretched my fingers around the steering wheel and took a deep breath. "Yeah. I'm ready."

My heart rate increased with each step as I approached the door. I closed my eyes, inhaling deeply, and knocked. Nothing happened. I knocked again, and was met with a distant, "Who's there?"

It was Grace, without a doubt. I recognized the upward inflection she used when she was anxious. And if it was her that answered, then her parents must have been elsewhere, which was good news for me, but made her situation all the more dangerous.

"Gra—uh—Ma'am! My name is detective Herman Powell! I'm with the Austin Police Department! Could you please come to the door? I need to speak with you!"

There was more silence. Sonny raised an eyebrow. *"Please come to the door?* You're supposed to be a cop, not a dictionary salesman."

"Wow, you are old, huh?"

"You need to be more forceful."

"She hasn't broken the law, it's not like we're here to arrest her."

"I still think the circumstances call for something a little more urgent than 'please'."

I shook my head and turned back to the door, just catching a glimpse of Grace peering through the window blinds, before they snapped shut.

"Ma'am! I need you to come to the door! It's about your fiancé, Bill Baker!"

Her voice called out, much louder this time.

"Obviously it's about Bill! Why else would you be here?"

"Ma'am, you're in danger here! Mr. Baker has escaped custody! We need to move you to a safe location!"

I looked expectantly back at Sonny, having sounded—in my opinion—much more authoritative. He gave me a thumbs up.

"Detective Herman Powell, is it?" Grace called back.

"Yes ma'am, I'm with the Austin Police Department."

There was a brief beat of silence before she asked, "Would you mind showing me your badge, Detective?"

"Uh—"

"Just hold it up by your head, I'll see it."

I looked back at Sonny, hoping he'd have a solution, but his eyes went as wide as mine. This was clearly an oversight in our master plan.

"What's the matter?" called out Grace. "Can't find it?"

"I, uh—I seem to have left it back at the station."

"Oh, well in that case—"

The door flew open, revealing the long metal barrel of a shotgun pointed directly at my chest.

"I'm going to have to ask you to back the fuck up!" Grace announced.

I jumped in retreat, nearly falling down the steps. Sonny tripped over himself as well, despite being both invisible and immune to bullets. Even with the gun between us, I felt a moment of elation at the sight of her. Her ginger red hair was up in a tangled mess and her cheeks were flushed, but she was still the most beautiful thing I'd seen since this adventure began. My elation faded when she pumped the shotgun.

"Whoa, whoa! What are you doing?" I shouted.

"Jesus, Bill!" Sonny said. "This is the girl you were gonna marry?"

Grace took a step forward, her eyes narrowing.

"If my fiancé escaped custody, why would they send an officer all the way from Austin instead of calling the station here?" Before I could think of an answer, she continued. "And sending a non-uniformed detective with no partner, no badge, and from the looks of it, no gun to protect me, doesn't sound like standard operating procedure. Did you honestly expect me to believe you were a cop wearing a yellow polo and flip flops?"

I looked down at my attire, embarrassed.

"Now," she continued. "You're going to stay there while I call the actual police and see what the hell is going on."

My brain scrambled for some explanation or excuse, and this

time, punching someone in the face was not an option. Sonny continued to make useless hand gestures and shrugs while Grace pulled out her phone. I was running out of time.

"Wait!" I said. "I know this all seems...suspicious—"

"Shady as fuck," she corrected. Her thumb hovered above the call button on her phone.

"But I swear, I really am here to help you."

"Why should I believe you? You've been lying from the second you opened your mouth."

"It's true, I'm not with the police, but I do know what's going on with your fiancé, and I know that the police won't be able to hold him for long. I'm not even asking that you come with me anymore, just—just leave town. Go somewhere no one would think to look."

Something changed in Grace's eyes. They were less intimidating, more cautious. "What do you know about Bill? I've been watching the news all day and they haven't released anyone's name. How did you find me? Have you been stalking me?"

"No!"

"Did you have something to do with what happened to Bill? Did you threaten him?"

"No, I mean, I—"

"Did you give him something? Did you drug him before the wedding?"

"I promise, I didn't!"

She cocked the shotgun again, really just wasting a shell. "Stop lying to me!"

"GRACE!" I shouted louder than I intended and the anger in Grace's face momentarily turned to fear. "Grace," I said again, calmly. "I do know the reason your fiancé behaved the way he did, but I promise you, I had nothing to do with it."

Her eyes narrowed. "Tell me."

"You're, uh—you're probably not going to believe me, at first."

"I don't care, just tell me what's wrong with Bill!"

"Okay." I looked once more at Sonny who vigorously shook his head. "He's been possessed by a demon."

Sonny sighed heavily and stepped off the porch in order to get a better look at Grace's reaction. In about one second, her face went from anger, to despair, confusion, and finally back to anger.

"Do you wanna run that by me again?" she asked through gritted teeth.

"Well, technically he died first. You see, the demon killed him and took over his body—"

"Alright," she said. "I think I've heard enough."

I was losing her and decided to play the only card I had left. "Alright fine, you want the truth?"

"I don't think she can handle the truth," Sonny added, unhelpfully.

"I'm Bill! I'm your fiancé, reincarnated."

Grace squinted her eyes and her jaw fell. She slowly put her phone back in her pocket and I thought she might actually be entertaining the notion, but then she pointed her shotgun at the ground in front of me and pulled the trigger. The blast rang in my ears, causing me to fall back and land hard on my spine.

"I swear to you, it's true!" I said, wincing from the pain.

"How dare you? Do you have any idea what the past two days have been like for me? How much I've prayed for an explanation for what he did? And then you come along and just twist the knife in my side!"

"I'm not trying to trick you!"

"Then you're just insane!"

"I'm not insane!"

Sonny leaned over me. "You are acting pretty insane."

"Shut up, Sonny!"

Grace looked around the yard in confusion.

"Who's Sonny?"

"No one. He's the reaper who took my soul. You can't see him.

He's invisible."

There was an awkward silence in which I realized what I just said.

"Okay," Grace began. "Listen up Herman Powell, or whatever your real name is—"

"Bill."

"I've put up with this sideshow for entirely too long, so I'm going to give you till the count of three to get off my property, before I scatter you across it."

"This isn't even your property! It's your parents'!"

"One."

"Will you at least do what I asked and get out of town?"

"Two."

"Alright, you know what? I don't care." I pulled myself up from the ground and kneeled with my arms straight out to make myself a bigger target. "Do it. Shoot me! But when I come back in another body, then will you listen?"

Her hands trembled around the gun. Her scowl intensified, but she didn't fire.

"Go ahead," I urged her. "I'm not afraid to die again. Not if it means keeping you alive."

"Will you just shut up!" she shouted.

"Wait, wait, wait," I said. "Just ask yourself one thing before you kill me. Do you really believe, deep down, that Bill would do those things? Do you really believe I *could* do those things?"

Her whole body was trembling at this point, but in an instant, it stopped. She let out a heavy sigh, lowering the gun just slightly.

"Fuck."

"That's a good 'fuck' right?" I asked.

"I don't know," she said. "I've been through a lot in the last two days, and I don't particularly want to kill a man on my front porch this morning. So how about you just get the hell out of here, because I am gonna call the cops."

"Will you at least leave here? Go somewhere I'd never think to look?"

"I have an inclination to do that already if you're going to show up again with this bullshit."

"Then I'll go," I said. "I just want you to be safe."

Grace furled her brow curiously. "Yeah, so you say."

In the midst of all this, Sonny bounced suddenly on his heels as an idea struck him. "Oh! Wait! Why don't you do that one thing they do in movies?"

"What?" I asked.

Grace looked confused. "So you say?" she repeated.

"No, not you." I turned to Sonny, furthering her confusion.

"You know," said Sonny. "That thing where they have the person answer a question that only they could know."

I turned back to Grace and echoed, "Before I go, how about we do that thing where you ask me something only I could know?"

She took in a deep breath and closed her eyes, taking one hand off the gun to grasp at the air as if she were trying to physically grab the words she was looking for.

"This is supposed to make me believe in ghosts and possessions?" she asked.

"You do believe ghosts exist, you've told me dozens of times."

"Not like this! I meant—" She paused, realizing that she had been indulging the idea that I was Bill for a moment. "I wouldn't even know what to ask," she said.

"It can be anything, just make sure it's not something like the date of our first kiss, or something like that. I'm terrible with dates."

She frowned, thinking. Then her eyebrows raised as an idea came to her.

"Fine, I've got one. Before we moved in together, we got locked out of Bill's apartment in Waco. It was too late to call the apartment office, and I didn't want to pay for a hotel—"

"Yeah," I chuckled. "So we opened a bottle of wine and decided to spend the night in my car."

Grace blinked a few times and shook her head, continuing. "At some point, Bill turned on the radio and we danced in the parking lot. So, tell me—what song did we dance to that night?"

Sonny looked at me and frowned. "Oh geez," he said. "I can't remember the last song I heard on the drive here. How the hell does she expect you to remember that far back?"

I smiled. "It was 'The Way You Look Tonight'. After it ended, you looked it up on your phone and played it again."

She stared at me, her face unreadable. "This is insane. You're making me feel insane."

"I'm sorry," I said, sincerely.

Her cheeks were so flushed that her freckles had disappeared. She quickly rubbed away the tears welling in her eyes. "If I promise to leave town, will you please just go away? I can't handle this right now."

"Yes, of course. Hopefully it will just be for—"

Grace's cell phone started buzzing in her pocket.

"I think your phone is going off," I said.

"It's my mother. She went to Brookshire about a half hour ago."

"What about your dad?"

"Work. Apparently, your son-in-law committing murder and going on a rampage through the city doesn't merit time off."

"I'm surprised he didn't go after me himself."

"Oh, he wanted to—go after Bill, that is."

The phone stopped and Grace sighed. "I should call her back or she'll worry, and you need to leave. Now."

"Right." I said, standing back up. "You will listen to what I said, right? I'd never forgive myself if anything happened to you."

"I said I would. Now go, unless you want to be here when the real cops show up."

I nodded solemnly and retreated to the car. Grace kept an eye on me until I had closed the door to the Corvette before finally going back inside herself.

Sonny sat next to me and patted my back. "I thought that went remarkably well."

"Thanks, Sonny," I said, dejected.

"She didn't shoot you. That's a plus."

I nodded and smiled, doing my best to remain optimistic. At the very least, I shouldn't have to worry about her safety anymore.

"Wait!" Grace called out from the front porch. I was so excited to see her running towards us that I didn't notice her holding up her phone until she hit the speaker button.

"Ms. Evans! This is Officer Park with the Austin Police Department. Mr. Baker he—Aghh! . . . Ms. Evans, please. You have to get out of town! You need to ge—"

There was a muffled gurgling noise and the message ended.

9

BLOOD IN THE WATER

IT MAY HAVE taken sudden mortal peril, but at least Grace was no longer trying to chase me off. I suggested we get into the Corvette and leave right away, but she still refused to go alone with me, and her mother had taken her own car. Grace paced around the yard, trying her mother's cell, but not getting through.

"Goddammit. Why does she even have a phone if she never checks it?"

"Does your dad have any more guns in the house?" I asked.

"Yeah, but I don't exactly feel comfortable handing one to you."

"If you still think I'm a threat, then why did you ask me to stay?"

"I don't know! Okay!" she cried. "I'm just freaking out a little bit."

Sonny nudged me. "What about the water? If this thing does show, we'll need to weaken it."

"Grace," I said as another call failed to go through. "Is there like a bucket I can use in your parents garage?"

"I don't know," she rubbed her tears away. "Maybe? What do you need a bucket for?"

"For water."

She made a puzzled expression.

"It's important, trust me." I said.

"Fine, whatever. You can check, but I've still got you in my sight." She balanced the shotgun against her hip. "Inside, I'm right behind you."

Sonny followed us through the house and into the garage. "In hindsight," he said. "We should have called the real police earlier and made a fake threat, or something. They could have come and gotten her somewhere safe."

"Thank you for your aptly timed input," I snapped.

"Please stop talking to yourself," Grace said. "I'm already on edge."

"Sorry, have you already called the local police?"

"No. Fuck. Just stay in there." She turned and dialed 911, briefly leaving me to search through her parents' junk. After a couple minutes, I located a blue bucket filled with bungee cables hidden behind some stacked bins. Just as I was able to free it however, I suddenly felt an all too familiar ringing in my ears. "I think Haniel is trying to call us!"

"I noticed!" Sonny shouted back, his hands clasped to his head. "Just ignore it! We don't have time to talk right now!"

I mimicked Sonny, covering my ears and trying not to focus on the ringing sound. After a few seconds, the noise subsided.

"What do you think he wanted?" I asked.

"Probably telling us that the demon's nearby. Doesn't matter. We can give him the good news once we finish this thing."

Grace reappeared in the doorway, holding up her phone. "They're sending a unit. I guess Austin PD already managed to contact them."

"Perfect," I said. "Is there a faucet I can use?"

"Follow me," she said, and led me back through the house and into the kitchen. I pulled the little hose out of the sink and sprayed inside the bucket, full blast.

"Enlighten me," she said. "How is a bucket of water supposed to help us?"

"You can't hurt a demon unless it's wet," I answered.

She let out a defeated sigh. "I can't believe I'm indulging this."

Suddenly, there was a knock at the door.

Grace and I looked at each other wide-eyed. My bucket was full enough, so I followed her back to the living room and stood at the ready with Sonny beside me. Grace stood apart from us, her aim fixed on the door. Then there was a noise. It sounded as if the creature was scratching at the lock, trying to get in—and succeeding.

"Grace," I whispered. "Remember, it may look like me, but that's not the real Bill on the other side of that door. You can't hesitate to shoot."

She didn't respond. Her arms were shaking and beads of sweat started running down her brow.

The lock clicked. The handle turned. The door swung open and Grace's mother stood, trying to collect all her groceries from the porch. Grace went bug-eyed and tossed the gun on the couch. I could hardly do the same, so I just stood there, stupidly holding a bucket of water.

"Grace! Couldn't you hear me knock—Oh!"

She dropped one of her bags at the sight of me, but luckily Grace sidestepped quickly into her field of view.

"Mom! You're home!"

Her mother continued to eye me suspiciously, then noticed the shotgun on the couch. I rattled my brain thinking of something to say, but Grace was quicker on her feet.

"Mom, this is Detective Powell with the Austin PD. He's come to escort us out of town."

Hearing that I was with the police seemed to put her at ease. "Oh, well, hello Detective Powell. I'm Carol, Grace's mother. Forgive me, I'm just a little frazzled. You're here to escort us somewhere?"

"Yes, ma'am," I played along. "You see, Mr. Baker has escaped custody. We need to get you and your daughter to a safe location."

"Oh my God!" Carol exclaimed. "And you think he'll come here?"

"Without a doubt, ma'am." I tried to speak with as much confidence and authority as I could muster.

"Okay, let me just get all this inside and—uh, I'm sorry, is there a reason for the bucket?"

I looked down at the water and began stuttering when Grace, once again, came to my rescue.

"His engine overheated. It's been happening a lot this summer. You know how hot it's been."

"Oh, of course," Carol said. "That must have been your police cruiser I saw across the street. I was wondering why it was there."

"Exactly." I said. "I'll just take this—wait, I'm not in a cruiser. I came in a Corvette."

"Are there other officers here? I could have sworn—"

The window shattered, followed by the entire wall. The couch exploded into broken wood and torn leather from the force of a two-ton police cruiser barreling into the living room. Grace darted to her mother, knocking her away from the flying debris. I was knocked on my ass by a high-speed pillow, spilling the bucket of water all over myself. Sonny's head poked out of the roof of the police car, having been standing in the exact location the vehicle stopped.

"I think the demon is here!" he announced.

"No shit, Sonny!" I tossed the cow-skin pillow away from me and searched through the thick cloud of dust to make sure Grace and her mother were alright.

The cloud dimmed as a silhouetted figure appeared on top of the rubble. As the dust settled, more details came into view. The tuxedo was torn to shreds, ripped apart by bullet holes and lacerations. The body was covered in blood, but had no visible wounds. On its face, the imposter wore a sinister grin that stretched from cheek to cheek.

"Honey! I'm home!" it yelled in a voice that barely resembled my own.

"Oh great," Sonny said as he phased out of the police car. "It has a sense of humor."

"A reaper?" The demon cocked his head. "Aren't you a little early? I want to have a little fun with this bunch before you're needed."

Sonny may have had a retort, but it was inaudible over Grace's mother, who began screaming at the top of her lungs. The demon hopped off the rubble, chuckling at the sound.

"Good to see you too, Mom. Can I call you Mom? I feel like we've reached that point in our relationship."

With its attention fixed, Sonny took the opportunity to locate the shotgun in the debris. I rose to my feet and hurled a piece of broken wood at the monster's head, which did nothing but adjust the direction its hair pointed in. I hadn't expected to harm it, but I did get its attention.

"Hello." It slowly turned its head to face me. "Who have we here?"

"What? You don't recognize me? I'm the guy who loaned you the tux."

Its smile stretched even longer. "Well, well. Bill Baker, I presume. That's a fine new meat suit. It does you justice. Pudgy and worn down—perfect for a man as insignificant as you. My thanks for your spare. I've poked around your memories and I think I've made a greater impact with your body in one day than you have in your entire life."

My ears flushed and I tightened my fists. It knew exactly how to push my buttons, but I needed to maintain my cool for a minute longer. Behind the demon, I watched Grace carefully usher her mother, on hands and knees, out the open door. I let out a fake laugh. "You think so? Because from what I've heard, you spent most of your time in a jail cell. Big bad demon subdued by a bunch of human cops. What'll all the other goblins and ghouls say?"

It dropped its smile, taking a step towards me as Grace and her mother finally crawled out of sight. "If you don't mind my asking," the imposter snarled. "How is it that you're here? I was under the impression that death on Earth was a permanent condition."

"Maybe I'm a little more *significant* than you thought. I am the man who's going to kill you after all."

It burst into manic laughter. "You? Yes! I can see the writings now! The next biblical hero is an emotionally codependent desk worker, with social anxiety! The Book of Bill! That'll be a page turner!"

As the demon bent over in laughing fits, I nodded to Sonny, who quickly tossed the shotgun to my outstretched arm.

"I don't know," I said, taking aim. "I'd read it."

I fired at the demon's head, but only managed to put a few pellets in its shoulder. Its eyes snapped wide open and before I could get another shot off, it lunged with lightning speed, thrusting its arm into my chest and propelling me through a surprisingly thin wall, into the kitchen. The force of the blow had knocked the shotgun from my hands, and may have broken a couple of my ribs for good measure. The demon strolled casually through the hole in the wall, reaching into its shoulder to pull out the bloody pellets.

"That hurts, Bill," it said. "Not the gunshot, I don't really feel pain, but the betrayal. I thought we were bonding. I was just going to fillet your fiancée a bit, maybe press hot coals to her eyes—you know, classic demon stuff. But now I'm thinking it might be more fun to make you do it yourself. You think you won't of course, but you'd be surprised by what you're willing to do to make the pain stop."

Everything slowed down, except my heart, which thudded painfully against my broken ribcage. I leaned my head back against the kitchen sink, where—just above me, I saw the nozzle of the hose dangling off the counter. I needed a distraction.

"Sonny! Now!" I shouted. Sonny wasn't there, but the demon didn't know that. It turned around to meet the nonexistent attack, allowing me to grab the hose. When the demon swiveled back to me, it was met with a spray of water directly in the face.

"Drink up, you body snatching-bastard!" I screamed, doing my best to hide the excruciating pain in my chest. However, what I heard in response was not what I expected. The demon was laughing again.

"You idiot! I'm in a vessel! Water can't hurt me! Nothing can!"

I closed my eyes in preparation for whatever torture was about to begin, but instead, I heard a loud boom, followed immediately by a warm wet spatter against my face. I opened my eyes to see my former body standing over me with a bloody stump for a neck. It fell limp to the floor, revealing Grace pointing a smoking shotgun through the hole in the kitchen wall.

I let out an exasperated breath. My eyes darted back and forth between my own bleeding corpse and the woman responsible. "You shot me," I said in disbelief.

Her eyes bulged, welling up with tears as the strength in her arms faltered. She let the gun fall at her feet and she dropped to her knees. "I did. I shot you. I killed my fiancé."

"Hey, you didn't—" I tried to get up too fast and immediately leaned back in pain.

She tore her eyes away from the corpse and saw me cradling my ribs. She crawled over, around the body, and held my hand. "But I didn't really, did I?" Tears streamed down her cheeks. "It is you in there, somehow. You are Bill."

I struggled to smile. "Ta-da."

Our respite was short lived. The headless body began squirming. Out of the bloody neck stump, the true form of the demon began clawing its way out. By the time I snapped out of my horrified stupor, it had already managed to wriggle its torso free. I reached behind me for the hose, but the monster shoved the nozzle away. It emerged fully, wailing in anger. I'd almost forgotten how enormous the beast was, and wondered how it possibly managed to squeeze itself into such a comparably small human form. Without giving me a second look, it sprinted on all fours out of the kitchen.

"Jesus Christ!" Grace screamed.

"What? You saw it?" I asked.

"Yeah I saw it! What the fuck was that?"

"Guys!" Sonny yelled as he ran into the kitchen.

"What the fuck are you?!" Grace screamed again.

"Oh, she can see me now," Sonny said. "No offense taken, by the way."

"Grace, that's Sonny," I winced again and held my side. "He's the invisible guy I've been talking to." Now that the immediate danger had passed, the pain in my ribs was almost unbearable.

"Why isn't he still invisible?" Grace asked, obviously horrified by my companion's appearance.

"You had too many doubts," Sonny said. "Blowing your fiancé's head off was, apparently, quite a leap of faith."

Grace covered her mouth with her hand, mumbling inaudibly to herself as she looked back and forth between Sonny and the corpse on the floor.

"Hey," I nudged her. "I know it's a lot. But it's okay. We're almost through this."

Her eyes stopped bouncing back and forth and she held my gaze for a moment, finally taking a deep breath and nodding.

I pulled myself to my feet, nearly passing out from the pain. Breathing through it, I peered into the living room. "Where's the demon?" I asked Sonny, not wanting to waste any more time.

"It rabbited," he said. "Took off through the hole in the living room."

"Wha—where would it go?" Grace asked.

"Where would you go if you just lost your only protection from something that covers seventy percent of the planet?" Sonny asked rhetorically.

"It needs a new body," I said. "It's headed into town. If we take the car, we can head it off."

From behind us, we heard the sudden sound of shifting rubble. We turned quickly to see Carol stumble into the kitchen, wide-eyed and delirious.

"Mom, I told you to stay outside." Grace rushed to her mother, trying to lead her out of the room before she saw the headless corpse of my former body.

"There were gunshots. I had to—I needed—Oh, good God!"

It was too late. Spotting the body on the floor sent her back into a panic. Sonny tapped on his wrist. We needed to leave soon if we were going to catch that monster, but I hated abandoning Grace with her sobbing mother in the ruins of their shattered home.

"Grace," I said.

"I know." She held her mother's face and looked her in the eyes. "Mom, listen to me. I just need to talk with the detective for a minute. I'm going to take you to your room, and you're going to stay put. I already called the police, but you should call Dad. Can you do that?"

Carol nodded, eyeing the pool of blood that slowly seeped toward her feet.

"One second," Grace said to me before leading her mother away.

I took a moment to catch my breath, but could only manage a painful wheeze. My feet began to feel damp. I looked down to find that my flip flops were missing, and the pool of blood draining from my old body was now surrounding my toes. I stepped out of the puddle and wiped my feet off on the kitchen mat. Grace emerged from around the corner, loading new shells into the shotgun with a whole box of them under her arm.

"You're gonna need these," she said, handing over the munitions.

"What about you?" I asked. "Do you have something in case it circles back?"

She pulled a large, silver revolver from the back of her shorts.

"Whoa. Where did you even get that?"

"These are just the ones not locked up in my dad's safe. I'd offer to switch, but I think you need the spread. No offense, but you can't shoot for shit."

I let out a painful chuckle, but it didn't matter. She definitely believed who I was now.

"Okay," I said. "We need to get going."

"Right. I just—I'm sorry. I'm sorry I didn't believe you."

"Hey." I put my hand on her shoulder. "You'd have to be pretty crazy to believe a story like that."

"Does that make me crazy now? I feel crazy."

"Welcome to the club." I smiled at her, and despite herself, she smiled back.

"Okay, go," she said. "And try not to get yourself killed again."

"Don't worry, I won't." I pulled her in for a kiss, to which she made an uncomfortable noise.

"What's wrong?" I asked.

"Mustache." She shrank back.

In the moment, I had forgotten that I was in another man's body, one that was nearly twice her age. "Sorry. Love you!"

With that, I followed Sonny out of the house, trying to walk as quickly as possible without putting stress on my ribs. I'd have preferred a better farewell, but it was all the more reason to come back in one piece.

Police sirens howled in the distance and I didn't want to be anywhere nearby when they arrived. Once we were both in the Corvette, I gunned it. Sonny nearly lost his grip on the vehicle, grabbing my forearm to stay in place.

"I assume you have a plan?" the reaper asked.

"There's a creek that cuts through downtown. If we lure it there, we can finish it off."

"How do you expect to do that? It knows to avoid water. There's no way it'll willingly go in."

"I'm sort of making this up as I go. We'll deal with that when we get to it."

I was forced to slow my speed as the road began winding through a neighborhood. Sonny looked all around us, scanning for screaming bystanders or general mayhem.

"You think it'd go into any of the houses?" he asked.

"I doubt it. If it has my memories, then it knows this neighborhood is mostly dead during the day. The closest guarantee for population is Main Street."

We screeched around another curve and, as suspected, spotted the demon making a mad dash for the Sugar Shack on Main. I hit the gas.

"Bill, you need to slow down."

I sped up.

"Bill, what are you doing?"

"Hold tight."

Sonny's eyes went wide and his hands dug into the leather of his seat. I hit the brakes just as we reached the curb, hoping to send the demon hurtling into the building. Instead, we passed straight through it—to no effect—demolishing the front of the store. My seatbelt gripped my chest, sending shockwaves of pain through my broken ribs until my whole chest went numb from shock. I could barely fill my lungs with air and the only thing keeping me conscious was the sheer amount of adrenaline pumping through my veins.

Loose jelly beans rained into the open car as I searched for the shotgun in all the debris. After an initial scream, the cashier rushed around the counter, asking if I was okay. I found the shotgun, holding it aloft before telling the girl to run. She listened.

"Bill Baker!" the demon howled. Its own voice was far more resonant than my puppeted vocal chords. It reverberated in my stomach like heavy bass from a concert speaker. The monster lifted up its massive arms and slammed them down on the trunk of the Corvette. The front end lifted, and Sonny fell through the bottom, having suddenly lost his focus on his seat. Before the car leveled out, the demon grabbed it by the doors and hurled the entire vehicle into the street.

The car landed sideways, passenger side down. I hung from the driver's seat, suspended by my still latched seatbelt. Thankfully, I no longer had feeling in my chest, but unbuckling and falling onto the road hurt in new ways I wasn't braced for. Sonny rushed around the wreck as I crawled through the broken glass.

"Come on, Bill! You gotta get up! Let's go!"

People started running out of the shops to see what all the commotion was, but when the cashier began yelling about a man with a gun, they all cleared away. My attack may have failed, but at least I managed to scare off any potential vessels for the demon to escape into.

I was still a little delirious from the wreck and was unable to get on my feet. Sonny tried to buy me some time by drawing the demon's attention elsewhere.

"Hey! Asshole! You are the most repulsive son of a bitch I have ever seen. That why you bailed back at the house? Afraid we'd see your fuck-ugly mug?"

The demon didn't seem to be listening. Sonny tried shouting at it again, stepping closer to the beast. Without looking, it lashed out its arm and sent Sonny flying into one of the shops across the street. I looked around for anything I could use to defend myself. Littered among the broken glass, I spotted the shotgun, the accompanying box of shells, some road trip snacks that fell from the console, and a shaken-up Dr. Pepper. I grabbed the bottle.

"It's over, human." The demon stood tall over me on its hind legs, blotting out the sun from my view. "I was hoping you could take part in your fiancée's torture, but you've been enough of an irritant. You'll just have to imagine the horrors. Now, do the world a favor and stay dead this time!"

I removed the bottle cap as the demon lifted its enormous clawed foot over me. Fizz erupted from the soda and I whipped it at arm's length, sending most of its contents upward. Steam bubbled from where the liquid made contact and the beast fell backward, howling in pain.

I reached out to grab the shotgun and planted the barrel in the road to help pull myself up on my feet. Now was my chance. At point blank, I was far more accurate, blowing apart chunks of charred flesh from its purple hide. After only a couple blasts however, the steam vanished, and the next shot no longer made contact.

Something I hadn't considered was how quickly liquid would

evaporate in the dry heat. It was midday, in Texas, during a summer drought. I fired one last shot, hoping that my previous miss had been the result of poor aim. When the pellets passed through, I knew I couldn't stick around. I grabbed the box of shells and hobbled away, wincing with each step.

I made my way to the antique shop across the road, certain that I was about to be pounced on. Then, from down the street, I heard a refreshing voice.

"Hey fuck-face! I'm not done with you yet!"

The demon was still recovering from its wounds and hadn't seen where I'd escaped to, but it sure as hell saw Sonny. It galloped down the road to reach him, seething with malice. That's when I realized that Sonny had a plan of his own. When the demon was just a few feet from pummeling him across the state, the reaper tore open a portal to Hell—right in front of it.

A look of panic came over the monster. It skidded to a stop, avoiding the portal by a millimeter. Watching it come so close, my heart sunk. Out of danger, the demon grabbed Sonny by his cardigan and snarled in his face. Once again, Sonny was flung through the air, landing directly into the shop I had just hidden inside. He rolled to a stop at my feet and wearily opened his eyes to see me.

"Oh. Hey, Bill."

"Hey, Sonny." I was in the process of loading new shells into the shotgun.

"I almost had it, man. We were so close."

"I saw. It was a good idea. Can you open a portal underneath it?"

"If I want it to fall on top of us. I could open it *from* Hell, but I can't track its location. I'd be blind."

"Damn. Did you at least see what I did with the Dr. Pepper? It worked."

"Wait." He jumped right back up. "Are you serious?"

"Yeah, can you believe that? I guess any liquid will work."

"Score one for the good guys."

"I need you to go back to the candy shop," I instructed. "There should be a fridge filled with soda and stuff. You can douse it while I try to make for the creek."

"I can do that. Did you say: *The doctor is in?*"

"What?" I asked.

"When you hit it with the Dr. Pepper!"

"I hadn't exactly planned it out. Next time I'm fighting a giant monster, I'll be sure to think of something witty."

"I'm gonna hold you to that."

The demon crashed into the shop through the window. Evidently, it never learned how to use doors. Sonny jumped away from me, once again trying to draw all attention to himself.

"Hey, dick-weed! Check this out!" He opened a small portal and reached his hand through. Above the demon's head, Sonny's hand reached down and flicked it between the eyes. The beast roared with rage. Sonny sprinted through the wall towards the candy shop, laughing all the while. The demon followed, not even noticing that it leapt over me in its pursuit.

When the shotgun was fully loaded with six shells, I got up and limped out of the store, making a beeline towards the bridge that passed over the creek. Behind me, I heard the demon wail again. I cocked the shotgun and kept hobbling. Sonny caught up to me, holding at least eight glass bottles of soda in his arms. I turned around and saw the beast galloping toward us, creating a trail of steam in its wake. I fired behind me—missing the first time, but knocking it back the second. We passed another shop; one more until we reached the bridge. Sonny lobbed another open bottle at the demon, dousing it once again. Anytime it got close, I fired off another shot. I knew that if I could get it into the water, it'd be weak enough to force into Sonny's portal.

It got close, and I fired. It got closer, and I fired again. As I reached the bank of the creek, I used my last shot. Sonny had already run out of bottles. *Maybe I can still make it*, I thought.

The demon lunged forward, knocking me to the ground. I reached for the box of shells, but the demon brushed them aside. Sonny jumped into the creek.

"Hey shit-stain! Is that the best you got?"

It laughed deeply and heartily. "A valiant effort, but you've already failed." The demon drove one of its long claws into my midsection. It was a sensation I remembered vividly from my first death.

Sonny rushed to my aid, but the demon swiped him away with its free arm.

"No!" the beast yelled. "His soul stays with me, where I can take good care of it."

It twisted the monstrous claw in my stomach and stretched its mouth into the closest approximation of a smile its deformed face could make. My vision blurred. Over the sound of Sonny screaming obscenities, I thought I heard a rush of water. Suddenly, I no longer felt anything, and when I looked up, all I saw was a bright sky—until that too faded away.

10

OUT OF THE PAN

I FELT A flash of excruciating pain as my soul was ripped from its body for the second time, and suddenly, I was back. Sonny released his grip on my spine and dropped me to the ground next to the battered corpse of Herman Powell. I ran my hands down my sides and was relieved to find that I was still wearing the suit I went in with. I had my own body again, at least, spiritually. My physical body was still lying headless in my in-laws' kitchen.

"What happened?" I asked. "Did we win?"

"I wouldn't say *we won* so much as *I won*." Sonny smirked.

I sat up on the bank of the creek and looked around for any sign of the demon.

"What happened? Where'd it go?"

"Complete disintegration. Not only did water hurt the thing, it melted it like a damn vat of acid. Sorry you missed it actually, it was super gross."

"Don't be," I said. "But I don't understand, how did you get it into the creek?"

"You actually gave me the idea. I told you I couldn't open a portal from Hell because I needed to be able to see the demon. Well, I had a great view from the water. Dropped the whole thing right on top of me. Thanks for keeping it still by the way."

I instinctively grasped at my stomach where the beast had stabbed me. "Don't mention it."

Sonny helped me to my feet and was courteous enough to keep his gloves on this time. I looked down at the body I had temporarily inhabited and wondered how the hell the police were going to explain the involvement of a college professor who was pronounced legally dead the day prior—and in a completely different state. More than anything, I just hoped his death wouldn't cause any trouble for Grace. The headless corpse in her parent's house could easily be dismissed as self defense, but if they found Herman's blood in the crime scene— what would that even imply?

I was eager to return to her as soon as possible, just to let her know that the danger was over, but before I could voice my desire, I felt another intense ringing in my ears. Haniel was evidently not content to wait for us to call him back.

I allowed the angel into my head and promptly heard Sonny shouting at him. "Dammit Haniel! There has got to be another way to contact us! At least give a warning or something!"

"This is urgent. It couldn't wait. I need you two back here, now."

"We were on our way already, you dick."

"Then don't delay," the angel said.

The noise faded out and I let out a sigh. It seemed that my reunion with Grace would have to wait.

Sonny walked over and tapped my shoulder. "Hey, don't worry," he said, as if sensing my concerns. "You guys'll be walking down that aisle again in no time."

"Thanks, Sonny."

"Anytime."

"No, really. I know that you're getting a lot out of this too, but you put Grace's needs—my needs, first. You didn't have to do that."

"The demon was coming here anyway. Even if I didn't—"

"But you did. I owe you more than I can ever repay, so again—thank you."

"Alright, alright. You know I hate this emotional sincerity bullshit. If I say you're welcome, can we call it square?"

I smiled and shook my head. "Sure, Sonny."

"Awesome. Now let's go bring Haniel the good news."

Sonny sliced through the air with his hands, opening a portal to Haniel's Office. I hesitated to step through, remembering the intense pain that scattering my atoms across space-time inflicted. Sonny decided to help me out by pushing me the rest of the way.

I rematerialized, stumbling into the room and nearly knocking over the angel's ficus. Sonny joined me a second later and closed up the portal. Haniel stood up and put his hands flat on his desk. Something about him had changed since we'd last been here. His suit was rumpled, his hair fell in his face, and he kept bouncing his fingers uncontrollably on his desk. His perfect, angelic aura had faded, revealing an unkempt, overstressed bundle of nerves.

"What took you two so long?" he demanded. "I called earlier and you completely ignored me."

"Oh, sorry about that," Sonny began. "We were a little busy, you know, killing a demon and all."

"What are you saying?" Haniel asked. "You've already encountered it?"

"And killed it. I feel that it's very important to reiterate that point."

"That can't be right. Just yesterday, we knew nothing of the creature's physiology. Surely, you would have informed me if you had discovered such information, so that we could formulate a plan together."

"We didn't need any hand holding to get the job done. We did just fine on our own. Isn't that right, Bill?"

I smiled apologetically to Haniel.

"I see," said the angel. "Well then, might I inquire as to how you discovered the beast's weakness?"

Sonny smirked. "We just—"

"Not you," Haniel interrupted. "Mr. Baker."

Sonny's eyes darted to me. I hate lying, but I knew Sonny wished to keep the lost books hidden from the angels. At the very least, I could omit some of the truth.

"We were going to tell you first thing," I said. "We just didn't have the time. Our first stop was to go warn my fiancée that she was in danger, but the demon was already there. We only learned its weakness by accident."

"Accident? How is that?"

"Well, as it turns out, it was water. When the demon attacked, it knocked me into the kitchen. If I hadn't busted up the sink, it wouldn't have gotten sprayed, and we'd have never been able to stop it."

Haniel sat back down in his chair and stared off into space, contemplating my story.

"Water." He let the word sit on his tongue. Sonny leaned over the desk and waved his hand in front of Haniel.

"You doing okay there, chief?"

"What? Oh. Yes, I'm fine. Are you positive it was the water? Not something in it?"

"Pretty sure," I said. "Why? I thought it made sense."

"It does make sense. It makes too much sense. That's what's bothering me. Every second-rate horror film down on Earth uses holy water as a means to battle demons, and yet I couldn't find a single reference to it in The Library. There are entire shelves—no, aisles of books dedicated to water and its spiritual properties, but not a mention of demons."

"Nothing in *his* library at least," Sonny whispered to me.

I ignored him. "You did say those books might be restricted, didn't you?"

"I wouldn't know," Haniel said, irked. "Apparently there is a great deal of information accessible only to the higher-ups. My supervisor denied my request for greater access. They said the circumstances did not merit emergency clearance."

"The circumstances?" I asked. "A rogue demon isn't considered an emergency?"

"Not to them. And it's worse than that," Haniel replied, glumly.

"Well, it doesn't really matter anymore," Sonny said. "The demon is dead. Job's done."

"So it would seem." Haniel frowned. "However, I'm sorry to say, we must postpone our celebration a bit longer."

Sonny and I exchanged looks, but we remained silent.

"I didn't call you here with news of *your* demon," Haniel continued. "Within the past few hours, my office has been flooded with reports of similar deaths. They began slowly, isolated in Texas, but have now begun to spread throughout the entire southwest. Demons are escaping from Hell at an alarming rate. Yours may well have been the first, but the problem is far from solved."

My heart sank. I remembered something Professor Widdick said: *A single rogue demon can be a grim portent of things to come.* "How are they getting out?" I asked.

"We don't know. That's the problem. And while your aquatic discovery is certainly helpful, it only raises more questions as to why this is all happening. Demons may not be the brightest of creatures, but they should know better than to come to a dimension where it may rain poison from the sky at any moment."

"That is a tricky one," Sonny commented. "I do hope you're able to work it all out, but if you don't mind, I'm more concerned with collecting my reward, now."

"Don't you understand? This is paramount. If this reaches a global scale. There is a standing directive to—"

The phone on Haniel's desk began to ring.

"That's probably another demon attack." He picked up the phone. "Yes?... What, here? Right now?... I'm in the middle of—Alright, fine.

Send him in." He hung up and addressed us again. "Forgive me, apparently there's another reaper here, who is demanding to be seen."

"Demanding?" Sonny asked. "If he wants to see you so badly, why not just portal inside?"

"Because some people actually use the system we set in place, Sonny. The one designed to keep people from just barging into my office."

Sonny puffed air out of his nostrils. Behind us, the door opened and another reaper entered.

He was a short man, with most of his skin unblemished by decomposition. He wore old workman overalls and had an awful bowl-shaped haircut. His appearance may have been a remnant of whatever era he died in, but I'm not sure if that was ever a good look. Though he was obviously younger than Sonny, everything about him was far more archaic.

The new reaper took large, heavy strides with his chest puffed out in a vain attempt to increase his stature. When he reached the center of the room, he looked us over, one-by-one.

"So," he said. "Seems you're already privy to the problem."

"I beg your pardon?" Haniel replied.

"I'm referring to the soul that was snatched during my shift. This one, to be precise." He pointed a finger at me—to which I, and everyone else, raised an eyebrow.

"What are you talking about?" Sonny asked. "I collected Bill's soul yesterday morning during *my* shift."

"There's no sense in lying, Sonny. Haniel can pull the tapes and see that—" he glanced down at the small scrap of paper in his hand. "—Bill Baker was killed only minutes ago. And surely, he will also see you stealing the soul for yourself. Did you honestly think you would get away with it? I figured that after Josiah caught you at it—"

"Hey! Josiah and I are square!"

"I think there's been some sort of mistake here," Haniel interjected.

"You got that right!" Sonny spoke up. "Who the hell are you anyway?"

"Nelson! Nelson Cooney!"

"Have we met, or something?"

"Yes!"

"Mr. Cooney," Haniel said. "Please calm down. Like I said, there's been some sort of mix up."

"Poppycock! This punk is a thief and a liar!"

"Poppycock?" Sonny commented. "I realize you probably didn't socialize much on whatever farm you came from, but you may want to think about updating your lexicon."

Nelson tightened his fists and scrunched his face, giving him a distinctly pig-like appearance.

Haniel stood up from his chair again. "Alright, that's enough! Sonny, stop talking. Nelson, listen up. Mr. Baker was, in fact, reaped yesterday during Sonny's shift. However, due to the extenuating circumstances surrounding his death, he was allowed to return to Earth and settle his affairs. He died a second time while in my service."

"What extenuating circumstances could possibly—"

"Hey Napoleon," Sonny interrupted. "If he wanted you to know, he would have told you. Top secret."

"It's Nelson!"

"That's what I said."

"Mr. Cooney," Haniel said. "If you wish to be compensated for Mr. Baker's soul, you will have to return when I am finished speaking to Sonny. I have something I'd like to discuss with you, anyway."

The reaper nodded and walked to the door, taking time to scowl at Sonny before exiting. Sonny shook his head the whole time.

"What a tool."

"I apologize for that interruption," Haniel continued. "Now, if we can get back to the issue at hand—"

"No need," Sonny said. "Our issue is resolved and I'd like my reward now."

"I don't think you understand—"

"I understand perfectly. Half off my quota: that was our deal, and you owe me."

"I owe no such thing. You haven't fulfilled your end of the deal yet."

Sonny's eyes went bloodshot. "You want to run that by me again?"

"I promised you payment for your service—yes, but unfortunately, further service is required."

"No, no, no, no, no. We have a contract. You wrote it up yourself."

Haniel produced said contract from his desk and slid it towards Sonny. "You're right. And if you take a look, it specifically states that you will receive your compensation upon the capture and/or termination of any *and all* escaped Hell-spawned entities, until such time as the crisis is ended. I can highlight the phrase 'and all', if you like."

Sonny scanned the document. The room became silent as he read it over to see if there was any room for argument and I couldn't help replaying everything Sonny had told me about the angels in my head. *Never trust anyone in the afterlife, especially the angels.* Sonny had gone above and beyond for them, and despite my initial repulsions, I'd begun to think of him as my friend. Denying him on some sort of technicality seemed grossly unfair.

After a few minutes, Sonny whispered just loud enough for Haniel to hear. "You sneaky son of a bitch."

"Sonny—"

"You dishonest, slimy motherfucker!"

"Silence!" Haniel rose, once again dimming the lights. The office shook as the angel lifted into the air. I shriveled into the corner, but Sonny stood his ground.

"What? What are you gonna do?" the reaper shouted. "Are you going to punish me? Terminate my service and send me to Hell? Go ahead! It's better than an eternity of service for a weasel like you! Fuck, shit, piss, cock! I'm cursing in your office, Haniel! What are you gonna do about it?"

The room stopped shaking and Haniel descended. As the lights returned to normal, Haniel's anger turned to guilt.

"I'm sorry," the angel said. He looked at his feet, embarrassed by his own behavior. "You have every right to be upset. You have to believe me Sonny, I'd like this to be over, just as much as you—"

"Oh, I *sincerely* doubt that."

"I won't force you to hunt down all of these demons, I just need someone to help me figure out *why* this is happening. When we discover the source, we'll be able to put a stop to it."

"Send someone else. Get another reaper to do your busy work."

"Don't you think I've tried? I have to be careful about who I tell, so that word doesn't spread. And the reapers I have asked don't want to risk missing their shifts for a mission that might not pan out."

"Gee, I wonder why?" Sonny mused. "It's almost as if this whole system is broken or something."

Haniel slumped in his chair and sighed. "The truth is, I'm bending the rules already. My supervisor was furious when he found out I'd waited to alert him of the demon. If it were just up to me, I would fulfill your whole quota for this, but that wouldn't go unnoticed. If my supervisor learns that I'm offering you any sort of deal, not to mention what I've done for Mr. Baker, there will be dire consequences. For all of us. The most I can do is give you half of what we agreed on, now— as a good faith payment. Twenty-five percent of your remaining quota. That is, as long as you agree to continue the investigation. Once we discover the truth, I promise I won't try to enlist you further."

Sonny folded his arms. I could tell he wasn't done yelling, but he hadn't been prepared for Haniel to make any kind of concession. Instead he looked at the floor and pouted. After a few seconds of this, he spoke again.

"What about Bill? He didn't exactly sign up for an extended tour when he got sucked into this whole mess."

Up to this point in the conversation, I had been so wrapped up in

Sonny's treatment, that it hadn't even occurred to me how this might affect my own deal. Was I stuck to the same contract? I could feel my whole body tighten as I awaited Haniel's answer.

The angel considered the reaper's words. "Given that Mr. Baker has been cheated more than anyone by these events, not to mention the emotional toll placed upon his loved ones, I'll ask no more of him. He never owed us anything."

I breathed a sigh of relief, but immediately felt a wave of guilt overtake me. I was free to go, but something about it just didn't sit right.

Sonny looked at me, dejected, then back at Haniel. "He doesn't owe anything, you're right. But I do? Haven't I given you people enough?"

"As a matter of fact, you haven't. Otherwise you'd have moved on by now, and I'd be negotiating with someone far less volatile. But if you don't want your twenty-five percent, I can't force you to do anything."

"You make it sound like I have a choice."

"You always have a choice. Perhaps it's time to start making the right ones."

Sonny opened his mouth, as if he had more to say, but for whatever reason, he held it in. He sulked off to the back of the room and leaned against the wall.

"Mr. Baker." Haniel switched focus to me. "We should probably discuss the nature of your return." He started typing something into his keyboard. I only half paid attention, too distracted by my thoughts. Of course, I wanted to return more than anything, but that would mean abandoning Sonny. In his state, who knows if he'd be able to complete his mission alone? I'd never have been able to take on the demon without his help. Would I deserve my happy ending if it meant he was deprived of his?

"According to my records," Haniel continued, "your body is currently in the possession of the local authorities in Salado. It's also—Oh dear. You cut off its head?"

"Huh? Oh no," I said. "It was Grace, my fiancée. She shot me."

"Mhm. Right. Well, as you can imagine, that presents a number of difficulties. We can't have you springing to life during your autopsy, not to mention regenerating your head. I've never done anything so extreme. We may have to abandon it entirely and do a full body recreation. I'll have to ensure that your old body is cremated quickly. After that, we'll need to wait a few days, to avoid suspicion. I hope you don't mind staying here in The Library. There's plenty to do. Obviously there are lots of books, and we'll get you a food voucher since you have nothing to pay with—"

"No," I said.

"Oh, well, if you're not hungry, that's fine. But spirits don't really get the same hunger sensation, and I really do recommend—"

"No, I meant, I'm not going to stay here. I'm going with Sonny. I want to help him with his mission."

Sonny perked up. I looked back and gave him an encouraging smile. Haniel stared at us both, puzzled.

"Are you sure about that? I was under the impression you wanted to return to your fiancée as soon as possible."

"I do, but I owe this to Sonny. He helped me when I needed it, and now that he's being pulled back into this—"

"Dragged," Sonny added.

"—I think it's only right that I return the favor. Besides, you said that it would be a few days before I could return anyway, right? Maybe we can wrap this up by then."

"And if it isn't wrapped up by then?" Haniel asked. "I can't exactly hold your body on ice. Do you intend on continuing the investigation after you return to life?"

"I don't know. Maybe."

"As I said, I've broken many rules allowing you to return to Earth. If you get killed again, I can't keep bringing you back. I'm offering you a second chance. You won't get a third."

"I understand. This is just something I have to do."

Haniel said nothing for a while, considering me. I couldn't be sure if it was just his aura of angelic pleasantness, but for a second, I thought his lips curled into a smile. "Very well. I wish you two the best of luck."

11

THE CANTINA

IF I'M BEING honest, there was more to my decision to stay with Sonny than obligation or fear. I hadn't realized it until I was confronted with the end, but this mission had given me an enormous sense of accomplishment. I've never been particularly driven in life. I often struggled to feel wanted or even noticed growing up, and it was an insecurity that I never fully shook in adulthood. Now that I was dead, I found myself filled with purpose. Of course, I still ultimately desired to get back on the path of quiet bliss with my fiancée when this was all over, but in the meantime, perhaps I could do something to earn the happy ending that slipped through my fingers only days ago.

We departed Haniel's office and retreated deep into The Library. I assumed Sonny intended to do more research before we set off, but when we reached an adequate distance, he collapsed against a bookcase and sat flat on the floor. I reached down to help, but he jabbed a finger in my direction, prompting me to back away.

"Hey man," I said to the reaper, who stared blankly at the books in front of him. "Are you okay?"

"Do you want the truth? Or am I supposed to say that everything's fine?"

"The truth, I guess."

"I'm fucking spectacular, Bill. Never felt better."

Still sitting on the floor, Sonny raised his hand and slashed a vertical line through the air, opening a small portal through which I could see tiny specs of distant light in a sea of black. He stuck his head inside and screamed without making a sound. When he pulled his head out, I couldn't help but ask:

"Was that space?"

"Yeah."

"Does that mean you can—"

He shot me a look that made it clear he wasn't interested in conversation, so I shut up and sat down next to him, waiting for his frustration to abate. After a while of sitting in silence, my mind drifted back to Grace. Surely the police had arrived by now and explained what happened to Herman Powell. She probably assumed the demon had defeated us and got away. Leaving her in suspense gave me knots in my stomach, but clearly my companion needed a moment before whisking me off to assuage my own anxieties. Then I remembered where I was. The Library of Eternity contained an up-to-the-minute recording of every soul in existence.

I pulled a book off the shelf, hoping to find Grace's, but instead, grabbed my own. I placed it back, thinking to myself, *No, not mine.* On my second attempt, I pulled a thicker book titled: *The Book of Benito*, which I recalled from the first time Sonny led me through The Library. Intrigued, I opened the cover—only for Sonny's hand to push it back down.

"Do not open that book," he said, gravely.

It occurred to me that I now held, in my hands, the life story of my grim companion.

"I'm sorry," I told him. "I meant to check in on Grace."

"Her soul needs to be present, like mine is. Only the angels can access everyone's records."

"I didn't mean to pry. If I knew, I wouldn't have opened it."

"I actually believe you." His expression was still sullen, but at least he was talking to me.

I slid the book back onto the shelf, noting the difference between his and mine.

"This is a hefty tome. Did you have the most interesting life on Earth, or does it keep recording after you die?"

"It's recording everything, all the time. Right now the last line probably says: *He's just sitting there, tired and wishing spirits could die for good.*"

I winced. "Kind of a bummer ending."

"I've led kind of a bummer life."

"The whole thing? You've been around—what? Two-hundred years or something right? What about when you were alive?"

"This may be a shock, but wartime-era Mexico was not an ideal time to grow up."

"Come on, I refuse to believe you had no joyful times. What about romance? You're way too confident to have been single forever."

He actually laughed. "Believe it or not, I actually used to be more timid than you when I was alive. Not saying that held me back too much, mind you. There were a few local girls, a couple of discreet cowboys who passed through town. But I never did settle down."

"You know," I said. "My family's lived in the southwest for a while too, and even you mentioned I may have a mixed heritage. Who knows, maybe one of those girls is my great-great-grandmother or something."

He looked over at me and raised his brow. "It's a pretty big country, Bill."

"Whatever you say, gramps." I smirked.

Sonny shook his head, but I had managed to elicit a smile, so I was satisfied. He looked back at me, more present. "You're probably worried about your own romance right now, huh?"

"Oh, worried doesn't begin to describe it."

He nodded and pulled himself up. "I guess we should let your girlfriend know that she isn't in active peril. She's probably gonna be pissed at you though."

"Me? Why?" I said, standing up next to him.

"You promised not to get killed again, and you blew that about as hard as you could." He took a quick glance at his list before swiping his arm through the air, creating a portal for me to walk through.

Thankfully, my hesitancy to warp through space-time gave me a moment to look through the portal before I jumped. On the other side, I could see Grace sitting in a small, featureless room with what looked to be two detectives. I stopped myself.

"Wait. We can't go yet."

Sonny frowned. "Why not?

"She's giving a deposition or something. If we were to burst into the room right now, she might freak out in front of the cops."

Sonny craned his neck to peer inside. "Oh yeah. I guess she did kill you. Maybe we *should* jump in, get her off on an insanity plea."

"Sonny."

"Yeah, yeah." He wiped the portal away. "Well that could take hours. What should we do in the meantime?"

"I don't know, get a drink?" I joked, but Sonny didn't laugh. He knit his brow and held his finger up, deep in thought.

"That's not the worst idea."

"What? We can do that?" I asked.

"Do you remember when Josiah jumped on our car yesterday?"

"I don't think that's the type of thing you forget."

"He said something. I thought it was a jab at—well, I thought he was trying to push my buttons, but he mentioned a rumor going around at the cantina. That there was a horde of demons running about. Either they were exaggerating, or someone at the cantina knew about this invasion before Haniel."

"What is the cantina?" I asked.

"Somewhere to get a drink."

WE EMERGED FROM Sonny's portal into a dank alleyway. It was grimy and smelled too foul to be the result of a few overcrowded dumpsters. It was an other-worldly stench. I had to be careful not to step in anything that looked unnatural enough to somehow stain my soul.

"Is there uh—a reason we picked this spot to portal to?" I asked, looking in every direction.

"It's hard to pinpoint the location," Sonny said, running his hands along the wall in front of him, touching each of the bricks. "Technically, the cantina isn't supposed to exist. The angels would shut it down if they ever caught wind, so its exact coordinates are scrambled in The Library database."

"They can do that?"

"If they know the right people upstairs."

"What, like some kind of criminal angel?" I asked to an empty space.

I turned around to find that Sonny had disappeared. I'd only looked away for a second, and I hadn't heard the sound of a portal tearing open. He was just gone. I walked over to the wall he had been touching, thinking he'd unlocked some sort of secret door. As I got closer, his head popped out, prompting me to yelp.

"What are you doing out here? Come on." He pulled his head back through the bricks.

I approached cautiously, first sticking my arm in to make sure it was safe. Something on the other side grabbed my hand and yanked me through the wall, into a dim tunnel. I yelped a second time, to which Sonny released my hand and rolled his eyes.

The source of the odor was now apparent. Along the floor and the walls was a sickening black ooze. As I followed Sonny, careful not to step in any of the sludge puddles, I thought I heard the faint sound of jaunty piano music. When we reached the end of the tunnel, I was able to make out a thin strip of light underneath a wooden door with no handle. Sonny phased through and I followed quickly, eager to leave the sludge hall behind.

After all I'd seen in the past couple of days, I didn't think there was much that could still surprise me. I gasped at the sight of thirty plus spiritual creatures, mingling in what looked to be a magical speakeasy. They came in every shape and color. I knew that the Compendium listed a good number of spirits, but I never conceptualized it in a literal sense. There were plenty of reapers, small impish-looking creatures, red-skinned monsters with horns, monsters without eyes, monsters with too many eyes, and—well, you get it. There was variety.

Sonny never broke stride. He walked straight up to the bar and sat down next to something that looked like it crawled out of the Black Lagoon. I took the vacant seat on his other side—next to a short, grey-skinned, bald creature with pointed ears. I tried not to look directly at anyone, for fear that eye contact would result in unwanted confrontation.

"What'll it be?" The bartender addressed us in a faint Irish accent. She was a reaper herself, with about the same level of decay as Nelson. As a matter of fact, I didn't see a single reaper that looked more decayed than Sonny.

"Nothing for us, Saoirse. But I would like to buy a glass of Jesus Juice for my friend in the corner booth."

I craned my neck to see who Sonny was referring to. Staring back at me, nodding in recognition, was Josiah. I waved.

"Wait a minute," Saoirse said. "Is that you, Sonny? I haven't seen you in a decade! You look godawful."

"More and more, every day."

Saoirse pulled out a fresh glass and began filling it with a viscous, green fluid from the tap. "You sure you don't want nothing for yourself? Used to be I'd have to keep a whole extra barrel in stock just for you."

Sonny sighed and gave a forced smile. "I'm fine. Thanks. You got a pen or something?"

Saoirse handed him one from behind the bar as Sonny pulled out his list. Several names appeared on the paper, all crossed out. Sonny circled only one and wrote beneath it: *Pay in order to Saoirse Quinn, 1922.* He then reached across the bar and the two reapers shook hands. As soon as they made contact, some sort of energy passed from Sonny to the bartender. I looked down and noticed that the name had vanished from Sonny's list. Saoirse pulled out her own list to ensure the name had transferred.

"Much obliged." She slid the green beverage over and Sonny stared into it, his fingers hovering around the glass.

"How about your friend here? He want anything?"

Sonny looked over at me and shrugged. "What do you say, Bill? I think you've earned it, if you want a glass."

I watched a drop of the thick, green Jesus Juice fall from the tap. "Thanks, but I'll pass."

"You look fresh from judgement," the bartender noted. "You ever get bored during one of your six-day weekends, you should come by and try some. I know a guy who works in the in-between. He gets this stuff straight from the higher dimensions. But seeing as this is your first time here, I should advise you to use discretion. I have a couple patrons who'd be more than willing to digest you for a few months if you ever mention any of this to the angels."

I didn't doubt her for a second.

While I contemplated the experience of being trapped in a monster's digestive tract, forever unable to truly die, the music behind me faded out. When it picked up, it was accompanied by a hauntingly beautiful singing voice. Her dulcet tones fell on my ears and made my whole body numb. I turned around, looking beyond the tables of various creatures, where I beheld a face that entranced me. I dared not look away, lest I miss a second of her radiance. It wasn't until Sonny jabbed me in the side that I realized I had started walking towards the stage.

"Careful, Bill. I don't think Grace would appreciate the way you're ogling that siren."

"I've never felt more—"

"Infatuated? That's the general response. The first time I heard one, I climbed on stage to profess my love to her—that is, until the bouncer pulled me down and knocked me on my ass. I could give you a nice beating, if you like. That'll snap you out of it."

I made no response. I was completely transfixed.

"Oh come on, Bill. You're embarrassing yourself. Tell you what? Look at her feet."

"Huh?"

"Her feet, Bill. Look at them."

"I'm not really into that."

"Would you just look?"

I managed, with great effort, to pull my gaze away from her face and recoiled immediately, falling back against the bar. Emerging from the bottom of her dress, digging into the stage, were two enormous clawed feet. I then noticed that, instead of hair, she grew long multi-colored feathers on her head and arms. In fact, her face was the only human feature she possessed.

"Why didn't I—" I began to ask.

"Notice what she really was? Let's just say, if you'd have spotted her before she started singing, you'd have caught on right away. Now, come on."

He placed his hand on my back and led me away from the bar, drink in hand. I took one last look at the siren and wondered how I could let myself become so enamored by another woman. I may have had no control over it, but I still felt guilty. The two of us sat down in Josiah's booth, and Sonny set the glass in front of himself.

"To what do I owe such a generous gift?" Josiah smiled.

"Who says it's for you?" Sonny asked.

"You haven't had a drink in years. Unless it's for your friend, but he didn't sound too eager to try it."

"You been eavesdropping, Josiah?"

"Come now, Sonny. What do you take me for?" Josiah tilted his head, briefly revealing a tiny portal next to his ear, before it vanished.

Sonny flashed a grin and pushed the glass across the table. "That's a handy trick. I'll bet you hear all kinds of stuff in a place like this."

"A glass of this certainly helps to loosen lips. Cheers." He took a long sip from the drink and turned his attention to me. "Didn't expect to see you again, Bill, especially in your true form. Last we met, you were a little more rotund."

"How do you know I'm the same Bill?" I asked.

"You were just as skittish then. And I've never known Sonny to keep much company. Two friends in two days is unfathomable."

"I resent that," Sonny defended. "I'm sitting here with two friends right now."

"Oh, you want to be friends, now?" Josiah smirked. "Here I thought you wanted a favor."

"I can multitask."

"If you're looking for help dealing with that demon, I'm going to have to decline."

"No, no, no. That problem's been dealt with."

"You don't mean—"

"Damn right I do. Thing didn't stand a chance against me."

I cleared my throat.

"Oh," Sonny said. "Bill helped a little too."

"I'm impressed," Josiah admitted. "Here I thought you'd be mostly bones after going up against it."

"Your faith is inspiring. No, what I need from you is information."

Josiah set down the glass. "What kind of information are you in the market for?"

"Yesterday, you said something that didn't sit well with me. Secrets going around and such. And if I recall, you specifically mentioned *demons running rogue*, plural. I let it go, assuming you misspoke, but I now have reason to believe you didn't."

"So, it's true then." Josiah raised an eyebrow. "Interesting."

"I want to know how you heard about multiple demons before the angels did, and from who."

"The trading of secrets is a valuable commodity. What makes you think you're entitled to anything?"

"Cut the shit. You're getting two extra shifts, thanks to me. With this heatwave, in my region, that's worth a fortune."

"This is true. I might just have something for you. Bear in mind, it could be completely unrelated." Josiah lifted his glass and drank the rest of it in three large gulps. "Yesterday morning, I was down here before my shift, taking in the atmosphere. It was uneventful, for the most part, and I was ready to head off when I saw an unusual pair enter the bar."

"You're gonna have to be more specific," Sonny said. "Unusual is the usual here."

"Nephilim."

The hair stood up on the back of my neck. "Nephilim?" I asked, leaning in so that I could better hear.

"Two of 'em. Came in and took a booth in the back. I don't want you to think I'm the kind of person who sticks my nose in the business of every strange creature that comes in here. I don't have enough noses. But Nephilim are a rarity in an establishment like this. They don't like to mingle among us common spirits. They think we're beneath their higher ancestry."

"So, what were they doing here?" I asked, taking over the conversation from Sonny, who raised his brow at my sudden interest.

"That's precisely what I wanted to know," Josiah replied. "From what I could gather, they were planning on meeting someone, and not another Nephilim. It can be difficult to read non-human spirits, but I suspected they were nervous. Whoever they were meeting sounded like bad news."

"You didn't see them?" I asked.

"Never got a chance. My shift began, and my curiosity only extends so far. All I know is that the Nephilim had found something, something the mysterious third party was interested in."

"What did they find?" I pressed.

"They didn't say much about it, but they did say it would take them a while to search through all of it—whatever that means."

"So where exactly do the demons come into this?" Sonny asked. "Could they have found some kind of doorway to Hell? Were they searching for a way to open it?"

"Possibly," Josiah said. "I only bring this up because one of them was concerned about the authenticity of their discovery. The Nephilim were afraid that this third party might 'sick his beasts' on them, if they were mistaken."

"And you think those beasts are the demons?"

"At the time, I didn't know what to think. After all, what kind of beast is scary enough to frighten a Nephilim? But when I heard about the incident in Texas, it made me wonder."

"What else did they say?" I implored.

"Nothing. At least nothing useful. They started complaining about the cantina and quietly made prejudiced comments about every spirit in the room, including yours truly. I left around that time."

"Great," said Sonny. "So, what you're telling me, is that you saw some shady figures talk about something vague, and you then assumed the rest?"

"Nephilim don't associate with just anyone," Josiah said. "And they did come in here on the same day as a demon attack. But like I said, it could all be unrelated. Maybe the whole world is just going to Hell and there's no rhyme or reason to any of it."

I was sold, but Sonny looked unconvinced. "I don't suppose you know anyone else who may have seen this meeting go down?"

"I'm not sure who was here when I left. Doyle might've seen something."

"Doyle?" Sonny asked.

"He works the bar when Saoirse is out reaping. New guy, young. I think he's supposed to take over when Saoirse hits her quota."

"Well, that can't be for a while though, right?" Sonny insisted. "I mean, she only took over the bar—what? 50 years ago?"

"Business has been good. From what I hear, she's planning to move up sometime next year."

"That is some horseshit!" Sonny shouted over the music.

Chatter around us quieted down as a few other spirits turned to look at Sonny's outburst. Sonny waited for them to return to their conversations before speaking in a hushed tone.

"There's no way they'd let her advance if they knew how she'd been getting those souls."

"Like you're not hunting these demons for some kind of short cut too. Let me guess, Haniel offered you a deal?" Josiah smirked.

"That's different."

"Sure. Never mind that you contributed quite a bit to Saoirse's quota back when you were a regular. You didn't seem to have a problem with it then."

Sonny folded his arms and stared down at the table. I leaned over to ask Josiah another question. "Do you know where we can find this Doyle?"

"I can write down his full name for you, that way Sonny can track him. But it may be a while, he should be in the middle of a shift."

He pulled a pen out from his jacket and scrawled the name down on a napkin. It occurred to me that for Josiah to carry a pen on him at all times, it would either require his constant focus, or it was some kind of ghost pen. In fact, in order to be useful, everything in this bar, from the glasses to the napkins, must have come from one of the spiritual planes. I suddenly had a million questions about the logistics of this business, but felt that the timing was inappropriate. I could ask Sonny later.

Josiah handed over the napkin, which Sonny stuffed in his cardigan pocket. "I'm very grateful for the work shifts you've given me, Sonny, but as of now, my debt to you is paid. Should you require anything else from me, it'll cost you."

"Oh yeah. I managed to trade two-to-three dozen souls to you for a hunch. Thanks a lot." He stood up to leave, but as I slid out of the booth, Sonny turned back to Josiah. "Actually, one more thing. Did you mention us to some snot-nosed little reaper—what was his name? Norman?"

"Nelson," I remembered.

"Yeah, Nelson something."

"You may find it hard to believe," Josiah said. "But some of us reapers actually like to communicate with each other more than once in a decade. So yes, I've talked to Nelson. He's a nice kid."

"How do you even know that guy?"

"You know him too."

"I do?"

"He's the one who took over my shift in Texas, after I was transferred to Alabama. You've met him at least twice."

"Oh, he's *that* kid? I think I may have tricked him into giving me some shifts when he first started out. Jeez, no wonder he was pissed that I didn't remember him."

Josiah flashed a grin and chuckled. "Always a pleasure. Let me know if you learn anything else of value."

Sonny nodded and I gave a short wave. As we walked away, I took another glance at the stage. The siren caught my eyes and gave me a wink that turned my face red. I kept my head down until we exited the bar. After emerging in the dark hallway, Sonny turned to me.

"Well, that was a bust."

"You don't think this Doyle guy knows anything?"

"I doubt it, besides—" Sonny took out his list and the napkin with Doyle's full name scrawled on it. "Josiah's right. His position keeps moving. He's on a shift. We're not gonna be able to get anything out of him for at least a few hours."

"What about the other thing he said? The Nephilim had found something. It sounded important."

"Probably, but what are we supposed to do? Start shaking down every Nephilim we find for information?"

"Maybe there's a way we can search The Library. If human actions are recorded in a book, maybe theirs are too?"

"No, that wouldn't work. We don't know the Nephilim's names. And we can't just randomly search through every book about—wait a minute." Sonny pursed his lips, thinking. "Josiah said something else. Yes, the Nephilim found something, but it would take them a while to search through all of it."

The same realization dawned on me. "And they were worried about the authenticity. Probably because—"

"Because the books are hand-written. They found the books. They found Widdick."

12

SHADOWS IN THE DARK

DESPITE PROFESSOR WIDDICK'S unique access to a wealth of knowledge beyond human comprehension, the man was severely lacking in sense. Upon appearing inside the professor's home, Sonny and I were greeted with ear-splitting screams, followed by a barrage of objects flung at us from the dark. Everything passed through us of course, but with only candle light to illuminate the space, Widdick failed to notice. Given the sheer volume of trash that cluttered the living space, he could keep up his assault for hours if we didn't find a way to calm him down.

"Professor! It's me! It's Bill!"

"That's a very common name!" He shouted as he hurled a printer at me. It smashed into a pile of broken junk, indistinguishable from the rest of the garbage that littered the floor.

"I was here yesterday, with Sonny! We asked about your books!"

"Everyone's after my books! And the Bill from yesterday looked nothing like you!"

"He was wearing your friend Herman at the time," Sonny said.

"What?" Widdick paused, snow globe in hand, ready to be launched.

"He means that I was possessing Herman Powell's body. Remember?" I asked.

Widdick's eyes narrowed and he lowered the snow globe. The professor walked over and stared into my eyes. "You're the soul that possessed Herman?"

"Yes!" I shouted. "You asked us to come back!"

His gaze turned vacant, the anger replaced by sorrow. "Right. Of course. I apologize, I've had a rather rough night and I thought you might be someone else."

"We know," Sonny said. "That's why we're here."

"It's pretty clear that you've seen other spirits in your house," I said. "What can you tell us about them?"

Widdick didn't answer immediately. He shuffled through the trash strewn room and peered between his boarded windows. He picked up one of the candles and carried it out of the room, beckoning Sonny and I to come along. We followed Widdick down a hallway, past the living room, and into a tiny, pitch black space. Once inside, he closed the door and turned on a battery powered lantern, allowing me to see where he had led us.

"It's a bathroom," I observed.

Sonny looked around, irritated. "If you have these lanterns, why do you even use all those candles? There's loose paper everywhere!"

"I don't want to waste the batteries," Widdick replied. "I keep this one in here so I don't miss the toilet."

"Why did you bring us here?" I asked, trying to get back on track. Widdick looked around again, as if someone else could be hiding in this cramped space with the three of us.

"I'm being watched," he spoke in a hushed tone.

The hair stood up on the back of my neck. It had never occurred to me that Nephilim would potentially be in the house with us when we arrived.

"Did you see them?" I asked.

"I heard them. Whispers coming from inside the house."

"Whispers? What did the whispers say?"

"I don't know. I couldn't understand them, but I do know they weren't human."

"How do you know?"

"Aside from my keen prophet intuition?"

"This is the same intuition that told you to throw a printer at an intangible spirit?" Sonny inquired.

Widdick glared at him. "Yes, well, there was something about their voices, something ethereal, like they were talking through a long tunnel. I came downstairs and saw nothing, but I could still hear them whispering—right in front of me. I shined my flashlight and the whispers stopped, but one of my books lay open on the back of the couch."

"You're positive you saw nothing?" I asked, needing to be absolutely sure. "Not even for a split second?"

"No. In fact, it was quite disorienting. I've lived in total blackness for several months, and my eyes have become adept at seeing in the dark, but as I drew closer to the whispers, details of the room seemed to fade. Even the flashlight failed to illuminate the space."

The bathroom was silent, save for the hum of the lantern on the sink. Sonny let out a sigh and nodded. "It's the Nephilim. The ones from the bar."

"Nephilim?" Widdick asked. "Angelic offspring?"

"Afraid so." Sonny said. "They're shadow creatures, absorbing the light around them like a black hole. "

Widdick nodded. "At least I know I'm not going crazy."

That was debatable, but I wasn't one to talk. Every time someone even mentioned these creatures, my whole body tensed and I felt insane. Yet at the same time, part of me wanted—needed to know more.

"What do you mean by angelic offspring?" I asked. "Josiah said something about higher ancestry and it didn't make sense to me. I thought you said Nephilim were monsters."

"No," Sonny said. "I said they were abominations."

"I'm afraid your companion's assessment is accurate." Widdick said. "Do you know what a giant is—in the biblical sense?"

"Yeah?" I replied, confused. "Like David and Goliath?"

"Do you know where the giants came from?"

"Honestly, I thought it was just Goliath."

Sonny rolled his eyes, but the professor continued, "The giants were an entire race of people. Goliath was supposedly the last of them and the first were the offspring of man and angel."

"Angels can mate with humans?" I asked, astonished.

"They used to. In the ancient days, angels could change their appearance, sex, even species to attract a human mate. In fact, it's likely they were the inspiration for mythologies all over the world for this very reason. Eventually, their escapades grew out of hand and the powers above had all their sexual organs removed."

Sonny and I both gulped. "I always knew they were dickless," the reaper said.

Professor Widdick waved away the comment. "Regardless, the problem remained. The giant offspring began breeding with mankind and spreading like wildfire."

"So, were the giants evil or something?" I asked. "I mean, why was it such a big deal?"

"It doesn't matter if they were evil," Widdick said. "This planet was created for human souls, but the giants didn't have souls, not proper ones anyway. They were never supposed to exist, so their spirits were corrupted—mangled. As they spread, humanity was dying out. Eventually there would be nothing but giants and corrupted souls, so it was decided to wipe them from the face of the Earth."

"The flood," I said.

"Otherwise known as the second apocalypse," Widdick confirmed. "The flood wasn't sent to cleanse the wickedness in the world.

It was to save mankind as a species. However, once the giants died, their corrupted spirits were left on Earth with nowhere to go. You see, the reaper is right. These nephilim are true abominations, the unwanted children of man and angel, abandoned and resentful. If they are after my books, I shudder to think of their intentions."

We sat with those words in silence for a moment. I'd hoped that learning more about the monsters that haunted my dreams as a child would help me overcome my fear of them. If anything, it only made the threat feel more imminent.

"What if they come back?" I asked. "What can we do?"

"They're mean," Sonny said. "But they're skittish. I don't think they'd confront us directly. I'm more worried about if they bring their demon pets with them."

Widdick's eyes went wide. "I thought you two were supposed to vanquish the demon?"

"We did," I said. "One of them anyway."

"Turns out, we weren't given the full scoop," Sonny added. "There's dozens of 'em now. All over the country. And I'll bet you can guess who the angels sent to deal with it."

"Dozens?" Widdick stared blankly at his shower curtain for a moment. "Oh my, that's not good."

"Yeah," Sonny said. "That was my general assessment as well."

"You don't understand. We may be running out of time. If what you tell me is true, we could be on the precipice of a global event. It's something I recall from my writings. If our world is at risk of falling to the creatures of Hell, then the dominion of men will be forfeit, and the angels will be forced to intervene directly."

"About damn time, if you ask me," Sonny said, shrugging his shoulders. "Something to get them off their asses."

"No, you fool! Did you listen to nothing of what I said? Both times the angels have interfered to wipe out an invading force resulted in an apocalypse. If the angels descend to do battle on Earth—mark my words, the third will be upon us!"

"Apocalypse?" Sonny and I both asked at the same time.

"Yes! And once it begins, there's no reversing it. Unless you two figure out how to stop these demons, we may be living in the last days on Earth as we know it."

"No, no, no," I protested. "I'm supposed to be getting married when all this is over. I'm supposed to get a fresh start."

"I hope you don't mind your fresh start happening during the years of tribulation, because that's what we have to look forward to."

Sonny looked panic-stricken. He whispered a quick "fuck" to himself and phased out of the bathroom, muttering expletives up and down the hallway.

I grabbed Widdick by the shoulders and looked him in the eye. "It's not too late though, right? We still have time?" I was sweating, and my voice quivered with desperation.

For as much knowledge as he possessed, there were some questions Widdick couldn't answer. He shook his head. "I suppose we have as much time as we're going to get."

What a terrifying notion.

I sat down on the edge of the bathtub. It occurred to me that this was the very calamity Haniel had tried to warn us about before we stormed off. To think, I had just been enjoying the feeling of purpose that this mission gave me. I wanted to feel important, and now I was saddled with the most important task imaginable. I already missed my insignificance. Outside the bathroom, I could hear Sonny break something made of glass.

"Is your friend okay?" Widdick asked, softly.

"No, I can't imagine he is."

"That's understandable. You'd think at my age, with all I know about the universe, I'd be ready for the end. The truth is, I'd very much like to stay here a while longer."

I nodded. I wasn't as old as Widdick, but that didn't matter much when faced with the prospect of eternity. Even though I was now aware of life after death, I had no idea what to expect once I moved on from the in-between. Would Grace and I even be allowed to remain together? Would we remember our lives on Earth? And if our days were numbered, would it be selfish to spend my remaining time with the woman I loved rather than foolishly try to postpone it?

"Nothing's changed, though," Widdick said.

"What?" I looked up from the bathroom floor.

"Just because we know what's at stake, doesn't change whatever you came here to do. Maybe we have exactly as much time left as we need."

I sighed as deeply as I ever had. He was right, of course. If there was the smallest chance we could still succeed, I owed it to Grace, Sonny, and everyone else to at least try. I had no time to wallow, even if it's all I wanted to do. My nerves bubbled beneath my skin and my chest felt tight. I forced myself to stand up from the bathtub and felt as if my legs would collapse in on themselves. "Okay then," I began, hoping that just talking would jump-start something in my brain. "Let's use this time. You have all those books and that knowledge in your head. Where do we start? What are we missing?"

Widdick pouted his lips. "I used to tell my students—when tackling a difficult problem, first you must determine why there is a problem at all. We need to figure out *why* these demons are coming here. Maybe then, we'll learn *how* they're doing it. What do you know about them? Tell me what you've discovered."

I recounted my first confrontation at the wedding, followed by everything we learned from the Compendium, and finally, our battle in the streets of Salado. When I finished, Widdick took a moment to respond.

"Curious." He stroked his chin as he sat on the toilet, in complete concentration. It was an amusing image to me, in spite of the circumstances.

"These dozens of demons," Widdick said. "Are they popping up randomly, or could they be originating from a single source?"

"I don't know. Why?"

"There used to be pathways between the worlds, but if I recall correctly, they were sealed off long ago. If the demons are coming into our world at the same junction, then it's possible that one of those pathways has been reopened."

"That sounds bad."

"Perhaps. But it may offer a simple solution. A single junction can be closed off. Sporadic materialization implies something more elusive. Either way, it seems unlikely that demons could accomplish this on their own. Someone is letting them out."

Sonny phased back into the bathroom and grabbed me by the arm. "I'm in big trouble, Bill. Big, big trouble."

"I know, Sonny. We're all going to be in trouble if we don't figure this out."

"You don't understand. This is especially bad, specifically for me."

I nearly pointed out how selfish he was being for making the actual apocalypse about himself, but then Widdick backed him up.

"I'm afraid he's right. The same goes for all reapers. You and I may already have our spots saved, but any soul not fit to move on to the higher planes will be left behind to suffer."

"Wait," I said. "You mean, if we fail—"

Sonny grabbed me by the shoulders. "Then I'll have given two-hundred years of service for nothing." His voice shuddered, and suddenly, my concerns felt quaint.

"You must relax, reaper," Widdick assured him. "Just as I told your companion, we need to continue as though we have all the time we need."

"That must be real fuckin' easy for you to do, old man. You're not predestined for eternal damnation!"

"The professor is right," I said. "Nothing is predestined, unless we let it be."

Sonny wasn't listening. In a repeat performance, he plopped down with his back against the wall and placed his face in his hands. "I'm just so tired of this. All of it. Every time I scrounge up a sliver of hope, it gets snatched away. Why are we even bothering? We can't stop an apocalypse. We could barely stop one demon!"

I reached over and placed a hand on Sonny's shoulder. "We did stop it though. Going up against that thing felt impossible too, but we figured it out. Now, I'm not ready to take on an army of those things, but we don't have to. All we have to do is figure out who has the means and the motive to free the demons, and then maybe we can stop them all at once."

"You reapers," Widdick said. "You have the ability to open portals to any plane of existence, do you not?"

Sonny lifted his face from his hands, glaring at the professor. "What are you suggesting?"

"If we're ruling out suspects, we have to consider—"

"I'll stop you right there," Sonny said. "You can rule out any motive for us. No reaper is stupid enough to ensure their own damnation."

"Unless they were coerced," Widdick suggested.

"That'd have to be some coercion. The only thing that could possibly benefit a reaper would be the fulfillment of their quota, and the only—" Sonny's eyes went wide. "It's an angel."

I frowned and looked to see if Widdick found his assertion as unlikely as I did. Instead, the professor rubbed his chin in contemplation.

"Think about it," Sonny continued. "They can travel instantaneously, just like us—and angels have already broken into Hell before. Who's to say they aren't doing it again?"

"Why would—" I began to ask, but realized the answer to my own question. "You don't think they're trying to free Lucifer?"

"It's the only motive that makes any sense," Sonny said. "Why else would anyone kick-start the apocalypse if it wasn't at the behest of the last guy who tried to do it?"

"The reaper makes a compelling case," Widdick said. "We may have a why, but we still need the how. Angels can pass between

Heaven and Earth at will, but Hell is forbidden for the very reason you mentioned. Reapers are the only creature I know of with that kind of access."

"So there's some reaper out there being used as a pawn in exchange for their freedom," Sonny said. "For all we know, they aren't even aware of what they're really doing."

"That's at least a start," I said. "So what's our next move? We can't just go around questioning every reaper, that would take years."

"We have to anticipate their next move," Widdick answered. "Suppose you're right, and they do intend to free Lucifer from his prison. Simply starting the apocalypse wouldn't accomplish that. The Fallen are held in the deepest pits of Hell. Reapers only have access to the upper layer. In order to reach them, they would need—"

"THE BOOKS!" All three of us yelled in unison.

"That's why the Nephilim were looking for them!" I yelled, excitedly. "They must be working for the angel behind this."

"The mysterious third party at the bar," Sonny said. "Sounds like Josiah was right on the money. If that other bartender can I.D. the angel who met with the Nephilim, then we can report him to Haniel, case closed!"

"You see?" Widdick smiled. "Enough time, after all. Can you go visit this bartender now?"

Sonny retrieved his list and examined it for a few seconds before sighing. "Not yet. But it should be soon. He's been mobile for a while. In the meantime, we probably need to do something with all these books in your house before the Nephilim come back. Are all the books here?"

"They should be," Widdick said. "I assume you brought back the one I gave you yesterday?"

"Th—the book from yesterday?" I stuttered.

"Yes, *The Compendium of Ethereal Entities*. You do have it, don't you?"

"I—um, well, we—"

"Shit," Sonny blurted out. "I think we left it in the car that we crashed."

"You lost the book?!" Widdick shouted.

"Hey, we didn't lose it," Sonny said. "We can get it."

"And you crashed my car?!"

"Now, that was unavoidable. Besides, you haven't left your house in six months, what good was it doing you?"

Widdick sighed heavily and pressed his fingers against his temples "Fine. It's done. It's fine. But you must make certain the book is safe. For all we know, it could provide exactly the information that this mysterious angel is looking for. Do you know where it is now?"

"If I were to guess," I answered, "it was probably taken by the police, as evidence."

"Evidence?"

"We may have caused a public incident during our fight with the demon," I explained. "But it's okay! We should be able to just walk right through the walls and grab it."

"If you're certain it'll be that easy." Widdick sounded unconvinced. "But once you do obtain it, don't bother bringing it back here. You'd have to move it physically and that will take far too long. You either need to hide it somewhere no one else can find it, or destroy it."

"Destroy it? What if we need the information inside?"

"Better than letting that information fall into the wrong hands. Just be prepared to do what you need to. I'll start working on a way to transfer the volumes I have here. If I had electricity I could scan them, but perhaps the university has some equipment I can use."

"What if the Nephilim come back and see what you're up to?" I asked. "You can't fight off a spirit. Sonny should stay and help you with the books."

"Me? Why should I stay?"

I didn't want to admit that coming face-to-face with another Nephilim had been my greatest fear since childhood. Even thinking about it made my legs feel weaker. I knew that if it came down to it, I would be even more useless in a fight than Widdick.

"Because," I said, thinking of a better reason. "You know more about them, and you have powers. You stand a much better chance. Besides, I still need to talk to Grace."

Technically, that was all true, especially the last bit. Sonny grimaced, but nodded his agreement.

"Professor, do you have a working phone?" I asked.

"My cell phone bill should be paid automatically. I haven't charged the blasted thing in months, but I can probably find a working plug somewhere."

"Okay, I'm going to have to memorize the number so I can call you when I'm ready. That way Sonny can just open a portal for me to come back." I reached out for my reaper companion and looked him dead in the eye. "Remember, don't let the professor out of your sight. If he is being watched, then the Nephilim may know we're on to them. Who knows what they'll do?"

Sonny scoffed. "We'll be fine as long as you don't spend too much time holding hands with your girlfriend."

"She's not my girlfriend. She's my fiancée."

"Oh she is? This is the first time you've mentioned it."

I shook my head and turned back to Widdick. "Okay Professor, let's hear that phone number."

13

GHOST HEIST

AS THE DEMONIC invasion escalated to a national scale, the public began to take notice. Panic spread in response to the wave of gruesome crimes that seemed to spring out of nowhere. The media surmised that there was a new drug on the market, turning ordinary men and women into superhuman killing machines—or maybe it was a virus that disrupted the brain and nerves. Two corpses were brought into the coroner's office in Bell County after displaying similar superhuman behavior. Nearby, in the Salado police department, Grace was being questioned about them both.

She was nearing the end of her deposition when I arrived. Sonny had dropped me off just outside the interrogation room, so that I didn't startle her further by appearing in thin air. The room conveniently had a window that looked into the bullpen of the station that allowed me to peer inside. With her were two detectives, a friendly-looking dark-featured woman, and an older sunburned man with a sour face. I tried to imagine him playing the 'good cop' and found myself unable.

Since they were still speaking, I took a moment to scope out the building. Being a relatively small and quiet town, Salado didn't merit a large police station, and the talk in every corner was of the carnage left behind at the Austin Police Department. On one hand, the officers seemed relieved that Grace had managed to put an end to my imposter's killing spree, but they also seemed uncomfortable with anyone connected to this case being held in the station—lest they provoke a similar attack. This was, after all, happening all over the state. At the very least, they likely didn't want to hold her for much longer.

It didn't take me long to finish my search, noting the location of the security tapes and the evidence room—conveniently in the same hallway as the bathroom. I began to formulate a makeshift heist of sorts, when I noticed the two detectives finally exit the interrogation room. I rushed over and stuck my head through the wall. "Grace!"

She was understandably startled. She let out a quick, high pitched scream and immediately sucked her breath back in. The detectives glanced at her through the window, to which Grace gave a nervous smile. When they returned to their conversation, Grace addressed me in a hushed tone. "Bill! Is that you? The real you?"

"Sort of," I said. "I'm a spirit, technically."

Her look of surprise morphed into frustration as she struggled to keep her voice at a low volume. "Do you have any idea how worried I was? I thought you were dead! Like, ghost-dead!"

I phased all the way through the wall and sat down in the chair beside her. "I'm so sorry. I would have come sooner, but we got called back by the angels—and then you got taken by the police and I—"

"The angels?" Grace stopped me. "Like real angels?"

"Less majestic than you're imagining, but yeah."

She shook her head, seemingly unable to process the concept. "What about the demon? Is it still loose?"

"No, actually. It's gone. It really is ghost-dead."

She let her head fall back as she breathed a sigh of relief. "I was convinced it was going to burst through the door at any moment disguised as my mother."

"Well, you shouldn't have to worry about that anymore. Hopefully."

She raised her head back up. "What do you mean 'hopefully'? It's dead isn't it?"

I winced. "That one is. Turns out there may be more than we initially thought."

She leaned over the table. "How many more?"

"Lots."

"Shit."

"Yeah."

"Does that mean they're going to keep coming after me?"

"No, no, no! They shouldn't. The first one only wanted you because it had my memories. The rest—well, God help whoever they're after."

My assurances did little to ease the concern on her face. "So, this is just reality now—never knowing if a person is actually a demon in disguise."

"Probably best to avoid anyone screaming obscenities and attacking people in public, but that isn't exactly a new rule."

A faint chuckle escaped her lips. "I guess. God, can you believe we're supposed to be on our honeymoon right now?" she asked, wistfully.

"Hey," I said. "Look at me." I placed my hand above hers on the table and concentrated. I directed all my focus on it, making her skin the only thing that existed in my mind. Then, I felt a wave of elation as I made contact. She let out a light gasp and the tension in her face lessened.

"We'll get that honeymoon," I said. "I promise."

"Does that mean—" she began to say. "Do you get to reincarnate in another body like last time?"

I smiled broadly. "Better than that. I get my old body back. Well—not the same old body. That one got a little damaged."

Grace winced at the memory.

"No," I continued. "I get a newly constructed body, all my own. But first I need to finish what I started, and this time I need your help."

Before she could ask how, the door opened, and the two detectives made their way inside. I jumped out of the chair, not wanting to accidentally get stuck inside one of them if they decided to sit down. Grace leaned back in her seat and tried to look like she hadn't been conversing with a ghost. I'm not sure how one accomplishes this successfully, but she started twiddling her thumbs and shooting her eyes in every direction but forward. They'd never guess what she'd actually been doing, but she sure as hell looked suspicious to me.

"Ms. Ev—" The female detective began to talk, but another officer opened the door holding a beige file and mumbling something inaudibly. The detective looked back to Grace. "Just one more moment," she said before they all exited the room, again.

I waited until the door clicked shut to speak. "We had a book in our car when we came to see you," I explained. "A very special book that we need to get back."

"The car that you—"

"Crashed into the candy store, yes."

"That's gotta be police evidence by now."

I pointed my finger at her. "Bingo! That's why I'm here. I need you to help me get it out of the evidence room."

"What?" Grace whisper-shouted and went bug-eyed. She quickly glanced at the door to make sure the detectives hadn't heard her before continuing. "You've got to be out of your mind. How am I supposed to get in there without being seen? I'm being detained."

"I've been listening to some of the chatter around the station. They're gonna let you go any minute. I can grab the book from evidence. What I can't do is walk out of the station with it. I might be invisible, but anything I hold won't be."

"They'd see a floating book."

"Exactly. So, once you're released, you need to ask to use the restroom. The evidence room is right on the way. I'll leave the door open and pass the book to you on your way out."

"And then *I've* got to be the one to walk out of here with police evidence in my hands. How is this supposed to work? I don't have my purse, I'm wearing minimal clothing, and I'm gonna go out on a limb and guess that this book is not pocket sized."

I looked at the floor, slightly ashamed of what I was about to admit. "It was written on printer paper."

"Oh, perfect. I—a person of interest—just need to walk out of a building filled with police officers while holding a fucking textbook related to the case that they're all working on, *right now*. This can't possibly fail completely and catastrophically."

"I'm open to other sugges—"

The door clicked open and only the female detective entered the room, leaning against the open door frame. "Too late," I muttered. "I'll get the book, just find a way to the bathroom." I phased through the wall, keeping watch through the window to monitor when Grace would be ready for the handoff.

"Detective Reyes," Grace said. "Did you have more questions?"

The detective crossed her arms. "Not at the present time. Ordinarily, we'd hold you for something like this, but I managed to convince my partner that wasn't necessary. He's not convinced, but in light of your situation and what's been going on at nearby stations, I think it's for the best."

"You mean I'm done?"

"You're free to go, for the moment. Though I'd advise you not to leave the immediate area. We may need to bring you in for further questioning."

"That's okay," Grace said, standing from her chair. She caught my gaze in the window and raised her eyebrows. "I do live out in Cedar Park, though. Hopefully that's not too far."

"Oh, you will not be returning to your home at the present time.

After the incident with your—uh, Mr. Baker, your home is being treated as an active crime scene."

"A crime scene? Where am I supposed to go? My parents' house was nearly destroyed. In fact, where are they supposed to stay?"

"I'm well acquainted with the owner of the inn down the street. I'll see if we can put you up for a few days while everything is sorted out."

"Oh. Thanks. I guess."

The detective shifted her footing and moved her gaze to the floor. "You should know, it's not just out of the goodness of our hearts. We don't know what Mr. Baker, or this Herman Powell were up to, but we have reason to believe it may be bigger than this. You and your family could still be in danger."

"You want to keep an eye on us."

"Just until we know what's going on."

Grace subtly nodded at me through the window. "Before I go, would it be possible to use the bathroom? I haven't had a chance since this craziness started."

"Oh, of course," the detective said. "Straight down this hall, third door on the right."

I took my cue and disappeared into the evidence room, if you could call it that. It was more of a closet that contained a couple of lockers and a white fold-out table with four plastic baskets on it. The book was in a two-gallon Ziploc bag in the second basket. In the others were Grace's shotgun, some of the contents from Professor Widdick's glovebox, and several empty bottles of soda.

I focused hard on my hands so that I could interact with the corporeal world again. In an improvised attempt to fool the police, I also took half of the contents from Widdick's glove box and swapped them with the book. Hopefully they wouldn't realize anything was missing until far too late. Once ready, I stuck my head through the adjoining wall to the bathroom.

Grace stood hunched over the sink taking deep breaths. Any time she got nervous, her cheeks would flush so much that her freckles would fade. Right then, they were barely visible.

"Psst! Grace," I whispered, but she jumped anyway.

"Jesus, Bill. Is there a ghost-bell you can put around your neck?"

"Sorry. I've got the book. I'll leave the door slightly ajar. Just stay close to the wall and reach back as you pass the room. I'll slide the book into your hand, and you can just walk out."

"I'm still not clear on how I'm supposed to *just walk out*."

"They're busy, they won't even notice you."

"Easy for you to say. You're invisible."

"Maybe I can draw their attention," I suggested. "We've got to hurry. Good luck!"

"I'd rather not rely on it!" she yelled out, but I had already sunk back into the wall.

I cracked the door, as I said—just enough to slip the book through, but not so much that anyone else would immediately notice. After a few seconds of waiting, I saw a shadow block the sliver of light from the hallway, followed by a small freckled hand poking into the room. I carefully handed off the book to Grace, easing it into her grasp so that the weight of it wouldn't make her stumble. Now she just had to get out unnoticed.

I wasn't a complete fool. I knew it'd be difficult to smuggle an object of that size through the station, even if the other officers were busy. Grace needed a distraction. Luckily, I was in an excellent position to provide her with one. While Grace moved quickly down the hall—head down and book gripped tightly behind her back—I took a shortcut into the bullpen where most of the officers were congregated. Grace would have to walk right past them in order to reach the public entrance, and it's where she was most likely to be caught. Officers buzzed around me as I scanned the space for the best possible disturbance. When I saw Grace round the corner, I had to work on instinct. I grabbed the first object I saw and threw it at a computer screen. Turns out, it was a very full cup of coffee.

Honestly, I think I did the station a favor. Those computers were clearly ancient and in no shape to be handling important work of any kind. Regardless, the plan worked. Everyone in the room gathered around the now-useless box of soaking junk, perplexed by what had just happened—except for the sunburned, sour-faced detective, who rushed over shouting furiously. He flung papers from his desk and started accusing every person in the room of the act, adequately drawing the attention of everyone in the building, and buying Grace enough time to walk away unnoticed. By the time the fuming detective allowed anyone to defend themselves, Grace had reached the front desk and was only a few more steps away from the exit. She maneuvered the book to her side so that the officers at the desk wouldn't spot it on her way out. Luckily for her, even they had abandoned their posts to get a better look at the commotion from the bullpen. It looked as though she was home free, when a voice called out.

Grace froze, and I was certain that we were caught. Detective Reyes walked right by the commotion to catch up to her. For lack of a better idea, I rushed over and swiped the manilla folder out of the detective's hands to buy Grace a few seconds of time. With Reyes briefly distracted, Grace quickly slid the book onto the front desk, using her body to block it from the detective's view. The interaction was out of my hands now and I made a silent prayer that the front desk officers would remain focused on the chaos in the other room long enough to miss the piece of evidence sitting next to the sign-in sheet. After gathering up her scattered papers, the detective caught up to Grace.

"Did I do something wrong?" Grace asked. "I thought I was free to leave."

"You can," Reyes replied. "I just wanted to—Look, I know what it's like." The detective placed her hand on Grace's shoulder, prompting her to quickly glance at the counter. Reyes continued, oblivious. "It's an awful thing to experience, having the person you most care about turn on you, hurt you. Just don't let it stop you from living your life. It gets better."

Grace's expression softened. "Don't worry about me, I'm tougher than I look."

"Oh, I believe that, Ms. Evans."

The two chuckled together, and I tapped my wrist to remind her that we were in the middle of an active heist.

"You probably have a lot of work to get back to," Grace said.

"Don't you need a ride to the inn?" the detective asked.

"Oh, uh, that's okay," Grace stammered. "It's pretty close. I can probably just walk."

"It's sweltering outside, I insist."

"I don't—"

Grace was saved at that moment by a shrieking woman. "Ah! Grace!"

"Mom?" She turned around, only to be immediately engulfed in her mother's arms. "What are you doing here?" Grace asked through strained breath. "The house—"

Carol released her grip and grabbed her daughter's face, examining her tousled hair and bruised skin. "Some officers came and started setting up police tape. After they questioned me, your father came and picked me up. He's down at the inn now, trying to get us a room. What about you? Are you okay? The officers just took you away and I didn't know if you were under arrest or what!"

Grace grabbed her mother's hands to stop them from rubbing dirt off of her forehead. "I'm fine, Mom. The police just needed to ask me some questions. I've only—" She paused, glancing in my direction and raising her eyebrows to signal some kind of message to me, though I couldn't determine her meaning.

"You only what?" Carol asked.

"Huh? Oh—nothing. Can I borrow your purse for a second?"

Carol looked down at her shoulder bag and I suddenly understood why Grace had signaled me. It was just large enough to slip the book into. Without waiting on an answer, Grace grabbed the strap and reached inside.

"I just need to borrow a brush," she said. "I'm sure my hair is a wreck." She pulled out the small travel brush that her mother always carried with her and made a big show of brushing out her hair. When she finished, she held onto the purse, draping it behind her. I got the message. With the detective still looking at Grace's mother, I snuck around and eased the book off the counter—into the open bag. Grace sighed.

"I'm sorry, but is my daughter free to go?" Carol asked the detective.

"Yes," she replied. "But we'd like to keep her under surveillance. It's likely that this incident is over, but if anyone else comes around that may be affiliated with Mr. Baker or his associate, it'd be better if there was a squad car posted nearby."

"You don't think that'll happen, do you?" Carol sounded mortified.

"She just said the incident is probably over, Mom," Grace said in a rushed tone. "It's just a precaution. Why don't we let the detective get back to work. I'd like to lay down anyway. I'm exhausted from all of this."

After another round of *Thank you's* and *Goodbye's*, Grace finally managed to get out of the police station, book in tow, and I let out a sigh of relief. I still had a lot of work ahead of me, but at the very least, Grace should be out of danger for good this time.

14

HITCHHIKER'S GUIDE TO THE AFTERLIFE

I NEVER DID hear which room at the nearby inn Grace and her family would be staying at, and in my present condition, I couldn't exactly ring the front desk. Luckily, it was a quaint establishment with only a few rooms arranged in a square around a central garden. After phasing my head through four doors, and averting my eyes at one very naked old woman, I managed to find Grace and—to my dismay—her parents.

I had dreaded an interaction with Frank and Carol Evans since this whole enterprise began. They were like a second family to me, and the fact that they certainly hated my guts now was almost as painful as being stabbed in the chest by a demon's claw. When I entered the room to signal Grace, I braced myself for what I might overhear.

"If anything, I'm just glad it happened before the wedding!" Frank spouted off. He was pacing the room, unable to stay still.

"Frank! At least *try* to be a little more sensitive," Carol pleaded. She sat on one of the two beds in the cramped space. Despite her protest, her look of shame indicated that she partially agreed with her husband.

"You saw the maniac. If that damned church had allowed me to carry my gun, I might've taken him down then and there, saved us a lot of trouble. I told you I wanted to bring my revolver. What did I say before we left?"

Carol turned to Grace, who was leaning against the bathroom door frame. From the look of her, she probably could have fallen asleep right there. "He did say he wanted to bring the gun," Carol told her daughter, who wearily blinked in reply.

"Exactly," Frank said. "Then we could have avoided all this mess."

"Yeah," Grace spoke, without looking up. "And you could have been arrested for shooting an unarmed man in a church."

"Last I checked, I can shoot a man who threatens my family, anywhere."

"What about outside of Texas?" Grace muttered.

"Honey, I think we're getting off topic." Carol turned to Grace once again. "I'm not saying it needs to become a regular thing, but one session certainly won't hurt. I mean, after all, you've been through such an awful experience."

"For God's sake, Carol. She doesn't need to see any psychiatrist. The man was a murderous lowlife. There ain't no shame in killin' vermin like that."

"She did love the man, Frank. I should like to think that if I went off the rails, you'd at least have some mixed feelings about blowing my head off." Carol immediately covered her mouth with her hands. She looked mortified with herself.

"Oh Grace," she said. "I'm so sorry. I didn't mean to bring that up. I'd never—"

"It's fine, Mom."

"See, you hear that?" Frank said. "She's completely fine. Didn't even faze her. And why should it? The man was a monster. Even before the wedding, I had my suspicions. What kind of man turns down multiple free hunting trips? I'll tell you, the kind who'd rather kill a person than a deer."

"That's like, the opposite of what a killer would do," Grace whispered.

This didn't seem to be winding down any time soon, so I decided to clear my throat, in order to make my presence known to Grace. I'd been standing with my head through the door for the entire conversation, but she hadn't looked up yet to see me. When she did, she turned wide eyed and stood up straight.

"I'm going for a walk," she announced.

"Oh Grace, your father didn't mean to upset you."

"Mmhm. It's fine. I'm just gonna go get something from the vending machine. It's sweltering in here." She stopped. "Actually, I'll need some quarters, do you mind if I take your purse?"

"Well, I suppose."

I backed out of the door and waited for Grace to meet me outside. As soon as she closed the door to the hotel, she reached into the purse and partially revealed the Compendium we'd just gone through so much trouble to steal.

"I got it out," she said. "But just barely. I caught your trick with the coffee cup. Nice going."

"Thanks." I smiled.

"I thought I was dead when that detective stopped me though." She looked me over and muttered, "Well, not dead like you, I guess, but—"

"I know. You don't have to clarify. It's not as if 'dead' is some kind of slur for us ghosts." I thought about that for a moment. "Well, actually, it could be. I'm not really an authority on the subject. I'll have to ask Sonny."

She shook her head. "This all sounds so casual to you already. Just a few days ago, you would get anxious if someone tried to strike up a conversation at the grocery store. Now you're running around with some strange corpse man, fighting monsters."

"It's been a whirlwind." I nodded. "But I'd take fighting monsters over making small talk any day."

She chuckled. "What took you so long anyway? I thought you were right behind us when we left the station."

"Oh, I had one more thing to do. I figured if the police noticed the missing evidence, they would probably check the security footage, so I destroyed the tapes. And by the way, not an easy thing to do as a ghost. It's hard enough just holding things, but smashing them takes a lot more out of you."

Grace leaned against the wooden fencing that overlooked the central courtyard. She ran her hand through her hair and slumped. "I hadn't even thought about the security footage. I could have gone to jail for real."

"At least you found possibly the nicest police officer in Texas. That could've gone a lot worse."

"Yeah, but now I'm stuck in the hotel with my parents until this whole thing blows over. I was starting to lose my mind after one day in their house. Now we're sharing a room. And my mom is talking about psychiatrists—if she keeps up with that shit, I'll ask that detective to find me an empty jail cell."

"Actually, I didn't think it's all that bad of an idea."

"Getting myself arrested?"

"No," I laughed. "The psychiatrist."

"Careful, Bill. Just because you're dead doesn't mean I can't hurt you."

I thought for a moment that being dead *absolutely* meant she couldn't hurt me, but I didn't want to test the theory. Grace had defied logic more than once since I'd known her. "I just meant—you've been through a lot in the past couple days. Several people around you have died, including me. On top of that, you were almost murdered multiple times, you've literally seen ghosts—oh, and there's that whole blowing my head off with a shotgun thing. That can't be a good mental image to have in your brain."

Her face scrunched up as she scowled at me. It was her go-to expression when she knew I was making sense, but she still didn't like it. "And what about you?" she asked. "You've gone through all the same and worse. You're the one who actually had to die, twice by my count. I don't see you rushing off to a shrink."

"Believe me, I've got *a lot* of therapy in my future. There's just some stuff I need to handle first."

"You make it sound like you've just gotta run some errands. I don't think all the therapy in the world is going to put our lives back to normal."

She was right, of course. It wasn't like I'd be able to walk back into town after everything that happened. How would we explain it to Grace's parents, or my job? I cleared my throat and did my best to sound sincere. "Maybe the angels can make it so that none of this ever happened."

"You don't think this was some kind of bad omen? Like, a sign that we shouldn't be getting married?"

The mere suggestion sent a spike of anxiety into my brain. "Of course not. What are you saying? You don't want to get married?"

"I do. It's just—when something supernatural intervenes moments before your wedding, it's hard not to think about the meaning of it all."

"Hey," I said, reaching out and touching her chin. "I'll tell you what it means. Nothing—not even the forces of Heaven and Hell— can keep us apart. I came back from the dead to see you again. Doesn't that mean something, too?"

She gave a faint smile. "You do have a way of making the worst experience of my life sound romantic."

"You'll see," I promised. "Once I finish my work with Sonny, things will be better again. They have to be."

Grace nodded absently, doubt in her eyes. She then pulled *The Compendium of Ethereal Entities* from her mother's purse and gazed at the cover. "I'm not finished yet either, am I? You can't exactly take this book with you in your—well, your current condition."

I shifted my weightlessness uncomfortably. I had been planning on explaining the rest of our mission to her, and unfortunately, it did require her cooperation. "I don't want to involve you any more than we have to, but you're not wrong. I can't take the book, nor should I. We think someone, or something, is after them. There's a whole house filled with books like this that we need to hide. I think it's safer if this one stays with you. That way, you'll have it if we need it again."

"Should I do something with it? If someone's looking—"

"Just keep it out of sight and obviously don't mention it to any-one, even your parents."

She ran her fingers over the title on the cover and then along the edges of the pages. The more dangers I presented about the book, the more fascinating it seemed to become in her hands. "Can I look at it? I'm not going to summon some kind of monster if I read a passage, am I?"

I chuckled. "No, you should be fine. Read it if you want. You might learn something that can help us. But whenever you're not read-ing it, make sure it's safe."

"I will." She tucked the book back into the purse and looked up at me solemnly. "I guess this is the part where you have to leave me again?"

I wanted to assure her that I would never leave her side again, but unfortunately, she was right. I'd already spent too long away from Widdick as it was. I needed to get back as soon as possible to help him and Sonny. I looked at Grace through crestfallen eyes. "First I have to make a call."

It would have been easier to borrow Grace's phone, but unfortu-nately Prof. Widdick and I never established an alternate line to com-municate over. If the police decided to check Grace's phone records and noticed a call placed to a man with direct ties to Herman, things might start to look suspicious.

All of the rooms were occupied, which was ridiculous on a weekend afternoon. Then again, I suppose no one wanted to be out in the heat. Grace went to the main office and found the owner of the inn, a nice elderly woman whose attire was more arts-and-crafts project than clothing. She lied that she had lost her cell phone and that her room phone didn't seem to be working. The old woman seemed hesitant about letting Grace use the private phone upstairs, but her mood changed considerably when Grace mentioned her name.

"Oh, you must be the Evans girl," the innkeeper said in a strangely cheery tone. "Valerie mentioned you'd be staying here. Room five with your parents, isn't that right?"

"That's right." Grace nodded.

"I imagine you have quite a few calls to make, after all that's happened. You take as much time as you need, dear." The innkeeper handed Grace a key to the door at the top of the stairs, and I followed her up.

The upstairs was considerably nicer than the room Grace and her family had been crammed into. The furniture was all late Victorian with heavy, ornate curtains draped across the windows. The phone was also old, though not an antique Alexander Graham Bell telephone as the aesthetic of the room might suggest. It was a beige rotary phone with a cord that could probably have stretched all the way downstairs at full length. It wasn't exactly before my time, but I hadn't seen one since I was a kid.

"Do you need me to dial?" Grace asked, wiggling her fingers in the air.

"That's okay, I think I'm starting to get the hang of this." I was only slightly right. I shoved my fingers through the phone several times before finally getting a solid enough grip on the rotary. I only prayed that Prof. Widdick had managed to find a working plug to charge his cell phone. There was a ring.

"Bill!" The professor's voice came through the receiver. "Did you do it? Did you find the book?"

"We got it. It's safe. How are your books coming?"

"Slowly, I'm afraid. I've been cataloging pages with the camera on this phone, and tossing anything that seems unimportant into a burn pile. At this rate, it's going to take a few days at least."

"Maybe we can pick up a couple more cameras and speed things up," I suggested. "How'd you get a plug working in the house?"

"I didn't. Not exactly, at least. I found a long extension cord in my garage and I have it hooked up to my neighbor's house. I'd like to wrap this up before he notices."

"Fair enough. Tell Sonny to open up a portal for me."

For a moment, all I could hear was static. "That's going to be rather difficult. You see, the reaper isn't here right now."

"What?" I shouted into the phone. Grace widened her eyes and mouthed to me, asking what was wrong. "Where is he?" I continued.

"Well, I don't exactly know. He'd been fidgeting with that list of his, and all of a sudden he got very excited and told me he needed to meet someone."

"The bartender. Dammit, Sonny. How long?"

"Nearly twenty minutes now."

I was fuming. If he had only waited a little while longer, I could have been there to wait with Widdick while Sonny met with the contact, but now he was putting the entire mission at risk—not to mention that he'd also stranded me five hundred miles away. I was just thankful that the Nephilim hadn't attacked already. I told the professor to wait somewhere safe, and that I would try to get back as soon as possible.

I hung up the phone and Grace stared at me expectantly. "Well? What was all that about?" she asked.

"Turns out my ride won't be coming to get me."

"Why not?"

"Because he's selfish, and impatient is why! If the world ends because he couldn't wait twenty minutes, I'm gonna find his soul in Hell, just so I can strangle him myself!"

"Whoa!" Grace put her hands up and took a step back. "I thought you were just trying to kill some more demons. You didn't say anything about the end of the world!"

I stumbled over my words. I hadn't wanted to frighten her, but in my anger with Sonny, it just kind of slipped out. There was no point in backtracking. She deserved the truth. I explained to her our theory for the demon invasion and the possible culprits behind it. "If it is an angel," I continued, "then we have no way to fight it. That's why we have to hide these books. Maybe if we can keep the knowledge hidden, we can stop whoever's orchestrating all of this from finishing it."

Grace was sitting on an old chair next to the phone, but she shot up to her feet as soon as I finished. "Then you need to get back and hide the rest of those books! Like, right now!"

"I know that, but I can't exactly drive there. It was hard enough trying to hold the phone."

"That's too slow anyway. You need to get there now."

I shrugged dramatically. "I'm open to suggestions."

"Come on, think! There's gotta be someone else who can take you."

"I'm still new to this. I've met a couple other reapers, but I have no idea how to get in touch with them. It's not as if there are spirit phones that can—wait."

As of that point, I'd only communicated with Haniel one way—through his loud and invasive phone calls to my head. When I thought about answering, it just worked. So, I figured if I wanted to make a call from my end, the concept had to be similar—right? I focused on my memory of Haniel's phone, sitting on his desk. I chanted over and over again in my head, "Haniel, pick up. Haniel, pick up…" until finally, I heard a click deep within my thoughts.

"He—hello?"

"Haniel!" I shouted in my mind, which to Grace, probably looked like I was having a migraine. "It's me, Bill."

"Bill?" There was a long pause, and then, "How did you get this number?"

"I didn't. I just called out to you in my head. I wasn't sure if it would work."

"I'm surprised that it did. I've gotten calls from higher up, but nothing from Earth. Certainly never with a personalized ringtone, screaming at me to pick up."

"Sorry, I just needed to ask you a favor."

"I have to say, you're running up a long list of favors from me. Letting you return to Earth, allowing you a second chance to live, repairing your damaged body—"

"Hey, I provided a service for those favors!"

"As opposed to the one you're about to ask of me, which you expect me to do pro bono?"

Grace watched me in utter confusion. She knew what I was doing, but it's hard to tell how a conversation is going when all you can see are rapidly changing facial expressions and hand gestures. "It's not like those other ones," I thought. "I just need a ride."

"A ride? Why? You're still a spirit. Sonny should be able to take you anywhere, instantly."

"Sonny is unavailable at the moment." Even in my thoughts, there was a tone of bitterness to my voice.

"Why aren't you two together? What is he doing?"

I considered explaining the lost books, but if it really was an angel looking for them, I didn't know who I could trust. I had to be careful not to formulate those thoughts into words for Haniel to hear. He probably heard me sputter a few random words in my head as I scrambled to think of a reason for our split. I started with a half-truth. "I wanted to check on Grace and make sure she wasn't in too much trouble after we left her in Salado. Sonny wanted to follow up on a lead about the demons, so I suggested we split up, but I forgot to set up a phone number I could call him at, and I have no idea when he'll be done with his lead."

Haniel considered this for a moment. "Very well. You're actually in luck. Nelson just finished his shift and you're right in his territory.

He'll take you wherever you need to go."

"Thank you, Haniel. I owe you one."

"Just figure out this demon nonsense and we'll all owe you a lot more."

There was a click and then silence. I looked at Grace, who had given up trying to decipher how the conversation was going. "That went well," I said out loud.

She jumped a little, apparently unaware that the call had ended in my head.

"So it's all good then?" she asked. "Your angel friend is going to send someone to help you."

"Yeah, I guess I have to go pretty soon."

"How long till they get here?" She looked at me, her eyes pleading for more time.

Before I could even open my mouth to speak, a short dead man stepped through a portal in-between us. Grace yelped. She was really going to have to start getting used to people appearing out of nowhere.

"Somebody call for a ride?" Nelson asked. His overalls looked dirtier than when I saw him last. I wondered what kind of supernatural filth someone had to go through to mess up their spirit clothes.

"That was fast. Were you already in the room with Haniel or something?"

"Nah, just taking some souls down under for the permanent stay. Time runs differently there. And I meant Hell, if that wasn't already clear. I was not in Australia."

"Yeah, we got that," Grace said.

Nelson turned around to look at her and then turned his head to me.

"Can she see us?"

"It's a long story," I said. "Don't worry, she's not gonna report you to the Ghostbusters or anything."

"The what?"

"You know, the Ghostbusters. From the movie."

Nelson scratched his jaw and stared at me blankly.

"Forget it, it was a joke."

"Yeah, well joke or no, the living ain't supposed to see into the spirit realm. Messes with their heads. This one's gonna need a therapist."

"Thanks, Mom," Grace rolled her eyes.

"You see what I mean?" Nelson asked. "She's delirious."

"I'll keep that in mind," I said. "Is it okay if I say goodbye before we go?"

"You couldn't have said your goodbyes before you called Haniel?"

Grace and I glared at Nelson in unison.

"Alright," he said, throwing his hands up. "Just make it quick, will ya? I got places to be."

A kiss would have been awkward to attempt in my state, but I'd gotten pretty decent at solidifying my hands. I touched Grace on the cheek and looked into her eyes. "I'll be back soon. Be safe, and try not to get arrested again."

"No promises," she smirked. "Try not to get yourself killed a third time."

"Definitely no promises." I took my hand back and her smile faltered. "I love you."

"I love you, too."

Nelson tapped on his wrist. I was starting to share Sonny's disdain for the short reaper.

"Relax, I'm ready," I said.

"Good. Where are we going?"

"Alabama. You know how to get to Opelika?"

"Don't need to, friend. The idea is enough."

He made a wide arc with his hand and a new portal opened before us. "I assume you've done this before?" he asked.

"Still not used to it," I replied and walked through. Once the last of my particles reassembled on the other side, Nelson stepped out behind me. We ended up near the college campus, in a small wooded area next to an empty construction lot. I must have looked queasy from the portal because Nelson took one look at me and backed away.

"You're not going to throw up, are you?" he asked.

"No, I'll be fine. Do the portal things hurt you too? Sonny barely reacts."

"You do get used to it, but don't let Sonny's act fool you. It smarts something terrible every time, even for a reaper."

"Sonny's act? You think he's pretending to not be in pain all the time?"

"Why not? His whole life is pretend."

"What does that mean?"

"You've been around the guy. You know what I'm talking about. He's got that whole *everything's a big joke and nothing ever gets to me* attitude. That's all new. He used to be a completely different person. I don't know exactly what he did in his human life, but whatever it was—stayed with him for decades."

I straightened up and looked at the reaper, intrigued. "What do you mean? What was he like?"

"Oh, he was a veritable mound of self-pity. First time I met him, things were real bad. When he wasn't late for his own shift, he was stealing souls from others to catch up. There was talk of revoking his reaper status."

"What happened? What changed?" I asked.

"Not sure. One day he gets called in for a meeting with the angels. Nobody hears from him for a little, and I assume they finally decided to send him to Hell. Then he comes back a few days later with a new name and a new attitude. Like we're all gonna forget what a belligerent drunk he used to be."

"Drunk?" I asked, remembering the comments made at the cantina about Sonny's past.

"Yeah, worst I ever seen. He'd've drank himself to death years ago, if he wasn't already dead."

"Is—is that how he died originally?" I asked. "Was it alcohol related?"

"Reapers in general don't like to advertise their manner of death, and Sonny keeps to himself more than most. No one knows for sure how he died, but among those who talk, that's the consensus."

I nodded, not sure how much to believe about my friend from a guy who clearly despised him. After a moment of standing around awkwardly, I was hoping Nelson would be on his way so that I could head to Widdick's house unseen, but he just leaned against a tree—looking at me expectantly. "So, be honest with me Bill. Where is Sonny, really?"

"He's—" I was about to give the same excuse I gave to Haniel, but I remembered that Nelson didn't know about our mission. "He's just busy right now. You know, *extenuating circumstances.*"

Nelson smirked. "Oh, right. I almost forgot about your super-secret arrangement with Haniel. Well, you can drop the act. I know all about the demons and Sonny's deal."

I wasn't sure if he was serious or if he was just grasping at straws, hoping to shake some information out of me. "I'm not sure what you're talking about."

"You think Haniel is trusting the fate of mankind to the two of you alone? He asked me to help out right after you left his office. Same deal. I'd expect he's asking all the reapers he can. Lord knows the angels won't help, even if they were allowed to."

"What is that supposed to mean?"

"You really don't know nothing, huh, Bill? Say hi to Sonny for me when you find him. And you can tell him not to get his hopes up about his deal, I'll have this demon thing wrapped up in no time."

With that, he vanished—leaving me alone in the woods, angry and confused.

15

BOILING POINT

AS FRUSTRATED AS I was with Sonny, I still didn't want his deal to get swiped from under him, especially by a guy like Nelson. The stout reaper seemed fairly confident in his ability to solve this whole thing on his own, but there was one thing he was missing: only Sonny and I had access to a prophet.

I had hoped that Nelson would drop me closer to the professor's house, but I couldn't specify where without giving away our little secret. Still, it was maddening to jog from campus, knowing that Widdick was unprotected for every second that I was gone. It also didn't help that the temperature was over a hundred degrees outside. Spirits may not need food or air, but for whatever reason, heat was a sensation that bore down on the soul. I stopped a couple blocks away to rest in the shade for a moment, when I heard sirens approaching.

I jolted alert, paranoid that the police were still after me, before I remembered that I was no longer in Herman's body. Then I realized that the sirens were not from a police car—they were from a fire truck.

The panic returned.

I sprinted the rest of the way, now plainly seeing the smokestack rising above the neighborhood. As soon as Widdick's house came into view, my worst fears were realized. The whole thing was ablaze. I didn't understand. I had spoken with the professor less than an hour ago. How could this have happened so quickly?

I rushed through the front door, immediately reminded of the difference between uncomfortable heat, and unsurvivable heat. Thankfully, I was already dead, otherwise the smoke would kill me in minutes.

"Professor!" I shouted at the top of my lungs, but the fire raged so loudly, that any reply would be lost in the noise. I ran through the house, straining to see through the smoke for any sign of life. When I reached the bathroom—hoping to find Widdick huddled in the tub—I instead spotted a thin trail of blood on the tile, leading away as if someone had been dragged out. This fire was no candle accident. Someone else had been here.

I crawled on my knees so that I could follow the trail of blood below the smoke. It led all around the living room, and it was only then I realized that most of the furniture had been knocked over in some kind of struggle. The trail led me into the kitchen, and as I passed through the threshold, my hand touched the fire eating up the wall. I howled in pain, shocked to discover that ordinary fire could burn a soul just as easily as hellfire. Feeling the heat close in on me, I crawled as quickly as I could out the back door.

The smoke billowed off my body as I pulled myself to my feet. Firefighters were beginning to swarm around the house and one of them looked peculiarly at the man-shaped column of smoke that rose from where I stood. I stumbled away from the house, desperate to distance myself from the flames. I was hunched over the grass, needing a moment to get my bearings, when I noticed the tire treads. The tracks left Widdick's yard through his neighbor's, and then onto the road. The professor may have been taken alive.

I heard a scream behind me and turned in time to watch Sonny dive out of the burning house, patting down his flaming cardigan.

"Sonny!" I rushed over and pulled him up.

"Bill? What are you doing here? What happened?"

"The professor is gone! He was taken. Do you remember anything from before you left? Did you see anyone around the house?"

He looked right through me, his mind wandering elsewhere. I lightly slapped his cheek until his vision focused on me and I repeated my questions. It seemed to come at him in waves.

"Widdick?" he murmured. "Where did he—no he wasn't—I was just here. There was no one, it was fine!"

"Did Widdick see anything? Did he mention anyone?"

"What happened to the house?" Sonny panicked. "Did he do this himself?"

I snapped my fingers in front of his face, doing my best to keep him on task. "No, Sonny. He was abducted. The place is trashed and there are tire marks leading away from the house. Whoever took him must have wanted him alive, so we need to find him now."

Sonny stared at the fire for a moment before turning to me. "Weren't you in Texas?"

Even over the burning smell, I noticed the same scent from Sonny's breath as I had from that green gloop at the cantina.

"Were you drinking?"

He didn't answer, and we didn't have time to deal with it.

"Sonny," I said. "You need to focus. Use your list and take us to the professor."

There was a brief period in which he just stood completely still, staring at nothing, and I thought he might throw up—if that were possible. But then he shook his head, reached into his back pocket, and pulled out his list. Sonny held the yellow paper at arm's length and stared at it intently. Nothing happened. He then grasped it with two hands and increased the intensity of his stare—which is to say he frowned harder at it. Still nothing.

"Something's wrong," he said.

Yeah, I wanted to say. *You're drunk off your ass and you're trying to use angel magic.*

"I'm gonna try something else," he said. Before I could ask what, I saw my name appear on the slip of paper in a heavy script followed by my exact location in relation to Sonny. He shook the list and then Grace's name and location replaced mine. He shook it once more, and then nothing. We both stared very intently at the paper, frowning at it even harder than before.

"I don't understand. What's going on?" I asked.

"I don't—This doesn't make any sense."

"Do you need to sober up a little first?"

"No, no, no, it shouldn't make any difference. It should be saying something, right? It did for you and your girlfriend. It's not saying anything now!"

"Has this ever happened before?"

"Of course it hasn't fucking happened before!"

"Alright! Settle down," I said. "We'll figure it out."

"This doesn't make any sense. I can find anyone! Where's The Rock? Oh look! There he is! Where's Professor Widdick? Fucking nowhere! He doesn't exist!"

"So, is he dead?" I asked, wincing.

"I can find dead. You're dead. It's like he was never even alive."

I did my best to keep a cool head while Sonny fell apart next to me. I thought maybe the list wouldn't work because Widdick was a prophet who wasn't meant to be tracked down, but then I remembered that we had used the list to find him already. Drunk or not, Sonny was right. None of this made any sense.

"Let's not panic, we can still track him down," I suggested.

"How?" Sonny pleaded, thoroughly unconvinced.

"There's tire tracks. If we keep portaling from track to track, we might be able to go fast enough to catch up to the car that took him."

Sonny gripped his head with both hands and shut his eyes tight, pacing back and forth. He was panicking again and I didn't have time to comfort him as I had before.

"Hey!" I grabbed him by the shoulders. "Listen to me, it's not over. We can still do this, but I need your help!"

"How? How can we do this? Whoever took him has what they need now. We lost! All reaper contracts are void, and I'm going to Hell! Forever!" He tore open another hole in space, but I held him back.

"Stop! You can't do that! You can't just resign yourself to misery every time you hit a bump in the road. We still have time, but not if you walk through that hole. I can't do this alone."

He paused. I could see something in his eyes. He understood the gravity of the decision that lay before him. He knew that I was right and that by giving in to self-pity, he'd only be dooming himself. Maybe there was still a chance that we could pull this off. I could see all this dawning on him, which made it all the more heartbreaking when he said, "I'm sorry, I'm just so tired."

He stepped through. Before I had time to process what happened, the portal closed up behind him and I was left standing in front of the burning house. I wanted to spend the next hour screaming and kicking the ground where Sonny disappeared, but I hadn't given up hope yet. I still had to try.

The trail was easy to follow. It looked as though whoever was driving had been swerving and leaving skid marks all the way. If I had been tangible, I could maybe try to steal a car and hasten my pursuit, but I could barely touch a vehicle, much less hotwire one. I kept running through the ways my situation would improve if Sonny hadn't abandoned me. We may not know Widdick's exact location, but he could at least jump us ahead faster. Even if that seemed impractical, he could find another dead body to shove me in, like he did with Herman. Hell, just having someone with me to make lighthearted, sarcastic remarks would make the experience far less dreary. Instead I was alone, running down the road, chasing tire marks while the sun continued to grow impossibly hotter with each passing second.

After a while, I noticed the tracks veering off the road into a large wooded park. The vehicle had flattened a path through the dirt and leaves. There were portions of bark scraped off of the trees where the abductors had failed to maneuver well enough around them. They wouldn't get far in these woods in a vehicle. *At last*, I thought, *a chance to catch up.*

I was right. The forest grew denser, with almost no room to squeeze a car through, and sure enough, I found a beat-up van just a little further. It was jammed between two trees and had most of the paint scraped off the doors.

I peered into the windshield, finding no driver. The back windows were tinted and I couldn't see in. Instead I would have to phase through the vehicle to look inside. It then occurred to me that I had just chased this van down without any plan of action for when I caught it. If Widdick had been abducted by demons, I had no way of confronting them. They'd laugh and then rip my soul to shreds—sending me to the super afterlife where everything is just as shitty, but the sun was somehow even fucking hotter.

Regardless, I leapt into the back of the van, hoping to at least catch the abductors off guard. There was nothing. Well—not nothing, I guess. There was blood. There was too much blood for it not to be a problem, but there were no demons and there was no Widdick. That's when I heard a yelp from outside.

I stuck my head out of the van and saw two figures in the distance. Once again, I had no weapons or physical strength to speak of, but I ran in their direction regardless. The figures spotted me and began to flee, making no noise as they did. As I drew closer, I realized that I had not seen silhouettes of men, but empty forms in the shape of men. *Nephilim.*

I stopped, paralyzed with fear. For some reason, I had been prepared to take on two demons with my bare hands, but the idea of getting any closer to those shadow nightmares was enough to strip away any ounce of courage remaining within me. I watched the shapes fade into the woods, wondering what had made the yelping sound I'd heard. On the ground to my right was the answer. Professor Widdick lay with his back against a tree, blood dripping from his face.

It felt like someone punched me in the stomach. I dropped to the ground and crawled over to check Widdick's body for any signs of life. I shouted at him, solidified my hands to shake him. Nothing.

"Bill!" I heard Sonny call out through the trees. "Bill, where are you?"

My fists tightened at the sound of his voice. I slowly stood up and walked toward the reaper, staring daggers all the while.

Sonny turned to see me, his eyes red and swollen. "Bill?"

"What are you doing here?" I asked.

"I'm sorry. You were right. I wasn't thinking straight."

"No, you were right. It is too late."

"What are you talking about?"

I stepped aside so that Sonny could see the display behind me. When he laid his eyes on Widdick's broken body, he fell to his knees.

"Oh God. This is all my fault."

"Right again, Sonny," I spat.

"I was only gone a little while. I thought he'd be fine."

"Over an hour, Sonny. You left him alone for over an hour. And now he's dead. You couldn't just wait for me to be finished. You couldn't even pull me back early. I had to get a ride back from Nelson."

"Nelson?" Sonny stood up. "What did you tell him?"

"What does it fucking matter what I told him? None of it makes a difference anymore. We have no prophet, no books, and no way of solving this—because of you!"

Sonny's face tightened. He wouldn't look at me. "I'm sorry."

"You're sorry? I could have forgiven your impatience, your recklessness, even your stupidity—but when I asked you for help, what did you say to me?"

He turned his head, silent.

"You said you were tired. Well I'm tired too, Sonny. I'm too tired to put up with your bullshit for one more second. Take me back to Haniel."

He was shaking, digging his fingers into his palms. "Why don't you get a ride from your new friend, Nelson?"

"Are you seriously going to pull this shit with me right now?"

He looked back at me, tears filling his eyes as he glared into mine. "I am. I don't have to take this. I didn't ask you to come along!"

"I came along to babysit you." My glare intensified. "To make sure you didn't screw up, but the moment you left my sight, you couldn't help yourself. You're a pathological fuck up! You ruined my life, and everyone else's, so you could fuck off to the bar and have some drinks!"

He shoved me back, full force. "Fuck you, Bill!"

"No," I said. "Fuck you!" I punched him, colliding the top of my knuckle with his tooth. He stumbled back, wiping his bloodied lip, aghast. Before I knew it, he leapt forward, tackling me into the leaves. We rolled together until I gained the leverage to sit over him and slam my fist down. He reached up and clawed at my face, but I felt nothing but blind rage. I kept punching until he managed to get his knee up into my crotch. I rolled off of him in pain and he managed to tear open a portal. Before he could escape however, I grabbed his pant leg and followed him through. We ended up in an alley somewhere, still grappling with each other. I was more disoriented coming out of the portal, so Sonny was able to land several good blows to my gut. I grabbed him by his long, stringy hair and slammed his head into the brick alley wall. I was about to do it again, but another portal opened in the bricks, and we both went tumbling in.

I was suspended, and freezing. We were suddenly submerged deep beneath the surface of an ocean. The salt water rushed into my open mouth as I struggled to maintain my hold on Sonny. He had spent centuries as a spirit and no longer tried to breathe as a reflex, but my lungs rapidly filled with water. It couldn't kill me, but it felt like I was going to drown, burning my lungs like a fire inside me. The reaper attempted to shake me off, but I held my death grip on his shirt collar. I wasn't going to let him get away, especially if it meant I would be abandoned in this ocean to drown forever.

We were off again, this time free falling in the sky. It was impossible to tell where. The world was spinning around me. The water that soaked my hair and clothes was blown dry by the torrential wind. Sonny may have hoped that the sudden fall would make me lose my grip, but at risk of plummeting to the Earth, I only held on tighter. Still, he had one last trick up his sleeve. We fell straight into another portal, shooting out the other end at terminal velocity. We had come out sideways and began tumbling and bouncing downhill. Finally, we each skidded to a stop at the bottom of a sand dune in the middle of a vast desert. We'd separated on our way down and were now several feet apart.

By this point, both of us could barely stand. I coughed water out of my lungs, which was instantly absorbed by the hot desert sand. I looked over and made eye contact with Sonny. He wearily clawed open a new portal, but I closed the distance and fell into his legs before he could get through. We rolled again, away from the portal, and I managed to get back on top of him. I hit him again, mustering any strength I had left. I was mostly just letting my fists fall down, too tired to add any additional force. He didn't fight back anymore and I had nothing left to throw at him.

I sat there, cooking in the scorching desert sun, too tired to move. The rush of anger faded away, and all I was left with was a horrible stinging in my knuckles and the lingering sensation of my body being stretched around the globe. I looked down at Sonny. His eyes were open, but just barely. I imagine the only thing that kept him from going unconscious was the fact that he was physically incapable of doing so. Frustration had been bubbling up inside of me since the day I died, and finding Widdick's body was the boiling point. Sonny became the target of all that frustration. As it dissolved, guilt took its place.

"Bill," Sonny managed to say through his blood-filled mouth. "I'm sorry."

I wasn't even sure which part he was apologizing for anymore. Part of me wanted to forgive him and apologize back. I'd never meant for this argument to get so out of hand. Instead, I stood up and glared down at my former companion. "Take me back to The Library. You're on your own from now on."

16

SUPERVISOR

I HAD A hard time finding reasons to defend Sonny after that. He was always an asshole, but I had tricked myself into thinking that his behavior was a cover, hiding a good man underneath. When I pulled back that cover, however, all I found was self-pity and cowardice. He didn't care that Widdick was dead, not really. He saw him as a means to an end. He certainly didn't care about me. I was just the soul he got stuck with.

I told Haniel everything. Once I was back in his office, I sat in the chair across his desk and explained every detail of our adventure. I was no longer concerned with keeping Sonny's "privileged information" a secret anymore. Perhaps if we had been open with Haniel from the start, Widdick would still be alive—and we may have even discovered the identity of whoever was orchestrating this plot. My only remaining hope was that we could salvage something useful from this mess. Widdick may be dead, but his soul might remember details that could help us.

Haniel didn't know where to begin. His voice was equal parts angry, excited, baffled, and curious. He couldn't believe that there was a living prophet on Earth, let alone that the lost books from The Library of Eternity were real—and inside a human man's mind. After scolding me for withholding vital information for so long, he implored me to reveal everything I could remember from the lost books. I told him to ask Widdick himself.

"Yes!" Haniel exclaimed. "I simply must speak to this mysterious man. Tell me, has a reaper already collected his soul?"

"I don't know," I said, slumped in my chair. From what I'd heard about the way reapers operate, one could have been in and out before I even found the body in the woods. "I didn't see anyone. Can't you check on your magic computer, or something?"

"Please, the divine nature in which our technology is constructed can hardly be compared with *magic*. I suppose Moses' Staff was nothing more than a big wizard wand to your pop culture obsessed generation, but I'll have you know that the inner workings of such a device—"

"Can you find him or not, Haniel?" I snapped. After a few seconds' pause, the angel confirmed that he could check his computer. I leaned my head back and stared at the ceiling. I was exhausted, and didn't know what a spirit could do to alleviate the sensation. After a bit of typing, and some mumbling to himself, Haniel spoke up. "Mr. Baker, are you certain this Professor Widdick is a real person?"

"I'm pretty sure?" I said, confused.

"It's just that I'm not getting any information on his soul, at all."

"Are you saying he's still alive?" I asked, a glimmer of hope evident in my tone.

"No, quite the opposite. I'm saying that he doesn't appear to have ever existed. Every search for every version of the man you described to me isn't coming up with anything."

I stared across the desk at Haniel's matter-of-fact expression. "That doesn't make any sense, Haniel. I just saw him. I found his body."

There was another moment of silence before Haniel asked me with a deeply condescending tone, "Are you sure?"

"Yes, I'm fucking sure! You think I found some other old college professor lying dead in the forest?"

Haniel winced. "Please, the cursing. And I'm not saying the man you met isn't real, I'm merely suggesting that his identity wasn't what you believed it to be."

"What, that he lied to us? Why would he do that?"

"Well, I don't know the man, but could it be possible that he wasn't fully present? If he had truly peeked behind the veil, there's no telling what it could have done to his mental state. I'll admit, I was intrigued by the possibility of a prophet in this day and age, but perhaps it was no more than a grandiose delusion of his mind."

"No," I denied. It suddenly hit me how crazy Widdick's behavior had been from the start. He lived in complete darkness, with no communication to the outside world, growing increasingly paranoid that strange forces were out to get him. Was he really just making it all up? Were his books just the ravings of a mad man? No! That would be ridiculous! He wasn't just paranoid. I followed the van myself. I saw the figures that abducted him. Sonny even found him with his list—his list!

"Haniel," I asked. "Why would someone appear on a reaper's list one day, and be untraceable the next?"

The angel considered this for a moment. "They couldn't. A reaper's list identifies the very presence of a soul. It can be traced anywhere."

"Can a soul be killed?"

"Of course not. Souls are eternal. Hell would sort of lose its impact if it all ended the first time you were eviscerated and feasted upon."

I grimaced. "A *no* would have been fine, but thanks. What I'm saying is that Sonny used his list to find Widdick before—but just a little while ago, he couldn't. What does that mean?"

Haniel considered. Then, after a few seconds, a thought dawned on him. "Oh good God, could we have been so blind?"

"Blind to what? What are you talking about?" I asked.

The angel stood from his desk, walking around the room and rubbing his chin. "This is going to sound a little strange at first, but could Sonny be the culprit we've been searching for?"

My brain didn't even register his suggestion as a possibility. "What?"

"Every action of every soul is logged within The Library of Eternity at all times. That's how the list works, it pulls information from The Library. So, if someone wanted to invent an identity, they wouldn't use a real one that could be traced to a book."

"Invent an identity? You think Sonny invented a college professor?"

"Not necessarily, but it is possible. Imagine—you're an elderly man living alone for years when a spirit appears before you and proclaims you to be of great cosmic significance. He gives you a new name, and then he warps your mind with knowledge that most Earthly souls aren't prepared to accept."

"Then how did Widdick know about things that weren't even in The Library?"

"That's actually the simplest detail. Despite what Sonny claims, there are no lost books from The Library. That's just a conspiracy theory started by reapers who lack access to books restricted by the higher authorities. In all likelihood, Sonny stole some books from The Library himself and filled this professor's head with volumes of knowledge until his mind snapped. I had thought it suspicious that entire categories could be missing. For them all to be restricted seemed unusual, but stolen—"

"But why? Why would Sonny—Why would *anyone* even think to do that?"

"If I were to venture a guess, for leverage. I've been racking my mind for days trying to figure out who stood to benefit the most from this demon invasion, and now the answer seems clear. Sonny invented a problem that only he could solve, so that he could leverage a deal to finish his quota."

It made no sense. Haniel's explanation contradicted so much of what I knew to be true, and yet I couldn't get past that one unchanging fact: a soul can't just disappear.

"No, no!" I stood up from my chair. "Sonny is a son of a bitch, but he wouldn't do that! It doesn't add up!"

"Think about it, Mr. Baker. A reaper could easily open a portal to hell, and the first demon *was* released under his watch. That's the reason I chose him for the assignment. Maybe he hoped I would fulfill his whole quota, and when I wouldn't budge, he released the others."

"No, it still doesn't make sense! Why would he let it go this far only to give up on everything now?"

"Perhaps it got out of his hands. Or maybe he realized that I was never going to meet his demands. Of course, he couldn't turn himself in, so he had to get rid of the evidence. He had to kill your friend in the woods."

"Sonny wouldn't—"

"Did he help you chase down the professor? Or did you say he left before you could find him?"

"He said he was tired, he—"

"He needed a head start."

"No! There were Nephilim! They were working for a third party. Someone else wanted to find Widdick."

"Yes, I remember. You told me these Nephilim met with this mystery person in an illegal spirit bar—which is a whole other matter I will have to deal with after all this. You two were supposed to speak to a witness together—yet, Sonny chose the moment you were indisposed to go by himself. Why would he leave your prophet unprotected to do this? Why was he so desperate to speak to this witness without you? And how would those Nephilim know the perfect moment to make their move without being told to do so?"

I had to sit back down. My head was spinning. Had every moment since my death been part of an elaborate grift? What about

Herman's memories of the professor? Sonny chose that body for me to take. Could he have fabricated Widdick's identity long before Herman's death, just to implant memories of him? Every explanation only offered up more questions. I still felt deep down that Sonny couldn't have orchestrated this, and yet the mere possibility made my blood boil. It was hard to think straight. Haniel was saying something, but I couldn't focus on it. I ran through my memories, desperately searching for anything that could absolve my former partner. Anything to prove that the only friend I had wasn't a monster.

"Mr. Baker," Haniel called out "Did you hear me?"

"What?"

"I said you look like you need a break. We can continue this discussion after you've had some time to recuperate."

HANIEL CLARIFIED THAT his entire theory was only that: a theory, but I was angry, and ready to accept it as the truth. It wouldn't take long for the angels to gather the necessary evidence of Sonny's schemes, as all of his thoughts and movements would be recorded in his soul book. Once Sonny was confirmed as the perpetrator, he would be stripped of his reaper status and condemned to Hell.

In spite of everything, I regretted how I left things with him, especially if it would be the last interaction we ever had. His actions were unforgivable, but I didn't believe he had any intention of jump-starting armageddon. Even if he was guilty, he'd only wanted to avoid eternal damnation. When faced with that ultimate punishment, what would anyone be willing to do? What would I do? In spite of his betrayal, our friendship *felt* sincere—or perhaps he was even better at deception than I gave him credit for. Still, I felt a measure of relief that my part in this escapade had ended. With the apocalypse no longer on the horizon, I could return to my life with Grace without the burden of impending doom.

My new body was still in the process of materialization, and Haniel was adamant that I could not return to Earth for the duration of my wait. Instead, I spent an indeterminate amount of time wandering around The Library of Eternity. It must have been several days, but without the visual marker of a rising or setting sun, coupled with an absence of sleep, it was impossible to say for certain.

Haniel had also provided me with food vouchers during my stay, despite my inability to feel hunger. I was, admittedly, curious about trying afterlife food, but I had no idea where I could possibly locate a restaurant in the labyrinthian library. Lo and behold, the moment I decided to search for one, I turned a corner to reveal a large clearing among the bookshelves where a food court was nestled. There were several restaurants advertising "angel food", but a cashier turned me away. He warned that my human soul wasn't equipped for it, and that a single bite would cause me to shoot flames from every orifice until all that remained of me was a shriveled husk. I backed away, horrified, until another customer assured me that the cashier was being overly dramatic. The food was just really, really spicy.

I settled on a small sandwich shop and ordered the same sandwich I ordered at every sandwich shop: grilled chicken on white with lettuce, onions, tomato, and deli mustard. It's a safe choice that rarely disappoints me, and I've found that the best way to compare restaurants is to order the same thing everywhere you go. I'm sure it goes without saying, but it was the greatest sandwich I'd ever tasted.

In fact, everything in the in-between realm was vastly superior to its Earth counterpart, but no matter what I did, I could only experience a dull satisfaction. *Of course the food was good. Of course each room smelled unique and wonderful. Of-fucking-course long dead artists were making incredible new entertainment without the limitations of time or money.* The longer I stayed, the more annoyed I grew. It wasn't as if I'd ever get to experience any of this when I returned to life, so what was even the point? It would only make me more bitter about my own mundane existence.

Of course, most of my time was spent actually exploring The Library itself. I had all the knowledge of the universe at my fingertips.

I looked into any famous conspiracy theories I could remember, but was disappointed to learn that they all had fairly boring explanations. Coca-Cola did make New Coke taste worse on purpose to sell more Coke Classic though. That one is one-hundred percent true. After satisfying my curiosity for life's great questions, I decided to read about the current events of Earth in my absence, which only plunged me deeper into misery.

The demon attacks were growing in number and severity, with no indication of slowing down. The media couldn't make heads or tails of the potential cause—blaming everything from drugs, microplastics in the brain, and online cults. One particular theory blaming the recent heatwave stuck out to me, however. Curious, I cross-referenced with a book of ongoing weather patterns and was able to confirm that the demon attacks were only occurring in areas affected by drought.

It made sense, considering their physiology, and it was too convenient to be a coincidence. Digging further, I could see that the drought was projected to keep expanding at an alarming rate—and more interesting still, I could trace the beginnings of the weather phenomenon to a single point—located in a town just a few miles from my wedding venue. If Sonny was truly the culprit, how could he instigate a global drought on his own? Did he have the help of a rogue angel, after all?

"HELLO, MR. BAKER. I have good news." Haniel smiled pleasantly. "You'll be able to return to Earth today."

I'd been summoned to the angel's office shortly after my discovery. I sat across his desk, searching his face for any hint of deception. Of course I wanted to tell him my theories about the drought, and the possibility of angelic interference, but how could I be certain that he wasn't the angel who had interfered? Perhaps he had only laid the finger on Sonny to distract attention from himself. I hated being so distrusting, but this whole affair had made me question everything and everyone.

Before I could decide whether or not to present my findings, the door opened behind me. I turned my head to see a tall, dark featured man in a perfectly tailored angelic suit. He had vibrant amber eyes and a neatly trimmed beard, so short it looked painted on his face.

"Hello, Haniel," the new angel said. His angelic aura made his voice sound smooth and sensual to my ears. "I apologize for my tardiness. I trust you've informed the human of the situation."

"Not quite. Mr. Baker, this is Ansiel." Haniel gulped. "My supervisor."

I stood up to shake his hand, but he immediately walked past me to stand behind the desk.

Haniel pursed his lips, contemplating his next words. "As I said, you may return to Earth today. However, before we release you—do you recall if Sonny gave you any indication of his plans before you parted ways?"

"I told you everything he said. Why? Haven't you caught him by now?"

"Um, truth be told, we're still looking for him."

"Still looking?" I asked, perplexed. "Can't you just search your computer?"

"Evidently," Ansiel spoke up, "your reaper friend has discovered a way to remove himself from our database. It's likely the same trick he used to erase the identity of your false prophet."

"I thought Haniel said that wasn't possible."

"Haniel, it seems, was wrong." Ansiel put his hand on his subordinate's shoulder and gripped him tightly.

"So, you still have no way of proving whether Sonny is even responsible then," I said.

"If anything, Mr. Baker," Ansiel began, "his lack of cooperation has proved evidence enough. But seeing as you have no knowledge of his whereabouts, we have no need to prolong your stay." He tightened his grip on Haniel's shoulder. "As we discussed."

Haniel was fidgeting with his cuffs and seemed unwilling to look at me directly, which I found highly suspicious considering my past experiences with the angel had included an uncomfortable amount of eye contact. "It would seem that I overstepped in my assertion that your life could be returned to normal," he said, maintaining a strained smile.

"What are you saying?" I asked.

Ansiel stepped forward before Haniel could speak. "We will return you to Earth in a new physical form, as promised, but you can never go back to your previous life. You will have a new name, new DNA, new fingerprints. Your appearance, we will allow to remain mostly identical, with subtle changes to avoid suspicion, of course. Everything else however, anything that could make someone definitively identify you, will be erased."

Small changes, I could live with. I had only one concern. "Will Grace still recognize me?"

This time, Haniel just looked down at his desk. Ansiel remained unfazed. "Actually, you will not be allowed to have contact with Ms. Evans any longer."

My stomach sank. "What?"

"Ms. Evans is a direct link to your previous life, and a person of interest for the local police department. For you to be seen with her would raise too many questions and, quite frankly, we are done cleaning up your mess."

"My mess?" I leaned forward. "I've been helping you guys!"

"What you've been doing out there is causing mayhem and incurring a considerable amount of work for us. We are in the midst of a crisis and I had to come down here *in person* to set things straight— seeing as Haniel appears to be incapable of handling it himself."

Haniel slunk into his chair, looking away from the both of us.

"I don't understand," I said. "If the only reason I can't see Grace is because of my appearance, then just change more. You can make me look like anything, can't you?"

Ansiel smirked. "We can, yes. But this department has devoted far too much energy into accommodating one soul. The body is prepared, and it will not be altered further. In addition, you are not to be granted any further leniency in the event of another untimely death, regardless of who or what is responsible. You die again, you remain so."

I was furious. Whatever angelic aura this angel had initially projected was completely faded by now. I wanted to crawl over the desk and punch him right in his perfectly groomed jawline. I doubt I could do him any harm, but it would have been enormously cathartic.

Instead, Ansiel snapped his fingers, prompting a portal to open up behind me. I felt the familiar sensation of a reaper reaching into my soul and grabbing my spine. The office I was standing in stretched out in front of me until it was just a pinprick of light in my vision. The illumination rapidly grew larger and the world snapped back into focus, but it was far from the world I recognized. I was someplace darker and colder than the one I left. Out of the corner of my eye, I caught a mysterious reaper creating their exit.

"Wait!" I pleaded. "Where am I?"

The decaying figure said nothing and disappeared before my eyes. I found myself on top of a stiff mattress in a wood paneled room. It was quiet, and I was alone.

17

SECOND LIFE

MY FIRST INSTINCT was to race to the door in order to determine where on Earth I'd ended up. This was a mistake. I shot off the bed and threw open the door, only to be blasted by a gust of freezing wind against my naked body. I crumpled to the floor, my legs feeling as if they had been transfigured into Jell-O. I crawled back desperately to get away from the cold, and when I was out of the path of the swinging door, I kicked it shut. Every motion of my body was a chore, as if I were using my limbs for the first time. Then I realized, I *was* using them for the first time.

I was in a new body, but unlike my previous experience taking over the recently deceased Herman Lewis, this body was unused. There was no flash of memories or influx of chronic pains. Somehow, Haniel had manufactured a fully formed adult body that felt as fresh as a newborn. The transition was so smooth, I hadn't realized I was no longer a spirit until I was shivering on the hardwood floor, feeling very much alive.

Eventually, I crawled back to the bed and grabbed a blanket to pull over myself. I was too sore from my initial burst of movement to stand, but I warmed myself up by flexing my new muscles as much as I could handle, slowly building my strength enough to sit back on the bed. It took me nearly an hour to get fully upright without toppling right back down, during which time I was able to survey my surroundings.

The house seemed to consist entirely of one large room with a small bathroom and closet. Judging by the bare wood that covered every surface, I surmised that I was in a log cabin, somewhere very far north. That would explain the unbearable cold. Aside from the twin bed pressed against the back wall, the house contained only a chest of drawers, a small kitchenette, a circular bistro table with one accompanying chair, and a 32-inch television precariously mounted on the wall.

Across the room, I spotted a wallet on the counter of the kitchenette. I stumbled over to it, leaning against the countertop for support. Inside the wallet was $40 cash, five gift cards to various restaurant chains, and a driver's license that bore my new face on it. I hadn't had the opportunity to look at myself in a mirror, but right away, I could see small alterations to my appearance in the photo. My eyebrows had grown slightly thicker and my nose was thinner. I thought that I might have had a new mole on my neck, but I couldn't recall whether it had been there all along.

After thoroughly scrutinizing the photo, I noticed the name on the license: Bob Butler. This was, perhaps, the worst thing I'd learned about my situation. Call me crazy, but I've always believed in the power of names to shape someone into who they are. Every person I've ever met named "Steve" has always represented the universal personality of what I perceived a "Steve" to be. Similarly, I've never met an accountant named "Salazar". This is why, for my entire life, I held a private disdain for my own name. I believed that people subconsciously projected their perceptions of a "Bill" onto me, and in turn, affected my own perceptions of myself. Now, presented with the opportunity to get a fresh start with a new name, I was instead saddled with a name virtually indistinguishable from my old one.

I know Haniel probably chose this new identity in order to make things easier for me, but it was the straw that broke the camel's back. I was fed up with the angels and their rules. They didn't tell me if there would be repercussions for disobeying them, but I didn't care. I was going to ignore the only thing they told me not to do. I was going to call Grace.

The angels had evidently anticipated this course of action and set out to make the task as difficult for me as possible. There was no phone in the cabin, and my brief exposure to the outdoors had indicated that I was far from civilization. I would have to venture out into the cold and attempt to locate a nearby town.

Gaining more strength with every second, I buzzed around the cabin, collecting supplies. I found plenty of warm clothes, an up-to-date passport, and cabinets miraculously stocked with food. I hadn't really thought about it until then, but I was hungrier than I could ever remember being. My new body had literally never eaten before. I gorged myself on anything that needed no preparation (mostly chips and crackers) until I was sufficiently filled enough to embark on my journey. I grabbed a couple of Pop-Tarts for the road.

As I suspected, there was no vehicle anywhere near the cabin, so I set out on foot. It soon became apparent that I had overreacted in my initial assessment of the cold. True it was much chillier than I was used to, but I had to abandon my winter jacket as I walked down the dirt path to the main road. I hoped that I'd be able to hitch a ride with someone headed to town, but I walked for hours without seeing a soul.

At long last, I spotted a sparsely populated area at the foot of whatever mountain I'd trekked down. There were maybe twelve buildings if I'm being generous—and not one of them looked as if they'd been built in the last fifty years. Still, at that moment, it was an oasis.

I made my way to an authentically retro diner, intending to use the phone, but seeing as I'd just spent the entire day walking down a mountainside, I decided that a glass of water was more pertinent. I sat down at the nearest open booth and let out a gratifying sigh.

"How ya feeling today, Bob?" a voice asked suddenly. I looked over to see a middle-aged woman in a red and white striped apron standing by my booth with a notepad. "You're not looking so good. Everything alright?"

Of course. The angels knew how to cover their tracks. They couldn't just drop an adult man on Earth without anyone noticing. They implanted fake memories into the local townsfolk so that I wouldn't raise any suspicions. And clearly they chose the smallest town possible to create less work for themselves. Typical.

I eyed the waitress' name tag and smiled at her. "I'm fine, Moreen. Just misplaced my car last night and had to walk into town."

"Walk? That's gotta be almost ten miles! Why didn'tcha call Dave? He'd've brought your truck 'round from the bar."

"My truck?" Ansiel clearly wanted to slow me down by separating me from a vehicle, but naturally, it would be insane for me to live in these woods with no way of traveling back and forth. "Now I'm starting to remember. Don't worry about me, Moreen. I could use the exercise, and perhaps a glass of water, too."

"You don't say? After that morning stroll?" She chuckled and whisked away to the kitchen.

I took the opportunity to grab a packet of Pop-Tarts from my jacket pocket. Being dead for so long, I'd almost forgotten what it was like to need food all the time. I was just taking a bite out of the wild berry rectangle, when I noticed a figure appear opposite me in the booth. It was Sonny.

I started choking on the dry pastry, waving away concern when another patron craned their neck to look at me. After regaining my composure, I whispered, "Sonny? What the hell are—" Moreen came back around and I pretended as if a literal ghost hadn't just materialized in front of me.

"There ya go," she said, setting a tall glass of iced water down on the table. "Just gimme me a shout if you want something to nibble on." And with that, she was back to the kitchen.

I maintained my smile until the moment she was out of sight. "What the hell are you doing here? You almost gave me a heart attack."

"I'm sorry," Sonny said. "I wouldn't have come at all, but I need your help."

"My help? I told you we were done, and I meant it. You're—" I paused to take a sip from my water as Moreen brushed past my table. "You're lucky I don't contact the angels right now and tell them where you are."

"You have to believe me," the reaper said. "Whatever they're accusing me of, I'm innocent. I can explain everything."

I huffed. "Really? And why should I even entertain the *notion* that you're telling the truth now? As far as I'm concerned, everything you've ever told me was a lie."

"Because if I'm not lying, then the real culprit is still out there, and we're getting closer to judgement day with each passing hour."

I considered this for a moment. "Fine. You have until I finish my water, then I'm washing my hands of you."

"I'll make it quick."

I took a large gulp from my glass and set it down, half empty. "Go ahead."

Sonny looked at the glass, sighed, then took a deep breath. "When you went to find the Compendium at the police station, I got a little antsy. I kept checking my list to see where you were. I also checked on Doyle, our witness. He finally ended his shift, and I couldn't get Widdick's words out of my head."

"What words?"

"Maybe we have exactly as much time as we need. *Exactly as much*. As in, if it came down to the wire, every minute we could save was precious. So I made—in retrospect—a terrible decision. I decided to question the witness myself, hoping that I would be back before you finished, and we'd have saved the trouble of two separate missions. Well, Doyle was less than cooperative. He wouldn't even acknowledge he was there that day until I started buying him drinks, and once he started drinking, he wouldn't say more until I joined him."

I took another gulp from my glass, looking over the rim with doubt in my eyes.

"I'll admit," Sonny continued, "I didn't fight him much on it. It had been so long, and it felt like the universe was giving me permission. It doesn't matter. I didn't realize how much time had passed, and when I got back to Widdick's—Well, you know what happened."

"And what about this Doyle?" I asked. "Did he tell you who met with the Nephilim?"

"No. It turns out, Doyle didn't know much. He confirmed the Nephilim were in the bar—just like Josiah said—and he saw *someone* sit at their table, but he never got a look at their face. He said they kept it hidden, with a cloak."

"So you got nothing," I said. "Nothing we didn't already know."

"Not nothing. He didn't see the guy's face, but he saw his hands. They weren't angel hands. They were decaying, like mine. A reaper."

"Okay. We already theorized that a reaper was involved. I don't see how that information was worth losing the professor over."

"It wasn't. You're right. It was a bust." His face became somber, and I had to remind myself that he may just be putting on an act, like he always did. I took another sip.

"So," he continued, "when I returned to find Widdick missing, his house on fire, and nothing of any value to show for my efforts, I panicked. I was drunk, and I'd run out of hope. I know that's no excuse. I have no excuse."

"Then why did you come back in the forest?" I asked.

"I had a moment to think about it, clear my head. And I remembered that you stuck with me when Haniel gave you the opportunity to quit. I regret leaving the professor more than you can imagine, but—" Sonny grabbed his neck and looked out the window. "I guess I regretted abandoning you even more."

There was a pause in the conversation as some customers walked by our booth. I looked at my glass, almost empty, and decided I wasn't thirsty enough to take another sip, just yet. "Then what?" I asked.

"When I dropped you off at The Library, you know, after—"

"I remember."

"Right. When I dropped you off, I wandered around for a while, thinking about everything that happened. I still couldn't get over how Widdick just disappeared from my list. It didn't make any sense. Any soul with a book in The Library should appear on the list. That's when it occurred to me. What if the book *wasn't* in The Library? What if whoever took Widdick made sure his soul could never be found?"

"You mean, they just took Widdick's book off the shelf?" I asked. "As simple as that?"

"You're not far off. I had to test my theory sooner than I expected. Not long after dropping you off, a gang of reapers tried to nab me in The Library. I managed to grab my own book and fled to Earth, but they kept finding me. So, I tried one last gambit. I burned my book. After that, I was off the grid."

Suddenly, Haniel's version of events seemed less concrete. "Do you know why they were after you?" I asked.

"I found out. Overheard chatter that some dickwad angel named Ansiel had put a price on my head. Ten thousand souls for whoever brought me in. Who'd've guessed I was so valuable? They actually thought I was the mastermind behind everything. Can you believe that?"

I cleared my throat. "It certainly stretches the imagination."

"You're tellin' me. I didn't know whether to be frightened or flattered. In any case, I knew that the only hope I had of proving my innocence was completing the mission and finding the true culprit."

"And that's why you need my help? No offense, but we're in even worse shape than we were before."

"No, I'm getting to it. If Widdick's death proved anything, it's that the culprit wants his books, desperately. See, I don't think they burned down Widdick's house. I think Widdick did that himself. He figured out what I only just discovered."

"Which is?"

Sonny smirked and opened a small portal over the booth. He reached in and pulled out *The Compendium of Ethereal Entities*, resting it gently on the table.

My eyes went wide. "How—"

"That's some book ya got there," Moreen commented, approaching with a refill for my water glass. "I didn't notice it earlier. Did you lug that thing all the way down the mountain?"

"Uh, yeah. Sure did," I lied. "Thought I might do some light reading."

"Mmhm. Well, are you sticking with the water, or would you like somethin' to go with it?"

"I might need some coffee, now that you mention it."

"Comin' right up!"

As soon as she stepped away, I leaned toward Sonny. "How did you do that? This is a physical book! Even the waitress can see it!"

Sonny smiled. "This is a special volume, my friend. Let me ask you, what do you know about the books in The Library?"

"I don't know. They're like magic, or something. They open to where you want, and they write themselves."

"It's not magic, Bill. It's intelligence. Everything is connected by souls. There's a book for each person that has ever lived on Earth and they are constantly changing. The books aren't magic, they're *alive*."

"What, like, the books themselves have their own souls?"

"More like they share a soul. I burned my book, so my soul is no longer connected to The Library database. But each book is bound to someone. That's how the information keeps updating. They're being written by our actions. So, when Widdick became a prophet, he didn't just receive the knowledge in the books, his body became the vessel for the thousands of souls contained *within* the books. Souls he imbued into each volume he recorded. That's why he burned the house down. If the wrong person got a hold of his books, they could reconnect one to the Library database and track its counterpart. They'd be able to find the next prophet."

It was so much to take in. I gulped down the rest of my water, ignoring my previous threat to cut Sonny off at that time. Moreen came around just in time to take my glass and set down a cup of hot coffee before she fluttered to the next table.

"How did you get this?" I asked.

"Beg your pardon?"

"This book, it was with Grace."

Sonny sank in the booth. "I um—I know you'd rather keep her out of this, but I went to see her. I told her you uh—that you sent me to pick it up."

I took a sip of coffee, which tasted far more bitter than I expected on my newborn tongue. After a moment of staring at Sonny through narrowed eyes, I set the mug down. "Okay."

Sonny breathed a sigh of relief. "Didn't really have a choice, you know?"

"It's fine. How is she?"

"Good, I guess? She's not in jail."

"That is good." I drank more of my coffee while Sonny looked at me expectantly.

"So, what do you say? Will you help me?" he pleaded.

"I'm sorry, did I miss something?" I asked, genuinely confused. "What are you asking me to do?"

"We find the next prophet. They have a target on their back, and it's up to us to protect them. Plus, since we know this mystery reaper will try to strike again, covering the prophet is our best chance of learning their identity. And if they never show, then at least we can postpone their goal long enough to figure something out."

I grumbled to myself, mulling over my coffee.

"What?" Sonny asked. "I'm sorry if I don't have a more direct plan, but right now, I think finding the prophet is the best course of action."

"It's not that," I said, finishing off the coffee. "Even before Haniel convinced me that you had been duplicitous from the start, I already felt betrayed. And now you're here and everything feels like it did before, but that doesn't change what happened."

The reaper lowered his head. "I know. I guess if you already believed what the angels are saying about me, it must be hard to trust anything I'm saying now."

"I didn't want to believe them, and maybe I never really did. I think I was just so mad that I would've accepted anything. And lord knows I don't trust the angels much anymore."

"You mean after they dumped you in the middle of fuck-all?" Sonny asked.

"Amongst other things," I said, remembering how I was sent to Earth the moment I began making headway in The Library. "So, no, I don't think you're lying about everything. But that doesn't mean I can rely on you. I want to help, I really do, but I need to be able to trust you again."

"Yeah, I get it," Sonny sighed. "What do you need me to do?"

"To start, I need to know that you trust me."

"I could've come to anyone in the world, Bill. I came to you because you're the only person I do trust."

"Then no more secrets. No more facade. I want to know what you did in your life that was so bad, it's still affecting you two hundred years later. I want to know the real you." Sonny tapped his fingers on the table, visibly unsettled by the idea of revealing the details of his life to me. "That's a long story," he said.

I pulled some cash out of my wallet and set it on the table. "I'm sure, but I'm willing to bet we got a longer drive ahead of us."

18

THE BOOK OF BENITO

DURING THE 1840'S, Mexico was in the midst of an invasion from the United States that became known as the Mexican-American War. During this time, American soldiers would routinely raid villages, gradually making their way deeper into Mexican territory. In one of these villages, in the northern region of Mexico, lived a man named Benito Olguin Estevez.

Benito spent his entire life in the village of Don Fernando de Taos, inheriting a ranch from his family. He was well-liked in the community, but lived a solitary existence, content to entertain himself with fiction.

He read every volume that he came across, even learning to read in English in order to expand his selections. These stories engrossed him in a way that real life could not compete. To him, each one was a new life he was privileged to experience. He particularly enjoyed stories of war and great heroes, often dreaming of embarking on his own noble adventure. As he grew older however, the American threat drew closer to home, and his affinity for these stories waned. Suddenly, the call to action was less appealing when it could arrive at any moment.

In August of 1846, the territory of New Mexico was taken by the United States after the Battle of Santa Fe. The army was forced to march through the Apache Canyon, a narrow pass over ten miles long, and the perfect location for an ambush. However before the American army was even in view, the local governor sent word of his surrender to the opposing general. His own men insisted that they hold their ground, but he ordered them to stand down. The Americans marched through the pass without a single shot fired, and the governor fled to the city of Chihuahua, where he was tried for cowardice and desertion.

Now under American occupancy, a new governor was placed in charge of the region. Charles Bent took up residence in the finest house in town—expecting to govern these people, who had been stripped of their lands and their goods, without complaint. Benito himself had been allowed to remain in his family home, but the surrounding ranch and cattle were seized to aid the war effort. Like many others, he felt powerless to do anything about it. Instead, he accepted his new reality and resigned himself to escape into a different one.

In the months that followed, life in the village continued to decline. Each time Benito returned, he saw fewer vendors. Hardly anyone had been allowed to retain possession of their farms, and those that remained barely had enough food to provide for the rest of the town. The people were hungry, and Benito could feel the growing tension in their air.

"PUT THAT AWAY," said an elderly woman behind the fruit table. Benito had taken some of his last remaining savings to pay her for a basket of mangoes. "You look like you haven't had a meal in days. Take it, and maybe one day you can pay me back."

He was stunned. It was true that he had been stretching his money and eating only when he needed to. The basket would get him through another week without starving. "I—I don't know what to say.

Thank you."

"In times like these, we need to be able to lean on each other. Take care of yourself, Benito."

He smiled at the woman and felt a pang of guilt. He wasn't sure if he would ever be able to repay her kindness if things continued as they had. As he departed the market, a passing man caught him by the arm.

"Follow me," the stranger whispered. At first, Benito wasn't sure if he'd heard him correctly, but as the man walked off, he discreetly nodded in his intended direction. Benito didn't like the idea of wandering after such a suspicious character, but he couldn't dismiss the curiosity he felt. It was like an encounter from one of his books. At the very least, he could see where the stranger was leading.

They weaved through the marketplace, winding their way behind a neighboring building. The man approached a partially concealed back door and quietly knocked a deliberate melody. The door creaked open and the stranger held it for him. Benito was far too curious now to not follow through. The two entered a cramped space, crowded with thirteen more men wearing spiteful expressions. Each one turned to examine Benito and he already wondered if it was too late to back out now.

"For those of you who don't know me—" One of the better dressed men shimmied to the center of the room and stood up on a short wooden stool. "My name is Pablo Montoya. I called this gathering because our homes and our livelihoods have been pillaged. These Americans have no respect for the rights of our people. To them, we are less than human. They feel entitled to our land and our possessions because they do not understand that the world does not belong to them. They are like children in this way, and they must be taught a lesson."

Benito was certain that he needed to get out of here as soon as possible, but the group tightened and he became trapped.

"We have been in contact," Montoya continued, "with neighboring farms and villages who support our cause. My friend, Tomás

Romero, has reached out to the Pueblo and they have agreed to assist us in our revolt. We will push these Americans back and reclaim what is ours."

There it was. The word "revolt" had changed the temperature of the room. The righteous anger of the crowd was palpable, and Benito felt as if he would suffocate in it. He squeezed his way through the men, trying desperately to reach the back door.

"Señor!" Montoya called out. All eyes were now on Benito, who stood frozen in his tracks. He turned to face the crowd, his head low. "Ah, Señor Estevez. I've not seen you for many weeks. I feared the soldiers had taken you. How is your ranch?"

Benito wouldn't raise his gaze for fear of meeting anyone's eye. He quietly mumbled just loud enough for Montoya to hear, "It's not my ranch anymore."

"I thought not." Montoya spoke to him like a priest to his flock. "So why is it that you wish to leave now? Why do you not want to hear these words? I understand that you keep to yourself outside of town, away from the troubles and concerns of others."

"I don't want to be part of any revolt. I don't think that makes me selfish."

"No. A selfish man may not care about the well-being of his neighbor, but even he would fight for what is rightfully his. You're not willing to do even that. You are a coward."

The rest of the men grumbled and nodded to one another. Before he stepped into that room, he had always just been the quiet loner who read too many books. Now, in the eyes of everyone he knew, he would forever be Benito, the coward.

"It's not cowardice!" he lashed back. "The Americans won't just pack up and leave because of one revolt! You said it yourself, they believe this land belongs to them. They will send wave after wave of soldiers until every hint of insurgency is wiped clean, and then there won't even be a village to take back. The governor was smart enough to see that. Why can't you?"

Montoya's confidence actually fell from his face for a split second. He didn't answer the question, he only warned Benito not to get in the way of what needed to be done.

WHEN WINTER CAME, word of the planned revolt had reached the governor's ears and the military's presence strengthened significantly. The townsfolk glared now when they passed Benito in the street, but he didn't bother to defend himself. No one would believe that he wasn't the snitch. Obviously, his words had gotten through to someone else at that meeting and he just hoped that would be the end of it.

It was not. On January 19 of 1847, the revolt began in earnest. Montoya had never given up his plan to take back the town, he had only postponed it while he accumulated more support from the neighboring villages. He led the insurrectionists into the heart of Don Fernando de Taos while his associate, Tomás Romero, led a Native American force to the house of the new governor. The insurrectionists swept through the town killing every military officer and government official. By sundown, the town had been fully purged and the streets were filled with the sound of celebration. Benito could hear the commotion from his home, but he never stepped foot outside.

Montoya continued his campaign, liberating nearby villages and gaining support with little to oppose him. There was even a moment when Benito dared to hope that he had been wrong about the revolt. Perhaps the Americans would simply abandon their conquest and let these people live in peace.

One morning, while tending to his reclaimed animals, Benito saw Montoya's men returning home. At first, he was ecstatic. In his mind, if they came back alive, it could only be in victory. But it soon became apparent that the men were not marching triumphantly, they were running in retreat. He contemplated fleeing, but if he were caught, the Americans would just assume he was an insurgent and a deserter. The only option remaining was to wait in his home and try his best to cooperate.

The ensuing battle was brief. The insurgents did their best to hold the town, but the Americans had greater numbers and superior weaponry. By the end, cannon fire had demolished the adobe church where many insurgents took refuge. It wasn't long after the battle ended that Benito heard a knocking on his door.

"I'm unarmed!" Benito shouted immediately, raising his hands in case the soldiers stormed in. "I'm going to open the door now. Please do not shoot." He kept one hand in the air while he reached for the lock. Before he could pull the door open, it swung towards him. He snapped his other hand back up as five American soldiers entered the room, guns pointed directly at his chest.

"I swear I had nothing to do with the revolt. I've been here, tending to my ranch."

None of the soldiers said a word. After a few seconds, a sixth man entered the house bearing a sword on his hip. He was a heavier set officer with such prominent sideburns, it was difficult for Benito to look at anything else.

"Do you speak English, my boy?" the man asked.

Benito, realizing he had been shouting in Spanish, struggled to find the right English words to respond. "I speak... small English."

"Excellent. I hate using the translator. It's much more satisfying to talk man-to-man. Forgive me, I've not introduced myself. My name is Colonel Price." The colonel gestured for Benito to sit at the wooden table beside him, taking the other seat himself. "Word around town is that this is the home of Benito Olguin Estevez. Am I speaking to the right man?"

Benito felt silly continuing to hold his hands in the air, and so he slowly lowered them on the table, where everyone could see, and nodded.

"Then you're exactly who I want to talk to. Gibbs, go and find us something to drink, will you?" Price gestured towards Benito's kitchen and one of the armed soldiers lowered his rifle to search the cupboards. The man named Gibbs returned shortly with two glasses and the remainder of Benito's last bottle of tequila.

"Ah!" Price exclaimed. "Do you get this in town, or does it come from the city?"

"It is made here."

"Wonderful." Price poured them both a glass and pushed one over to Benito. "Now, about this revolt—"

"I did not—"

"Don't interrupt me, son. It's not good for your health. I know you didn't take part in the revolt. That's the only reason we're having this discussion over a drink, instead of on your knees."

Benito glanced at the guns pointed directly at him and failed to see a large difference between the two scenarios.

Price took a sip from his glass and let out a deep grunt. "That's good stuff. Now, the reason I came to you is because I have it under good authority that you were present at the initial planning of this revolt, and I want to personally thank you for alerting the authorities about it."

Benito raised his eyebrows, just slightly. He had not, in fact, alerted the authorities of anything, but the colonel didn't need to know that. The whole town had treated him like dirt after it happened, and the soldiers had likely made a note of it. He decided it was best to play into the assumption. "I did not want… pain… death."

"I don't blame you, son. War is an ugly thing. And I assume after you ratted them out the first time, you weren't informed of the later attack. You were probably just as surprised as poor Governor Bent. But that doesn't mean you can't help us now."

Benito shuddered at the thought. He took a big swig from his glass and swallowed hard. "I will...try."

"That's good. For starters, you can tell me how many other men were at that meeting to plan the revolt?"

"Catorce." Benito blurted it out without thinking. He could have said any number, but in his eagerness to make this end, he gave the truth and possibly endangered more lives than he needed to.

"Cator-say? What is that? Fourteen?"

"Yes, sir," one of the soldiers confirmed.

"Okay, fourteen. Good. One more question, son, then we can put all this behind us. What were the names of the men at that meeting?"

Here it was. He'd already committed to the number, but now each name he gave was tantamount to killing the men himself. Benito didn't know if it was fortunate or not that he truly did not remember the names of most of the men there, only familiar faces that he'd seen around town.

"I do not…" He struggled with the word, looking at the soldier who had translated 'fourteen'. "Recuerdo."

"He doesn't remember, sir," the soldier responded.

"Yes, I gathered that." Price was silent for a moment. He tapped his fingers on the table in a way that made Benito extremely anxious. "Perhaps something got lost in translation. I'm going to ask you one more time and you're going to tell me the truth. What are the names of the men who planned the revolt?"

"I do not know names."

"Aw, hell," Price said, calmly. He then flipped the table across the room, shattering the bottle of tequila and glasses against the wall. He stood and kicked Benito in the chest, knocking him to the ground. Before Benito could even process what happened, he felt the barrel of a revolver pressed against his forehead.

"I'm not gonna ask you again! What are the names?"

"Please! Please, no!"

"The names, boy!"

"Caras! Caras!"

"What is that?" Price looked back at his men. "Is that a name?"

"I think he's saying 'faces', sir."

"Faces? Is that right? You don't know the names, but you can point 'em out? Is that what you're telling me?"

Benito felt the gun press harder into his skin. Tears welled in his eyes and he tried to formulate words without hyperventilating.

"S–Si! Yes! Do not shoot! Please!"

Price considered him for a moment and finally released the pressure on his forehead. "Now, that wasn't so hard, was it?" He got up and holstered his revolver under his jacket. "Parker, go find Hendley. See if the rest of the insurgents have been rounded up. Gibbs, place Señor Estevez in custody and find him a jail cell. I don't want him skipping town before tomorrow's festivities. He's going to be the guest of honor."

NOT ALL OF Montoya's men were captured at the church. A good number fled to the town of Mora before the attack began, but every last one was rounded up by Captain Hendley before being brought to Colonel Price. Meanwhile, Benito languished in his cell, kept awake both by his anxiety and the sound of banging hammers that persisted all night. He had an idea of what the Americans were building in the town plaza, but prayed he was wrong.

The light was disorienting when they dragged him into the morning sun. As his eyes adjusted, he was able to see a long, wooden gallows with fourteen equally spaced nooses looming in the plaza. Across from the gallows stood a crowd of over a hundred men, bound in chains, looking sullen at the ground. At the front of the crowd was Pablo Montoya and Tomás Romero, on their knees—guns trained on the back of their necks. Armed guards surrounded the crowd, ready to act if any of the prisoners stepped out of line.

"Señor Estevez!" Price's voice called out from behind the gallows. Benito recognized him from a distance by the size of his sideburns. Price had been inspecting each trapdoor, to ensure that his demonstration would go off without a hitch. He approached Benito with a wide grin. "I hope your cell was not too uncomfortable. If it was, don't blame us, your town built it!" He let out a deep guttural laugh that gave Benito goosebumps. Price grabbed him tightly by the arm and led him to the crowd of prisoners. Benito could barely keep the pace with his ankle shackles on, but Price didn't seem to notice or care.

Up close, Montoya and Romero looked terrible. Their faces were swollen and bruised, and their clothes were spotted with blood. "Obviously you have no need to identify these men." Price said, as if he were delivering a joke. "We'd have liked to have them corroborate your accusations, but they both seem intent to die in silence. That's okay though, I trust you can point out the remaining twelve just fine on your own." Price slapped Benito on the back, the force causing him to drop to his knees. Before Price could pull him up, his gaze met with Montoya's. He could feel the man pleading with his eyes, and Benito never felt more ashamed in all his life.

Montoya and Romero were yanked up and led to the far end of the gallows. Price then took Benito down the first row of prisoners. "Alright, boy. Your time to shine."

Benito peered into the first man's face. Did he know that his life was in Benito's hands? The man's visage was definitely recognizable, but to Benito's immense relief, he did not remember seeing him at the meeting. It was a futile relief, of course. Sooner or later, all fourteen men would have to pass his judgment. He went down the row, looking each face over, seeing the terror in their eyes. It wasn't until he was halfway through the second row of men that panic flooded his brain. This was the same man who had brought him to the meeting in the first place. For a brief second, Benito thought of lying. He could shake his head like he had for all the rest, but inevitably, Price would demand fourteen lives, guilty or innocent. The man in front of him did not look afraid like the others. In his eyes, Benito could only see malice. He hated Benito for his cowardice, for betraying his own people. Price stepped forward eagerly.

"What do you say? Looks to me like we have ourselves a winner."

Benito turned to face Price and slowly nodded. The man was taken to the gallows and filled the third spot in line. Nearly an hour passed in dead silence as Benito went from man to man, occasionally condemning one to death before carrying on. By the time he was halfway through the crowd, he was no longer mortified to see his next victim. He was numb to it.

Thirteen men stood up on the gallows by the time Benito reached the last man in the crowd. He barely glanced at his face before turning to nod, but forced himself to do a double take. This final man was not, in fact, one of the conspirators. Benito looked around, confused.

"What's the matter?" Price asked. "Is he one of them, or isn't he?"

"No."

"Well, did you skip one? Because I don't know if you've noticed, but we're a man short."

Benito racked his brain. He had looked at over a hundred men, but he made certain that each one was innocent before moving to the next. These were the people he'd seen in town throughout his entire life. He knew their faces, even if he'd never bothered to learn all their names. He could go through them again, but he doubted that it would do any good. The fourteenth man was almost certainly killed during the revolt. Quite frankly, Benito was shocked he was the only one missing.

"Not here. I think... dead."

Price let out a deep sigh. He pointed at his officers and made a gesture for one of them to come over. Captain Hendley approached.

"Hendley, you sure this is all the Taos townsfolk?"

"Yes, sir. We've searched every building and all the surrounding areas. Unless they're blending among the Pueblos, this is all there is."

"Your men kill many of the insurgents while you were rounding 'em up?"

"Just a few who wouldn't stand down. It's possible one of them was the fourteenth man. I can have the bodies brought over, but it might take a few hours."

"No, I think we've all been out here long enough. I'm getting stir crazy waiting to drop these ropes. I think I have an alternate solution, anyway. You can return to your post."

"Yes, sir." Hendley gave a salute and returned to his spot in front of the gallows with the rest of the officers. Price stared at the last empty noose for a few seconds before turning his gaze to Benito.

"Señor Estevez. I'd like to thank you for your cooperation in identifying those who would conspire against the United States. You see, it is my belief that unless those responsible are punished publicly and definitively, we will never be able to hold a position of power in this region. According to you, fourteen men were present for the planning of a doomed revolt, and so fourteen ropes await them. As it stands, there are only thirteen men present at the gallows and yet, I find myself looking at a fourteenth man who was also present on that day."

Benito didn't understand immediately. He was still translating the words in his head when two men grabbed him by the arms. Suddenly, it all clicked.

"No! I helped! I helped!"

"That you did, and I'm certainly grateful, but in the end, it doesn't really matter if those men up there are the real conspirators or not. We need to send a message, and an empty noose just ain't gonna cut it. If it helps, take pride that you will give your life for the betterment of your new country."

Price gestured towards the gallows and Benito was hauled off. He kicked and squirmed with each step that drew him closer to the wooden death trap. Within moments, his neck was secured tightly at the end of the row. His hands and feet were bound, and a gun was aimed squarely at his chest from below. There was no hope of escape.

Price walked up and down the gallows, making a grand speech about justice and social order. Benito couldn't hear a word of it. The only thing he could process was the same thought, repeated over and over again. *I don't want to die.*

Price stepped down, satisfied with himself, and Benito looked at the row of men he had condemned one last time.

Price gave the signal.

Benito opened his mouth and shouted, "I don't want to die!"

BY THE TIME Sonny finished his story, we had crossed the Canadian border and re-entered the United States. I didn't even know we were in Canada until we were leaving it. The truck had been exactly where the diner waitress directed me, and the keys were already inside. Sonny started talking as soon as we got on the road and only paused to give directions.

"You pretty much know the rest," he said. "I dealt out death in life and was forced to deal it out for centuries as punishment. One-hundred thousand souls. Of course I probably would have reached that number by now if I hadn't spiraled. I must have lost years of hard work trading souls in that cantina, trying to forget what I'd done. Then one day, I finally decided that I had enough punishment. Changed my name, changed—everything. I didn't want to be associated with the man I was before."

"You can't blame yourself entirely for what happened," I said, fully engrossed in his story. "You were put in an impossible situation. They would have killed fourteen men regardless. What were you supposed to do? Let him choose at random?"

"It's not what I did, it's why I did it. I didn't condemn those men to prevent others from dying. I did it so that I could live. I was driven to betray men I admired and respected because of fear. Hell, it was fear that prevented me from joining their cause in the first place. A lot of good it did me."

"But you were right, weren't you? The American forces were too strong. Fighting was futile."

"Maybe. But Montoya knew that too. He knew the odds were stacked against him, and he did what he thought was right anyway." Sonny stared blankly out the passenger window and chuckled. "I think that man would have faced the whole of the American army by himself if it came down to it. He must have been scared shitless the whole time, but he was never a coward."

I stared out at the open road, thinking about my last encounter with Sonny, what I'd thought of him when he abandoned me.

"For what it's worth, Benito—" He flinched when I said the name. "I don't think you're a coward. You can be selfish sometimes—a lot of times. But you're making an effort. I'd say the odds are stacked pretty high against us now, and yet, here you are."

"Yeah, well, it's not as if I have anything to lose."

"I don't just mean: you're here, still working this case. I mean you're here with me. After the way we left things, I'm surprised you want to be anywhere near me."

"I can't exactly do this alone," he said.

I nodded. "Yeah, I suppose that's true."

He folded his arms and let out a deep sigh. "And I guess, I don't mind having you around. It's been a while since I met someone who didn't hate me, and it didn't feel spectacular when you finally did."

I smirked at him. "I don't hate you. It might take me a little while before I'm fully ready to forgive you for what happened, but I am glad you came back."

He uncrossed his arms and looked over at me. "How long is 'a little while?'"

"Are you serious?"

"I just wanna know how long I gotta deal with Stoic Bill."

I chuckled. "How long until we get where we're going?"

"The new prophet lives in Oklahoma."

"Then I'm thinking somewhere around Kansas."

He started laughing and I joined in. It was the first moment of happiness I'd had since we'd split. I settled into a smile as we continued down the road.

"Oh, and Bill?" Sonny perked up. "Before I forget, can I ask you a favor?"

"Go ahead."

"Don't ever call me Benito again."

19

MEANWHILE, IN OKLAHOMA

AS THE LAST flicker of life faded from Professor Widdick's body in Alabama, nine hundred miles away, a young woman named Maya Kabua fell to her knees. It was the most intense migraine she'd ever experienced. For a moment, she feared she was having a brain aneurysm, *but no*, she thought. *You're not supposed to feel an aneurysm as it's happening, it just happens and then you die, like that lady who fell face-first into her morning cereal.* At least, that's what she had read. She may have been a medical professional, but she was just as susceptible to clickbait articles as anyone. Then, just as quickly as it had come on, her migraine disappeared. She suddenly felt silly, kneeling in the middle of a hallway at work. She rose quickly to her feet and continued her rounds, bringing each patient their medicine and making sure everyone felt comfortable.

Maya hadn't envisioned herself working in a nursing home when she got her degree. She had always imagined herself in a bustling hospital, rushing from room to room, saving lives, and showing the young doctors that they weren't such hot shit. In all fairness, that expectation only emerged after binge-watching the first seven seasons of *Scrubs*. She never finished the eighth season, though. She didn't like any of the new characters and couldn't really get into it.

Her dreams for working at a big hospital were quickly dashed when she learned that the only hospital in her home of Enid, Oklahoma wasn't hiring. She could seek employment outside of town, but couldn't afford an apartment in the city, especially without her parents' help—and they would never support her moving away.

Maya was a third generation American whose grandparents immigrated from the Marshall Islands. She wasn't entirely sure why the original Marshallese immigrants came to the middle of Oklahoma—a state as far away from any ocean or cultural hub as you can find—but once they did, the town of Enid became a magnet for dozens of Marshallese families. Of course she had dreams of seeing the world, or just anywhere outside of Oklahoma, but her family was adamant that they should all stay together. So, while it was no busy hospital, she felt grateful that she could find employment at the only other place in town that needed nurses.

Her place of work wasn't nearly as exciting as an emergency room, but unfortunately, it still saw its fair share of death. There was nothing Maya could do to stop it. These people were old, and most of them were at death's door by the time they were brought in. She smiled at them, fluffed their pillows, and snuck in their favorite snacks whenever she could, but one day she would inevitably walk in to find that they had passed on. It was a depressing reality that she had mostly grown used to.

On that afternoon, after Maya's brief migraine incident, Mrs. Wagner had passed away in her room while watching *Family Feud*. Maya would have rushed in immediately, but Mrs. Wagner had figured out how to lower the volume on her heart monitor, in order to better hear the television. As a result, Maya wasn't mentally prepared to find a dead body when she entered the room, and even less prepared to see a spectral corpse with its hand in Mrs. Wagner's cold chest.

The entity was partially-decayed and wearing 1980's business shoulder pads. It leaned over the bed and pulled out an ethereal, naked replication of the elderly woman. Then, before Maya could react, the corpse tore open a hole in midair and disappeared into it. The hole sealed itself up, and Maya was left alone with Mrs. Wagner's dead body.

It had all happened so fast, Maya wasn't sure if it was real. It could have been a quick flash of imagination. She took a few deep breaths and then rushed to Mrs. Wagner's side to prove to herself that she was only seeing things. Of course, to her dismay, Mrs. Wagner was already dead. *That's okay. I mean, it's not okay, a woman has just died, but it doesn't mean that what I saw was real.*

She went about the rest of her day and tried to put the incident out of her mind. She was sad about Mrs. Wagner, but far more concerned about the implications of her possible hallucination. Either it wasn't real and she needed to see a psychiatrist, or it was, which was far worse. Luckily, there were no other medical emergencies for the rest of her shift, nor was she brought to her knees by any other mysterious head pains. Maya drove straight home from work, hoping some sleep would remedy her mental hiccups.

She was glad to live alone. Sometimes she wished for the company of a roommate, but that night, she felt socially exhausted. Her parents would have preferred she lived at home, but she had convinced them that she needed her own place if she was going to be dating. The truth was that Maya had never seriously dated anyone, and possessed little interest in men or women, but her parents didn't need to know that. The mere suggestion that their daughter may produce a grandchild was enough to keep their questions at bay, lest they jinx it. *Maybe I'll fake a pregnancy and adopt a kid one day*, she would often think. *I'll claim the father ran off with the delivery doctor, tie up all the loose ends.*

Maya got into bed, which was more a collection of stuffed animals than a mattress at this point, and attempted to rest. Surely her hallucination had been a result of her insomnia. After twenty minutes of frustrated turning, she grabbed her phone off the nightstand and scrolled through it for the next few hours.

The next morning was like any other. Maya made herself a bowl of off-brand cinnamon toasted squares, no milk, and sat crisscross on her couch with the bowl nestled in her lap. She wouldn't begin eating until she found something to watch, settling on a cartoon from her childhood that she had been revisiting. By the time her show was over, she had less than an hour until she needed to be at work.

It's worth noting that, as Maya moved about her apartment, she was surrounded by pop culture paraphernalia. The apartment contained very little in the way of furniture, but on every available surface, Maya had covered the place in knick-knacks and figurines. She put up posters like they were wallpaper, with only slivers of her bright neon paint showing between them. Sometimes she would think about saving some money to buy a coffee table for the living room, but inevitably, she would find an expensive plush character online that would look perfect at the foot of her bed. She didn't regret a single purchase. These things made her happy.

After brushing her teeth, taking a shower, and putting on her dalmatian-patterned scrubs, Maya hopped into her faded green minivan and made off to work. Her daily routine had helped her to forget the unpleasantness of the day before, and by the time she had arrived at the nursing home, terrifying hallucinations were the last thing on her mind. After all, the odds of someone dying two days in a row were pretty slim, even for her workplace.

There were two deaths at work that day. Maya had been unfortunate enough to be nearby for both of them—and just like before, a mysterious corpse-person emerged from thin air to steal the soul of the deceased. There was no way these were only hallucinations. She had read somewhere that auditory hallucinations don't usually occur simultaneously with visual ones. She could hear each time these corpses tore into the room, so she knew they had to be something else.

Things continued to get worse throughout the week. Seeing corpses appear for a few seconds was bad enough, but she soon began to encounter other creatures as well. There weren't many, but every now and then she would walk into the store and see what looked like a sasquatch with bird legs strolling through the aisles. Over the weekend, Maya had gone to the movies with Kelly, a friend from work, only to see a pale woman with pitch black eyes and swirling black hair patiently waiting for the film to start. Kelly had suggested they sit in the center of the aisle, oblivious to the fact that one of those seats was already taken by the specter. Maya insisted that they sit in the back. *Where I can keep an eye on that thing in case it tries anything.* Despite the distraction, she still enjoyed the movie.

After a week of this, Maya seriously considered seeking out professional help, but she couldn't afford a psychiatrist on her own, and no part of her wanted to involve her parents. They worried enough about her as it was, and may even force her to move back home. Besides, it wasn't as if the spirits were threatening her in any way. Perhaps she could just learn to live with them.

Then one day, she got through an entire shift without a single undead incident, and wondered whether the whole ordeal might be over. As much as the specters initially startled her, the idea that they may be gone for good gave her a tinge of melancholy. Sadly, the sudden appearance of ghosts was the most excitement she'd experienced in her entire life in Enid, Oklahoma.

As she left work that night with Kelly, she received a text message from her mother, asking if she was off work yet and to text when she got home safe—just like she did every night. Her friend continued to her own car as Maya replied to the message.

"Have a good night Maya!" Kelly shouted as she pulled out of the parking lot.

Maya waved her friend off when she heard another voice call out from the parking lot. She turned to see who was shouting at her, and locked eyes with a corpse.

20

COME WITH ME
IF YOU WANT TO LIVE

ACCORDING TO SONNY'S list, the newly awakened prophet was a woman named Maya Kabua who lived in a seven-mile-wide town called Enid, Oklahoma. Having lived in a bustling city all my life, I found it hard to imagine how anyone could survive in such a sparse environment without going stir-crazy. On the bright side, Oklahoma is only one state above Texas and I became increasingly convinced that the origin point for the demonic invasion resided there. Of course, I wanted to be able to relay my theory about the drought to Sonny, but it was too soon to trust him completely. Perhaps after he proved truthful about this new prophet, I could get his opinion.

We stopped at around three in the morning, just after crossing into Colorado. Like we'd done on our previous road trip, I pulled into a rest stop and leaned my seat all the way back to get some sleep. When I awoke six hours later, Sonny was nowhere to be seen. I walked around the rest stop, but couldn't spot him anywhere. I felt uncomfortable leaving without him, but remembered that he could easily locate my soul no matter where I was. After about an hour of driving alone, Sonny popped into the passenger seat, scaring the living hell out of me. I'm not sure why, as I had been expecting him to do just that, but it's not a phenomenon that's easy to get accustomed to.

"Relax," he said. "It's just me. I'm surprised you're up so early."

"Never really got comfortable," I said. "I woke up with the parking brake jamming into my side. Where'd you run off to?"

"Oh, I was in Sydney, watching a film. Well, a few films. Everything was closed here in America."

The reality of that statement was hard to wrap my mind around. I knew that Sonny didn't sleep, and I shouldn't have expected him to wait around for me to wake up, but traveling to the other side of the world for quick entertainment would never have occurred to me.

"Did you vanish as soon as I fell asleep?"

"Pretty much. I would have returned sooner, but I don't check my list in the theater. It's rude.

"Aren't you invisible to everyone in the theater?"

"Not to other spirits, no."

That's an idea I'd never get out of my head. How many times had I gone to the movies and sat right next to a reaper—or some other creature without realizing it?

We had a much shorter drive ahead of us that second day, but we still didn't roll into Enid until the sun went down. Sonny directed me to the northern side of town, into the parking lot of a nursing home. I knew that Widdick had been an older man, but I'd hoped the next prophet would be a tad more spry. It was going to be difficult to protect her if we also had to provide medical care while on the move. I rolled down my window and tried to peer inside the facility.

"So how old are we talking about here?" I asked. "Seventies? Eighties?"

"I don't know, man. This isn't her dating profile I'm looking at. I just know that she's in there."

"Well, can't you just zap next to her exact location?"

"Yes, if we intend to scare the life out of her. Don't forget—Widdick could see me, so it stands to reason she can too. It took two days to get here and I don't want to have to search for another prophet because we gave this one a heart attack."

"So, what? I just go in there and start yelling the name Maya Kabua and hope someone raises their hand?"

Sonny pursed his lips and furled his brow. "You know, that wouldn't not work."

I was in the process of rolling my eyes when two young women in ostentatious scrubs exited the building. One of them stopped to check her phone while the taller blonde woman went to her car. As she began to drive away, she shouted, "Have a good night, Maya!"

Sonny and I perked up. We both leaned out our windows to get a better look. Maya Kabua was not, in fact, elderly. At first glance, she couldn't have been more than twenty-five. She was also exceptionally short, 4'11" at the most. I needed to get Maya's attention before she reached her own car, but I wasn't sure how to do that without scaring her off. I was, after all, a large and mysterious man waiting outside of her place of work in the middle of the night. It didn't scream *safe*.

Before I could formulate a plan, Sonny shouted, "Are you Maya Kabua?"

The tiny woman turned, panic-stricken, and immediately started fumbling with her keys. At first, I was afraid she was trying to make a quick getaway, but instead, she tightly gripped a bejeweled canister of pepper spray.

"No," she lied. "Why? What do you want with her?"

Sonny retreated back to his seat where she couldn't see him, so the question fell on me. Not once during the two-day drive did I think of a sensible answer to that inevitable question. I stuttered a bit before blurting out, "You're in danger! We need to take you away!"

Her eyes bulged and she ran for her car. I was about to ask Sonny what our plan B was, when he vanished from the passenger's seat and emerged right in front of Maya. She reacted as anyone might have, by screaming and shooting pepper spray at his face. The spray went right through him, obviously, but that didn't stop her from trying a couple more times.

"Oh God!" she exclaimed. "You're one of them! Are you here to kill me? Am I already dead?" She pointed at me. "Did that creepy guy in the truck murder me somehow?"

I dismissed being called 'creepy guy' given the circumstances. I also tried to decipher what she meant by *one of them*. Had she already encountered other spirits in such a short time?

"You're not dead," Sonny assured her. "I'm not here to take your soul, or anything like that. Please try to calm down."

"My soul?!" she screamed, again.

"No, no, no! I'm *not* here for your soul. Just the opposite really! My friend and I are here to protect you."

I did a little wave from the truck.

"Is that why you keep coming here?" she asked. "You've been watching me?"

That didn't bode well. If someone else had been keeping tabs on her, then it could have been our mysterious bar patron who sent the Nephilim after Widdick.

"Uh, not to scare you further," Sonny replied, "but I have no idea what you're talking about. Have you seen others like me? For how long?"

Maya finally lowered her arm, realizing that the pepper spray wasn't going to be of any further help. "It's been happening all week. I thought I was losing my mind. Horrible, disgusting people, appearing out of nowhere. Every time they show up, one of our residents passes." She wearily looked Sonny in the eye. "You haven't been killing them, have you?"

"Whoa, easy. First off, 'disgusting' is kind of rude. We may be dead, but we have feelings. Second, this isn't my territory. I haven't killed anyone, and nor has whatever reaper you've been seeing. We don't kill, we escort."

"Reapers? Like the Grim Reaper?"

"Sure. Minus the cloak and harvest equipment."

"Then why do people keep dying?"

"What am I, a doctor? I don't know. They're probably just old. This is a nursing home isn't it? Do people normally come here because they're young and nubile?"

All this excitement was a bit much for Maya and she started to look as though she might faint. I opened the car door in case I needed to help catch her, but she snapped out of it as soon as I did. She then aimed the can of pepper spray in my direction.

"Who is he?" she asked Sonny. "Why doesn't he look like the rest of you?"

"Oh, that's Bill. He's not a reaper, he's just a twice resurrected mortal who's been helping me out. Don't worry about him, he's harmless."

She glanced back at me with a great deal of doubt. "So, if I'm not dead, and you aren't here to kill me—what do you want with me?"

Sonny and I exchanged dreary looks and I decided to be the one to break the news. "We think someone else might be looking for you. Someone who might actually want to—uh—hurt you."

Maya muttered something in a language I didn't understand and proceeded to faint. I lurched forward and managed to catch her just before she hit the pavement. Immediately, her eyes snapped open to find me holding her like a kidnap victim. She yelped in surprise and squeezed her can of pepper spray. The blast struck me in the face prompting me to yell in agony, as well as drop her to the ground. Worse yet, the spray ricocheted off of me directly downward onto her. As the two of us rolled in the parking lot, wailing in pain, Sonny stood over us shaking his head.

WE SAT ON the curb outside of a nearby gas station called the Sooner Stop. Sonny had taken the liberty of shoplifting a small bottle of milk and administered it to our eyes, which helped reduce the stinging only slightly. At the very least, the experience seemed to convince Maya that we were not immediately trying to steal her soul. As she laid back with a milk soaked cloth over her face, Sonny attempted to explain who we were and what was happening to her. By the time he finished, most of the swelling had gone away and I found myself able to see again.

"You know," Maya said, lifting the damp cloth from her face. "If you guys had shown up a week ago, I wouldn't believe a word of this."

"Yeah," Sonny said. "We ran into that problem with Bill's girlfriend."

"I thought I was having a psychotic break when these things first started showing up, but either this hallucination is more vivid than I thought possible, or it's all very real—which is somehow far more terrifying.

"If it's any consolation," I said, "you're handling this far better than I expected."

She sat up and wiped her face with a napkin. "I fainted, and then I pepper sprayed myself."

"And Bill," Sonny pointed out.

"Right, I am sorry about that," she said, wincing.

"You don't have to apologize. My fiancée tried to shoot me with a gun when we told her."

"Technically," Sonny said. "She did shoot your head off."

Maya's mouth hung open.

"It's not like that," I assured her. "I wasn't using it at the time."

She shook her head. "Okay, I have about a million questions for the both of you—especially you," she nodded at Sonny. "But can we go somewhere to wash off? I'm sticky and smell like milk."

I WAS ASTONISHED at how well she was adapting. Widdick had six months to adjust to his new abilities, and it clearly broke something in his brain. Maya had only been seeing things for a week and here she was, excitedly chatting with a rotting corpse-man in the break room of a nursing home. The facilities offered a shower and a change of scrubs for her, though we had to keep our voices down when she emerged to hear the rest of our story.

She was fascinated by every detail, and appeared noticeably worried when we got to the part about Widdick's death. Sonny had already explained to her that she was the new prophet—chosen after the death of the previous one, but hearing why he died was another matter. We tried to cover everything we could, but we skipped some of the personal events, like our big fight in the woods, as well as Sonny's traumatic past. Neither felt relevant to her current predicament.

Over the course of the night, we learned details about her life as well. She told us about her family and how dull she found Enid, Oklahoma—as if that wasn't obvious to anyone with eyes. More than anything, Maya expressed a deep desire to leave this town behind and travel the globe. She'd never even been outside of the state. Luckily with us, she might have the opportunity to fulfill her dream, albeit to flee for her life.

We asked if she'd been experiencing any visions or sudden bursts of knowledge like Widdick had, but she didn't recall any instances. The most significant change in the past week was the sudden presence of reapers in her workplace. She admitted that it was possible that she had mistaken a vision for a casual daydream, but it was hard to tell because of how often she found her mind wandering.

Without meaning to, the three of us talked all through the night. As the sun began to rise, we prepared to leave the nursing home before any of Maya's coworkers showed up. She made an offhand comment about how exhausted she would be when she returned for her shift later—which concerned me. Obviously we couldn't force her to suddenly drop everything, but I feared that she didn't grasp the immediacy of her danger. If someone had convinced me a month ago that evil spirits were searching for me, I think my work schedule would be the last thing on my mind. I wanted to get her off the grid as soon as possible, and I happened to have recently acquired a lovely cabin in

Canada that would serve as a great hideout.

I followed Maya in my truck to her apartment on the other side of town. She asked Sonny to ride with her so that they could continue their conversation, evidently unfazed by his less-than-photogenic appearance.

As we passed over a set of train tracks, I couldn't help but notice a change in the atmosphere. Every storefront and home now had bars on the windows. Broken bottles filled the gutters and shirtless men just wandered around aimlessly. It was here that we finally arrived at Maya's apartment. The building was two floors of stark white concrete. Outside, there were a couple of children with Super Soakers, running around barefoot on the hot parking lot pavement. I couldn't stop visualizing one of them slicing their foot on a piece of broken bottle, but it wasn't as if they'd listen to some weird stranger telling them to be careful. Maya drove past the kids and pulled into a parking space, still talking to Sonny as I pulled up beside them.

"So how long do you think it'll take these nympho-things to find me?" Maya asked, making her way up a flight of stairs.

"It's tough to say," Sonny replied. "As far as we know, they didn't catch up to Widdick for about six months, and he was pretty public with his findings. As long as you're able to keep a low profile, you should be alright."

"That's good to hear. As much as I'd love to travel, I don't think I'm ready to pick up and leave just yet."

Maya unlocked the door to her apartment and held it open for us. I'd expected to see a dull, dreary interior to match the aesthetic of the rest of the building. Instead, I was assaulted by color. The walls were neon pink, covered with enough pop culture posters to make an entire college dormitory envious, and every surface appeared to be lined end-to-end with some kind of plushie or vinyl figurine.

"You guys can make yourselves at home," she told us.

I stepped in, still transfixed by the decor. I wanted to say something, but I couldn't find the words. Luckily, Sonny had his own opinions.

"This place is great! Did you paint the walls yourself?"

"Yeah, tenants aren't supposed to paint, but my landlady hasn't come by since I first moved in, so what she doesn't know won't hurt her."

Sonny skipped around the room like a child in a toy store, examining each figurine in a row. "I didn't even know they made some of these! It's good to see a human spending their money on something worthwhile for a change."

Maya laughed. "Yeah some people buy impractical things like clothes and groceries, but I focus on the essentials."

Sonny nodded, agreeing in full sincerity. "Do you have any other figures in your bedroo—" He was about to walk through the door when a towering empty void of a figure emerged from the other side. The Nephilim reached out and grabbed Sonny by the neck, its arm coiling around him like a tentacle. Maya screamed.

"What is that?!"

I was speechless at the sight of the creature. My legs turned to jelly, and I felt as though I'd lost the ability to make sounds from my mouth. I was useless, staring as it enveloped Sonny in darkness.

Maya had a far more interesting reaction. Her panic dropped as a wave of eerie calm came over her face. She maneuvered swiftly to the bathroom, opening the door to reveal a second Nephilim waiting inside. It lurched forward to grab her, but hadn't anticipated her small size. Moving as if in a trance, she managed to duck under its arms and passed right through its body into the bathroom. The Nephilim was quick to turn around, but Maya had already found what she was looking for. In her outstretched hands, she held a long-necked lighter and a can of hairspray. She deployed both. Fire spit from the makeshift weapon, engulfing the shadow's head. The black void that made up its body receded away from the flames, revealing a disfigured black skull underneath.

Maya stopped briefly, her eyes suddenly wide and mouth agape.

She seemed to have only just realized what she was doing, as if she had been operating on autopilot. The darkness began to form back around the skull, creeping up from the neck into its previous shape. Maya snapped back to action, lighting the creature up from head to toe, leaving the darkness with nowhere left to recede. It let out an unholy wail as the fire revealed a full skeleton of twisted bones. The wailing was unbearable to my ears and it drew the attention of the other Nephilim attacking Sonny. As it witnessed its compatriot engulfed in flames, it loosened its grip enough for Sonny to regain his faculties—and the use of his arms. The reaper used the little bit of freedom he had to open a portal between him and the creature, severing its arm clean off.

Maya's can of hairspray sputtered and ceased, ending the jet of flames. Even still, all the darkness had burned away, and the monstrous skeleton collapsed into a dusty pile in front of her. The other Nephilim had no intention of waiting to see if Maya had truly run dry. It used its remaining arm to shove Sonny aside and bolted out the door, leaving the three of us bewildered.

21

TRIPLE THREAT

I SAT IN the corner of Maya's living room with my knees to my chest. Shame washed over me, not just of my inaction, but for the anger I'd held onto for days. My behavior proved that even if I had been present when the Nephilim attacked Professor Widdick, the result would have been the same. I'd have just crumbled and let them take him. That didn't absolve Sonny, but it did color my reaction in a much harsher light. The Nephilim almost got away with another prophet under my watch and I was too petrified to do a damn thing about it.

Sonny rubbed his neck where the creature had wrapped a shadowy tendril a moment ago. "Thanks for the help, Bill. We got saved by the person we came to protect, again."

"I'm sorry," I said. "I don't know what came over me." That wasn't entirely true. I had always been deathly afraid of the Nephilim, even before I knew what they were. Seeing one so unexpectedly shot my mind back in time to my tenth birthday.

I rose to my feet and approached Maya, only now realizing that she was still frozen in place with her hands outstretched over the pile of bones. "Maya?" I asked. "You doing alright?"

Her head twitched a little and she began sputtering out nonsense words. She had to take a deep breath before she could relax her body and speak. "Was tha—was that one of the Nympho things you warned me about?"

"Yes," Sonny answered, cheerfully nudging the bones with his foot. "Nice job with this one. To be honest, I didn't know Nephilim could be killed."

Maya's expression went blank and she began speaking in an eerie monotone. "Spiritual beings cannot be fully destroyed. The essence of a spirit may be scattered, but in absence of divine intervention, the entity will inevitably reform." Her eyes fluttered and her expression returned to normal. "I'm sorry, I think I spaced for a second. Did you ask me something?"

Sonny and I exchanged confused looks before saying in unison, "The books."

"Huh?" Maya cocked her head.

"What do you think just happened a minute ago?" Sonny asked. "Do you remember anything you did?"

Maya's eyes darted around the room. She glanced down at the hairspray and lighter in her hands and then back at the bedroom door where the first Nephilim had appeared. "I remember seeing a huge shadow-thing walk through that door and attack you. I wanted to help, but then everything got fuzzy, and I found myself standing here—holding hair spray?"

"That's it? You don't remember the second Nephilim?"

"There were *two* shadow things?" she asked, horrified.

Sonny paced around the room, trying to piece everything together. "So the books are definitely in there, but the knowledge inside them is only accessible when it's needed. Widdick was different though, he felt the weight of the knowledge, at least until he put it into writing. Why would it work so differently now?"

"Maybe it isn't," I suggested. "Could be that Widdick started out this way too. He did say that he would have memory gaps during his lectures."

"Maybe," Sonny said, doubtfully. "But the books are alive, in a way. They have a soul. It could be that they adapt with each host. Widdick's writings put him in danger. Maybe now the books have learned to hide themselves a little better."

"Does that mean no more skimming through thousands of pages for what we need?" I asked, hopefully. "We can just ask Maya like some kind of human Alexa?"

"One way to find out." Sonny cleared his throat. "Maya, why did fire hurt the Nephilim so badly?"

Maya scrunched her nose and frowned. "I'm a little lost here. Can someone tell me—" Her face slacked, yet again. "Nephilim are an amalgam of human souls corrupted by angelic ancestry. Such corruption is particularly sensitive to cleansing forces designed to pierce the veil of the ethereal plane."

"Cleansing force?" I asked. "You used hairspray and a candle lighter."

Maya shook her head. "What?"

"Fire." Sonny noted. "Hellfire can burn humans and angels, so it stands to reason regular fire is a cleansing force too. Funny that demons live surrounded by fire and are sensitive to water. Maybe we'll run into a spirit who is weak against leaf attacks and we can battle them."

"Why would we want to do that?" I asked.

Maya and Sonny chuckled together. "See?" Sonny gestured to his compatriot. "She gets it. Seriously, Bill, don't be such a geezer."

"You're like two-hundred," I pointed out.

"But still in touch."

"Not that I don't appreciate the banter," Maya interjected, "but I feel like we're glossing over the fact that we were almost killed in my apartment a second ago. I thought you said that if I laid low, this sort of thing wouldn't happen?"

Sonny and I looked at each other, puzzled. She was right, the Nephilim had discovered her exceptionally fast. As far as we knew, they had tailed Widdick for several days before attacking him. If they were so desperate to get ahold of Maya now, our time was running short.

"They must have followed us," Sonny deduced. "If they'd known about her any other way, they'd have attacked before we even got here. They've probably been keeping tabs on us ever since the Widdick incident."

"Thank God we didn't drop her off here last night. If we had—"

"She could be dead, or worse," Sonny finished.

For a moment, I had forgotten that Maya was standing right next to us. She backed into her couch and sat down, staring off at nothing.

"Oh—uh—Maya?" I said. "Are you okay?"

She didn't answer, but began breathing rapidly

Sonny sat down next to her. "Hey now. It's over, there's nothing to worry about."

Maya shot a look at Sonny. "Nothing to worry about? Nothing—" She began fully hyperventilating.

I was experienced enough with panic attacks to recognize one coming on. I knelt down next to her and locked eyes. "Hey, it's okay. Just breathe. Deep breaths."

She closed her eyes and nodded, trying her best to listen to my advice.

"Can I get you anything?" I asked.

"Water," she said between breaths.

I raced to her fridge and found a water filter pitcher, quickly pouring a glass before rushing back. "Here, drink some of this."

She grabbed the cup and gulped down the entire thing in a matter of seconds. Her breathing finally slowed, and she leaned back on the couch. "Thank you."

"Do you need anything else?"

"No, I just—I need a moment to grasp all this. First, I start seeing ghosts popping up and I think, 'Maybe I'm losing my mind?'. Next, I'm abducted in the middle of the night—yes, by you two, but it was still scary! Then, you tell me that I'm some kind of human encyclopedia, something that causes me to lose control of my body and experience memory lapses, so that's fun. And finally, I discover that I'm being hunted by literal monsters, and possibly will be for the rest of my life! I have to abandon my home, my job, and my family to go on the run with two guys whom I've only just met, one of which is a ghost. But yeah, nothing to worry about, right?"

Sonny was silent for a moment as he pondered the right thing to say. "I'm not actually a ghost, that's a whole other thing."

I shoved Sonny aside and knelt back down to Maya's level. "I know things are bad right now, and believe me, I definitely know what it's like to have your life uprooted, but this isn't forever. We're going to figure out who's behind all this and we're going to put a stop to it. After that, you can come back here, or do whatever you want with your life."

I don't think anything I said could have calmed her down completely, but I saw a gleam of hope appear in her eyes, amidst the anxiety.

"Yeah, and look on the bright side!" Sonny pitched in. "That's one Nephilim down and only one to go. Hell, for all we know, we scared it enough to abandon its mission altogether. I mean, it's not as if one Nephilim can take the three of us by itself."

Something about that last sentence gave me a bad feeling in the pit of my stomach. Sonny was right. The Nephilim couldn't kill us, not alone.

"Maya?" I asked.

"Yeah?"

"Do you own a gun?" She looked at me, confused and shook her head. "No. Just my pepper spray. I have replica swords, but I don't think they're sharp."

"Is there a place to get guns in town?"

"I—uh—I'm not sure. I don't really—"

"We're in the Bible Belt." I looked her dead in the eyes. "Someone is selling guns."

"There's a Walmart on the west side of town?"

"That'll do." I grabbed her by the arm and pulled her off the couch.

"Did I miss something?" Sonny asked. "What's going on?"

"I have a feeling we're about to get some familiar company."

"Company? From—" Sonny's eyes went wide with realization. "Bill's right, we gotta go."

We were down the stairs and back in Maya's minivan within seconds. I was about to pull out of the parking lot when I saw those kids playing with their Super Soakers again.

"Hey, kids!" I shouted out my window, pulling up to the two boys. Sonny looked at me like I was crazy, but kept quiet.

"We're not getting in that car, weirdo," said the boy in the T-shirt featuring a black Sonic the Hedgehog wielding a handgun. He and his friend lifted their plastic weapons, ready to fire if I tried anything suspicious.

"No, I was just admiring your water guns. What would you say if I gave you twenty bucks for both of them?"

"Man, one of these costs more than that," the other boy in the *Dragon Ball Z* shirt said.

"That can't be true," I protested. I looked at Maya in the backseat who just nodded to confirm the validity of their claim. "Fine. How much do you want for them?"

"Fifty."

"Fifty bucks?" I exclaimed in disbelief.

"Each."

"Look, kid. I don't have a hundred dollars. I can give you, like— thirty."

"Go ask someone else then."

"Who am I sup—Is this how your parents raised you? To rip people off?"

"Maybe."

I held my tongue and pulled out my wallet. As I suspected, I only had thirty-five dollars left from the money in my cabin. I turned back to Maya. "Do you have any cash?"

Maya pulled out a wallet in the shape of some yellow cartoon dog I didn't recognize. She fumbled around with it before pulling out twenty dollars. "This is all I have."

I took three fives and handed it to the kid with my thirty-five. "Here. I'll take one."

The kid snatched the money and tossed me the soaker. He smiled and ran off with his friend.

"You're welcome!" I yelled out to them. "Little brats."

Sonny snickered as I got back onto the road.

"What?" I asked.

"You're gonna be a great dad someday."

"Shut up, Sonny."

I knew he was joking, but the comment gave me pause. Even if we managed to stop the end of days, it would be years before Grace and I could return to a degree of normalcy. Who knows whether her parents would ever forgive me, but if things somehow all worked out fine, *would I still want children*? It's not really a question I'd ever asked myself. It always seemed to be inevitable that I would settle down, have kids, and live the American dream, but things had changed. I'd changed. Perhaps I was destined for another life.

"Bill!" Maya yelled from the backseat.

I snapped back to what I was doing. "Sorry, what was that?"

"I said you need to get in the left lane. Your turn is at the next light."

"Thanks," I said, flicking my blinker.

"So, is anyone going to tell me what we're running from right now?" Maya asked. "Or why you just paid a kid fifty dollars for a toy?"

"It's like Sonny said." I glanced down at my newly acquired weapon. "Demons are sensitive to water."

Maya gulped, holding tight on the overhead hand grip.

I scanned the road ahead and saw the Walmart sign approaching. Checking my mirror to get into the turn lane, I found myself doing a double take. Sprinting on all fours, like a gorilla, was a massive demon. It was the size of an SUV, which was evident because it shoved a similar sized car aside as it barreled towards us. Maya and Sonny turned to look at the sound of screeching tires and clanking metal.

"Holy shit! Is that it?" asked Maya.

"Bill!" Sonny alerted me.

"I see it."

The demon was quickly gaining on our van, and I knew I wouldn't be able to outmaneuver it while surrounded by traffic. Instead, I waited for the beast to get closer before swerving and then jerking the wheel—slamming into the monster from the side and nearly colliding with an oncoming truck. I glanced at my driver side mirror, and saw the beast still holding onto our minivan with its hooked claws. It had evidently made itself intangible at just the right moment to avoid collision. We needed to force it onto the physical plane.

"Maya!" I yelled. "Take this!" I tossed the water gun into the back seat and sped through my turn, narrowly avoiding a T-bone in the intersection. The minivan screeched, clearly not built to take turns at such high speeds.

The demon pried its claws into the back left door and ripped it away from the van, sending the hunk of debris careening down the road behind us. Maya screamed as it reached its enormous gnarled hand to grab her. She held tight to her water gun and pulled back the pump, blasting the demon's eyes. The backseat filled with hot steam as the monster howled, losing its grip. It rolled into the Walmart parking lot where it was immediately struck by a sedan.

"Oh my God!" Maya held up her neon weapon. "This thing is like a proton pack!"

"Did you kill it?" Sonny asked, looking behind him.

Maya poked her head out of the gaping hole in the side of her van. "I don't think so. It just flipped that car over."

"Yeah, that sounds pretty not-dead," Sonny agreed.

I pulled the minivan onto the curb in front of the garden center and hurried out. The three of us rushed inside the building as a flurry of customers ran in the opposite direction, fleeing the Walmart as if their life depended on it. We skidded to a stop in time for a large ceramic pot to fly past our heads and shatter into a pile of fertilizer. Blocking our path to the automotive department was another demon.

"Oh, fuck this!" Maya yelled. "Now there's two of them?"

"Maybe I can get its attention," Sonny suggested. "Lure it into a portal like a matador."

"Didn't you try that last time?" I recalled.

"This one is smaller."

He was right. It was about half the size of its partner, sickly skinny and covered in protruding hooks and spikes. It didn't wait around for us to finish formulating a plan. The lithe creature leapt onto all fours and hurdled over rows of plants to get to us. Maya shoved the water gun in my hands and ran out of sight. I lifted the weapon and unleashed a blast at the monster. The stream skimmed its side, throwing it off balance.

It collided with a table and emitted an ear piercing screech. I pumped the soaker for another blast, but the demon lifted the table by the legs and wielded it like a shield, continuing to advance on us. We were now down to Sonny's matador idea.

Before he got a chance to open a portal however, water suddenly sprayed from the ceiling. Somehow, the sprinklers in the garden area had been activated. No table was big enough to shield the demon from an assault on all sides. It collapsed on the ground, squealing in agony and crawling towards the exit.

We wasted no time. Demon Two was incapacitated, but the first would soon be hot on our heels. Sonny and I ran to the automotive section, followed closely by Maya.

"Where did you scamper off to?" Sonny asked her.

"The sprinklers—they're set to water all the flowers and plants. I just had to find the switch."

"Was this prophet Maya or nerdy Maya?"

"This was middle-America Maya who knows half the employees here."

"Great," Sonny said. "I hope the next Maya knows Kung Fu."

We ran past the devastation wrought by the loose demon. Aisles were knocked down, and more than a couple of bodies lined the way. I can only imagine what the mayhem must have looked like to bystanders who couldn't perceive the monster unleashing it. As we ran, I heard a tremendous crash, followed by more screams. Demon One was inside, and closing in. I needed to buy us more time.

I broke off from the group, shouting back, "Get the guns, I'll loop around!"

Maya tried to stop, but Sonny ushered her along while I rushed back in the direction of the screams. Demon One wasn't hard to find. It was rampaging through the kitchen appliance aisle, swiping at anyone unfortunate enough to wander near it. I primed my Super Soaker and fired a small spray at the demon's back to get its attention. I didn't want to waste the whole tank until we had real fire power. I saw steam rise as the water made contact, and the demon turned to glare at me.

"Hey asshole!" I taunted it. "Looking for someone?"

Demon One snarled, but didn't attack. "You must be the one they call Bill." It spoke in that familiar vibrating resonance.

"I didn't know I was so famous."

"You're the human who killed a demon. Your reputation has spread far throughout our realm." I nearly pointed out that it was technically Sonny that killed the demon, but that seemed ill advised. "Did you know that time moves differently in Hell, Bill? We've had months to talk all about you. I've been hoping I'd be the one to find you." The monster started inching toward me, little by little. Sweat beaded on my forehead and I wondered how much time Sonny and Maya would need to get back to me with the real weapons.

"I'm flattered." I gulped. "I can't wait to hear what they'll be saying about me once I've killed two more demons."

Demon One smiled, revealing a grotesque display of gnarly teeth. "Two more? Don't you mean three?"

My eyes widened and I glanced away from the beast in the direction of Sonny and Maya. That was all it needed. It barreled forward and swatted me away, like an insect. All the air escaped my lungs as I slid on the tile floor for twenty feet, stopping in the paint aisle. I could barely breathe, grasping for the water gun that I'd lost in midair. Failing that, I grabbed a bucket of white paint and attempted to shimmy it open with my fingernails. The demon was bearing down on me in no time, so I gave up—flinging the can of paint at the monster and hoping against hope that I might get lucky.

The demon swatted the can out of the air, causing it to split open on impact. The paint splattered the beast from head to toe and I hooted in triumph. My cheers ceased when I realized that the demon wasn't howling in pain like before. One second, the monster was drenched in paint, and the next it went incorporeal. The paint fell off its hide and splattered on the tile, leaving the demon bone dry. Evidently, the water content of common house paint is far more diluted than in a Dr. Pepper.

The demon solidified again and raised its fists to smash me to a pulp. It took one step forward and slipped on the wet paint, falling backward into the puddle. After a moment of shock, I leapt to my feet, racing around to scoop up my water gun before sprinting to the hunting section.

The store was almost entirely empty now. I may not have been to this particular Walmart before, but if you've been in one, it's not hard to navigate another. I found Sonny hiding behind the rifle counter. The glass display case was busted and he sat on the floor, carefully trying to load one of the shotguns. I hopped over the counter to join him.

"Where's Maya?" I asked, nearly out of breath.

"Oh good. You're alive. Maya ran to the toy section."

"What? Why?"

"To get more water guns. Don't worry, she can handle herself."

"Handle herself? I can't even handle *myself*."

"I never suggested you could."

Part of me wanted to rush over to make sure she was still alive, but Sonny was right. Of the three of us, her prophetic trance made her the most capable of surviving. Plus, I didn't feel like moving at the moment. Having a chance to sit down made me realize that my abdomen was in enormous pain from being swatted through the air. Instead, I resigned to help Sonny load the guns, shoving some of the ammo into my pockets in case we needed to move before we finished.

"This remind you of anything?" Sonny asked.

"What do you mean?"

"Just like old times."

"You mean Salado? That was last week."

"Feels like yesterday."

"Except it was only one of them then," I pointed out. "Now there's three."

"I thought there were two," Sonny said, dismayed.

"There could be. I'm not certain a demon is a reliable source of information."

"Doesn't really matter. The more there are, the easier they'll be to kill."

"How the hell do you figure that?"

"It's like the rule of bad guys. The first *Alien* was nearly invincible, but in *Aliens*, they were cannon fodder. Applies to any monster."

"Well, call me crazy, but I'd take my chances with less demons over more."

Suddenly, I heard footsteps running toward us. Assuming it was Maya, I kept loading guns. The next second, a woman hurdled over the counter, landing just a few feet away. It was not Maya. Sonny and I both yelped and pointed our guns in her face. She yelped too.

"Please don't!" the woman pleaded, holding her hands out, as if to block the bullets with them.

I immediately lowered the gun and crawled over, shushing her quietly. She was a blonde woman, around my age and she looked absolutely terrified.

"It's okay," I whispered to her. "I'm not going to hurt you, we're hiding too."

She opened her eyes and lowered her arms. "Do you know what's going on?" she asked, her voice shaking.

Of course the answer was yes, but I couldn't tell her that, so I just shook my head.

"Can I wait here with you and your friend, until help comes?" the woman begged. "I'm really scare—"

Before she could finish, a deafening sound erupted behind me, and a huge hole opened in the woman's chest. Blood sprayed across my face and she was knocked back into the counter, dead. I was horrified to turn around and see Sonny pointing the smoking gun.

"Jesus Christ! What did you do?"

"She said 'you and your friend'. She could see me."

"What does that—" Then it dawned on me. I looked back at the woman's corpse to find it shaking, violently. From the hole in her chest, an arm began clawing its way out. I snatched my water gun and blasted the emerging monster. Steam billowed and the woman's body split in half as Demon Three crawled out.

Sonny was about to open fire, when a claw—dripping with white paint—reached over the countertop above us. Demon One was back as well. I pointed the water gun up, but it was ripped from my hands and thrown across the store. Sonny's theory about monsters being weaker in numbers was turning out to be bullshit.

Demon One shrieked and I closed my eyes in anticipation of death. When the shrieking continued, I realized it wasn't a blood curdling war cry, but a shriek of pain. Maya had returned with her own super soaker, nearly half her size—with a second one strapped around her back. She unleashed a torrent of water at the demon, giving us ample time to grab our new weapons and crawl over the counter to join her. Sonny and I held up the shotguns and opened fire, blasting Demon One apart while the steady stream of water kept it solid. After three shots, each at point blank range, the shrieking stopped. The monster's skin began to bubble, and the whole thing disappeared into steam, leaving only a puddle of ectoplasmic goo and white paint.

"One down," I said.

"Thanks for the assist," Sonny nodded to Maya. "Now we just need to work on your timing."

"Sorry. I couldn't get these things out of the box, so I had to run over to office supplies to get scissors, then to the bathroom to fill them up—"

A deep roar echoed through the air. About twenty yards away, near electronics, Demon Two had finally recovered. At the same time, the cracking of broken glass alerted us that Demon Three was now free from its dead host. This one was lanky too, but much taller than either of its friends. The two creatures closed in on us from opposite sides, but this time we were ready for them. Sonny laid his shotgun on the ground next to me and took Maya's oversized water gun for himself while she unstrapped her spare. The two stood back to back, weapons trained on opposite enemies. I took a few shells out of my pocket to reload the gun in my hands. Once the demons were in range, we began.

The dual jets of water slowed down both advances. I started with Demon Three, who was closer. I fired a couple shots at its legs, causing the beast to fall forward on its face. Three more blasts into the top of its head finished it off. Once the creature began to dissipate, I swung around and fired my last shot into Demon Two, who now had two jets of water on it. The first shotgun spent, I swiped up Sonny's from the ground and continued the barrage. It only took a couple more shots before the final demon collapsed into goo. All in all, it was over in less than twenty seconds.

There was a moment of stunned silence before Maya began to chuckle. Soon we were all laughing, without really understanding why.

"You guys made this sound way harder," Maya said, lifting her nearly empty soaker. "I could blast monsters all day!"

"It's like I told Bill," Sonny replied. "Bad guys are always easier to kill in groups."

"We had better tools, and we actually knew what we were doing. That logic still makes no sense." I was adamant. "Besides, you guys got to go shopping while I nearly had my ribs cracked. Wasn't so easy for me."

"Sorry," Maya said. "That's why you're not supposed to split up. That's like Scooby Doo rule one."

"I thought that was the rule for slasher movies," Sonny said.

"I don't watch those," Maya grimaced.

Out of the corner of my eye, I thought I caught movement. I shot a look to the clothing department in case another demon had been lurking about, but found the area empty. Thinking I was just on edge, I dismissed the thought, only to turn back and see Sonny scowling. "One moment," the reaper said, vanishing into a portal.

Maya looked at me expectantly, but I was just as confused as she was. A couple of seconds later, Sonny reemerged, this time clutching a struggling Nephilim.

"What the hell?" I exclaimed as I watched the reaper pin the shadowy creature to the ground. It was nearly twice his size, but it submitted, clearly terrified.

"Spotted this lookie-loo watching from behind a clothing rack," Sonny grunted. "Making sure your goons finish the job, huh?"

Watching the Nephilim squirm under Sonny was an unusual experience for me. I had instantly recoiled at the sight of the creature, but seeing it like this felt different. It was genuinely afraid—not just of Sonny, but of us. A little of its power over me died and I felt as if I might be able to talk to it.

"Wh—Who are you working for?"

"Do not speak to me human!" The Nephilim's voice echoed as if he were shouting from the bottom of a cavernous pit.

Sonny grabbed what looked like the creature's face. "Hey now, I take offense to that. I used to be human myself."

"You are the scum of the universe!" the shadow screeched. "Nothing but a failed science experiment. You are beneath me."

"Hmm. That's funny," Sonny forced a chuckle. "Because from where I'm sitting, it looks like I'm above you."

The Nephilim snarled.

"Correct me if I'm wrong," Sonny continued. "But aren't you half human yourself? Sounds like you're being a little hypocritical."

"I will answer none of your questions."

"Oh, you will if you don't want to end up a nice little pile of bone and ash like your buddy."

Even for a smoky void, the creature's trembling was unmistakable. "You no longer possess the mobile flame," it said, denoting an air of mysticism to a candle lighter and hairspray.

"That's true," Sonny admitted. "But I don't need jack shit to drop you into an active volcano, do I? Now answer my friend's question. Who are you working for?"

The Nephilim was utterly defeated. It looked in my direction, and even through its featureless visage, I could feel its contempt for me. I took another step back.

"Even if I tell you," it said, "nothing will come of it. The years of tribulation are upon us."

"Humor us," Sonny demanded.

"He will know," the Nephilim whispered. "He hears all."

"So, it's an angel then?"

"No, not divine. Portals. Always listening to me… to you."

Sonny and I exchanged grim looks.

"He wants—"

The floor opened up, swallowing both the Nephilim and Sonny. Orange light emitted from the hole, and just as quickly as it appeared, it vanished.

"SONNY!" I fell to my knees and clawed at the tile he had just fallen through. A second later, another portal opened overhead and Sonny fell crashing to the ground. He was groaning, and his clothes were darkened by soot.

Maya and I crowded around him. "What happened?" she asked. "You didn't actually drop that thing into a volcano, did you?"

"No." he coughed. "It wasn't me. Someone else was listening— opened the portal. Apparently, our rogue reaper doesn't like being gossiped about."

"Listening." I looked around, puzzled. "Has it been here the whole time?"

"I don't think so. Any reaper can track us with their list. If they want to, they can listen in on our conversations with portals so small, we wouldn't even notice."

"Like Josiah did at the bar," I remembered.

Sonny released a dejected sigh. "Yeah."

"You don't think—I mean, did you get a look at him when you fell through the portal?"

"No, it was too fast, and there was fire everywhere. Needless to say, I don't think that Nephilim will be able to give us any more information."

"So what can we do now?" I asked.

"Run," Maya suggested.

"What? How will that help us?" I asked

"It'll help by getting us away from the police," she replied.

I suddenly became aware of the approaching sound of sirens in the distance. Within minutes, cops would be swarming us. We took Maya's advice.

22

BOOK BURNING

THE WALMART WAS still emptying when we got to the exit, allowing us to easily blend in with the crowd. We left the guns behind—as my new fingerprints were not yet in any database, and Maya had not actually touched any of them. We did, however, hang on to the water guns. Yes, we were technically stealing two of them, but that hardly seemed to matter in the grand scheme of things, nor were we the only people to grab items as they fled the store. Maya's minivan was still parked in front of the garden section, and we managed to pull away just as the police arrived. We'd have surely been stopped, but there were so many cars attempting to flee, there was just no point in chasing down anyone. Once we were clear of the exiting traffic, we made straight for Maya's apartment.

"Won't they be able to identify us from the security cam footage?" Maya leaned up from the backseat, squeezing herself between Sonny and I in the front.

"I doubt it," Sonny said, "This was a big demon attack. Once word of it reaches upstairs, the footage will mysteriously become very fuzzy at the crucial moments."

"Fuzzy? As in tampered with? By angels?" Maya asked, aghast.

"Or their lackeys. You ever wonder how an entire spiritual plane can exist with almost no hard evidence of it? It's no accident."

"What about witnesses?"

"No one was paying attention to us. Besides, what are they gonna say? They saw you and Bill having an imaginary shootout with thin air?"

"You did shoot a woman," I chimed in.

"Yeah, but she was also split open into an unrecognizable heap of body parts. Hard to say what the cause of death is there."

"Wait, you shot someone?" Maya asked.

"She was already dead. No harm no foul."

It really was amazing to think about the level of influence the angels had over the human world. They were able to pull a lot of strings in order to bring me back to life without arousing suspicion, so I had to wonder what other tampering they were responsible for. Maybe the original photo of Bigfoot was crystal clear before they got their hands on it.

As I turned onto the main road, I glanced back in the rearview mirror and was reminded that one of the back doors was still missing.

"Hey Maya," I said. "Maybe you should sit down and put your seatbelt on. I don't want you rolling out of the side of the car."

"I'm fine, I won't fall out."

"You say that now, but Sonny's fallen out of the car twice now."

"Three if you count the time you hit that candy store," Sonny added.

Maya didn't need further examples to strap in.

Once we were a few miles away from the Walmart without being pursued, Maya finally became comfortable enough to release her pent-up excitement. Her play-by-play of our department store show-down consisted mostly of sound effects and hyperbole. I'd half-expected the entire experience to throw her into another panic attack, but having survived her trial by fire, her fears seemed to melt away. Perhaps the reason this unassuming girl was chosen as the next prophet was because she was born to the task.

I, on-the-other-hand, was far too worried about the Nephilim's final words to let my guard down. Some mysterious reaper could be—and likely was—listening to us at that very moment. Visual forms of communication might be safe, unless the reaper peered through tiny portals like a peephole. If I took the proper precautions, I was confident I could pass messages to Sonny that wouldn't be intercepted, but I couldn't even tell him that yet. We could give no indication of our intentions until we found some way to shield ourselves from surveillance.

I pulled into Maya's apartment complex, noticing that the kids from earlier were gone. They were probably on their way to spend all the money they robbed me of. Upon reaching her front door, I held Maya back, just in case there were any more surprises waiting for us. I readied a water gun in one hand and carefully turned the doorknob with the other. Maya got the idea and aimed her soaker at the door as well. I threw it open and pointed the weapon inside. We entered quickly and cleared the whole apartment. Once we were certain there were no more demons or Nephilim, all three of us collapsed on the couch.

Maybe it was the adrenaline from the battle that kept us so alert after a night of no sleep, but once I sunk into that cushion, my eyelids felt like manhole covers. The next instant, I felt Sonny nudging me while I moaned in protest. I just wanted a moment's rest, but the angle of the sunlight in the window told me that I had somehow already slept for hours. I noticed that Maya was still asleep, her head resting on my shoulder. The TV was on, displaying some show about people haggling over old trinkets in people's garages. Across from me, Sonny sat on the floor, using a turquoise pen covered in glitter to write on tiny scraps of paper. When he caught my glance, he pressed a finger to his lips, turned up the TV, and held up a slip of paper inches from my face. Taking a moment for my eye to adjust, it read:

Good Morning.

I raised an eyebrow. Sonny ripped up the tiny message and dropped the remnants into a metal cooking pot from the kitchen. He held up another slip of paper, careful to shield it from view.

Rogue Reaper could be listening. Can't talk out loud.

Sonny read my mind. I nodded my head, unsure of how else to communicate without waking Maya. He tore up the second slip of paper and grabbed the next.

I have an idea.

I felt as though he could be getting a little more mileage out of each message, but I was literally incapable of complaining.

Reaper is tracking us through list.

I nodded again, more slowly this time as I began to anticipate where Sonny was going.

I'm off the grid. You and Maya are not.

It was perfunctory at this point, but Sonny held up the next message, regardless.

We need to burn your books.

It was a good plan. Not only would we be safe from the reaper, but we'd also be invisible to the angels in case one of them really was in cahoots.

There is still danger.

Of course there was. At this point, I'd have been shocked if there wasn't.

If you are not in the system, I cannot track you.

That seemed to go without saying.

If reaper finds you, he can make you disappear, like Widdick.

Sonny tore up that last piece of paper and added it to the pot with the rest. On the TV, a man was having a difficult time letting go of a rusty bicycle that had been pulled from underneath a pile of scrap metal. I sat there watching this transaction play out while the severity of the situation washed over me. If this rogue reaper had managed to wipe Widdick's soul from the records, then that meant he could have hidden it literally anywhere and no one would ever be able to find it. Widdick could be millions of miles away, sitting alone on some distant planet for all eternity. Worse yet, he could be in literal Hell. I doubt they're doing spot checks to see if everyone belongs down there.

I truly felt bad for the professor, but it was my own soul that I feared for most. I know that sounds selfish, but I'm not going to lie about it. From the very beginning of the journey, my worst-case scenario was that I would have to move on to the heavenly plane before my time. That's not too awful, considering the alternatives. But now, I faced the very real possibility that I could be lost in eternal isolation. To my knowledge, souls can't ever die. I would be conscious of every waking moment of my exile, forever.

Across from me, Sonny picked up the pot filled with his paper messages. He then revealed Maya's candle lighter and set them all ablaze. This was what woke Maya.

AFTER HER INITIAL panic about a fire in her apartment, Sonny was able to calm Maya down with another written message—of which he had created a separate stack just for her. Oddly enough, he actually had one that said, *"Sorry about the fire"*. The rest of the messages were similar to mine, minus the last few, detailing the potential risk. I realized that Sonny only told me this because I still had a choice in the matter. I could walk away right now and not have to worry about demons, Nephilim, or reapers ever again. Maya wasn't so fortunate.

When Sonny finished his flashcard presentation, Maya grabbed a sheet of paper from next to Sonny and ripped off her own strip. She wrote something very quickly.

Can you fetch our books for us?

Sonny shook his head and pulled off a new strip.

Cannot pull books without your soul present.

I remembered looking for Grace's book in The Library. Without her, I could search that place for a thousand years without finding it. So the question remained: how could we locate our own books while we were still alive?

To be safe, Sonny grabbed all of the notes we had written and burned them in the pot. He then tore off a new strip and wrote down his message.

I have an idea, but you're not going to like it.

Sort of frustrated by the whole note-taking system, I blurted out loud, "That's not an incriminating piece of information. You can just say that, and then write down the next part."

Both Sonny and Maya shushed me ferociously. As a sarcastic gesture, I held my fingers to my mouth and mimed zipping it closed. Sonny wrote down the next message.

I'm going to have to kill both of you. You'll be dead for 10-15 seconds.

Having died twice before, I was more relaxed about this than Maya. She had never experienced death, and I hesitated to tell her that it did, in fact, really hurt. Sonny assured us—again in note form—that he would place our souls right back in our bodies before there was any brain damage. I think that even mentioning the possibility of brain damage only made things worse for Maya, but she agreed to the procedure, trembling all the while.

I volunteered to go first, in order to help familiarize her with the process. Sonny opened up a portal in the center of the room and a bright light shone on us from the floating tear in reality. I leaned back on the couch, preparing to go limp. Next thing I knew, Sonny's hand sank into my chest, where I felt that all too familiar grip on my spine. He yanked me out of my body and pulled me to my feet. I glanced back and saw myself sitting on the couch, eyes wide open and slack jawed. It was kind of embarrassing. I suppose nobody looks good when they're dead, but at least most people don't have to see it. Maya looked back and forth between my body and my soul, less terrified than before, but still utterly fascinated. Sonny wasted no time. He grabbed me by the back of my neck and led me into the blinding light.

We were in The Library again. I looked back through the portal and saw Maya waving from the couch. "I brought us somewhere remote," Sonny said. "We're about 500 miles from the front desks, so we shouldn't run into any angels."

He dropped the number so casually, as if that didn't imply more knowledge than there seemed to exist in the whole universe. I couldn't help but wonder—if entire categories really had been removed from The Library, just how many books did Maya have stored in her head?

Sonny grabbed the first book he saw off the shelf and held it for me to see. *The Book of Bill.* Evidently, whatever the angels did to my public records on Earth didn't impact the name of my soul. Sonny looked back at the shelf, and cocked his head, confused. He pulled a second book and ushered me into the portal. We jumped back into Maya's living room, two books in tow. I fell right through the couch, which gave Maya a quick scare. She was used to seeing Sonny interact with the physical world and had no idea how easy it was to just phase through things by accident. Sonny set my book on the couch and continued staring at the second one.

"Hey, Sonny," I said, standing next to my own corpse. "A little help?"

"Oh, right. Clear!" he yelled.

He reached into my chest and shoved my soul back into my body. I jolted to life, a guttural moan escaping from my mouth. I gasped for air and slowly returned to normal breathing.

"You see?" I said, still panting. "Nothing to it."

"That looked painful. Is it painful?" Maya asked, still trembling.

Sonny and I looked at each other in silence. Then in unison, "Nah."

I moved to get off the couch, but as I shifted, I felt an uncomfortable sensation underneath me. I settled back in and wiggled around to confirm my fears.

"Maya," I said. "Did you move my body when I was gone?"

"God, no. I don't want to touch a dead body. Why? What's wrong?"

"Oh," Sonny spoke up. "Bill's just upset that he shit himself."

"He what?" Maya asked.

"Yeah," I said, glaring at Sonny. "I what?"

"You shit yourself when you die. Were you not aware of this? You've died before."

"I know I've died before, but I've never shit myself!"

"You might've. A lot of people do."

Maya turned pale. "Oh my God, I completely forgot. He's right."

"You knew this?" I accused her.

"Well, yeah," she said, "I work in a nursing home. It's kind of a regular thing."

"Come to think of it," Sonny mentioned. "The other times you died, I pulled you out of the body right away. Even when I put you in Herman's body, he had just been cleaned by the hospital staff. I guess you wouldn't have known."

"You guess?" I was fuming.

"Hey guys," Maya said. "We probably shouldn't be talking out loud so much."

I scowled silently at both of them, and left to wash off. Thankfully, Maya had some extra stretchy sweatpants, though they only reached shin height on me. After cleaning out the bathtub, and lighting every candle that she owned, I finally rejoined the two of them in the living room.

"Okay, if I were you," I said to Maya, "I would sit on the toilet for this."

"Actually," Sonny said, "I was just showing Maya. She doesn't need to die at all."

"What?" I asked.

"Yeah, take a look."

Sonny handed me the second book that he pulled from the shelf. It was a red-violet color, with silver filigree. On the cover, it read: *The Book of Maya.*

I was flabbergasted. "I, uh—I don't—how—"

"It seems," Sonny explained. "Because I held the portal open, The Library recognized Maya's presence on the other side, so I could pull her book. Nifty huh?"

"Nifty? You're saying I didn't have to die at all? I didn't have to go through all this... shit? Do you have any idea how much having your soul ripped out hurts?"

"Hey!" Maya interjected. "I thought you said it didn't hurt!"

"Well, I lied!"

I sat down on the couch and folded my arms, feeling ridiculous in my undersized sweatpants. Maya and Sonny looked at me and then at each other before laughing hysterically. After a few seconds, my frown faded, and I started laughing too. There was really nothing else to do about it.

"Okay," Sonny said, calming down. "We should probably get this over with."

He grabbed the metal pot from the floor and placed the two books inside. It was strange to me that a book about my life would be so ornate looking. My cover was burgundy with gold, angular filigree decorating the borders and the spine. I wondered if each book was designed individually by an angel, or if they're a reflection of our personalities in some way.

As I watched Sonny ignite the lighter, I felt a sudden urge to yank my book out of the pot. I could drive to Salado to pick up Grace and take her to that cabin in Canada where I could live the rest of my life happily as Bob Butler. I watched the flames lick the pages and wondered if I could pinpoint the moment it was too late to turn back.

23

HELLO GOODBYE

IT WASN'T ENOUGH to erase the record of our existence. The rogue reaper may have lost his ability to track us, but he still knew our last location. If we didn't leave, the whole town would be crawling with demons, as if three weren't bad enough. Sonny and I assured Maya that the move would not be permanent, but truthfully, we had no way of knowing that for sure. She packed herself some clothes, toiletries, and snacks into a cat-shaped backpack, as well as a plush platypus that she claimed helped her to sleep.

She buzzed around the apartment, all the while chatting on the phone with her mother. Obviously, she could not reveal the truth of why she was leaving town, so the three of us concocted a story about traveling to meet some guy Maya was dating online. It was the only way, she claimed, her parents would let her go without prodding too deeply. Personally, I would have a lot of questions if my daughter suddenly ran off with a mysterious internet stranger, but then again, I met Grace before the popularity of dating apps. Maybe this was normal?

Maya's minivan had served its purpose, but wouldn't be much use to us anymore. It drove fine, but we'd draw unwanted attention going around with a missing door. We all crammed into the front of my three-seater pick-up truck and began to leave Enid behind us.

"I can't believe it," Maya said, looking wistfully out the windshield at the passing signs. "I've wanted to leave this town so badly for years. I thought my mom would blow a gasket if I ever tried, but she was totally cool with it. Why did I wait so long?"

"Well, multiple monster attacks in a single day is a pretty good motivator," Sonny said.

"Fair," she chuckled. "I don't know if it's the sleep deprivation, or brain overload, but I'm weirdly not as freaked out by that as I should be. Or any of it! Is that weird?"

"Yes," I said, truthfully.

"I think it would be weirder if you weren't prepped by thousands of years of spiritual knowledge floating around your head," Sonny suggested. "Probably softens the blow on your psyche, or drives you so insane that you don't know the difference."

Sonny's inflection indicated that he was joking, but I didn't want to tell Maya that he was just describing what had happened to the last prophet. In any case, she didn't seem too concerned by the possibility.

"By the way," she said. "Where exactly are we going?"

Sonny and I looked over her head at each other. "Uh—" the reaper began. "That's a good question."

"What, you don't know?" she asked.

"Actually," I spoke up. "I might have a suggestion."

Sonny smirked. "Let me guess. Texas?"

"What's in Texas?" Maya asked.

"Bill's fiancée."

"Oh neat. Are we picking her up too?"

I didn't answer right away. The truth of the matter was that I was driving towards Texas, but hadn't even considered seeing Grace there. Only a couple of days ago, I was prepared to defy the angels' explicit instructions in order to get back to her, but the moment Sonny re-entered my life, I no longer felt the same compulsion. The mission became my primary focus.

"I wasn't talking about Grace," I said. "I would like to see her, but I'm not sure if she'd be able to come even if she wanted to. Technically she's still a murder suspect."

"Your fiancée killed someone?" Maya's eyes went wide.

"Yeah," I said. "Me."

"Yikes."

"It's not like that. Sonny told you the story, my body was possessed."

"Oh, right," she nodded. "So then, where did you want to go, if not to see her?"

"There's a small town a few miles outside of Austin. I think it might be where this demon invasion originated," I said. "It's a long shot, but maybe if we snoop around there, we can find some way to stop it at the source."

The others looked at me wide eyed.

"And you were gonna share this with us, when?" Sonny asked, aghast.

"It's something I discovered in The Library. We weren't exactly on speaking terms. I didn't even tell the angels. I couldn't be sure—"

"If they were working with the rogue reaper?" Sonny finished my thought.

"Exactly. Pinning the blame on you didn't exactly inspire my confidence in them."

"So, what then?" Sonny asked. "What exactly did you discover?"

I told him all about the weather patterns I had correlated to the spreading demon attacks. The conditions of the drought were projected to spread around the globe, paving the way for a demon paradise without the fear of rainfall. But more importantly, I had learned that it all originated from one location, as if something there was physically sucking the moisture out of the air.

"Like a giant dehumidifier?" Maya asked, fascinated.

"Probably something more spiritual, but that's what I'd like to find out," I said. "At first, I wondered if it was the angels themselves affecting the weather. Sonny mentioned they might be able to do that. But why from one spot? Wouldn't it be easier—and less suspicious to cause multiple droughts around the world?"

"Indirect interference," Sonny said.

Maya and I looked at the reaper, eyebrows raised.

"The angels can't change the course of the natural world directly—at least not at that scale. Someone upstairs would notice and catch them. No, it would have to be done indirectly, a side effect of some kind of natural phenomenon like solar activity, or a volcano venting an absurd amount of heat."

"I think that kind of stuff would make the news," Maya said. "I haven't heard anything about Texas turning into Mordor."

"She's right," I said. "It would have to be something invisible to most humans. Something like a fire spirit or—" A thought occurred to me. "Didn't you say once, there used to be crossover points between Earth and Hell?"

"Sure," Sonny said. "but supposedly they were all closed up."

"And if someone were to figure out how to open one, and leave it open?"

Sonny tilted his head. "Probably get pretty hot."

IT WAS JUST a working theory, but it was the best lead we had. I was fairly confident we would find something at the origin point, even if it wasn't a gaping hell-mouth. We prodded Maya for information about how to close such a fissure—if one existed. The answer was always the same: Only the angels had the capacity to seal off an entire realm. We'd cross that bridge when we got to it.

Since the location of the origin point was just a few miles from my wedding venue, we agreed to stop for the night in Salado. It would give us a chance to rest up and allow me to see Grace one last time before we dove into God-knows-what the following morning.

Texas may have only been a state a way, but it was also the size of a country. Maya took the opportunity to get a couple hours of sleep. After stopping for gas, she woke up and offered to take over so I could rest as well. I agreed to try, but found myself unable to get a wink. My brain knew that if I slept, my mind would jump forward in time and be that much closer to seeing Grace. So, like a child on Christmas Eve, I just leaned against the door with my eyes closed, listening to Sonny and Maya joke around in hushed tones.

It was dark when we finally arrived. I pretended to wake up when Maya started complaining about the construction on the highway. I directed her to the small hotel on Main Street where Grace and her parents were last staying. With any hope, they would still be there. Once we parked, Sonny and Maya turned to look at me as I pondered how best to get Grace's attention.

"Do you know what room she's staying in?" Maya asked.

"Yes."

"Well, are you going to go see her?" Sonny chimed in. "Or are we going to spend the night in the car?"

"I'm thinking."

"Thinking of what?" Both Sonny and Maya asked me at the same time.

"Of how to handle this. I can't just go up to the door, her parents might answer. I should have called ahead. What was I thinking, not calling ahead?"

Maya pulled out her cell phone. "You can call her now."

I reached out and grabbed the phone, my hands shaking. I didn't know why I was so nervous. I had just seen her a week ago and it's not as though she hadn't known what I'd been up to. I suppose it had something to do with being able to physically touch each other for the first time since this whole debacle began. Not to mention, she would be seeing me in my new body. Would she notice the differences? Would she like the new me as much as the old me?

I dialed her number and waited. On the third ring, she answered.

"Hello?"

"Grace?"

"Bill? Bill, is that you?"

"It's me."

"I haven't heard from you in a week! Are you okay?"

"I'm fine. Everything is fine. In fact, I'm here now."

"What?"

"I'm right outside the hotel. Can you make some excuse to your parents?"

"They finally got their own room. It's just me here."

At that, I opened the door and stepped out of the truck. At the same moment, the door to Grace's hotel room opened and she stood before me, framed in light. We smiled at each other and hung up our phones. Behind me, the truck window rolled down and Maya poked her head out to see.

"Oh, she's pretty!"

Grace looked at the strange girl, mildly confused. I just shrugged and said, "Long story. I'll catch you up."

I walked forward, ready to embrace her as she stepped out of the threshold. Behind her, a portal briefly flashed. Her smile vanished. Her face went white. Over her shoulder, Nelson grinned.

"Howdy," the reaper said.

Three things happened at once: Nelson pulled Grace's soul from her body and fell back into a closing portal, Sonny reached into Maya's chest and held her soul in place to prevent Nelson from grabbing it, and I ran to catch Grace's lifeless form, ignoring Sonny's pleas to get back in the truck.

I reached her before she hit the ground, accomplishing little. I should have listened to Sonny, but all logic had abandoned me. I held her limp body, only vaguely aware of the shouting behind me. I had failed in the worst possible way. Then, I felt a hand grip the inside of my chest.

"Let's see you come back from this one," Nelson whispered.

My soul was ripped free, and I fell into a chasm, engulfed by heat.

24

INTO THE FIRE

I FELL INTO an ocean of flames. I could feel the flesh melt off of my bones only to reassimilate and burn away once more. I descended all the way through the lake of fire and emerged from the bottom, careening through the sky toward a small cluster of buildings. The pavement was rapidly approaching, but I was too relieved to be free of the heat to take notice. The respite was short lived. I impacted the ground like a meteor, only kept intact by whatever horrible magic healed my skin. I peeled myself out of the cracked asphalt and gazed into the air above me.

Flames filled the entire sky like a storm cloud, bathing this world in orange and red light. It was a barren landscape, interspersed with random structures few and far between. Hell, it turns out, was not all that different from Oklahoma. I had fallen in the middle of a dusty road outside of a dilapidated two-story house. The windows were boarded up and the front door was caved in. Inside, I could hear the creaking of floorboards. I wasn't keen on meeting any residents of this realm, but the only hiding place for a hundred yards was the house itself. I approached cautiously, prepared for anything—when a familiar sight appeared in the doorway.

"Grace?" I couldn't believe it. I thought I had lost her forever, but here she was, in front of me.

"Get inside! Quick!" she yelled.

I heeded her advice and helped to lift the broken door back up into its frame. We pushed an overturned wardrobe against the entrance, sealing it off from the malevolent forces that undoubtedly lurked outside. Grace panted heavily and then embraced me. Somehow, in Hell of all places, I'd found comfort.

"Bill," she pulled away. "What happened? Where are we?"

"Don't be too alarmed, but I'm pretty sure we're in Hell."

"Hell?" Her voice cracked as she tried not to scream.

"It's okay. We'll be fine. Sonny will still be able to track you. He'll be here in no time."

"Track me? How"

"Your soul should still be connected to the afterlife records."

"Is yours not?"

"Not anymore." I started walking around the house with Grace in tow, checking to see if anything was lying in wait to attack us. "We knew we were being watched," I told her. "So we erased our identities. We burnt our books."

"Burnt—oh God."

"What? What's wrong?"

"Whenever that—that thing pulled me out of my body, he didn't bring me here first."

"What do you mean? Where did he take you?"

"Some enormous library."

If I wasn't already dead, my heart would have stopped. I dropped to my knees and leaned against the creaking walls of the house. Grace knelt down beside me.

"No one's coming for us, are they?" she asked.

We both knew the answer, and I couldn't muster the strength to open my mouth and confirm it. I had never felt more hopeless, and we had only been in Hell for a few minutes. We still had an eternity of this to look forward to.

Then, we heard a knock on the floor—and no, I don't mean door. Something knocked on the hardwood floor directly underneath us. Grace and I looked at each other, panic in our eyes. I raised a finger to my lips and slowly lowered my head, pressing my ear against the floorboards. Nothing. I sat up on my knees and shrugged, right before the wood exploded upward. Between us, a great purple hand shattered through the floor. I reached out to Grace, but a second hand emerged behind her. The enormous limbs converged and gripped her by the torso. Her expression morphed into utter horror before she was heaved down into the darkness.

"GRACE!"

I crawled to the gaping hole and saw nothing but pitch black. Grace's horrified screams echoed in my ears followed by gurgling, and crunching—sounds I'll never be able to erase from my mind. I didn't know what to do, so I did the most foolish thing I could. I jumped into the hole after her. It was far deeper than I anticipated, and at the bottom, I landed in a pool of warm viscous liquid. When I surfaced for air, the light from the hole above barely illuminated a few inches of space around me. I could see the dark red fluid that I waded in, as well as solid red chunks floating around me. I had to hold back my urge to vomit as I paddled around, searching.

"Grace!" The foreign blood seeped into my mouth as I shouted. I spat it out and yelled again. "Grace!"

In front of me, a naked figure slowly rose out of the muck. It was her, dripping with blood, whole sections of her body ripped away by some clawed thing. She opened her eyes and looked at me.

"Bill. What have you done?"

"No!" I struggled to stay afloat. "I didn't!"

"You are a blight on my happiness. A burden on my life."

I tried to protest, but it became increasingly difficult to keep my head above the pool. Against all logic, I felt as if I needed to breathe. I knew I was dead, that I no longer required air, but it didn't matter. Blood filled my lungs. The fluid burned and tore at my insides and I feared this would be my existence forever. At last, my feet touched the bottom of the dark chasm and the chamber began to drain, leaving me curled up on the wet ground.

I coughed up most of the fluid in my lungs and tried to crawl, weighed down by my sopping clothes. When I wiped the blood from my eyes, I could barely make out Grace standing in a dim light, completely dry and clean. She smiled at me with a piercing, soulless gaze.

"Grace, what—what are you—"

She grabbed me by my hair and pulled my head back.

"Grace," I struggled to say.

She maintained her smile as she drove a knife deep into my neck and dragged it all the way across.

I SHOT UP, screaming. I was lying on an old couch in a dark room. Next to me sat Grace, surprised, yet relieved to see me awake. I grasped frantically at my neck, but found no wound.

"What's going on?" I asked. "What happened?"

"It's okay," she said. "You lost consciousness on the way down, or when you landed. Either way, I had to drag you inside before anything else found you."

"I was... unconscious?"

"Just for a little while. Do you know where we are?"

On the way down, she had said. So it wasn't all a dream. "We're in Hell."

"Yeah," she said. "That's what I thought."

I got up off the couch and looked around the room. It wasn't dilapidated or even messy. It looked like a perfectly ordinary living room, in a perfectly ordinary house. It didn't feel normal, though. Something about the tidiness felt sinister in a way the other house hadn't. *But there hadn't been another house, had there?*

"Wait a minute, I couldn't have been dreaming," I realized. "I'm dead. Spirits don't sleep."

"You fell out of the sky and landed on your head," Grace told me. "I think that's enough to put even a spirit out of commission."

"But I shouldn't be able to get knocked out at all. And the dream, it was so vivid."

"What happened in the dream?" she asked, innocently.

"A lot. It's kind of hard to explain. It was all so surreal. But it ended with you killing me."

"Well that settles it. Do you think I would ever hurt you?"

I rubbed my neck, the sensation of the blade still fresh in my mind. "No, I guess you wouldn't."

I walked over to the window and pulled back the blinds. We were in a neighborhood, in the middle of a cul-de-sac. There appeared to be only two types of houses, repeating one after another. The sky was yellow, but looked more like a sunset than a ceiling of flames. *Had I imagined that too?* Then I remembered something else from my dream.

"Grace, the reaper that killed you—did he bring you here directly? Did he take you anywhere else first?"

"No." She looked confused. "I was alive one moment, and then I was here the next. Why?"

I rushed over and took her by the hands. "We may be able to get out of this place," I said with a glimmer of hope in my eyes. "We just have to stay together. We can't get separated."

"That should be easy enough. I don't intend on leaving this house."

The moment after she said that, I heard a rumbling outside. I peeked out the window again to see a mob of people forming in the road. They were emerging from all the houses in the neighborhood and flooding into the center of the cul-de-sac where they began to light each other's torches.

I closed the blinds and turned back to Grace. "We have to get out of here, now." I grabbed her by the hand and led her through the kitchen, looking for a backdoor.

"Bill!" Grace pointed to the frosted glass door where shadows gathered on the other side of the curtain. Hands busted through, slicing themselves on the broken shards and grasping for the door handle. All throughout the house, I heard the sound of windows breaking and voices shouting. Soon, we would be overrun. I led Grace up a flight of stairs in the center of the house. Vicious chanting filled the air as we reached the top, as did the smell of smoke. We ran into a bedroom and locked the door, buying us a few seconds at best.

"Shit!" I yelled. "They're going to burn themselves up with the house!"

"I'm more worried about us!" Grace added.

I searched the room for anything useful, finding only a wooden chair in the corner. I pulled it over and shoved it under the doorknob. Meanwhile, Grace tried the bedroom window, but it wouldn't budge.

"Wait!" Grace said. "Give me the chair!"

I unlodged it and handed it to her, bracing the door in the meantime. Grace swung the chair with all her might and smashed the window. She started crawling out immediately, cutting her arms and legs in the process.

"What are you doing?" I shouted. "Be careful!"

Grace didn't answer. She managed to shimmy along the awning until she found a point where the roof dipped down low enough to climb up. I placed the chair back against the doorknob and followed her out of the window, also slicing my legs in the endeavor. When I reached her position, I was able to help lift her onto the higher level. Looking back, I could see smoke billowing out of the window we'd just crawled out of. Below us, the mob of people continued to rush into the house, flames and all.

"Bill, come on!" I took her hand and climbed to the roof of the burning house. After a good deal of effort, I sat down and let out a sigh of exhaustion.

"I don't understand," I said. "Sonny should have found us by now.

I don't know how much longer we can wait."

"Could be worse," Grace joked. "At least you're not drowning in blood."

I chuckled humorlessly. "Yeah. Wait, what are you talking about?"

"Like in your dream. I'd rather take my chances here than deal with whatever that was."

I stared at her face, the same face that I fell in love with years ago and had never stopped loving since. "Who are you?"

"Huh?" She looked genuinely perplexed.

"I knew it couldn't be a dream. That was you in that pool of blood, saying those things to me."

"Bill, I don't understand—"

I stood up and grabbed Grace by the collar. "What are you doing?" she cried. I dragged her to the edge of the roof and held her over the angry mob. "Bill! You're scaring me!"

"Where's Grace?" I demanded, tears streaming out of my eyes.

"Bill, it's me! Don't do this!" Her face was red, eyes wide with fear.

"What have you done with her?" I dipped her lower. If I lost my grip, there'd be no regaining her balance.

"Please, please don't do this. I love you." She wept openly. It was so convincing—so real, but something in my heart wouldn't accept that this was my fiancée.

Smoke began to cloud the air around us. The flames had engulfed most of the house. It was foolish to think either one of us was going to make it out of this situation, and even if we did, we'd still be in Hell. The obstacles would never end.

"Maybe you're telling the truth," I said. "Maybe this place is just messing with my head. It doesn't really matter though. We'll both be on fire or ripped apart by an angry mob soon."

"No! We just have to wait! Sonny will come!"

"No, he won't. Because you're not Grace. I'm not interested in playing your games. I won't draw this out any further." I released my grip and let her fall from the roof. Only she didn't fall, she simply hovered in the air. Suddenly, the mob ceased their assault, and the smoke began to clear away.

"Dammit," Grace said. "I was having fun with that one."

I glared at the imposter. "Where is she?"

"Not where you'll ever see her again."

"If you hurt her—"

"Bill, honey, you're in Hell. What is it you think we do here? Though, if you play nice, I could arrange to have you tortured together."

"The game is up!" I shouted. "I know what you're doing and I'm not going to fall for any more of your sick scenarios!"

"Maybe not for now," the fake Grace smiled. "But I think after a few years of excruciating physical pain, your mind will latch onto any hope we give it. Until then—" She blew me a kiss. She then took both of her hands and pulled open her jaw, like a snake. Out of her mouth came a familiar sight. The purple arm of a demon. It peeled Grace off like a rubber suit and tossed the skin off the roof.

I closed my eyes and waited for the monster to rip me limb from limb.

TIME WORKS DIFFERENTLY in Hell so it's impossible to determine how long I endured the physical torments. Hellfire may sound like a cliche, but it's certainly effective at inflicting unimaginable agony. Somehow, the demons always knew when my body began to grow accustomed to the pain and would switch tactics to psychological torture. I experienced sights and sensations that I have no interest in recalling in detail. If I could, I'd erase the entire experience from my memory.

In all that time, I never could get that demon's words out of my head. *You are a blight on my happiness. A burden on my life.* It was my fault that Grace got pulled into this mess, my fault that she had been killed. I told her that the forces of Heaven and Hell weren't enough to keep us apart, but maybe she had been right about our wedding being a sign. Maybe I had been trying to force a life that wasn't meant to be. I was, after all, expressly forbidden to see her. If I had listened, Nelson would never have found us.

Nelson. *That sniveling rat.* We spent all that effort making ourselves untraceable, and then we showed up at the one place he knew I couldn't resist. He'd probably been watching Grace from the moment we burned our books, just waiting for us to arrive. If I had anything left to be thankful for, it was that Sonny had managed to protect Maya from my fate.

It was brilliant of Sonny to grab on to her soul like that. Once they were away from Nelson, hopefully he could go after Grace's soul. If he was fast enough, he may have been able to restore her to life. That is, if Nelson didn't manage to get her book too. Even if I had to spend eternity down here—which was looking more likely by the hour—I could at least hold on to the hope that Sonny might bring him to justice. We knew his identity now. The angels could catch him and put a stop to his plan. He would lose.

EVENTUALLY, THERE WAS a respite from the horrors and the flames. I found myself back outside, in a barren desert stretching on with not so much as a cactus on the horizon. I laid in the sand, wondering how long it had been since I first arrived. Had it been days? It could just as easily have been weeks. For all I knew, I could have been in the burning pits for decades. *No, it couldn't be that long.* I wouldn't accept it. I couldn't become lost in this place. After all, there was still a lingering hope that Sonny had been able to catch Nelson. Maybe after that, the angels would be so grateful that they'd help him to locate me. Surely there was another way to find me without the books. There had to be. Sonny wouldn't abandon me here. Not forever.

"And why wouldn't he?"

The voice came from behind me. It was nasally and smug. The sound of it filled me with a loathing I'd never experienced before. I whipped around to confront him.

"You," I growled.

"Don't tell me *you* forgot my name, too." Nelson smiled. It was a sinister expression on his face, grotesque to behold.

"You're not here," I said flatly.

"You've really started to lose your marbles, kid. You're out here talking to yourself, you can't tell real from not—and you're still under the delusion that help is coming for you. Sonny's probably too busy drinking his sorrows away, like he always does. And even if he did catch me, you really think he'd waste a single moment looking for you? No. He'd take his reward and forget you two ever met."

It had to be an illusion. He couldn't have known what I was thinking, unless I really had been talking to myself. But I'd have known… wouldn't I?

"Leave me alone," I told the illusion.

"Oh, pardon me. Did I interrupt your eternal torture? You know, I'm the one who convinced them to let you out of the barbecue, so I think I deserve a little gratitude here."

"Gratitude?" I didn't care if he was real or not. I lunged at him. I wanted to rip his face off of his skull. He quickly opened a portal and sidestepped into it, leaving me to tumble to the ground. He emerged only a yard away.

"Yes, gratitude. After all, I'm your only hope of getting out of this joint."

I rolled onto my back, devoid of strength. "Says the asshole who brought me here."

"You didn't exactly leave me with a lotta options, Bill. You brought this on yourself when you took the prophet off the grid. I only needed one book! Is that too much to ask?"

"Oh, sorry for ruining your evil plan."

"I know you think I'm the bad guy, but you're not seeing the big picture. Yes, I threw you into Hell, and yes, I'm trying to instigate the end of the world, but I wouldn't do those things unless I had no other choice. I'm not heartless."

"Do you even hear yourself right now?"

"It sounds wacky, I get it, but it's the truth. I don't want to leave you here to rot. You have nothing to do with any of this. You're completely insignificant." He said this like it was a compliment. "You're not my enemy here, *this* is the enemy!" He reached into his pocket and held out his reaper's list at arms length.

"So toss that in the fire, and yourself with it."

"It's this system, Bill. Don't you see? I'm sure Sonny told you all about us reapers. We weren't goodie two-shoes in life, so we became indentured servants in death. We're forced to do the angel's dirty work for centuries so we can earn enough tin to buy our way up."

"No offense, but I don't think there's any way up for you after all this."

"Oh, I'm well aware. There hasn't been a way up for me, for Sonny, or any of us reapers for some time now. That's because the system is rigged. As soon as the third apocalypse kicks into gear, then it's curtains for everyone else. Our contracts get torn and the pearly gates get locked, permanently."

"I can see why you'd want to speed that along," I mocked him.

"Speed it? Oh, Bill. Have you not read the books yet? You haven't noticed the signs?"

"Is this speech part of my torture?"

"The end is coming, faster than you'd believe," he continued, ignoring my jab. "I learned the truth months ago, while working a job. I popped in to nab a soul from a motorcycle crash on the side of the highway. It was a particularly grisly scene, so I hung around after to give it a look. Doing this job as long as I have leaves a man pretty desensitized to that sort of thing, you know?"

"I think maybe you're just a sick bastard."

"Anyway, I'm looking around, and I notice this woman in traffic, staring at me. Me! I wobbled back and forth, thinking that she must have been looking at the accident, but her eyes were fixed. This woman could see beyond the veil. I chatted her up and it turns out, she'd been seeing strange things for a while, ever since she'd become the next prophet. I was fascinated. I took it upon myself to befriend this woman, and so gain access to her knowledge."

"You're not coming off as sympathetic in this story."

"She had written shelves of books, on every piece of paper she could find. They filled her home until she resorted to writing on the walls. It would have taken years to read it all, but I never got the chance. You see, I uncovered a very special book that had long been banned from The Library of Eternity. It contained the ever-growing record of an angel, cast out from his home, and plotting his revenge ever since. I found The Book of—"

"The Devil, right? You found Lucifer's book? That's what you were going to say?"

Nelson leered at me. "Yes. I found Lucifer's book. It was nothing short of a revelation. I was engrossed in the narrative of his existence. So many things I'd never known—things the angels would never allow anyone to know. This whole place was built as a prison for him, but he'd been freed millenia ago. Some rogue angels managed to rewrite the rules of this dimension using a very special book. They got caught, of course, but not before creating a direct path for him to escape."

The reaper kneeled down to speak at my level, lowering his voice. "But the book didn't end there. The last chapter of the book has yet to be written, and I was left on a cliffhanger that would change every-thing. You see, he'd been busy. Do you get it now, Bill? I don't have another century to finish my quota. I doubt I have another decade. The end is coming far sooner than anyone realizes, and there's nothing anyone can do to stop it."

I still didn't fully believe that Nelson wasn't another elaborate illu-sion, but his story didn't sound made up. Why would a demon be telling me this?

"So," Nelson stood back up. "Seeing as Hell has always been an inescapable eventuality for me, I was left with two options: I could either wait idly and watch the world slowly crumble on its own, or I could take action to make sure I didn't crumble with it. Have you ever heard of the expression, 'It's better to rule in Hell than it is to serve in Heaven'?"

"Yeah, in movies, from villains."

"I'm not a villain. I did what anyone would do. You've been down here for a while now. Be honest, wouldn't you do anything to make your time here better? To stop the torture, the mind games? Or should I ask again, after you're a little crispier?"

I didn't answer his question, though it was valid. What would I have stooped to in order to make the pain stop? Nelson could see it in my eyes. He nodded, knowingly.

"Maybe you've pieced it together by now. If I could get the demons on my side, to follow me, then I could ensure a torture-free eternity for myself in the new Hell on Earth. You see, they're all very antsy waiting around for the apocalypse. As far as they know, it could be centuries from now. So, when I offered up the chance to kickstart it early, they didn't hesitate."

"What about the Nephilim?" I asked. "What were they supposed to get out of this?"

"That was easy. They just wanted new bodies. Poor bastards have been dead for thousands of years. I promised I'd find 'em a couple of fresh corpses if they worked as my middlemen. Someone to talk to the demons and round 'em up when it was time to come out. Nephilim are a lot more intimidating than myself—what with the half angel thing they got going on. And to be honest, I'm not very fond of coming down here. But for you, I made an exception."

"So, you came to see me personally so that you could gloat about your rise to power?"

"No, you twit. I'm here to offer you freedom. I already told you, I don't take joy in this. You don't deserve to be here. I just need a little something before I can set you free."

"You want me to run errands for you, in Hell?"

He smiled a thin, annoyed smile. "You and Sonny are just two peas in a pod, ain't ya? No, Bill. What I need from you is information."

"Read a book."

"Oh, believe me, I'm trying."

That caught my attention. He really did want something from me, which meant this was no illusion I was talking to. This was happening.

"What do you want with the lost books anyway?" I asked. "You don't need them to start your apocalypse. You've basically done that already."

"You're not wrong. My plan is almost to its fruition—a little faster than I intended, thanks to you and Sonny—but before I'm ready to pull the trigger, I need insurance. I'd like to think the demons will uphold their part of the agreement to let me exist peacefully in Hell without torture, but they are demons. I need power over them, and those books contain the forbidden knowledge of reality—including the schematics of this place. See, there's no such thing as magic. These illusions they keep inflicting upon you operate on some kind of written code, and like everything else, they can be rewritten. One book in particular—the very same book used to free Lucifer—contains that code. Once I'm able to shape Hell to my designs, it ceases to be Hell."

"For everyone, or just for you?"

"For anyone I like. Or anyone you like, if you're willing to cooperate. Like I said, the apocalypse is coming, and your pal Sonny is out of time. You can make things a lot easier on him. I just need to know how to find the prophet girl."

"Why would I know that?"

"Don't be asinine, Bill. I know you and Sonny figured out a way to track the prophets. It would've taken me months to find the girl on my own, and you two morons found her in a week. I don't want to hurt her; I just need the book. Once she agrees to give it to me, you will be freed."

I pulled myself off the ground and wearily stood in front of Nelson. "What about Widdick, huh? You had no problem hurting him."

Nelson stuck his chin up and turned his gaze away from me. "That was different. I was resigned to sneaking about his house, reading what I could, but when the old man got a good look at me, I had to take action. I wanted him alive, but those idiot Nephilim crashed the van—with you hot on our heels. I had to cut my losses."

"Cut your losses? Is that what you did with the woman too—the prophet before Widdick? I noticed you conveniently left that little tidbit out of your story." I stood up straighter, now standing tall over Nelson.

"I didn't kill her!" His voice was weaker. He sounded offended by my insinuation. "She was vital to me. I wanted her to help me with my plan, but she didn't understand. She burned her books, and herself with them. It wasn't my fault."

I could see the sincerity in his eyes.

"You really believe what you're saying, don't you? You think that you're just some down-on-his-luck guy, standing up to the system—that the lives you've ruined aren't your responsibility."

"Hey, I told you. The system is out to get me, and all us reapers. They're the real enemy!"

"But you're not fighting the system. You want to be part of it. You want to be the one calling the shots, and you're willing to condemn your own friends to do it."

"Aren't you listening to me?" he shouted. "We're already condemned!"

"All of you? How many reapers would fill their quota before Lucifer's army marched? Twenty? A hundred? But you want to hold them down, so that you can lift yourself up. You think you're doing what anyone would do because you think everyone is as selfish as you are. That's why you're down here, talking to me now. You thought that I'd give up my friends to save my own skin, but you were wrong—about me, about Sonny, about people. And we're going to stop you, because no matter how you spin it, you are the bad guy."

Nelson trembled. He was absolutely enraged. He wanted to hit me, teach me a lesson for talking to him that way, but he didn't. Instead, he took a deep breath and opened up a portal.

"We'll see how long you feel that way." He vanished, leaving me alone once more.

Within seconds, I could hear the distant sound of cackling demons all around me. They would be on me in less than a minute. I had nowhere to go, but I ran anyway. They would catch me, but they would have to work for it.

DAYS PASSED. My mind was shattering. I had difficulty remembering which parts of my life had been real. At one point, it occurred to me that my entire adventure in the afterlife could have been a fabrication. I could have died on my wedding day and gone straight to Hell. There was no Sonny trying to save me. I just invented him as some kind of coping mechanism. That made more sense than me actually turning into some kind of hero. Who was I to think I could have fought demons and stood up to angels? I was just Bill Baker, not even special enough for a middle name. I was least liked in every friend group and never loved in any relationship. Had Grace been the same? Certainly she had only settled for me. Like my parents, we were destined for a loveless marriage because I was the safe choice. I was average.

When a new portal eventually appeared, I figured Nelson had returned to finish what he started. But as the earthly light dimmed, I recognized someone else kneeling down to speak to me.

"Bill!" he shouted. "Come on! We gotta get outta here!"

He grabbed me by the collar and dragged me across the ground. As I passed through the portal, I looked back to see a horde of demons in pursuit. Then the opening closed, and they were gone. I laid there, staring up at the sky—bright blue. My brain still hadn't grasped what happened.

Sonny came into view, looking over me. "Bill? Can you speak? Can you move?"

I groaned and lifted my arm to touch his face. It felt cold and disturbingly squishy. I remembered the same sensation when I grabbed his hand for the first time.

"Sonny?" I asked in disbelief.

"It's me, buddy. Let's get you up."

He helped me to my feet as I took in my surroundings. We were back in Salado, back in the real world. Somehow, I was free.

"You're really here?" I asked, my voice raspy. "Everything—did it all really happen?"

"I don't know what you consider everything, but I'm here. You were down there for a while, Bill. It might take some time before you're back to your old self. Do you remember what happened?"

I did. In the midst of all the horrors I experienced, my memory had become cloudy and unreliable, but now it came flooding back. I didn't know how I could have doubted it.

"Nelson. It was Nelson. Sonny, we have to tell the angels—"

"Hey, hey—relax. It's already handled."

"What?"

"How do you think I found you? As soon as I got Maya to safety, I went directly to Haniel."

"But Grace—"

"Don't worry. I got Grace too. She's fine. I grabbed her before her body even got cold. She's back alive and walking around like it never happened."

I couldn't believe it. That was amazing news, better than I could have hoped for. After so much hardship, I was utterly stunned.

"Are you gonna be alright, buddy?" Sonny asked.

"I—Yeah. I think I am. I'm sorry, how did you say you found me?"

"Right, so I went to Haniel and told him everything. Turns out, the angels can monitor exactly what's going on in Hell. They nabbed Nelson and voided his contract. He'll be taking your spot in that horror factory any minute now. As a reward, the angels agreed to help me find you. And here you are!"

"It's really over," I said. "I'd almost lost hope."

"That's not even the best part. In light of everything I've done, the angels have agreed to honor my deal, and then some."

"You mean—"

"Yep. My quota is complete. I can finally move on, and I'd never have been able to do it without you."

Sonny hugged me, and in my weakened state, almost knocked me over. All of this news was so much to comprehend. It felt like the universe was correcting itself to make up for what I'd been through.

"There's still one more thing we have to do though." Sonny let go of me and looked serious all of a sudden.

"What is it?"

"I didn't want to tell the angels about Maya. Who knows what they might do to get a hold of those books she has? Trouble is, I don't know where she went. I want to tell her the good news, but I still can't track her."

"So she doesn't know? She must be terrified."

"She's running scared. I already checked her apartment, her parents—nothing. Can you think of anywhere she might have gone?"

"Well, shouldn't you still be able to—" I stopped. Of course I knew we could track her by using the connected soul inside *The Compendium of Ethereal Entities*, but Sonny would have known that. Something felt off.

"Shouldn't I be able to… what?" Sonny asked.

"Sorry, I lost it. Everything is still coming back to me, after being in that place. You'll just have to give me a second."

"Oh, right. Of course. Take all the time you need."

I stumbled over to a nearby bench and sat down. Sonny sat next to me and began fiddling his thumbs impatiently. It looked to be about midday, but there didn't seem to be anyone else around. Salado was small. I could see most of Main Street from that bench. Down the road to my left, a bridge crossed over the same creek where we killed our first demon. To my right, I could just make out a little candy store, with a huge assortment of jellybeans in the window display. I listened for the familiar sounds of construction on the nearby highway, but it was silent. Nothing but wind and chirping birds.

"Awfully cool today, isn't it?" I asked Sonny.

"I don't know, you were just in Hell. It gets pretty hot down there."

"You are right about that. You know, I just remembered—"

"You did?" he asked, enthusiastically.

"You asked me to start calling you by your real name now. Benito." I smiled.

He looked deflated. "That's right, thanks for remembering that. You keep trying to recall stuff so we can find Maya. I'll bet she's worried sick."

I didn't have much strength, but I summoned all that I could and shoved my hand into the soft decaying tissue in Sonny's neck. I ripped out his throat, revealing a red-haired, purple hide underneath. The buildings around me melted into black goo and the blue sky ignited in flames.

25

HERE WE GO AGAIN

THAT'S WHEN IT really hit me. I was never going to leave this place. I had come to this conclusion several times during my stay, but part of me always held onto a glimmer of hope that there would be some dawn to this endless night. That hope melted away with the fake blue sky. The sun didn't shine on Hell, and no dawns were coming.

The demons never gave the impression that they had been holding anything back, but I suppose they were disappointed that their latest ruse had failed. For the next few days, they really went into overdrive. Psychological torture was put on the backburner in favor of good, old-fashioned maulings. They didn't even seem like they were having fun anymore. Now, they were just mad.

Like my time in the fire pit, eventually the whole experience became tedious. This was my reality for the foreseeable future, and one day, some other kind of torture would replace the monotony of this one. There was no sense in fighting it.

The demons would often tag in fresh talent in order to give everyone a turn. It was astounding just how many shapes and sizes they came in. I preferred the larger bruisers who would just knock me senseless over the scrawny ones that liked to focus on scratching and biting, but beggars can't be choosers.

I was faced with one of these slashers when I once again heard that old familiar sound: another portal. Before the creature could react, a torrent of water rushed down on the both of us. The sensation was so alarming that it jolted my consciousness out of whatever stupor I had fallen into. I rolled over, drenched in something other than blood for the first time in ages. Next to me, the demon was pinned by the downpour, howling in agony.

That's interesting, I thought. *I wonder how they're able to simulate water in this dimension? It certainly can't be real. Some kind of oil, perhaps?*

Through the steam cloud that resulted, I could hear Sonny's voice shouting, "Bill!"

Great, I thought. *This again.*

He spotted me on the ground and rushed over. "Oh my God, it's you! Let's get you up." He extended his hand to me, but I swatted it away.

"No!" I shouted at him. "Get away from me!"

He was baffled. "Bill, it's me."

I got to my feet and attempted to retreat from him. I made it about five steps before he portaled in front of me.

"Stop it! I'm trying to save you!" he pleaded.

I took a swing at him, which he dodged easily. He grabbed me around the neck and placed me in a choke hold. I struggled against him with all my might, of which I had very little left.

"Will you settle down?" he said. "We have to go! Now!"

"Why won't you leave me alone?" I managed to groan with his arm over my windpipe.

"Because I'm your friend, you idiot. I won't abandon you here."

We stood only a few yards away from the boiling demon. The portal above it disappeared and the torrent of water ceased. The creature rose to its feet, even uglier now that most of its skin had melted off.

"We don't have time for this," Sonny said. He released his hold of me and opened a new portal. "Come on."

I stepped away from him, but hesitated to run. This was definitely another trick, but even an illusion would be a nice break from excruciating physical pain. It's not as if it could be worse than sticking around here. I took a chance and followed him through the portal, narrowly avoiding the melted demon's outstretched claw. It wailed in anger just before Sonny closed the passageway.

I STEPPED OUT into a dark field, surrounded by longhorn cattle. As far as illusions go, it was an odd choice of venue. I heard a rustling in the grass and turned to see myself, or my body, walking through the field. They weren't even trying to keep this convincing.

"Son of a bitch," the other me said. "You actually found him."

Sonny plopped down in the dirt and let out a deep sigh. "Yeah, took some doing too. How long was I down there this time?"

"I'd say about fifteen minutes."

"Fifteen?" Sonny said in disbelief. "I will never get used to that time shift."

My doppelganger examined me, wincing. "He looks like shit."

"Yeah, he tried to fight me off," Sonny panted. "Who knows what they did to him down there. Still, we should probably get him back to his old self, so we can get moving."

I looked back and forth between the two in total confusion. Maybe I'd finally lost my mind. I was left with even more questions when Sonny reached into the other me and ripped out the soul of a reaper. The empty body collapsed, and Josiah straightened his jacket.

"Damn," he said. "I forgot how much that stings."

"I don't understand," I muttered. "Why were—What is this?"

"We'll explain everything in a minute," Sonny answered. "For now, we need to get you back on your feet."

I looked down, concerned. "But I am on my feet."

Sonny grabbed me by the sternum and shoved me down into my own corpse. Everything went dark, and the next moment, I was gasping for life.

"Breathe," Sonny told me. "You're back, Bill. You're alive."

Could this still be an illusion? Old sensations suddenly permeated my body, things I never felt in Hell. I was desperately thirsty, starving, and groggy past the point of sleep. It didn't feel like torture, it felt like life.

"Am I really here?"

Sonny smiled. "Yeah, you're here." The sound of rustling grass and moaning cattle arose, growing nearer. "And you're not the only one."

Both Sonny and Josiah grabbed my arms and helped pull me up. I was wobbly on my feet, but the reapers kept me steady. Then, stepping out from the herd of longhorns, Maya and Grace appeared. I narrowed my eyes, still not ready to accept what I was seeing. Grace rushed over and threw her arms around my neck.

"I thought I'd lost you," she whispered to me.

Obviously, this couldn't be real. Still, feeling her embrace helped to soothe my aches and I tentatively allowed myself to hug her back. I was almost certainly embracing a demon in disguise, but the sensation was so warm and familiar that it made my heart swell. I shuddered in her grasp, savoring every instant before it all melted away again.

"You two were supposed to be getting some sleep." Sonny crossed his arms in disapproval. "We gotta move come sunrise."

"Sleep was never a possibility," answered Maya. "I figured I could at least catch Grace up on what she missed, make a proper introduction, and such. You know she's never seen a single anime? Isn't that crazy?"

Sonny puffed from his nostrils. "That's what you guys were talking about?"

"Amongst other things." Maya's smile faded when she got a better look at me. "Where did you find him?"

"He was in Hell," Sonny said. "It was just like we thought. Luckily, he was the talk of the town among the locals. It took some tracking, but they eventually led me to him."

"He was fortunate," Josiah said. "There are much worse places he could have been taken."

That snapped me to attention. I released Grace and wiped the tears from my face. "I'm sorry, fortunate?" With no one to lean against, I felt as if I could collapse, but I was fueled by defensive anger. "What's the goal with this charade? To convince me that Nelson did me a favor?"

He was unmoved. "Nelson could have dropped you off in outer space, or the center of the Earth, and there'd be no way to find you no matter how long we looked. He put you in a place where you're practically a celebrity, and news travels fast. Still, I will admit that ten hours in Hell does sound unpleasant."

I stumbled back. "Ten hours?"

"Maybe not for you. Time works differently in Hell."

I laughed. "Sure. I guess this is supposed to renew my hope, right? That there's still time for someone to come rescue me? Torturing a guy isn't fun if he's given up, huh?"

Sonny and Maya looked at each other, concerned. Grace put her hand on my shoulder.

"Bill, this is real. You're really here."

"Of course. I'm definitely here. So, while I'm here, let's have a change of scenery. Can we set this thing in Paris? I've never been, so you don't have to get all the details right."

"He's been down there too long," Josiah said. "His mind is warped. It could take days before he starts to trust his surroundings—if ever."

"I appreciate the commitment to the bit," I dismissed him.

"Maya," Grace said. "Is there anything we can do to help him? Anything in your head that can ease his mind?"

"I don't think so. I'm not sure the books deal with this kind of thing."

Sonny walked over and slapped me in the face. "You feel that? That was real. We're all real."

I slapped him back.

"Ow!" he yelped.

"Sonny, why did you slap him?" Grace asked.

"He slapped me!" Sonny defended.

"You slapped him first!"

"Well, I don't see anyone else doing anything!"

"That's enough," Josiah said. "If what you all told me is true, then we've already wasted enough time locating your friend. He's safe now. Whether or not he believes it can be dealt with later."

"What are we supposed to do now?" Grace asked.

"I'm going to speak with the angels, in person. Something is going on up there, and I'm going to find out what." With that, Josiah disappeared.

Though I was unmoved in my assertion that this was all an elaborate illusion, my interest was piqued. "What's that he said? Something going on with the angels?"

Sonny folded his arms. "What do you care? It's not real, right?"

"We tried to contact them," Grace answered me. "Like you did when you called inside your head, but no one answered. So, either your angel friend is away from his desk—"

"Or they're not taking our calls," Sonny finished.

"So I take, in this little skit, Nelson is still at large for some reason?" I asked.

"Yes," they all said in unison.

"Okay. I think I'm following, but there's still one thing I can't figure out. Why am I not wearing pants?"

It was the strangest element of the illusion, more so than the herd of longhorns. My lower body was only covered by one of the jackets I'd left in my truck, tied around my waist. It draped in front of me, revealing my bare ass to the cattle behind me.

"You might've," Maya began. "Um—"

"You shit yourself again," Sonny finished.

"Ah. Of course. You guys are really going for realism in this one."

"We can get you some new pants at my parents house," Grace said. "It's still trashed, but it's empty for now."

"Yes," Sonny said. "And we should leave as soon as possible. I don't want to be here when some farmer notices we drove a truck through his cornfield."

GRACE SAT ON my lap in the three seater pick-up while Maya took the wheel. Sonny sat in the middle, pouting because he hadn't been allowed to drive. I was beginning to have doubts that I was still in some elaborate simulation. It was too specific, too weird. Still, I refused to let my guard down. Any time someone asked me a question, I remained silent, just in case that information would somehow benefit Nelson.

"Grace," I whispered.

She turned to look at me. "Hm?"

"Suppose I might be considering the possibility that this isn't all an illusion—and I really did make it out of Hell. If I was only there for ten hours, how long did it take for Sonny to get you out?"

Her expression turned warm, relieved to hear me engaging. "I was never taken to Hell," she whispered back. "I was thrown somewhere in the ocean. Sonny came and found me after a few minutes."

That should have been a relief, but I couldn't help feeling a tinge of jealousy. I'd happily take years in the ocean over what I'd received.

"What about your soul?" I asked. "Did Sonny—"

"Don't worry," Sonny leaned over. "We already burned her records. We grabbed her book as soon as I pulled her out of the water."

"A whole geyser of ocean water followed them back through the portal," Maya added. "That's when I got the idea for Sonny to use his portal as a giant water canon—in case he ran into any demons while looking for you. According to the info in my head, water and fire exist equally in the spiritual and physical planes, so they can pass through the veil. Cool, huh?"

"What about you?" I asked Maya. "What did you do while all this happened?"

"Well, after we lost Nelson in that corn field, Sonny reached out to that Josiah guy for help."

"And he just agreed?" I asked. "No conditions?"

"He was nice," Maya smiled. "At least, once Sonny told him I was a prophet. He had a lot of questions—made me do the human-encyclopedia bit, but he agreed to hold my soul until Sonny got back with Grace. Then, he possessed your body when Sonny went to look for you—you know, so it didn't suffer any prolonged brain damage. Turns out, bodies are pretty inconvenient."

I actually cracked a smile, agreeing. Then, the smile turned into a gasp of terror. Maya slammed on the brake and we all jerked forward. Sonny was, once again, flung from the car. He rolled over a few times, stopping at the foot of an angelic figure standing in the middle of the road. The reaper looked up to see great black wings silhouetted against the rising sun. I leaned forward to better see out the windshield and was startled to find Ansiel glaring back at me.

The road was still empty and fields stretched beyond sight. Ansiel folded his wings into his neatly pressed suit, leaving not so much as a wrinkle.

"Good to see that you're back on your feet, Mr. Butler."

"Who the hell is Mr. Butler?" Grace asked.

"Ugh, I think he's talking to me," I said. I opened the door and followed Grace out of the truck. Sonny pulled himself up and angrily dusted off his cardigan before rejoining us.

"I believe I gave you explicit instructions not to visit Ms. Evans again," Ansiel spoke. "And now it seems you've pulled another unsuspecting groupie into your entourage."

Maya lurched forward, held back by Grace. "Hey! I'm no groupie, bird brain!"

Ansiel rolled his eyes. "Humans, charming as ever."

It occurred to me, the way he dismissed Maya, that the angel had no idea what she was. If he had known he was speaking to the last prophet, he'd likely be far more interested in her.

"How did you find us, Ansiel?" I asked. "Did Josiah speak to you?"

"As a matter of fact, he did—though he refused to give up your location. Thankfully, the reaper has yet to join your little book burners cult, and it was a simple matter to track his last jump point and watch from the sky."

"Then you know everything," I said. "You'll help us stop Nelson."

"Actually, I've come here to stop *you*."

We all looked at each other, confused.

"Stop us from what?" I asked.

"From all of it. All your running around America, causing havoc, and trying to prevent something that shouldn't be prevented."

I squinted at the angel, speechless. Luckily, Sonny was not.

"You slimy son of a bitch, you're working with Nedry, aren't you?"

"It's Nelson," Maya corrected.

"Whatever."

"You're failing to see the bigger picture here," Ansiel said. "Rest assured, I'm not in league with that rogue reaper—though I must admit, I admire his ambition. He's doing more good for the world than most mortals could dream of. He's putting an end to the apocalypse."

"Okay, back it up," Sonny said. "You got your wires all crossed. We're the ones trying to end the apocalypse, not him."

Ansiel shook his head softly. "I'm going to let you all in on a little secret that most angels don't like to admit. The war between Heaven and Hell is not predetermined. True, we like to boast of the inevitable victory over Lucifer's forces, but when it comes down to it, Lucifer wouldn't be amassing an army in the first place if he had no hope of winning. That's the state of things. Lucifer possesses a very real chance of defeating the angelic forces, and that would be very unfortunate for all beings in the universe."

Even Sonny was stunned to silence. It was Grace who managed to step forward. "But that can't be. Surely your boss would step in—"

"Use your brain, girl. The Powers that Be, in whatever form They may take, do not interfere in the affairs of Their creation. They would idly watch as Lucifer slaughtered every angel in existence just as They allow your kind to murder each other with abandon. This isn't even the only Earth! There are limitless realities for Them to shift their attention to if this one goes belly up. In the end, we can only rely on ourselves."

It was a heartbreaking thing to hear from an angel of all beings, but I was beginning to understand where he was going. "So, if Nelson succeeds," I said, "then the war would start early, and Lucifer would be caught off guard. It's a guaranteed victory for you."

"Precisely. So, it's true that I could help you. I could rip up Nelson's contract and strip him of his reaper status without even having to track him down, just as I could have destroyed Sonny's when we thought him to be the culprit. But I didn't then, and I won't now. To do so would be to put both of our worlds at risk. Is that what you want? To postpone the inevitable, only to lose everything?"

I looked over at Grace and Maya, I could see the doubt on their faces. Ansiel was making a lot of sense. This whole thing ended up way more complicated than I ever imagined. Then, I looked to Sonny, the man who dove head first into Hell in order to pull me out. I knew what I had to do. I trudged towards Ansiel and dropped to my knees. "I guess this is it then," I told him. "Do it."

The angel raised an eyebrow. "Do what?"

"You said you're here to stop us. Do it then. Kill me."

Grace stepped forward. "Bill! What are you doing?"

I ignored the question, looking Ansiel directly in the eyes. "Did you think you could just come and stop me with a chat? I already defied your instructions once. What makes you think I'm going to listen now?"

"I am telling you to do the right thing, for the greater good."

"You're telling us to do nothing, but you know full well that when the apocalypse starts, Sonny is already condemned."

Ansiel became noticeably irritated. "I suppose for services rendered, and your cooperation, Sonny has more than earned the right to move on. Consider his quota fulfilled—*if* you agree to my terms"

I heard Sonny let out a small gasp behind me. That was a big deal for him. It was everything he'd been fighting for, but it still didn't sit right.

"And what about the other reapers? Josiah helped us when we needed him."

"Oh, do be practical, won't you?" Ansiel spat. "I'm being exceedingly generous about letting one reaper off his leash, you can't very well expect me to exonerate all your friends."

"I'm not talking about just our friends. I only really know three reapers. One is a sociopath bent on ending the world—I'll give you that—but the other two are good men. Even if only one out of every three souls is good, who am I to condemn them all?"

"So instead, you would condemn every soul in existence?"

"No—I would *fight* for every soul. I would fight so that everyone, even Nelson, could have a chance for redemption."

"Have you heard nothing I said?" Ansiel shouted. He reached down and grabbed me by my collar, lifting me to his level. "We could lose!"

"We could win!" I argued, dangling in his grasp. "You've spent all your days in paradise and somehow, you lost hope for the future. So, go to Hell, where hope is the only thing that gets you by."

My friends stared at me, bewildered. I felt good. Terrified, but good.

Ansiel narrowed his eyes and smirked. "And what does Sonny have to say about all this?" He let me drop back down to my feet. "Would you let this insignificant man take away your one chance at freedom?"

Sonny looked down, contemplating. He let out a sigh and walked over to stand beside me. "He's pretty fucking significant to us. And you, sir, can eat a dick."

Ansiel's nostrils flared. He adjusted his tie, even though it had never shifted out of place. "Am I to assume you all feel this way?"

Grace and Maya glanced at each other. Maya nodded, and Grace hesitantly followed suit.

"For what it's worth," Ansiel said, "I'm not afraid of getting my hands dirty. If I were permitted, I would squeeze the life out of each and every one of you." Ansiel's wings erupted from his back. The wind swirled around us like a tornado. His voice echoed in all our heads. "It makes no difference. You will fail, Bill Baker, and you condemn all your friends to the same fate." Then, with one enormous flap of his wings, we were knocked to the ground. The wind dissipated, and he was gone.

"You know," I said as I picked myself back up. "I'm starting to think this might all be real. I thought for sure the illusion would crumble after that."

Grace walked around and punched me in the shoulder.

"Ow! What was that for?"

Her eyes were bulging. "What did you do?"

"I don't know! What did I do?"

I thought she was going to slap me again, but instead she grabbed my face and kissed me as passionately as she ever had. Maya turned away awkwardly, and Sonny coughed into his fist. Grace released me, but looked no less freaked out.

"I can't believe you said those things to an actual angel."

"I'm confused. Are you mad at me?"

"No, I'm terrified for you. For all of us. I don't know if you did the right thing. I mean, I guess you did, but Jesus, Bill. That's a huge risk to take."

"I know." My eyes dropped. "I probably should have consulted with everyone before I said all that, but that guy really gets on my nerves."

"I'm just impressed," Sonny said. "If anyone was going to doom humanity to spite some prick angel, I thought it would be me."

"Humanity is not doomed," I said. "We may have to deal with a… larger problem in the future, but for now, we just need to focus on the problem that lies ahead. We have to stop Nelson."

Sonny pulled me into a hug. "It's good to have you back, man."

"I don't know if I'm fully back, yet." I stumbled, feeling light-headed. "It's sort of hitting me in waves."

"Well, either way, you're right. We've gotta stop that weasely little shit, but I think our best hope to do that just fluttered away."

"Don't be so sure!" A voice arose in the field to the side of the road. From behind a tree, surrounded by cows, Haniel stepped into the open. He clumsily crawled over a wooden fence and strutted triumphantly toward us.

Grace put her hands on her temples. "Where are all of these people coming from?" she asked, rhetorically.

Haniel answered enthusiastically. "I work in the The Library of Eternity, as an administrator. I don't really get down to Earth much, but I must say, it's absolutely wonderful to be here in person again. Last time I visited, it must have been during the reign of Constantine."

"Haniel," I addressed him. "Why are you here?"

"Because, Mr. Baker, I am an optimist. And as an optimist, I simply cannot condone the course of action that my superiors have chosen. Allowing such a heinous crime to occur in the name of good intentions—it goes against everything I believe in."

I grinned. "So you're going to tear up Nelson's contract?"

"Oh, heavens no—they would never allow me access."

I frowned. "Then what are you going to do?"

"Provide moral support, of course," he grinned.

26

THE WAR ROOM

WE HAD TO move quickly. Nelson was still seeking the books, but now that I was free from his prison, there was a very real possibility that he would forgo his insurance policy and unleash the rest of the demon hordes upon the Earth.

Haniel agreed to join us at Grace's parents' house to help formulate a plan. One would assume that he would fly ahead using his supernatural wings, but he opted to sit in the truck bed—as all the other seats were taken. The angel didn't mind at all. In fact, he was fascinated by the whole experience of riding in a human car. He looked over every side of the vehicle as the road raced by, grinning like a child.

We soon arrived at the dilapidated home of Grace's parents and climbed underneath the police tape. Haniel pulled Sonny to the porch, presumably to apologize for blaming the entire apocalypse on him, while I broke away to retrieve a pair of pants from Frank's closet.

After securing the oversized garment with a belt, I inspected myself in the mirror, looking less like a heroic figure in my mismatched outfit than I'd hoped. I noticed Grace enter in the reflection of the mirror and smiled as she approached. She smiled back, right before revealing a long kitchen knife and reaching around to slice my throat. I yelped, falling backwards onto the bed and grasping at my neck. I was fine. Looking around the room, Grace was nowhere to be seen. I heaved heavy breaths, hunched over on the edge of bed, trembling uncontrollably. It was just in my head. I was free of that place…*wasn't I?*

I took a moment to regain my composure. The world hadn't melted away, which was a good sign. Perhaps if I got some food in my stomach, I would feel a little better. I heard Maya rummaging through the cabinets as I entered the kitchen. Grace sat down at the small breakfast nook and sipped on a diet soda she'd found in the fridge, all the while staring at the hole in the wall where she'd fired a shotgun blast though my head a week prior.

I sat down beside her, ripping open a sleeve of fig bars that Maya had tossed onto the counter.

"How you doing?" I asked.

"I should be asking you that question." She offered a tense smile. "After everything you've been through."

"Oh, I'm terrible," I said, only half-joking. The vision of murderous Grace still fresh in my mind. "I don't think there's enough therapists in the world to fix my problems, and that's assuming this is even the real world."

"Still don't believe us, huh?"

"I think I do. Though, if I'm being honest, everything has felt like a walking dream since our wedding."

"God. The wedding." Grace rested her face in her open hand. "We should be getting back from our honeymoon about now."

She looked exhausted, worn down by the unending barrage of stress that had beat against her since the first day we were plunged into this chaos. I used to worry that I wouldn't offer the kind of excitement in life that she deserved, but now it was hard to imagine a future that wasn't plagued by constant threats. If anything, I feared that the excitement of my life exceeded anything she was prepared to deal with.

"You know," I said, "you don't have to do this anymore."

"Oh believe me, I have no intention of riding off into battle with the three of you."

"No, I just meant—"

Maya shuffled over with an armful of snacks, splaying them on the breakfast nook and tearing through boxes and bags. "God, I'm starving," she said. "I'm convinced these prophet powers burn up my energy like The Flash." She bit through a solid hunk of dry ramen noodles.

Grace and I smiled at one another, silently agreeing to continue this conversation at another time. "You know," Grace said to Maya, "the power still works. I can heat up some water for that."

"Take too long," Maya managed to reply with her mouth full.

Haniel finally entered the living room through the gaping opening in the wall and stepped up on the coffee table with a massive book in his hands. "If everyone is ready, we don't have a lot of time, and I'd like to go over the plan."

Maya and I brought our respective snacks with us as we flocked to the couches. Sonny leaned against the wall, his arms crossed. Once we were gathered, the angel stepped down and laid the book on the table. He opened it to the center page, revealing a familiar map of the United States with red concentric circles emanating from the Midwest.

"I know this book," I said.

"Yes," Haniel began. "Josiah mentioned your discovery in The Library, and I was able to locate it. For the rest of you—this is a book that tracks climate patterns around the planet. Those red circles on the map indicate unusual heat waves, and these—" He turned the page to reveal a similar map with yellow circles over the same region, "—indicate rainfall, or lack thereof."

"Well, we are in a drought," Grace said.

"Yes," Haniel replied. "And as Mr. Baker has correctly surmised, the conditions of this drought are not natural. In fact, using this book, we can pinpoint the exact coordinates it appears to be emanating from, and thus—put a stop to the cause."

"That's exactly what we were planning on doing before everything went haywire," Sonny said. "Is that all you brought for us? Directions to the hell-mouth?"

"While I'm sure I have no idea what a 'Hell-mouth' is," Haniel shook his head, "I do have a theory as to what does exist at this origin point."

"You've never seen *Buffy the Vampire Slayer*?" Maya asked the angel.

"Buffy the—This is a… person?" Haniel twisted his face in confusion.

"We thought the origin point might lead to a fissure of some kind," I explained, "possibly to Hell."

"Like in the TV show," Maya finished.

"I see," Haniel claimed, still visibly confused by the reference. "But I don't believe any such fissure exists. Crossover junctures are possible, but they wouldn't have as profound an effect on the Earth's atmosphere. It is my belief that we are dealing with a specific entity of enormous power, as described here." Haniel closed his large book of maps and slammed another book down on top of it. When he removed his hand, he revealed a pocket-sized Bible.

"Is that a, uh—magic Bible?" I asked.

"No. Believe it or not, there's only one copy of every book in The Library of Eternity, and I was not going to risk damaging ours. I bought this one at a local supermarket."

Maya cocked her head. "Do angels carry money?"

"I don't really need to carry anything. If it's a mundane item, I usually just have it when I need it. Like this."

He held up his hand, which was now grasping an enormous wad of cash. Maya's eyes went wide and she gingerly reached for the money, doing her best to appear nonchalant about it. "I'll just hold onto this," she said, stuffing the cash into her cat-shaped backpack.

"You couldn't have just summoned a Bible the same way?" I asked.

"Books are different. Even the most widely distributed text still bears a small piece of the soul who wrote it. I also can't do electronics, but that's only because I don't understand them."

I nodded, wondering if my car manual had a soul attached to it.

Haniel opened up the Bible to a section he had earmarked and began to read aloud. "*Behold now Behemoth, which I made with thee; he eateth grass as an ox.*"

We stared at him, expecting more.

"Sorry," he said. "I only marked the first time it's mentioned. The creature isn't discussed much in this book, but it does go on to say that the Behemoth consumes rivers—which I forgot to mark. I'm not used to these confounding Earth books." Haniel closed the Bible and tucked it into his suit jacket. "However, it is further described in the Book of Enoch and in the Haggadah. I would have brought them, but for some reason, they don't sell those in the supermarket."

"It's really fine. We'll just take your word for it," I assured him.

"Well, the gist of it is," Haniel continued, "the Behemoth is a primal monster that lives in a great desert and reaches the peak of its power during the summer months. Its counterpart, the Leviathan, lives in the sea and the two are destined to do eternal battle until the end times—and so on and so forth. The point being, the Behemoth is a force of nature, powerful enough to push back the seas and dry out the air. If unleashed before the Leviathan, it's more than capable of causing a global drought."

Grace sheepishly raised her hand.

"Yes!" Haniel said. "Ms. Evans?"

"Forgive me, I'm still catching up—and I'm just going off of what they've explained to me—but what does a drought monster have to do with this demon invasion? Is this evil reaper just releasing every monster in Hell?"

"It's the water," Sonny answered her. "Water burns demons on contact. Nestor clearly realized the key flaw in the movie *Signs* and realized he needed to make the Earth more livable to his demons. He probably brought this Behemoth thing here months ago to start the process. That's why the demon attacks began in the heart of the drought. Now they're starting to spread all over the country without so much as a drizzle to fear."

"And very soon, they'll spread to the entire world," Haniel finished. "Once they go global, we angels have standing orders to invade, and the war between Heaven and Hell will officially begin."

Silence overtook the room as we contemplated the enormity of the situation.

Maya and I looked mournfully at each other. Grace was the first to speak.

"*Signs*, as in that movie where the kid could see ghosts?"

"No," Sonny replied. "That's *The Sixth Sense*."

"Yeah, *Signs* had aliens and crop circles," Maya added. "It wasn't as good."

"Whoa, hold on now," Sonny objected. "I happen to think that *Signs* is an underrated gem in M. Night's filmography. It wasn't until *The Village* that he started going downhill."

"You didn't like *The Village*?" Maya asked.

"It was fine, I just didn't buy the twist at the end. If the father knew about the outside world, wouldn't he have just kept medicine available in town, in case of emergencies?"

"Guys," I interjected.

"But he didn't want any modern technology in the town!" Maya ignored me. "What if someone had found a prescription bottle and pieced together the truth?"

"He could put the medicine in a mason jar and say it comes from a special plant, or something. These people believe in forest monsters. They aren't hard to fool."

"Alright—fair, but I think we can both agree that his real downfall came with *Lady in the Water*."

"I, uh," Sonny stammered, "I kind of like *Lady in the Water*."

Maya and Grace shouted in unison. "What?!"

"It's a modern fairy tale!"

"Guys!" I screamed. "Can we please get back to the plan?"

They all shut up and looked expectantly at Haniel—except for Haniel himself, who looked expectantly at me.

"Well, Haniel?" I asked.

"Oh! Yes! I'm the one with the plan. Where was I?"

"Behemoth," we all said together.

"Right. The Behemoth is likely the cause of our unusual weather patterns. If it were destroyed, the rains would presumably return. Nelson won't be able to enact his plan worldwide, thus preventing the apocalypse."

"How long will it take for the rain to return?" I asked.

"Not sure, I'm not a meteorologist. Fairly soon if I can enlist some assistance from the fellows in the Climate Department."

"Wait," Grace said. "There's an entire department for angels who control the weather?"

"Not as intricate as all that. Angels are forbidden from overtly interfering in the natural state of affairs on Earth. The department is only authorized to give the weather a bit of a nudge, lightning bolts here or there, pushing a storm a couple of degrees north or south, that kind of thing."

"And you think they'll be willing to do something like this for you?" I asked.

"I do," Haniel confirmed. "They get really, really bored in the Climate Department. I suspect they'd be willing to bend the rules for little more than a dare."

"Perfect. So we just need to kill this Behemoth thing and let Haniel's friends handle the rest!" I exclaimed.

Finally, we had a real plan that could actually put an end to this nightmare. I felt a small portion of anxious dread fade away, and as I looked across the faces of my friends, I could see hope returning to them as well. The only face that remained concerned was Sonny.

"What's wrong?" I asked him.

"He's not telling us everything. Are you, Haniel?"

Haniel's smile sagged a little. "Well, there is a minor thing. The Behemoth is said to be invincible to human weaponry. Water likely won't make it vulnerable as it does to demons. And even if it did, the water would just evaporate before touching the monster's skin."

My face sagged too. "So then, how do we kill it?"

"Perhaps Sonny could open a very large portal? Put it back into Hell?" Haniel offered, as a real suggestion.

Sonny laughed. "Sure I can! And would you mind telling us how big this monster is supposed to be?"

The angel mumbled almost inaudibly. "...Roughly three to five stories."

"Three to five stories!" Sonny announced. "Yeah let me just whip up a portal the size of a department store real quick. Never mind that it'll see what I'm doing—I'm guessing around the five-minute mark—and easily step out of the way."

"It was just a suggestion! Do any of you know how to kill an ancient Hell-beast?" Haniel asked rhetorically, positive that we wouldn't answer. Maya did.

"An angel's primary means of defense is the wings. Allowing them to fly through the veil that divides realities, angel wings can also provide protection from both spiritual and Earthly threats. The layered feathers are tough enough to withstand a blow from any known force. In addition, there is nothing deadlier than an angel feather. Reaching up to four feet in length, a single feather can pierce through any hide, and is the only weapon capable of inflicting damage on another angel." Maya shook her head and began rapidly blinking. Haniel was staring at her, mouth agape.

"Sorry," she said. "I spaced out for a second. Could you repeat that?"

"It's you," Haniel said softly. "You're the prophet." He turned to look at me. "You said the prophet was an old man. A dead one!"

I had grown very protective of Maya during the short time I'd known her and felt uncomfortable acknowledging her identity to an angel, even if it was Haniel. "She became the new prophet when the professor died. Listen, you can't tell anyone about her."

"But she holds a vast wealth of information missing from The Library! If we could extract the books—"

"Haniel!" I yelled. "No one can know. There's no telling what the angels would do to get that knowledge out of her head, or how they would use it afterward. The books were taken from The Library for a reason."

"Plus," Sonny added, "if you mention her to anyone, we'll tell your boss that you went behind his back to help us."

"You're going to blackmail me? An angel?" Haniel was aghast.

Sonny and I looked at each other and shrugged. "Yeah."

Haniel crossed his arms and pouted. "Fine. But I want partial access. If I need information that could potentially save the world, I expect cooperation."

Sonny and I looked at Maya, whose eyes had been ping-ponging back and forth throughout the conversation. "Uh, that seems fair?" she agreed.

"Great!" Sonny exclaimed. "Now, time to fork over the feather."

"I beg your pardon?" Haniel's eyes went wide.

"You heard the lady," the reaper said. "Angel feathers can pierce through any hide. Let's have one."

"Oh, um—yes. I, uh—I suppose she did s-say that," Haniel stammered. "I won't say the idea hasn't crossed my mind. I had hoped, perhaps, there might be another way to battle the beast. Do you have any information on that, Ms. Kabua? Any other way?"

He looked expectantly at Maya, who slumped. "Did it work? Did I say anything?"

"What's wrong with the feather idea?" I asked. "Why do we need an alternative?"

Haniel frowned. "Do you recall, when we first met in my office, Mr. Baker? I said that if you failed to discover a method for facing the demons, I had a potential plan B?"

"I take it, you're referring to this?"

"Well, hold on," Sonny butt in. "You knew these feathers could kill demons all along? Why wasn't that Plan A? You made it sound like Plan B was some horrible, last-case-scenario type of thing, like a meteor or a plague—or something"

"This is a last-case-scenario type of thing," Haniel said. "Angel feathers are the most powerful weapons in the universe. Handing one over to a mortal—even for the sake of the Earth—is no easy decision."

"I know it's been a while since you've been to Earth," Sonny said. "But you do realize that humans have made nuclear bombs and shit, right?"

"Nuclear bombs can wreak physical devastation, but they do very little to the fabric of the universe. Angel feathers are the only weapons capable of eradicating a being, body and soul."

"And *soul?*" I asked, bewildered. "As in, no more afterlife? Just nothingness?"

The angel nodded.

Sonny shook his head. "That can't be right. Maya explicitly said that souls can't be destroyed. Not without—"

"Divine intervention," Haniel finished. "Angels fall under that umbrella, I'm afraid. During the great war, when an angel was lost in battle, there were no second chances. It's why the Fallen had to be stripped of their wings once they were defeated. If even one of these feathers found their way into the wrong hands, the results could be catastrophic."

"Do we have another choice?" I asked.

Haniel became silent. We all knew the answer.

IT TURNS OUT, Haniel was right to be weary. With no other options, he agreed to bestow one of his feathers to us. We cleared some space and he allowed his left wing to emerge from his jacket, launching with enough force to burst through the living room wall. Slightly panicked by our reaction, Haniel began spinning around the house, his wing still outstretched. The outer feathers scraped across the room, tearing through picture frames and shredding what remained of the furniture.

When we finally managed to calm Haniel down, we still had to physically pluck the feather from his wing. It was no easy task. Even with all our strength—minus Grace, who refused to touch it—we couldn't pull a single feather loose. Worse still, if we squeezed too tightly around the edges of the feather, it sliced our hands. It wasn't until Haniel offered to give it a try that the feather popped loose at his touch.

"There," he said. "That wasn't so bad."

I looked around at the utter destruction of the house and my exhausted friends' bloodied hands. Haniel folded his wing back in and handed me the shimmering white plume. It was nearly three feet long and straight to a sharp point. The stem of the quill was just the right size to grip firmly with one hand and the whole thing was as light as— well, a feather. It felt perfectly designed to be wielded as a weapon, and I was extremely uncomfortable to be the one holding it.

"Is there a—uh, a sheath I can put this in?"

"Wrap it carefully in a cloth," Haniel said. "And don't swing it around. One false move could be your last."

I gingerly set the quill down on the table, nervous just to be standing near it.

"Okay, my friends," Haniel clapped his hands together. "I believe you have the tools you need to get the job done. I've given Sonny the coordinates of the beast to track with his list. I'll get to work on the rain as soon as you've finished the job. Good luck to all of you."

He was about to unleash his wings again, but stopped himself. "Perhaps I should step outside." He walked to the hole in the wall and looked at us one last time before exiting. "Oh, and Sonny! Don't forget what we discussed earlier, about Neil."

Sonny laughed. "Do you mean Nelson?"

Haniel shrugged. "Whatever."

27

BOSS FIGHT

THERE WERE THREE of us on the road to potential annihilation. Grace remained behind, but had provided us with the entire contents of her father's gun safe, which we loaded into the back of the truck. I wasn't sure we would actually need any weapons beyond the soul-slaying angel feather, but it was always better to be safe than sorry. I suggested that Maya stay with Grace, seeing as both women were untraceable to Nelson now, but Maya insisted that she may be able to offer crucial on-the-fly prophet wisdom during the battle. She also proposed the possibility that she might enter a trance and kill the monster single-handed, while Sonny and I "bask in her glory".

In spite of the task that lay ahead of us, the young prophet was chatty in the middle seat of the truck, as if the possibility of utter defeat hadn't even occurred to her. Her upbeat attitude even helped to settle my own nerves as she recounted how much she felt like a protagonist in a video game—on their way to face their biggest foe yet. Oddly, the least talkative person in the car was Sonny, who offered little more than the occasional smile at Maya's enthusiasm. Eventually, she tapped my leg and nodded over to the brooding reaper, having finally noticed his dour mood.

"Hey, man." I glanced over at Sonny. "You okay?"

He straightened up, pretending that he hadn't slowly been slumping into his seat for the entire drive. "Yeah, why wouldn't I be?"

"You're being uncharacteristically quiet."

"I'm just psyching myself up. We're about to fight a monster, you know."

"And we'll kick its ass like we always do," Maya said.

"Alright, calm down Van Helsing," Sonny said. "You fought three demons. I wouldn't call you an expert yet."

"Oh?" She tilted her head. "And how many demons have you guys fought?"

"Four," I said, "Including the same three you did."

"Exactly," Sonny said. "None of us are qualified to take on something ten times the size."

I had to give him that. I was far more nervous about this encounter than I had been for our previous battles. Not so much for my well-being as for everyone else. I had already undergone pretty much the worst experience imaginable, so my own death barely registered on my list of concerns. Still, I sensed that Sonny's troubles were larger than the immediate conflict.

"Do you think we—I made the wrong choice?" I asked him. "Should I have taken Ansiel's deal? Free you of your contract and just step aside—allow the apocalypse to happen?"

Sonny took a few seconds to answer. "I think you did the right thing. It's the choice I wish I would make myself."

"But not the one you would have?"

"You know me, Bill. Probably better than anyone has known me—which is depressing, considering the time frame. I can know what the right decision is and still make the wrong one. That's how I ended up like this." He slipped off his glove and wiggled his decaying fingers around. "I'm selfish."

"You're too hard on yourself."

"Spare me. You know that if Ansiel offered me the same deal in private, I'd have taken it in a second—just like I took a deal to save my own neck on the gallows."

"The gallows?" Maya asked. Sonny's human past had not yet been revealed to her.

"Don't worry about it," the reaper told her.

I shook my head. "I don't know what choices you would have made, Sonny. What I do know, is that you had nothing to gain from leaping into Hell to find me. You've known me for a week and we weren't on the best of terms for most of that time. Still, you came for me. Doesn't sound selfish to me."

Sonny was quiet again for a moment. "It doesn't change anything. Part of me still wishes we'd taken the deal."

I let my head fall back against my seat rest, feeling disappointed and guilty. I believed we made the correct decision in rebuffing Ansiel, but it killed me that it came at the expense of Sonny's chance at salvation. Even if we succeeded in our mission, we'd pissed off a high-ranking angel. There was a chance that all of us would be condemned regardless.

"For what it's worth," Maya said, "I don't think it matters what you would have done alone. If it were just me, I'd probably have rotted away in Oklahoma for the rest of my life. There's nothing wrong with needing friends to make you stronger."

Maya held both of her hands up and alternated looks between us. I shook my head, smiling as I grasped her hand. Sonny rolled his eyes and did the same, prompting Maya to reflexively pull back.

"Sorry!" she said. "I didn't expect it to be so—"

"Oh God," Sonny said, quickly slipping his glove back on to protect her from his slimy flesh. "No, that's my bad."

He took her hand again and we all squeezed tight.

GIVEN THE ENORMOUS size of the Behemoth, I fully expected to see it towering over us as we approached the small roadside town. Instead, there were only a spattering of businesses and desert stretching on to the horizon

Maya stared out the window. "I know spirits are like—invisible to most people, but you'd think someone would notice a thirty-foot tall monster stomping around a populated area."

"It could be intangible," Sonny suggested. "That's probably why it hasn't crushed any buildings or cars when it walks."

"Still," I said, "we should be able to see it by now. Are you sure this is the right place?"

Sonny starred coordinates on his list. "Unless that book was out of date, the monster should be in that building up there."

Maya unbuckled her seatbelt and leaned forward to better see out of the windshield. "You're joking."

"Which building?" I asked.

Sonny leaned forward and pointed at the one-story, innocuous-looking Chinese restaurant, sitting in the middle of an otherwise abandoned shopping strip.

As we approached the restaurant, Maya read the name aloud. "China King II. What does the two mean? Can a restaurant have a sequel?"

"I don't understand," I said. "How can this be it? Do you think the Behemoth is underground?"

"Maybe there's a basement that Nelson stashed it in," Maya suggested. "You have to admit. This is the last place anyone would look."

"You're not wrong," I admitted. "Okay, let's go check it out."

We shuffled out of the truck and gathered around the back to retrieve our armaments. From Frank's gun collection, we had our choice of two shotguns, some kind of assault rifle I couldn't believe was legal, a magnum, and two smaller pistols—all pre-loaded. In addition, we brought along our Super Soakers and the angel feather—tightly wrapped in a bath towel so that it didn't slice through our hands on accident. We knew the other weapons wouldn't hurt the beast, but they may be able to distract it long enough for one of us to get close and stab it. I felt most comfortable with the shotgun, but grabbed the magnum and one of the pistols as backup. Maya took the other pistol, but opted for the water gun as her primary weapon. Sonny eagerly reached for the assault rifle.

Lastly, I picked up the towel and carried it under my arm. After closing the tailgate, I noticed Sonny folding his arms and raising an eyebrow at me.

"What?" I asked.

"I know you think you're the big hero here, or whatever, but if someone has to get close to that thing, maybe it should be the only one of us who can't actually die."

"You want the feather?"

"Fuck no. But—" He closed his eyes and took a very deep breath. "It's probably the right move."

I flashed him a smile. "Aw, you do care."

"Don't make me regret it."

I handed him the towel-wrapped feather and the three of us stood in a row together outside of the China King II.

"Alright," I said. "Let's go."

THE INTERIOR OF the restaurant was not at all what I was anticipating. First, it was far nicer than the exterior suggested, with low lighting, ornate carpeting, and murals featuring Chinese landscapes and wildlife. Second, it was absolutely packed with customers. There wasn't a single vacant table in the room and yet, there were still dozens of people walking around the buffet who seemingly had nowhere to sit. It looked as if the entire population of the town had decided to eat here at this exact moment, which was especially troubling as I didn't recall seeing a single car parked outside.

We hid our weapons behind our backs and tried in vain to conceal them under our clothes. A young Chinese woman approached us, grinning.

"Hello. Have a seat. Anywhere is fine."

Now, it was possible that she was distracted by the heavy crowd, but there was clearly a shotgun barrel sticking out the back of my shirt and—as far as she was concerned—a floating towel and assault rifle beside me. She ignored these obvious red flags and zipped away to attend to another customer. The four of us looked at one another in complete confusion.

"I'm not crazy right? That was fucking weird," Sonny said.

"There's definitely something sinister about this place," I said. "Don't stray from the group."

"We should probably make our way to the kitchen," Maya suggested. "If there's a secret basement, that's where I'd hide it. What do you think, Bill?...Bill?"

My eyes had locked in on a face in the back of the restaurant. Sitting all alone with a bounty of food before him was a frighteningly gaunt man with a ghostly pallor. He wore a pinstripe suit with a large napkin tucked into his collar. As soon as he entered my field of view, I was overcome with the unshakable feeling that I'd seen him some place before.

"Bill?" Maya asked again.

"I know that guy."

"Which guy?" Sonny asked. "There are—like, a hundred guys."

The man at the table looked up from his meal and smiled at me, gesturing for us to come over. I walked towards him.

"Wait, what are you doing?" Maya whisper-shouted at me, but I was already disappearing in the crowd, forcing the others to follow.

I'm not fully sure why I approached on-command. I don't believe I was under any kind of trance other than unbearable curiosity. *Why was this man so familiar to me? And among all the other tables in the restaurant, why was he the only person sitting alone?* I weaved through the crowd and arrived at the gaunt man's table, with my compatriots at my heels.

"Mr. Baker," he spoke with a soft voice. "What a pleasant surprise. Sit, please."

From out of the crowd, the hostess reappeared carrying a chair and placed it in front of me. I looked to Sonny for a piece of silent advice, but he only shrugged in confusion. I decided to take the seat.

"Who are you?" I asked.

"In a moment, Mr. Baker. I believe your food is on its way."

"I didn't order—" But sure enough, the hostess returned with two large plates and set them on the table. It looked as if she had smushed some of every item from the buffet onto the two dishes, resulting in a repulsive spread.

"Something is fishy here," Sonny whispered to the group. "They're not supposed to serve you at a buffet."

Maya looked at him. "That's what you find fishy here?"

"There's no need for private conversation," the gaunt man told us. "I'm fully aware of how strange this all must seem. I apologize to the rest of you, but there don't appear to be any more seats. There is plenty of food however, so feel free to dig in. I'm sure Mr. Baker won't mind sharing."

"We're not hungry," I said.

"What a silly place to visit with no appetite." The man started devouring his sweet and sour chicken. Everything from his tailoring to his manner of speech indicated wealth and class, but the man ate like an animal. He shoved handfuls of chicken into his mouth, and anything that fell from his lips, he smashed into the next handful. When the chicken was gone, he politely dabbed his lips with a napkin. "Are you sure you won't have anything? It really has been one of the most satisfying meals I can recall."

I looked down at the plates, and though I was disgusted by the man's display, I had to admit, the food did look more appetizing than I previously thought. Still, we had a job to do.

"We aren't here to eat," I told him. "We're looking for something. Or someone."

"Well, there are lots of someones here today." The gaunt man smiled.

I scrutinized his face as he began to shove sugar-coated dough balls into his mouth. Sure, he was an unsettling sight, but could he really be the monster in disguise? We knew that demons were capable of possessing human bodies, but was it even possible for a beast of such immense size to be contained in such an emaciated frame? Perhaps I should have just shot him to play it safe, but instead I asked, "Are you the Behemoth?"

The man started coughing up his doughnuts. He composed himself enough to swallow the remainder and resumed chuckling. "I realize I may have put on a few pounds recently, but I don't think I ever expected to be called a behemoth."

Despite my certainty that the man in front of me was a supernatural creature of some sort, I still felt awkward about the confusion. "No, I—I didn't mean—You're not—"

"Please relax, Mr. Baker. I believe I know what you're asking, and why you are here. Rest assured. I am not this Behemoth that you seek."

Sonny placed a hand on my shoulder and leaned over me. "How do we know you're telling the truth?"

"Blind faith, I suppose," the man said innocently. "I don't blame you for doubting me. I'm not oblivious to my manner or appearance." He gestured to himself, only then noticing a glob of sweet and sour sauce on his lapel.

"Oh, dear," he said. "I do hope that hasn't set in." He removed the napkin from his collar, revealing a small bowtie underneath. As he dipped the cloth in a glass of water and began dabbing the stain, I suddenly recalled exactly where I recognized the man from.

"You were there, at the church," I said. "You helped me with my bowtie."

The gaunt man smiled. "Forgive me for gate crashing, but I can never resist a wedding when I'm able. I have a terrible weakness for cake, you understand. I took a few slices; I hope you don't mind. I was afraid it might become damaged in the onslaught to come."

I felt my ears become hot. My fingernails dug into the table. It took every effort not to reach over and strangle this man with my bare hands. It wouldn't be hard with such a spindly little neck. "Who are you?" I demanded.

"I've been called by a few names. My given name is Atys, though as my life fell into legend, I became known as Tantalus. More recently however, I've been given the rather apt moniker, Famine."

Sonny lifted his gun and aimed it squarely at the man. Maya followed suit with her decidedly less intimidating plastic weapon. No one else in the restaurant seemed to notice, or care.

"You're a horseman," the reaper announced.

"Terrible nickname, really." Famine shook his head. "It's been over a century since I've ridden a horse."

My eyes narrowed. "Where's the Behemoth?"

"Still roaming the deserts of Hell, I would imagine. That is unless our mutual friend Nelson has grown more ambitious in his dreams of destruction."

"No," I told him. "It has to be here. It's the only thing that could be causing the—" I paused, the truth dawning on me.

"Drought?" Famine asked with a wry smile.

The smell of the food in front of me was beginning to grow more intense and I could feel my stomach grumbling. I resisted the urge to reach for a bite. "It's you. Somehow, you're the one doing all this."

"One of the side effects of my condition, I'm afraid. Where I walk, the rains cease, the crops wilt, and the animals die. It's a long process now that humanity can ship food and water around the world, but eventually, all succumb to the famine."

I shook my head. "A mindless beast I understand, but you? What do you have to gain from helping Nelson start the apocalypse? Don't you know—"

"That it's doomed to end in the catastrophic defeat of the armies of Hell? I have no stake in that war, I can assure you. I am merely a harbinger for the end of days, but regardless of the outcome, my fate remains the same. I will return to the underworld and spend all of eternity in an anguish I am all too familiar with by now. If some young troublemaker wants to kick things off a little early, so be it. He's given me an extra six months to indulge in my cravings. Perhaps you should take what little time you have left to fill yours."

As he said that, Sonny reached over and swatted Maya's hand away from the plate of food in front of me.

"Hey!" she yelled. "I'm starving over here."

I was too. The smell was intoxicating. I felt more hungry than I had in all my life. I wanted nothing more than to drop my gun and dig into the plate of Chinese food, face first. Sonny was the only one of us who remained unaffected. He kicked the table over, sending all of the food—including Famine's—crashing to the floor. That finally got the attention of the other patrons. They ceased all conversation and stared silently at the reaper.

"Why are you telling us all this?" Sonny shook his rifle in Famine's face. "What are you playing at?"

The horseman looked woefully at his scattered banquet and shook his head. "What a waste. I had hoped to be civil about this, but it's no matter. I'm sure Nelson will arrive shortly to collect the prophet girl. In the meantime—" He snapped his bony fingers and the entire restaurant stood up. "I seem to have found more seating for the rest of you."

Sonny had broken my hunger spell when he flipped the table. My attention was now diverted to all the unblinking eyes that surrounded us.

"Uh, Sonny." I tentatively reached for the shotgun strapped around my back. "Maybe we should regroup."

"Why?" Sonny didn't look at me as he spoke, his gaze was locked with Famine's. "We came here to kill a behemoth. The way I see it—" He dropped the assault rifle and reached into his cardigan, gripping the hilt of the angel feather. With his other hand, he yanked the towel away and flung it through the air behind him. Famine's expression darkened at the sight of the glimmering blade. "We over-prepared," Sonny said with a smirk.

Famine bellowed in a deep, guttural voice, "*Apóllymi!*"

Every patron in the restaurant roared. It was a familiar sound by this point, one that only a demon could emit. They swarmed on us.

Maya and I immediately opened fire while Sonny leapt towards Famine, his quill outstretched. The reaper was tackled in midair by the hostess before he could reach his target. The woman snarled at him before he sliced her head clean off. From inside her open neck, a pillar of black ooze erupted with the sound of agonized squeals. The demon inside had been reduced to ectoplasmic goop. Sonny examined the feather in awe before he jumped back into the fray.

The bodies I left behind were not so inert. Each person I shot exploded a moment later, revealing a larger foe underneath. Maya held them at bay with her water gun, but there were too many to do any real damage and she was quickly running low in her tank. Sonny was the only one making a real difference. He slashed the feather all around him, cutting through the demons like tissue paper. If the hordes weren't afraid to close in on him, we'd have already been overwhelmed.

Still, it wasn't enough. I fumbled to reload my shotgun and realized that I didn't have enough ammo to take on a tenth of the horde that remained. As ferocious as Sonny fought, he was not a trained swordsman. The demons were soon able to flank and swipe at him from behind. The feather flew from his hands, lost in the buffet. Sonny was pulled to the front of the restaurant where he disappeared under a pile of demons. I could hear him wailing as they tore at his body. Human souls may not be able to die, but they can feel like they're going to. I can personally attest to that.

I helped Maya onto a table in the corner booth as the demons, now mostly free of their vessels, closed in on us. I had about two shots left and I could see through the yellow plastic tank of Maya's water gun well enough to realize that it was basically empty. She aimed her weapon for show.

"Stop!" A voice echoed through the room. All of the demons turned to look at the source, and for a fleeting moment, I thought that maybe Haniel had returned to save us. The crowd parted and Famine appeared amongst them, holding a chicken skewer in one hand and the angel feather in the other. My heart sank. "Remember," he told the horde, "keep the small one alive. Slaughter the others."

There was a rumble of laughter amongst the crowd, as well as the telltale sound of a portal tearing open nearby.

Sonny emerged on the table just behind us, having managed to break free of the demonic dogpile. I winced at the sight of his face, which was entirely stripped of flesh. He finally looked like the Grim Reaper of legend.

"Thanks for the reprieve, horsey," the skeleton gestured toward Famine, before disappearing once more.

Suddenly, a long rip opened in the ceiling, unleashing a torrent of ocean water into the restaurant. The demons who still had human hosts panicked and fled to the entrance. Maya quickly abandoned her useless weapon and took aim with her pistol, attempting to pick them off before they could escape. For the rest, it was already too late. The noise of their cries was drowned out by the sound of rushing water.

Famine watched this all unfold, awestruck. The seawater quickly rose to waist-level and he lifted his arms instinctively, giving me the perfect shot. I leapt off the table and took aim, blasting the feather out of his hand. He turned sharply around and snarled at me, like a wounded animal. His pale skin was peppered with metal pellets, but each one popped out when he closed his fist, leaving not so much as a scratch. He flexed his newly healed hand and snatched me up by the neck, holding me aloft.

"Bill!" Maya called out. She jumped into the rising water and pointed her pistol point blank at Famine's face. He grabbed the muzzle with his other hand, prompting her to pull the trigger. The shot knocked his head back a little, but just like before, the bullet popped out of his face as if it never happened. He yanked the gun out of her grip and jammed it back, striking Maya in the forehead and knocking her into the water. I struggled wildly in his grip, kicking at the rising pool to no avail.

"I wondered why Nelson had such a problem with a random mortal." Famine glared at me. "Now I see! You're like a cockroach! You just refuse to die!"

I tried to respond, but with his hand squeezing my throat, it just came out as gurgles.

"After I'm through with you," he continued, grinning wildly, "there'll be no coming back. No Heaven, no Hell. I'm going to purge your soul from existence, and you've brought me just the tool to accomplish the task!"

Funny he should mention that tool. Maya emerged from the water, just behind Famine, having retrieved the feather from the watery depths. She plunged the weapon straight through his back, almost reaching my own chest on the other side. His grin remained, frozen on his face, but something changed in his eyes. His pale skin darkened, losing texture. The fingers around my neck turned gelatinous and his arm melted into sludge, releasing me. The feather erased him, reducing his essence to a column of black goo and a lump of chewed Chinese food that dropped into the water where he stood. I fell back, gasping for air.

The portal in the ceiling closed, ending the downpour. Maya stood triumphantly above the floating remains, more shocked than anyone that she had been the one to deliver the killing blow. "I didn't even go into a trance that time!" she said excitedly, probably hoping to see us basking in her glory.

Instead, she turned to see me collapse into the draining water. She rushed over and helped me into a booth where I could sit and catch my breath. I panted and let the reality of Famine's defeat wash over me. "We did it. You did it. We won."

The young prophet let out an exhausted laugh. "I told you guys," she said. "Easy peasy."

I chuckled along with her and surveyed the devastation we'd wrought on the restaurant. The water level continued to lower now that the ocean portal had been sealed. The demons were all gone, either dead or escaped. There were plenty of bodies floating around, but I didn't see Sonny anywhere.

"Where'd he go? Sonny?" I called out.

Maya laid the feather on the booth table and waded through the draining pool to the center of the restaurant. "I don't see him by the buffet. Could he have gone after the stragglers?"

Just then, a portal opened up next to her and I let out a sigh of relief. After seeing Sonny in such a grisly condition, I was worried we might have lost him for good. Out of the portal, a hand reached out and plunged into Maya's chest. Her body stiffened as Nelson emerged, one hand on her soul.

"No!" I turned to grab the quill, ready to slice him to pieces.

"Touch that feather," he shouted, "and I'll cast her soul into the sun."

I froze, my hand hovering over the weapon. "You wouldn't!" I yelled back. "You need her!"

"Wrong. I *want* the books in her head, but I don't need them. There'll always be more prophets. I've killed them before, what's stopping me now?"

The image of Professor Widdick lying bloodied against a tree trunk flashed in my head. I closed my fist and pulled my arm back. "It's over, Nelson. You've already lost. Just disappear and pray the angels don't come after you."

"There's more than one way to stir up an apocalypse, and with her help, it'll be a snap."

"You can't possibly think I'm going to let you walk out of here with her!"

"That's exactly what you're going to do! Unless you want this innocent girl to suffer eternal torment. It'll be awfully hard for you to rescue her soul now that you've erased her records."

Nothing could ever be easy. We'd had two seconds to celebrate our victory before the next crisis appeared. I couldn't let Nelson win, but what were my options? One false move and Maya would be lost forever. The thought of her going through the same torture Nelson had inflicted on me was unbearable.

Luckily, it wasn't a decision I had to make. As the water continued to drain out of the restaurant, I reached again for the feather.

"Stop that! I'm not bluffing here!" Nelson shouted.

"I know," I told him, taking the weapon in my hand.

"Have it your way!" He yanked Maya's soul about halfway out of her body, but it snapped back.

"What the Hell?" Nelson tugged at it, to no avail. "What is this?"

The last trickles of ocean water flowed out of the shattered restaurant entrance, revealing a previously submerged skeletal hand around Maya's ankle. No matter how hard Nelson pulled, the hand held her soul in place. In a flash, Sonny leapt from inside the floor and grabbed Nelson by his free hand. The shock caused Nelson to release Maya from his grip, and she stumbled away, disoriented.

Nelson struggled to pull free, but Sonny held his grip firm, shaking it vigorously.

"Let go of me!" Nelson whined, yanking with all his might. The two separated, and Nelson was horrified to see that Sonny's severed hand remained clasped in his. He shook the appendage loose and quickly made a wide motion to open a new portal. He fell backward onto the water-soaked carpet of the Chinese restaurant.

He attempted a second portal, but nothing happened. He swiped desperately through the air, over and over again, but the fabric of reality remained intact.

"What have you done? What have you done!" Nelson screamed.

Sonny reached for his pocket with his missing hand. "Whoops.

Gimme a sec." He stretched his other arm over and retrieved his list, holding it high to read aloud:

"*Pay to the order of...Nelson Cooney.* You hear that? I learned your full name for this."

Nelson blinked.

"Where was I? *Pay to the order of Nelson Cooney: 76,452 souls.* In other words, every soul that I've ever collected, minus a few that I traded for drinks here and there. Now, if I'm doing my math correctly, I do believe you've filled your quota! Congratulations, man!"

Nelson began to stutter. "B-But I—I don't—I—I refuse! I don't accept your souls!"

"Oh, it's too late for that. We shook on it, you see." Sonny waved his handless nub. "You're officially a free man."

Nelson pulled out his own list to verify Sonny's claims, as if his inability to create portals wasn't proof enough. As he studied the scroll, he noticed his skin begin to change. He no longer had the complexion of a bloated corpse, but was now as fresh as the day he died.

"No, no, no, no!" He crawled on his knees toward Sonny. "You can't take me to Hell, not after the promises I made. They'll do horrible things to me!"

"I think that's kind of the idea behind Hell, isn't it?"

I walked over to Sonny, who was nothing but bones, one eye, and a few strips of dangling flesh at this point. Maya leaned against me, still reeling from having her soul stretched back and forth. Nelson trembled at our feet. I didn't think the defeated reaper could make his expression any more pathetic than it already was, but somehow, he managed.

"Oh quit your pouting," Sonny told him. "As much as I'd like to, I'm not going to take you to Hell."

We cocked our heads at Sonny. "We're not?" Maya asked.

Sonny looked over at me, and even with one eye and no facial muscles, I gleaned his intent. Nelson stared up with great, pitiful eyes—and I did pity him. As much as I would rather have seen him as a monster, he was still a person. He made truly evil choices, but ultimately, his flaw was human.

"Sonny's right. We can't take him there."

Nelson's face lit up with shock and hope.

"Are we…sure about that?" Maya asked. "I mean, the guy had no problem dumping you there."

"I know. I know exactly how horrible that place is. He deserves to face justice, but how much is too much? If he's tortured for a thousand years, will he have paid his dues? Whatever you think a fair punishment is, Hell is beyond that. No one deserves to suffer forever."

"So, what?" Maya asked. "Is there like a phantom zone we can banish him to? What else can we do with him?"

I turned my head to Sonny, who nodded. "We'll give him a choice," I decided. "Nelson, we can either hand you over to the angels and leave your fate to them, or—" I held up the feather. "—you can choose to die, fully. No Heaven. No Hell. Just, gone."

Nelson whimpered. It was a terrible choice to have to make, but he wouldn't get a better offer. It didn't take him long to decide.

"Do it. It's a more merciful fate than what awaits the rest of the reapers." He looked directly at Sonny. "You might wanna do the same."

Sonny took a step back. He had just given away all his souls, so any hopes of finishing his quota before the real apocalypse began were pretty much dashed.

"Let's go, you bastards," Nelson barked. "It smells like moldy Chinese food in here."

As far as last words go, they were at least memorable. I raised the feather high. Nelson closed his eyes. Then, the room darkened and all became pitch black.

"Did you do it?" Nelson asked. "Is this oblivion?"

Dozens of voices echoed from every direction. "You do not belong to oblivion. You belong to us."

The darkness began to materialize in the shapes of men. Against all instinct and logic, I let the feather slip from my fingers in sheer terror. We were surrounded on all sides by a host of Nephilim.

"Wha-what do you want?" I struggled to ask.

The voices spoke again in unison. "Promises were made. This one broke his bargain, betrayed one of our own. He must face justice."

Panic filled Nelson's eyes. He reached for the feather that I'd dropped to the floor, but was ensnared by strips of smokey blackness. He screamed as the Nephilim swarmed past us, wrapping the former reaper in a blanket of abyss before melting away, leaving no trace.

28

THE BOOK OF BILL

THE DAYS THAT followed felt like a dream, and not only because I slept through most of them. I had been confined to Grace's hotel room, unable to step outside for fear of being noticed by literally anyone. She was concerned that, due to the heinous acts I committed at the Austin police department, I would be recognizable to any cop within a hundred miles, even with my slightly altered facial features. Until things cooled down, I had to stay under wraps.

Grace offered Maya the second bed in our hotel room, at least until we were able to return her to Enid, but she declined. She reasoned that Grace and I had been apart far too long to have to share a room with a third wheel. Though we protested, I was secretly grateful.

While things were slowing down on Earth, the afterlife was in an uproar. News of recent events spread like wildfire. Evidently, Josiah had leaked some juicy information about a particular high-ranking angel who tried to stage a cover-up of Nelson's actions. Soon, every reaper on the planet was threatening to go on strike and let the dead go on living indefinitely, unless big changes were made.

Ansiel was temporarily demoted down to Library front desk worker, under Haniel's supervision. He would be forced to interact with hundreds of human souls every day until he learned to appreciate the value of those he'd nearly condemned. I don't know how his appreciation would be measured, but I had a feeling that he would be there a very long time.

Meanwhile, the governing body of archangels agreed to grant an audience to a single representative of the reapers. The chosen representative would present a list of adequate policy changes to prevent any similar catastrophes from ever occurring again. Due to his recent actions—and physical disfigurement—Sonny had become the poster child for unfair treatment of reapers, and was unanimously elected as the representative. With assistance from Haniel, he drafted a series of new amendments to the laws that governed the afterlife. It was the first time a human soul had been allowed to meet with the archangels in over two thousand years.

To Sonny's shock, most of his proposed amendments passed. The effects of which were monumental to all afterlife service workers.

First, all worker contracts were to be nullified, requiring no additional time or quota in order to move on from the in-between realm. There would be a grace period in which the workers would still be expected to perform their duties while a new system was established, but no worker had to fear the consequences of another apocalypse scare. Their spots in Heaven were reserved.

Second, the standards for future advancement would be adjusted so that any souls who would previously have qualified for the afterlife service program, would now be allowed to move on directly upon their death.

Third, in order to maintain working institutions, a new rewards-based system would be established, in which current residents of the heavenly plane may volunteer their service in exchange for visitation time on Earth. I may have been the first human ghost to walk among the living, but I would be far from the last.

Fourth, in the event of a preventable apocalyptic scenario, angels would be given the right to directly intervene in the affairs of Earth, when deemed necessary by the governing body of archangels..

Fifth, souls in Heaven would have access to all Hollywood films at least one week prior to their release on Earth, provided the films are theater-ready by that point. Sonny snuck that last one in, without Haniel's knowledge, and the archangels didn't care enough to deny it.

The only amendment that did not pass was the one I had suggested. It would have placed a sentencing cap on all souls, past and future, condemned to Hell. The archangels maintained that allowing condemned souls into the heavenly plane, even after years of torture, would be unfair to those who had earned their peace. Had I been allowed in the meeting, I would have reminded them that anyone who deserved to be in Heaven, probably wouldn't wish eternal suffering on others out of "fairness". Progress had been made, but clearly there was more work to be done.

In addition to all this, Haniel delivered one more round of good news. After doing some research into the spontaneous appearance of portals outside the boundaries of earth, he discovered two anomalies that occurred in the past six months—both in the same location. In order to protect his secrets, Nelson had apparently stashed the soul of the first prophet he encountered on the surface of Mars. Later, he did the same with Professor Widdick, and the two souls had been wondering about the planet together ever since. Haniel had both of them recovered, and they now reside safely in the heavenly plane, where I hear they have remained great friends.

Lastly, though it would take some time to find enough volunteers to fully transition every reaper to the new system, Sonny was granted his freedom early—as a show of good faith. I was overjoyed for him when I heard, but I had hoped to see him one more time before he moved on. Once stripped of his reaper powers, he would no longer be able to return to Earth—unless of course he volunteered to work again. After two hundred years of service, I expected he would desire a long vacation.

As for Nelson, I still feel remorse for what happened to him. I understand that he was a deeply flawed person, but I also know what led him to the path he chose. He lacked empathy, and that made his decisions easier, but I don't think he was evil. I'm not sure what the Nephilim had in mind for him, but because he had burned his own book, it was impossible to locate his soul. Whatever punishment he deserved, he would likely receive much worse.

And then there's the apocalypse problem. In the wake of everything, I've received nothing but positive support for choosing hope over fear, but in doing so, I'd taken a big risk. According to Nelson, Lucifer had been walking free all along, and was planning to unleash the real apocalypse sooner rather than later. Was it possible that I had only briefly postponed the inevitable? And did I grant the fallen angels the time they needed to pose a more serious threat? I don't know if I made the right call, and I doubt I will until the consequences of that decision are upon us. Maybe my gamble will pay off, or maybe I condemned the entire universe. We'll see.

AFTER TWO WEEKS in that hotel room, it became apparent that I would have to leave soon. For one thing, our house in Cedar Park was no longer considered a crime scene. Grace's parents had been staying there for days while their own house underwent repairs, and it made no sense for Grace not to stay with them. Another issue was that my continued occupation of the room was becoming expensive. Salado may have been a small community, but it was also a wealthy one. Quaint hotel rooms on Main Street were not cheap. I also suspected that Maya would want to go home soon. It was an eight-hour drive that we had been putting off, and perhaps now was as good a time as any.

The morning of our trip, Grace came over early with a large purse filled to the brim with various things she insisted I needed before we set out. We sat together on one of the hotel beds as she presented them.

"This finally came in the mail for you. I had it ordered a couple of weeks ago." She gave me a credit card with the name Bob Butler on it. "It connects directly to a joint account. I'll be able to pay off any purchases you make on the road."

"Thank you," I said. "I do owe Maya quite a bit of money, so don't be too scared when you see some strange charges. She likes weird, nerd stuff."

"I'll keep that in mind." She laughed. She reached her hand back into her purse, pulling out more items than I thought could reasonably fit in it. "I brought you both some snacks. I don't know what Maya likes, so I got three kinds of chips, gummy candy, and chocolate candy. Figured that covers most bases."

"Thank you, now we don't have to get dinner."

She swatted me on the arm. "You have a new body now, try and take care of it."

"We've had pizza like five times this week."

"It's not my fault there's only two gluten friendly restaurants in town."

I smiled at her. "What else you got?"

She reached back into the bag and pulled out a small rectangular box. My eyes lit up.

"Oh my God! Is that a new phone? I've been losing my mind without one!" I tore open the plastic around it, frantically.

"Yeah, I figured next time you could text me before showing up at my doorstep with a new name and identity."

"You do realize I'm only going to be gone for one night, right?"

"Actually," she set her purse aside, "I wanted to talk with you about that."

My stomach sank. She had clearly buttered me up with the candy and phone. This was a conversation we had been putting off since things had calmed down. "Okay, what's on your mind?"

"It's just something I've been discussing with Valerie."

"Who's Valerie?" I asked.

"A friend from the police station. She's actually the reason I could afford this room for so long."

"Wait, the detective who questioned you? She's been paying for this?"

"Not paying. She got me a discount. I think she just feels sorry for me, being widowed in such a—dramatic fashion."

"I guess you are technically a widow. Hey, did my life insurance ever pay out?"

"You died while committing a crime. They don't pay out for that. Believe me I checked." She pouted. "Anyway, we were talking the other day and it turns out there's been a lot more cases like mine. They slowed down after the horseman's death, but they never stopped."

"Demons," I said. "But the drought is over, isn't it? They should be dying off." Then it dawned on me. "But not if they have human hosts."

"Exactly," Grace said. "And from what we've seen, these demons know how to hold grudges."

"You're worried they'll come after me," I guessed.

"You are virtually untraceable. I'm worried they'll come after Maya. They have attacked Enid before. They know where she lives. But if you were to stay with her for a while—"

I nodded, solemnly. "A while. Yeah."

"I'm not saying permanently," she assured me. "Just until things cool down, both with the demons, and with the police."

"Grace, we both know that day is a long way off. And you're right, I still have a lot to do before I can safely settle down anywhere."

She looked down, clearly not wanting to meet my eyes.

"I've been thinking," I continued, "and I'm pretty sure you have been too. You've put up with all of this for entirely too long. I think—" My voice caught in my throat, and Grace's eyes began to well with tears.

"Bill, we don't have to do this," she said.

"Yes we do. I know it's what you want. It's what you've wanted since I dragged you into this mess. I spent so much time trying to save you from monsters and the apocalypse, but I did all that so that you could live your life—the life you deserve, the one I can't give you anymore. I mean, be honest—what does a future with me even look like?"

She didn't protest. She only bit her lip and let the tears fall down her cheeks. "It's not like things are going to ever be normal for me either," she eventually said. "I'm always going to be the crazy lady who blew her fiancé's head off."

"At least I'll know you're safe. Who'd wanna mess with you?"

WE TALKED FOR a while, entertaining the notion that we could maybe do long distance, or eventually move away together to a place where no one had ever heard of us. It always circled back to one unchanging fact. There would always be threats, both to me and to Maya. The only way Grace could have a semblance of peace was to move on from me. And maybe, some day down the line, if I managed to thwart every escaped demon out for my blood, we could find each other again. Till then, I had a mission.

We laid in bed, holding each other for what could be the last time when there was a knock at the door. I assumed it was Maya, eager to get an early start on our road trip. When I opened the door however, it was Haniel who greeted me.

"Hello, Bill! Hello, Grace! I hope I'm not interrupting anything."

"No, actually. It's great to see you. I didn't expect—"

Before I could finish the thought, another man appeared in the doorframe.

"Didn't expect to see such a handsome face?"

"Sonny!" He had undergone a full transformation. His skin was tan and free of rot. His hair was full, falling just above his shoulders. He even had a short crop of facial hair. His eyes, on the other hand, were unmistakably his. He also still dressed like a hipster, which was a dead giveaway.

He held out his hand for me to shake. "Not slimy anymore."

I shook my head and pulled him in for a hug instead.

"What are you doing here?" I asked, pulling away so I could get another look at him. "I heard they already let you move on."

"Not just yet. There were a few more details I needed to iron out with the new policy changes. I'm supposed to move on today, but I asked Haniel if I could drop by here first."

"Hi, Sonny." Grace came to the door and hugged him as well. "How long can you stay? You know Maya will be here soon."

"I don't know," he said. "What's the verdict, warden?"

Haniel looked slightly confused by the nickname, but answered nonetheless. "We can stay for an hour or two. I'd like to have a word with Bill, anyway."

"A word?" I asked. "Am I in trouble?"

Sonny placed a hand on my shoulder and looked solemnly at me. "That's the real reason I've come, Bill. You died four times. I'm here to take your soul to Heaven with me."

"What?" Every hair stood up on my neck.

"Stop that, Sonny," Haniel told him.

The former reaper burst into laughter. "Oh man, I'm fucking with you. It's just some library business, or whatnot. Boring stuff."

Grace swatted at Sonny, but her hand passed right through him. I took a deep breath to calm down and looked back at Haniel.

"Why don't you guys come in and we can talk about it in the—" I looked into the cramped hotel room. "Uh, this doesn't need to be a private conversation, does it?"

"No, in fact, I'll have to go over it with Ms. Evans and Ms. Kabua as well."

I led Haniel to the bed on the far side of the room while Sonny jumped onto the nearer one, grabbing the remote. The man was about to go to paradise, and all he wanted to do was watch television. Grace sat down with him, giving Haniel and I some space to talk.

"So, what's up?" I asked.

"I've already gone through this with Sonny and the other two prophets. I'll have to speak with everyone who had their library books destroyed. You see, without being registered in The Library of Eternity, you won't actually be allowed into the heavenly plane when your time comes."

I glanced over at Sonny, who was still flipping through channels. "But clearly, there's a way to re-register, right? I mean, Sonny is going today."

"Yes! And thankfully, it's a relatively simple process. You just need to put your soul into a new book."

I blinked at him. "Would you care to elaborate on that?"

"Certainly. What you need to do is sit down and write something about yourself. It can be anything really, as long as it's personal. Sonny, for instance, wrote about how he died, and his regrets on the matter. Because of how important the writing was to him, he left a little bit of his soul on the page. Once his writing was placed in The Library, the rest of his story filled itself in. Now, you need to do the same."

"I have to write a story." I suddenly felt the familiar sensation of being assigned a college essay that constituted half my grade. "I've never really written anything before. Not like this, at least."

"That's okay, Sonny hadn't either. Just start putting words on the page and let your feelings come out."

"And it can be anything?"

"Anything at all! You can write a poem about your childhood, or a journal entry about a particularly bad day. It really doesn't matter, as long as it's meaningful to you."

I sat there, staring past Haniel, wondering where to even begin. How does someone reflect their very soul in writing? "When does it need to be done?"

"Anytime, really. Though, before your eventual demise would be preferable."

I had my whole life to write my story. What a nightmare. I hated projects without deadlines.

"Is that it?" I asked him.

"Yes. That pretty much covers it. Now, do you know when Ms. Kabua will arrive? I can leave Sonny with you for a while, but I'd like to get back to the office."

"Already busy?"

"Insurmountably. My new promotion places me directly in charge of Earthly affairs, which means I'm responsible for handling the fallout of all these demons that are running rampant across the country."

"I don't suppose you can just smite them with your new angelic authority?"

"In an apocalypse scenario, yes—thanks to Sonny's amendments. Unfortunately, or perhaps very fortunately, we are no longer in an apocalypse scenario. I've got to find an indirect method of mopping these demons up. Quite frankly, I don't imagine there will be a lot of volunteers for the job."

I was reminded, in that moment, that I had meant to return Haniel's feather the next time I saw him. I'd been keeping it in the bottom of my dresser drawer—under my socks and underwear. In light of my conversation with Grace however, perhaps it would be best if I held onto it. After all, it was a long drive to Enid, Oklahoma. Who knew what kinds of trouble might be on the way? Or even, what kind of trouble we might be able to find—if we looked hard enough.

After Haniel finished giving his spiel to Grace, Maya arrived with a tray of iced coffees she had just picked up. The young prophet was shocked and delighted to recognize Sonny in his current condition, joking that she preferred the old version better. At least I assume it was a joke.

It was nice being together, with everyone, before we all had to part ways. It was the first chance we'd had to just enjoy each other's company without the threat of an immediate apocalypse weighing over us. Maya already tore into the road snacks Grace had bought us, assuring me that we could pick up more if we stopped at Buc-ees along the way.

Haniel left early, as he said he would, promising to return for Sonny in a couple of hours. I never did return the feather to the angel. We spent our remaining time the best way we could: sitting together, on two beds, watching old reruns on TV.

ACKNOWLEDGEMENTS

FINALLY. At last I have finished this book that I've had ruminating in my head since high school. What started as a handdrawn comic strip I would pass around in class, has morphed into this physical printed text that can sit on my bookshelf. That makes it sound as if I've been writing it for over a decade, but rest assured, I spent far more time procrastinating by writing outlines for dozens of other books I also haven't finished. So after all this time, am I happy with it? Well, I've read it and reread it so much in my editing that I'm kind of sick of looking at it now, but hopefully you enjoyed it! Mostly I'm glad that I can mentally move on to other projects that hopefully wont take a decade to release.

In any case, I'd like to thank a few people, without whom I may never have assembled a functional version of this story. First off, my wife, Montana, who read my first draft years ago, has provided innumerable edits, and has had to put up with my agonizing over it for far too long. Without her, there is no book. Second, my best friend,

Mike, who is largely the inspiration for the loving, yet antagonistic friendship at the core of the story. He doesn't really care to read fiction though, so I guess he'll never see this tribute. I mean, I'm certainly not going to tell him about it.

I'd also like to thank my beta readers CJ Beshara and Claire Hiria. Without CJ, this story would be about fifty pages longer and feature several additional characters who would have added very little to the experience. I am extremely grateful for their insight and suggestions. In addition to general comments, Claire provided desperately needed editing to the final draft that helped me get my manuscript ready for publication. If you catch any glaring typos, it's not her fault, I probably messed something up in formatting it for print.

Finally, I'd like to thank the online writing community on Bluesky for helping to motivate me and providing enthusiastic support for all my excerpts and snippets. I had kind of resigned myself to abandon this project when I couldn't find a traditional publisher, but the positive responses I received from this community convinced me to polish it up and finally put it out there.

So, thank you all and I hope you'll continue to read more from me in the future!

ABOUT THE AUTHOR

Christian Akins was born in Okinawa, Japan in 1992 and has lived in many places, including all those mentioned in this book (yes, even Enid, Oklahoma). He currently lives with his wife and two pets and enjoys more hobbies than any reasonable person should. He also works as a professional graphic designer. To see his work, or learn more about his writing, please visit:

www.ChristianAkins.com